To
Everything
a Season

To
Everything
a Season

SHERRI SCHAEFFER

Becca's Journal

I'M SO EXCITED. I'm going to the singing tonight at the Fisher farm with my brothers. I know Jacob and David and others will be drinking in the barn but I don't have to venture there. I'll just stay in the house with my friends.

Jacob had just finished morning milking and was climbing into our buggy when I caught up with him yesterday. Where does he go in such a hurry sometimes? He frowned when I asked him if I could go with he and David to the singing but then mumbled, "All right." He was in one of his moods, gloomy and tense. What's with him these days??

It's my first singing since I turned sixteen last week. I'm finally in rumspringa and my running around years start now. I wonder what my future holds. Will I meet a boy I like, do some naughty things, like go to the movies or wear modern clothes? I hope John King is at the Fishers tonight. Out of the corner of my eye, I saw him looking at me after church today. Hmmm, that makes me a little nervous.

My whole life stretches before me, like a newborn calf's, eager but wobbly. Now maybe I can write more interesting things in you, since life may become more interesting. Or maybe not. Maybe I won't have the chance to taste a little bit of the modern world. But I hope I do.

1

J ACOB YODER LEANED against his grey buggy, a hand-rolled, brown-wrapped cigarette dangling from his mouth. The Sunday evening singing was over and as the young crowd began to disperse from the Fisher barn, he quickly harnessed Chestnut and stroked his mane. The early June evening was dark but redolent of honeysuckle and the lush smell of freshly turned soil mixed with the faint aroma of manure.

Jacob scanned the crowd, waiting for his brother David and sister Becca. He took a last puff of his cigarette, threw it down and crushed it into the dirt with the toe of his sneaker. He retrieved his wide-brimmed straw hat from its perch on the hitching post and placed it on his head, then bent and picked up his beer can from the ground, finishing it in one long swallow. He slid open the buggy door and concealed the empty can with the other half dozen on the floor underneath the front seat.

The Old Order Amish in Lancaster, Pennsylvania, the oldest Amish settlement in the country, advocate separation from the modern world by their distinctive old-fashioned dress, mode of transportation, and simple lifestyle. Yet Jacob and his Amish brethren also lived a life of contrasts, their farms of fertile soil located off idyllic country roads but set in the midst

3

of an expanding area of shopping centers, fast food restaurants, retail outlets, traffic-clogged main roads, and eight million tourists a year.

Jacob himself was a study in discord. He drove the traditional horse and buggy and sported the mandatory hat, straw in summer. Yet he flouted Old Order rules as he guzzled beer in contemporary clothing: black boot-cut Levi jeans, grey cotton t-shirt with pocket, and white Nike sneakers. The smoking was a blend of two cultures, the habit modern but the hand-rolled cigarette a nod to the tobacco grown on his family's farm for two generations. It was as if Jacob had schizophrenic feet—one foot firmly implanted in Amish soil, the other turned to bolt in the opposite direction.

He watched Becca walk toward him from the Fisher main house. She wore a deep purple below-the-knee-length dress and black bib apron, her long blonde hair parted in the center, braided, twisted in a bun at the back of her head, and covered by a white Swiss organdy *kapp*, strings untied and hanging freely. She had just turned sixteen, the beginning age of *rumspringa*, the few years during which Old Order Amish youth flaunt to various degrees the rules they live by.

Jacob knew his sister had taken part in the evening's singing but had not ventured to the barn where the drinking and general rowdiness had taken place. She was cautiously easing into her *rumpsringa*, unlike many of those gathered for the evening who were well into their fling with the so-called vices of the English, or non-Amish, world, enthusiastically experimenting with modern fashion and technology—cell phones, video games, computers, cars—as well as with alcohol and sometimes drugs.

Jacob grew up with the eldest Fisher boys, Jonas and Elam, both members of one of the more rebellious Amish youth groups, the Stonies, and it was not unusual for he and David and other *rumspringa* youth to attend gatherings sponsored by this group where cases of beer were stashed under the hay in the barn. Most Amish parents, including the Fishers and his own, were well aware of the general nature of their children's *rumspringa* exploits, if not the specific details, but chose to look the other way, convinced their sons and daughters would eventually get their flirting with the modern world out of their systems, baptize, marry, have a family, and settle down into the Amish way of life. So far, Jacob knew, he had sorely disappointed his parents' expectations.

"Jacob," Becca whispered when she reached his side, "I saw you with the beer. Did you drink much?"

"*Neh.* I only had a few. Don't worry. Here comes the happy couple."

Their brother David and Anna Beiler approached the buggy. Anna's dress was identical to Becca's, except green, and David wore black broadfall trousers—the front closed with buttons rather than a zipper—suspenders crossed in the back, and a tan, short sleeve, pocketless shirt. He was clean-shaven, as are all Amish males before marriage. A straw hat covered his hair, styled in the traditional bowl cut with bangs, unlike his brother's shorter modern cut.

Although there would be no formal announcement for several months, it was whispered with some certainty among the Amish community in their town of Hickory Hill that the two would probably marry that fall. Their heads together, they murmured to each other, then Anna walked away to join her brother Aaron.

"I told Aaron to wait a bit until the other buggies leave and we'll meet him at the end of the lane," David said. "I challenged him to a race to their farm."

Jacob nodded. "We'll beat him this time. He only won by a horse's nose the last race."

Becca climbed into the buggy's back seat. As Jacob climbed in, he tripped, landing hard on the front seat, his straw hat falling to the floor. David glanced sideways at his older brother as he climbed in beside him.

"Are you good to drive?" he asked.

Jacob scowled, jammed the hat back onto his head and grabbed the horse's reins.

"Light the kerosene lantern now," he instructed Becca. "We'll need to see when we get home. It'll be too hard to light while we race."

Becca picked up the lantern on the floor near her feet and David handed her a disposable lighter. She lit the lamp, placed it carefully on the seat beside her, keeping one hand on the handle, and returned the lighter to David.

"Jacob, you have any cigs?" David asked.

"My last one," Jacob said as he took a plastic bag containing a brown cigarette from his jeans pocket and tossed it to David.

David leaned out of the open buggy door and lit the cigarette, blowing the smoke into the balmy night air. The three patiently watched the orderly exodus of the other buggies from the Fisher farm.

THE BMW Z4 two-seater red convertible sped along the dark back roads of Lancaster. Taylor Loden wasn't sure where she was and regretted the decision to spontaneously turn off the familiar but congested Route 30 in order to save time.

Taylor was a vice president at Loden Media, a conglomerate founded and owned by her father, Connor Loden. The company, headquartered in Philadelphia, owned nineteen daily newspapers, four radio stations, and seven television stations in five Mid-Atlantic states and Washington, D.C. She had worked at Loden Media full time for the past two years, but had been a presence in the office ever since she could remember, including summers during high school, college, and graduate school.

Two hours earlier, Taylor had left her home in Philadelphia and was due to lead a panel discussion on "Media Ownership and Consolidation" at a conference the next morning at the Lancaster Hotel on Route 30. She had decided to drive up Sunday night because she knew the traffic exiting Philadelphia, as well as on Route 30, would be even worse early Monday morning. Plus, there wasn't much to keep her home on a Sunday night; she lived alone and could work as productively in a Lancaster hotel as in her Rittenhouse Square penthouse. She had hoped to arrive at the hotel by nine o'clock, giving her plenty of time to go over her notes for the panel and respond to the dozens of work e-mails she knew awaited her, even on a Sunday evening.

According to the clock on her dashboard, it was already nine-thirty and she had no idea how far she was from the hotel. Briefly, she considered stopping to activate the navigation system in her car but rather than waste time she chose to continue on, figuring the back roads would eventually connect to Route 30.

The spring night was warm, but the BMW's convertible top was up, as always, because her car was an extension of her office and it was difficult for Taylor to talk business on her cell phone with the wind blowing. Before the sun had set, she had driven through one of the most scenic areas of rural Lancaster, but she hadn't noticed. On both sides of the road stretched verdant farmland, rolling fields planted with corn, alfalfa, and tobacco that in late summer and early fall would spread over the countryside like a patchwork quilt, dotted with white clapboard farmhouses and red barns. Instead of enjoying the scenery, she had spent the last two hours on her cell phone, via Bluetooth, checking with all nineteen newspapers regarding end-of-May circulation figures and discussing with general counsel the legal ramifications of running a television piece based on the claims of a corporate whistleblower. The news never slept at Loden Media.

Taylor's life, at 28, revolved around work; she socialized and traveled but it always related to work. Her two cell phones—a BlackBerry and an iPhone, the former strictly for work calls and emails, the latter for personal use—and laptop were as essential to her as oxygen and she prided herself on her 24/7 availability. She measured the success of her days by the number of items she crossed off her *To Do* list, and her self-esteem partnered solely with her accomplishments.

This addiction to activity, helpful though it was to her career, diverted her from dealing with an emptiness she had yet to acknowledge. She wasn't prone to self-analysis and she didn't have, or take, the time to soul search. So she had never asked herself, at any time during the last several driven years of her life, what fueled this single-minded, all encompassing, manic level of motion.

THE PUNGENT SMELL of manure mixed with hay filled the barn earlier that evening on the Yoder farm. The cows moved restlessly in their stalls, mooing insistently, impatient to be milked.

Daniel Yoder looked around the barn for his father, who sometimes helped during the twice-a-day milking of the cows. Daniel's parents, Levi and Mary, lived in a grossdaadi, or grandparents' house, in back of the main farmhouse. Daniel was short-handed that night since sons Jacob and David were at the Fisher farm for the singing. Even with Levi's help, it would take him longer than the usual hour and a half to milk and feed the herd of thirty Holsteins, and Daniel was mighty hungry already.

He hooked up the double milking machine to Bessie and Lulu but his mind was on the task he and his sons had started on Friday and would continue the next day. Six acres of their forty-five acre farm were devoted to tobacco. The tobacco seedlings, planted in March, had grown to nearly the size of a man's hand, and each plant needed to be transplanted out of the seedbed into the field.

Daniel was grateful that his farm, as well as dozens of other Amish farms in Lancaster, participated in a three-year experiment with a new type of genetically modified tobacco. The brainchild of a small domestic cigarette manufacturer, the tobacco was modified to contain a gene that inhibits nicotine and would eventually be used to produce what the tobacco company called a virtually nicotine-free cigarette.

Over the last several years, Daniel had nervously watched the price for burley tobacco, used in cigarettes, dip as low as eighty cents a pound at auction, forcing him to sell his harvest in Maryland where prices were better. So two years ago, when the tobacco company offered to pay a dollar fifty a pound for the genetically modified tobacco, guaranteed by a three-year contract, Daniel jumped at the opportunity.

He had grown up harvesting tobacco on the very same acreage he now farmed; as the youngest Yoder son, he had inherited the farm when Levi retired. He figured even if the genetically modified tobacco experiment didn't pan out, he'd have a good income for three years, some of which could be put away for a rainy day. He could always go back to harvesting burley even though it didn't pay as well.

But lately, Daniel had been wondering if it was all worth it. Even with just six acres of tobacco, the labor was backbreaking. Daniel would soon lose one of his farmhands when David married Anna Beiler. David wanted his own farm but the Yoder's forty-five acres wasn't large enough to sub-divide and would eventually go to youngest son Joseph, and the huge Beiler farm would in time be split among Anna's three brothers.

Daniel knew David had been saving what little money he could for years to purchase land to farm and Daniel had saved some too, but it wasn't enough, what with the ever-increasing price of farmland in Lancaster. A hefty mortgage loomed in David's future.

As for his eldest son, Jacob had never shown a real desire to farm tobacco, or to farm anything for that matter. When Jacob finally decided on an occupation, Joseph would be the only son left on the farm, and they'd need more hands to harvest the tobacco. Hiring workers would cut into profits, especially if they had to return to farming regular burley tobacco. Daniel sighed in resignation. *God's will be done.*

"Daniel, your head's in the clouds," Levi said as he scraped cow dung into the grates behind the stalls. He had worked unnoticed near Daniel for several minutes.

"Just thinking about the tobacco," Daniel said. "And about Jacob. I worry about him. For some time now, he's been difficult. Moody, not focused on his work, disappears for hours at a time. He's twenty-two and without direction."

"*Ja*, he is lost. Maybe once David gets married, Jacob will come around. If he doesn't want to farm, he'll find something else. Maybe he'll even want to be baptized this fall with David. It will work out in time."

"Time is short," Daniel said curtly.

His late-blooming eldest son frustrated Daniel, and the community was beginning to talk. Amish religious custom required baptism into the faith as an adult, usually between age sixteen and the early twenties. As far as Daniel was concerned, Jacob had already stretched his *rumspringa* to the limit. It was time to end the running around, baptize, and commit to living the *Ordnung*, the unwritten code of conduct that is the foundation of Amish life.

Daniel heard his two youngest children yelling before he saw them run into the barn. Joseph's cobalt blue shirt was half hanging out of his black pants, despite the suspenders. Dirt smeared his freckled face and the hand he placed on his father's arm was filthy. He and his eight-year-old twin Emma had been helping their mother pick vegetables from the garden for dinner but as usual they spent more time bickering than helping.

"*Dat, Mamm* says supper will be ready in a half hour," Joseph said breathlessly.

"Hi, *Daadi*," he said to his grandfather. "And tell Emma to stop calling me a *dummkup*. She pushed me 'cause I pulled up a carrot that wasn't ready and then I fell in the dirt but I'm not a *dummkup*."

"Are too," said Emma.

Daniel held up his hand, his face stern.

"If you want to eat soon, the cows need feeding."

"I'll help," Joseph said. "I get to push the wheelbarrow with the hay."

"*Neh*, I want to push the wheelbarrow. You did it last time," Emma said, racing across the barn, Joseph at her heels.

SARAH RINSED THE fresh-picked carrots in the sink. She loved Sundays. No work was done on the Lord's Day in Amish country except for necessary chores such as milking and food preparation. The day was quiet, less busy, and she looked forward to the family sitting down to Sunday supper, even though three of her children were absent. She dried the carrots and began chopping them for the salad.

The kitchen bustled with activity. Middle daughter Katie finished the salad while Sarah sliced the pot roast, mashed the potatoes, and took a homemade apple pie out of the gas stove. Mary set the table, prepared the gravy, and seasoned a bowl of green beans, also fresh from the garden. She and Levi often ate Sunday supper with the rest of the family.

"The men and the twins should be coming in from the barn any minute," Sarah said as she set the roast on the table. At that moment, Joseph barreled into the kitchen, the screen door banging behind him.

"I am soooo hungry," he yelled. "Mamm, me and Emma helped feed the cows but Emma got to push the wheelbarrow."

"My little man, get right over to that sink and wash your hands and face. Your hair is all *strubley*," Sarah said as she tried to wet down his tousled hair. "You are a sight!"

Joseph laughed. "Wait 'til you see Emma. She fell in the hay bin. Hay all in her hair and stuck to her dress. *Daadi* was trying to clean her off."

Sarah and Mary chuckled. The family considered the twins their miracles. Sarah had suffered first a miscarriage and then a stillborn after Katie was born and had been afraid the large family she and Daniel had wanted was not to be. Then along came Joseph and Emma, a more-than-welcome handful.

The screen door banged again as Emma flew into the kitchen. Blond wisps of hair had escaped from the bun at the back of her head, stray bits of hay dotted her head, and her burgundy dress was torn at the sleeve. Right behind came Daniel and Levi, leaving dirt-encrusted boots by the door.

The family sat on benches at the large pine table handmade by Daniel's furniture-making brother Samuel and when Levi bent his head in silent grace, the others followed. Sarah felt peace and contentment as she sat surrounded by her family.

Thank you, God, for our bounty and our health, and may your will be done, she prayed.

CONNOR LODEN STOOD beside his sleek custom-made walnut desk, the phone on speaker, his hands in the pockets of his impeccably tailored navy pin-striped Brioni trousers. It wasn't unusual for him to be at work on a Sunday evening and he gazed out the window of his corner office at the twinkling Philadelphia skyline without really seeing it, intent on his conversation.

"I want the *Tribune News*," he said to legal counsel Alan Moore. "I don't want this sale screwed up because of legal paperwork crap. Figure it out."

"Connor, don't worry. It'll just take some time to work out the details. Then you'll have your twentieth newspaper, a nice round number. By the way, I just spoke to Taylor about the whistleblower story out of our station in Baltimore. She's on her way to Lancaster for the conference."

Connor smiled at the mention of his daughter. "I'm scheduled as the keynote speaker at the conference lunch tomorrow but will try to catch her morning panel discussion. We work in the same office but I've barely seen her the past few weeks. Keep me apprised of the *Tribune*. I want the deal done by the end of the month."

He trusted Alan to work out the sale; he had been with Connor since the beginning of the company, had helped him buy the first newspaper in Pennsylvania, his hometown *Kennett Square Gazette*, where he had been a reporter a couple years post-graduation from Princeton. In quick succession came a radio station in West Chester, several more newspapers, a television station in up-state New York, and before he knew it, he was on his way to becoming a media magnate. That was thirty-four years ago. Loden Media was now one of the last family-owned media groups in the country.

Alan and executive vice president Dan Burke comprised Connor's inner circle, the two men he relied on most in his company. He intended for Taylor to join the top management of Loden Media someday and she certainly had the brains, the ambition, and the stamina for the job. A chip off the old block, Connor thought proudly. But he worried about her breakneck pace of life. She worked constantly and travelled frequently among their thirty media holdings. As far as he could tell, she had no close friends, was not dating anyone, had no hobbies, and did nothing just for the fun of it. Her life was her work.

He last saw her three weeks ago when they had dined together at Barclay Prime in Rittenhouse Square for his birthday. While enjoying rib eye steaks, they had talked excitedly about the *Tribune News* acquisition and about business in general. Taylor had laughed and gestured animatedly with her hands, just like her mother, but Connor couldn't help but notice her eyes—those mournful, hazel eyes. Her eyes reflected only surface enjoyment, a happiness that didn't penetrate. And Connor didn't know how to help her.

He and Taylor had always been close, even more so after his wife Alexis had died from uterine cancer seven years ago, during Taylor's junior year at Yale. For the first year after her death, he and his daughter had clung together, mostly to save each other from suffocating grief. Connor had planned to semi-retire, at fifty, stay on at Loden Media as chairman but turn the day-to-day business over to Dan Burke to run until Taylor was ready. He and Alexis had talked about traveling the world, getting more involved in the community. He had even toyed with the idea of buying a sailboat, and Alexis, with her artistic bent, had wanted to paint landscapes and take up photography.

But after Alexis died, there didn't seem to be any point to retiring; for a while there didn't seem to be any point to anything. So he stayed with his daughter at the company, and continued to expand it and his wealth, enjoying a certain satisfaction as he watched his baby grow bigger. But sometimes, like that evening, he wondered if life could offer him more than a Sunday night in his office.

"LET'S GO," DAVID said as the last buggy left the Fisher's. Jacob lightly snapped the reins and started down the lane.

"There's Aaron, waiting off to the left," David said.

Jacob pulled the buggy next to the Beilers and David leaned out the door to speak with Aaron. Anna sat on the seat beside her brother.

"You ready to lose again?" Aaron teased. "Maybe I should give you a head start."

"Eat cow dung," David retorted. He winked at Anna, then glanced down the road to make sure the area was clear of buggies. The Beiler farm was a mile south from the Fisher farm on the opposite side of the road and the Yoder farm a half mile south of the Beiler farm. David raised his hand in the air.

"When I drop it, go."

He looked at Jacob, who nodded his readiness. David dropped his hand.

The buggies lurched forward together.

"Yee ha!" Jacob yelled to Chestnut. The buggies were head-to-head for several hundred feet, then each took turns inching ahead, their battery-operated headlights piercing the dark road ahead.

Becca sat nervously in the back seat, her hand clutching the lantern. She had been driving a buggy for years and knew they shouldn't be racing, although it wasn't the first time she had known her brothers to do so. She was anxious but also exhilarated by the speed. Boys will be boys, she thought.

David leaned forward in the front seat, his cigarette in his left hand.

"Faster, faster. They're catching up," he yelled. He alternated between yelling and taking a puff of cigarette, flicking the ashes out the open buggy door. David could just make out the split rail fence that outlined the Beiler farm on the left; they were nearly to the entrance of the lane leading to the farm.

Jacob glanced quickly to his left and saw Aaron pulling up beside them. For an instant, they locked eyes. Jacob saw Aaron grin, and then all he saw was the back end of the Beiler buggy. Although Jacob urged Chestnut on, the Beilers were more than a buggy length ahead when they began to slow down and turn into their lane.

"They won again," David said. "We'll never hear the end of it." He looked at Jacob, expecting him to slow down Chestnut. Jacob made no move to do so.

Becca opened her mouth to speak, then hesitated, fearing Jacob would be annoyed with her.

"Jacob, there's a stop sign up ahead," she finally said, referring to the familiar four-way stop at the intersection of Hickory Hill Road and Stoney Creek Road.

But Jacob stared straight ahead, stone-faced, and the buggy flew through the night.

∾

TAYLOR FINALLY ADMITTED she was lost and wasting precious time driving around dark country roads with no streetlights. According to the last road sign she saw in the glare of her headlights, she was on Hickory Hill Road. She pulled over to the side of the road, grabbed her Blackberry, searched for the number, and called the Lancaster Hotel, where she had reservations. She told the desk clerk who she was and explained she was lost.

"If I'm close to Route 30, can you quickly give me directions? If it's too complicated, then give me your address and I'll plug it into my car's GPS."

"Ms. Loden, do you know what road you're on?"

"I'm on Hickory Hill Road and I just passed through a covered wooden bridge," she answered.

She saw the headlights of a horse and buggy coming down the other side of the road, followed after a short distance by two more. She figured there must be an Amish gathering in the area and was thankful they weren't on her side of the road slowing her down.

Taylor didn't know much about the Amish—they kept to themselves, wore strange clothes, lived on farms without electricity, spoke a German dialect called Pennsylvania Dutch, and only attended school through the eighth grade. She remembered they had been in the news a few years ago when a non-Amish gunman had entered a one-room schoolhouse in Nickel Mines and massacred five girls and injured five others.

Taylor remembered the event had been a media circus and the circulation for the *Lancaster Post*, the local paper the Lodens owned, had been off the charts. The incident had reinforced Taylor's impression of the Amish as compassionate and strong of faith, but nevertheless provincial, uneducated, uncultured social misfits.

"Ms. Loden, I know exactly where you are," the desk clerk said. "You're not that far off Route 30. Since you just passed through the covered bridge, you'll be coming up shortly to Stoney Creek Road. Make a left onto Stoney Creek, and follow that for less than a mile. Make a right onto Route 340, then a quick left onto 896. Route 896 will take you to Route 30. The hotel will be just down the highway on your left."

Taylor pulled the car back onto the road.

"Okay. I'm stopping at a stop sign." She squinted in the darkness at the road sign to her right. "Good, this is Stoney Creek Road. I'm turning left here. Thanks . . ."

As she turned, Taylor saw the buggy careening toward her. She wrenched the steering wheel to the left but the buggy smashed into the passenger side of the Z4. Taylor felt the car spin around; she slammed the brakes, heard screams, the panicked neigh of a horse, then silence.

The BMW's headlights cast an eerie glow over the buggy resting on its side on the road, its frame twisted and mangled, two of its wheels still slowly spinning. A straw hat lay upside down nearby.

2

TAYLOR TOOK A minute to steady herself and determine her injuries. Her chest ached and her right knee throbbed. Her hands shook so much she had trouble unhooking her seat belt. She opened the glove compartment and retrieved a flashlight. The passenger door was crushed into the seat, the side airbag had deployed, and oval pebble-sized glass pieces from the shattered window covered the seat and floor. After carefully rummaging around, she located her Blackberry on the floor. She also found her purse wedged under the seat and managed to extricate it, placing it on what was left of the seat. She opened the door and gingerly eased out of the car. She limped over to the buggy, shining the flashlight over the wreckage.

"Hello, anybody in there? I'm calling 911 right now," she called out, her voice cracking.

No response. She peered into the upended open door of the buggy, but saw no sign of passengers. She walked away from the buggy, her flashlight illuminating the ground. It was then she wondered about the horse. Where was the horse?

Taylor gasped as she came upon a male body, lying face up on the side of the road. She was bewildered at how uninjured he appeared—his arms at his sides, no limbs splayed at odd angles, no blood. The only clue his body had been violently thrown was a white sneaker missing on one foot. For an instant, like a reporter gathering facts, she was curious about his black jeans and t-shirt, decidedly non-Amish clothes. She thought he might be dead but then saw his eyes flicker. She knelt, wincing at the pain in her knee.

"Are you all right?" she asked. Averting his eyes from the flashlight's glare, he struggled to speak; his lips moved but no words came out.

"Okay, take it easy. I'm calling for help now. Can you tell me if anyone was in the buggy with you?"

"My brother and sister," he finally managed to say.

Taylor froze. Oh no, she thought, two more bodies are here somewhere.

She dialed 911. To her surprise, the operator told her an ambulance was already on the way. The desk clerk from the Lancaster Hotel had called as soon as he had heard the crash while talking to Taylor on the phone and had directed them to the accident site. Taylor told the operator three were injured and the operator said she would send another ambulance.

She returned to her car. From what she could see from the glow of the flashlight, the entire right side of the Z4 was dented and part of the hood crunched. However, she was able to open the trunk. She pushed aside her suitcase and briefcase and grabbed the navy wool blanket she kept on top of the first aid kit. She returned to the roadside male and covered him with the blanket.

"Are you in any pain?" she asked.

"I don't feel . . . anything," he whispered.

TAYLOR WALKED ALONG the road, flashlight in hand, searching for the other brother and sister. She heard the wail of a siren in the distance, and then saw a female figure stumbling down the road away from the accident site.

"Wait!" Taylor called out. "Are you okay? Where are you going? The ambulance is on the way."

The girl, her left arm bent at the elbow and close to her chest, did not respond and continued to walk toward what Taylor then saw was a lane leading to a farmhouse.

Taylor's attention was diverted by a whooshing sound and she turned to see flames on the other side of the buggy. Ignoring her knee pain, she ran toward the fire, frantic to locate the second brother.

As she rounded the buggy, she saw him. He lay on his right side on the road, motionless, but as Taylor neared, she heard him moan. His face was bloody, his breathing labored. A flaming puddle on the road had spread to within a few feet of his body. Taylor bent over him.

"Can you get up?"

No answer. Carefully she shook his shoulder.

"Hello, hello, please, can you get up? The fire, the fire is coming. To you." In her rising panic, Taylor couldn't speak coherently. Still no answer.

The ambulance screamed louder and in the distance came the wail of the second. But there wasn't time to wait for help. Taylor felt the heat of the flames, inching closer.

She tossed the flashlight and her cell phone onto the embankment beside the road, gently rolled the brother onto his back, hooked her hands under his arms and pulled him, slowly at first, then more urgently, breathing hard from exertion, away from the flames. Unconscious before, the movement of his battered body brought him back. His scream so startled Taylor she nearly dropped him but she didn't stop moving until they were well away from the flames.

"I'm so sorry," she said as she knelt next to him. "I had to move you. I hope I didn't make your injuries worse."

Without the flashlight and with the blaze behind them, she could no longer see clearly but it seemed as if he turned his head and looked into her face.

"It's my fault," he said.

Out of the corner of her eye Taylor saw movement. A man and woman ran down the road toward them, a younger girl hobbled behind. Taylor stood. She recognized the girl as the one who had left the accident earlier. The man, older and bearded, and the adult woman both carried kerosene lanterns.

As they came closer, the lantern light illuminated the bone protruding from the young girl's elbow and the blood from the gash on her leg, the woman's white and terrified face, and the man's wild-eyed look.

"My sons, my sons," the man choked. "You *Englishers* and your fancy cars," he spat. "Look what you have done."

THE QUIET OF the rural country landscape was shattered and the night suddenly ablaze as the first ambulance and paramedic vehicle arrived, lights flashing. Two paramedics and two ambulance attendants jumped out. Within moments, a police car arrived.

"Call the fire department," the police officer yelled to his partner as he emerged from the car and saw the flames.

Quickly Taylor pointed the paramedics to where the brothers lay and nervously explained why she had moved the one. Taylor also pointed out the girl, and one of the ambulance attendants and a police officer approached her and the two adults as they stood by the road. Relieved that help had arrived, Taylor returned to her car and leaned against it, watching the attendants work.

One wrapped the gash on the girl's leg, put an inflatable splint on her arm, and quickly ushered her to the ambulance. Two transferred the brother Taylor had moved onto a backboard and placed a cervical collar around his neck. Inside the ambulance, Taylor could see him being hooked up to an IV and given oxygen. The ambulance doors closed and the brother and sister sped away, the paramedic vehicle with the adults aboard right behind. The couple's two kerosene lamps sat extinguished by the side of the road.

After radioing for a fire truck, the second police officer conferred with Taylor. She explained to the officer what had happened, he examined her car, and then left to investigate the buggy and the area of the fire, which by then had extinguished itself. The second ambulance arrived.

While paramedics placed the brother Taylor had discovered first on a backboard and gave him a cervical collar, an attendant approached Taylor. She told him her chest and knee hurt and he said she needed to go in the ambulance to the hospital to get checked.

"Okay, but I need to get my laptop and purse out of the car," Taylor said.

"We have to go now. You can get those items later from the police," the attendant said.

"No, I can't be without them," Taylor said. She grabbed her purse from the car and then retrieved her briefcase, which contained the laptop, from the trunk. She'd have to leave her Blackberry by the side of the road where she'd tossed it, but at least, she thought, she'd have the iPhone in her purse.

She climbed into the back of the ambulance with the first brother just as the fire truck pulled up. A paramedic climbed in back with them, closed the door, and with sirens screaming, they headed toward Memorial General Hospital.

TAYLOR LAY ON the stretcher and watched the reflection of the siren lights bounce around the inside of the ambulance. She couldn't decide whether the wail of the siren was a sound of hope or horror. The adrenaline rush she felt at the accident scene was gone and her body shook uncontrollably. She closed her eyes and, as the competent businesswoman she knew herself to be, attempted to come up with an action plan, but her mind, foggy and sluggish, froze like a computer screen, leaving her blank.

She glanced over at the first brother, thinking how jarring the speed and noise of the ambulance must be compared to a buggy ride, and was surprised to see him watching her. His dark eyes were wide and frightened but there was something about him that also suggested intensity and complexity. The paramedic adjusted the IV. Taylor struggled to sit up on one elbow and lean toward him; the pain in her chest seemed worse or maybe she noticed it more since she was stationary.

"I'm Taylor," she said, their faces only a couple feet apart. "What's your name?"

"Jacob."

"How do you feel, Jacob?"

Long pause. "I can't feel my legs."

The paramedic stiffened. Taylor lay back on the stretcher and wondered about the smell of alcohol on Jacob's breath.

THE TELEVISIONS IN the hospital waiting room blared the Sunday late night news. The room bustled with activity. Daniel and Sarah had been waiting for over an hour and had been given a pager so the emergency room staff and doctors could keep in touch. They sat next to the wall aquarium, heads bowed in prayer, ignoring the colorful fish, the televisions, and the stares and whispers—they were used to being gawked at by the hordes of year-round tourists who headed to Lancaster to see the Amish up close.

Earlier that night, when Becca had come screaming into the house, Daniel and Sarah had already been in bed. Daniel had grabbed from the bedroom floor the dirty and manure-smelling clothes he had milked the cows in earlier; his barn boots were only tied enough to keep his feet from walking out of them and the laces trailed the ground. Sarah, in a plain white nightgown, had snatched her black cape that needed darning off the bedroom chair; it had a noticeable hole at the shoulder seam. Her long blond hair tinged with grey fell down her back, and she had wasted no time looking for her black shoes—her feet were bare.

Under normal circumstances, Sarah would have been mortified about appearing in public in her nightgown and without her hair in a neat bun under a white *kapp,* and without her black nylon stockings and shoes. But right then, both cared nothing about appearances. Absorbed in their prayers and being unfamiliar with pager technology, they didn't notice the pager vibrate as it sat on the table beside them.

"Yoder, anyone from the Yoder family?" a doctor called. Daniel's head snapped to attention and he stood.

"I'm Dr. Branson. Two other doctors and I have been treating your sons and daughter in the emergency room."

"Are they going to be all right?" Sarah asked, rising to stand beside her husband.

"Becca was treated for the laceration in her leg and her left arm is fractured. We've called in an orthopedic surgeon. She'll undergo surgery as soon as the surgeon arrives. Pins will be placed in her arm to realign and stabilize the bone. The paramedics said she landed on the grass embankment and fortunately didn't receive the full brunt of being slammed against the road, as did her brothers. Assuming a successful surgery, she should be able to go home tomorrow. She's resting in one of the ER beds and you may see her before she's taken to surgery.

"David sustained three broken ribs and a collapsed right lung, as well as numerous abrasions on his arms, legs, and face. The right side of his body hit the road full force. He also has a mild concussion and a nasty bump on the right side of his head. We inserted a chest tube to help his lung expand. He should be in the hospital for three or four days and is being transferred to a room on the fourth floor. You may see him as soon as he's settled. Becca and David were very lucky. Their injuries are serious but not life threatening."

Dr. Branson paused. The Yoders stared at him, bewildered and overwhelmed.

"And our Jacob?" Daniel asked.

"Jacob is the most critically injured," the doctor explained. "He's in our neurological trauma unit now. He also has arm and leg abrasions. A CT scan shows a spinal fracture and swelling around the spinal cord. It's too early to tell the severity of the damage to the spinal cord but there appears to be some paralysis."

"What are you saying?" Sarah asked, her voice quivering.

"We won't know for sure until the swelling goes down and we get an MRI, which is a more in-depth look at the spinal cord, but the paralysis could be temporary or permanent."

Sarah leaned into her husband as Daniel's left hand grasped at his beard.

"What of the *Englisher*?" Daniel asked, a hint of anger in his voice.

"Her condition can only be released to a family member but we'll keep her overnight. You should know the paramedics told me Ms. Loden may have saved David's life. She apparently dragged him away from the flames heading toward where he lay on the road."

"*Ja*, we know," Sarah said softly. "We saw her."

"There's something else you should know." The doctor hesitated, knowing his next words would cause the parents even further anguish. "The paramedics and the ER doctors smelled alcohol on both David's and Jacob's breath."

3

W HEN JACOB WOKE, it was still dark. The clock on the wall opposite his bed read 4:45 but without looking he knew what time it was. Time to milk the cows. He automatically began to swing his legs off the side of his bed, his mind allowing him a few blessed moments of forgetfulness before he again heard Becca's scream, Chestnut's frantic neigh, and the solid crunch of the buggy smashing into the car. He again felt the buggy disintegrating around him, his body flying through the air, the smack of his bones against the road. He lay still while his confusion grew. He felt the IV hookup in his arm, the heart monitor wires taped to his chest, the bandages on his arms. What he couldn't feel were his legs. As his eyes adjusted to the dark, he saw the metal bed rails, the TV hanging from the wall, and the phone on the table by his bed. He realized he wasn't home. And he wasn't getting out of bed to milk the cows.

TAYLOR ALSO WOKE early and her first thought was to get out of the hospital in time for her conference panel discussion. The night before when she had called her father from the ER, she had instructed him to bring her, first thing in the morning, shoes and another suit since her suitcase was still in her car trunk. Connor had wanted to drive to Lancaster right then but she told him that wasn't necessary, she was fine, she had apparently banged her knee on the steering column and her chest on the steering wheel and the doctor was keeping her overnight only to make sure she didn't have an irregular heartbeat.

She slowly climbed out of bed in the predawn hours of Monday, her body stiff and sore under her hospital gown, and retrieved her laptop from the briefcase on the chair by her bed. A nurse had neatly folded the clothes Taylor had worn the night before and placed them on the chair. Taylor dared not even glance at those clothes, let alone put them on again. Just looking at them suggested reliving the accident and she didn't want to go there—not yet.

She spent the next hour and a half in bed reading over her notes for the panel discussion and responding to emails. She then headed for the bathroom. She wore a wireless heart monitor so she washed carefully by hand. No sooner had she stepped out of the bathroom than her father walked into her room, pantsuit and shoes in hand. He hung the clothes in the closet, then gently embraced his daughter.

Connor watched as Taylor walked stiffly to the bed and pressed the call button for the nurse. He saw the purple bruised area around her right knee and grimaced.

"Whatever needs to happen to get me out of here within an hour, please do it," she told the nurse. "And can you remove this heart monitor? I need to get dressed."

Connor sat beside his daughter on the bed. "You don't need to go to the conference. I'll call and tell them you've been in an accident. Bob Hayes, the editor from our paper here in Lancaster, he's on the panel too, right? He can take over for you. I'll stay with you until you're released and then take you home. Dan can step in for me and give the speech I prepared. He could be up here in plenty of time to speak at lunch if I call him right now."

"No, Dad. I'm going to the conference. I'm a little sore but otherwise fine. I need to get out of here, preferably ten minutes ago. I'm prepared for the panel and I'm going to get dressed and go."

Connor nodded reluctantly. "Can you tell me more about the accident? I didn't get many details from you last night on the phone. After all, I am a newsman; we're a very curious bunch, you know." He attempted a weak grin.

"I can't, Dad. Too soon. I need to keep busy, not dwell on it. So, I've got my laptop here but my panel discussion notes need to be printed out. I can do that at the conference. At some point today, we need to check on my car—Where is my car, by the way?—and get my suitcase out of the trunk. Also, I need a rental car. Maybe they can take care of that for me at the hotel."

She ignored the anxiety she felt at the idea of getting behind the wheel of a car.

THE YODERS SPENT the night with David, sleeping fitfully on chairs in his hospital room. Becca came out of surgery about three in the morning. When Sarah woke, she inquired at the nurses' station and was told Becca's room was down the hall from David's. Sarah quietly entered the room but Becca was still asleep. When Sarah returned to David's room, Daniel was awake.

"Your parents and the kids will be anxious," Sarah said.

"*Ja*, but not to worry," Daniel said. "They'll take care of what needs to be done while we're here. After we see how our three are doing, I'll call home from David's or Becca's room. Hopefully someone will hear and answer the phone in the shed."

The night before, as Daniel and Sarah flew out the door on their way to the accident scene, Daniel had banged on Mary and Levi's door and had hurriedly explained the situation. Daniel knew his mother would reassure the twins and Levi and Katie could handle the milking, at least for the morning.

David groaned and opened his eyes.

"How do you feel, son?" Daniel asked.

"My chest and my head hurt. How are Jacob and Becca?"

Sarah lightly kissed his forehead. "Becca will be fine, her arm is fractured," she said. "Jacob, we don't know yet, they need to do more tests, but he's alive. David, what happened?"

"*Mamm, Dat*, I . . . " David's voice cracked. "It was my idea to race against Aaron Beiler. Jacob was driving and he . . . I don't know why he ran the stop sign." He paused and swallowed hard. "We both drank beer at the Fishers, in the barn. Oh, God, what have I done?"

Daniel shook his head and frowned. "Your poor judgment has cost you, and us, much."

The room door opened and a police officer entered.

"Good morning, I'm Officer Reid. I'm investigating the accident and I need to speak to David—alone, please."

THE SUN CRESTED the horizon, casting a hazy glow over the Yoder farm, the dew shimmering on the fields like shards of glass, as Levi exited the barn. He and Katie had managed to milk the herd themselves but it had been slow going without Daniel and the boys. Levi had been stoic around Katie, who was worried sick about her siblings, but he felt the strain and the fatigue deep in his bones. He was sixty-seven but that morning he felt like a hundred. With heavy footsteps, he made his way to the house for the breakfast Mary had prepared.

The mood was somber at the kitchen table. Even the normally boisterous twins were subdued as they picked at the eggs and bacon on their plates.

Levi normally left the use of the storage shed phone, located on a corner of the property away from the house, mainly to his son, who only used it to call the vet, feed dealers or the like, but that morning had overcome his disdain for what he termed "a too worldly gadget" and had called various relatives to tell them about the accident.

As Katie distracted the twins after breakfast with a card game, Mary and Levi talked quietly in the kitchen.

"I could walk down the road to the Evanston's farm and ask Harold if he'll take me to the hospital in his car," Levi said. "It'll take too long to get there by buggy plus I can't drive down Route 30 with all that car and truck traffic."

"The Evanstons are good English neighbors," Mary said, gazing absently out the window as she cleaned the breakfast dishes. "They'll help if they can. I can't bear another minute without knowing how everyone is." Suddenly, a glass clattered in the sink. "Levi, we have a visitor. It's a state police car."

Levi walked outside and met the officer as he exited the car. They introduced themselves and the officer told Levi he was investigating the accident.

"I came here to talk to you briefly, if you can spare the time," Officer Mullen said.

"Do you know anything about my grandchildren?" Levi asked. "We haven't had any news yet from my son."

"I don't have details or any recent news, Mr. Yoder, but I do know that all three of your grandchildren were alive as of very early this morning," Officer Mullen said.

Levi ushered the officer into the house, where Mary hovered by the door.

"Everyone is still alive, as far as the officer knows," Levi told Mary as the two passed her on their way to the family room. The trooper eyed the room, large but spare, with plain off-white walls, an armchair in each corner, a compressed air sewing machine against one wall, a glass-fronted cabinet against another. A well-worn sofa and rectangular wooden coffee table sat on a frayed braided throw rug. On the coffee table were piles of the weekly Old Order Amish newspaper *Die Botschaft*, and several months of *Reader's Digest*, assorted farm journals, and the black and white Amish magazine *Family Life*. Levi motioned for the officer to sit as he stood in front of the windows, adorned with dark green shades pulled a third of the way down, which overlooked the front yard and a small pond.

"I'm curious about the horse that pulled the buggy," Officer Mullen said as he sat on the edge of the sofa. "No horse was found at the scene of the accident."

"Chestnut is here, in his stall," Levi explained. "He must've come home last night. We found him standing by the barn this morning. He was still dragging part of the torn reins and harness. He doesn't seem to have been hit by the car but he's skittish and has some cuts and bruises on his flank and legs. The vet's coming later today to check him over."

"Mr. Yoder, I know this is hard for you but I have two kerosene lanterns in my car and a white sneaker that were found at the scene. I also wanted you to know the buggy was towed to the Stoltzfus Coach Shop over in Paradise. It was too damaged for repair but the shop may be able to use it for parts."

DANIEL AND SARAH walked down the hall to Becca's room while Officer Reid talked to David. Becca was awake and a nurse helping her bathe told them Officer Reid had stopped by just a few moments ago and would be back. The Yoders asked at the nurses' station for directions to Jacob's room, then took the elevator up to the Neuro Unit on the fifth floor.

Sarah stared at her eldest son, his eyes closed, lying so still among the wires protruding from his body, and she clasped her hands together to steady herself. She and Daniel stood by his bed and after a few moments, Jacob's eyes opened. Sarah saw no trace of the remorse she had seen on David's face. Instead, Jacob's eyes were cold, his face expressionless.

"How do you feel?" Sarah asked.

"What I can feel hurts," Jacob replied tersely. "How are David and Becca?"

Sarah filled Jacob in on his siblings' injuries.

"David explained what happened," Daniel said. "Jacob, what were you thinking? What price for your recklessness?"

Jacob stared straight ahead and remained silent.

Daniel and Sarah moved back from the bed as a doctor entered their son's room. She nodded to the Yoders and addressed Jacob.

"I'm Dr. Mayes, your neurosurgeon. You have a spinal fracture but it's stable and doesn't require surgery. We'll be giving you steroids to reduce the swelling around your spinal cord. You're scheduled for an MRI later this morning, which will give us pictures of the fracture. Once we get the MRI results back, we'll know more."

Dr. Mayes drew down the bed covers. "Tell me if you can feel any of my touches," she said as her hand began probing Jacob's legs in various places.

Jacob clenched his fists and shook his head. No, he could not feel her touches.

Later, when Jacob looked back to the moment when his normal good sense flew out the window of the racing buggy, he realized three factors had clouded his judgment and caused him to suddenly snap: the beer, the stress of a dual life, and the secret he was keeping from his family.

DESPITE HER IMPATIENCE, Taylor waited more than an hour to be released from the hospital. A doctor checked her monitor, said her heart rhythm was fine, and approved her discharge. While she and Connor waited, Officer Reid visited. He explained he had already talked to David, Becca, and Jacob, as well as the desk clerk at the Host Resort, who had confirmed that Taylor had been stopped at her stop sign while asking for directions. He returned Taylor's cell phone and flashlight that one of the officers found by the side of Hickory Hill Road. He also informed Taylor her car had been towed to a local BMW repair shop.

"Ms. Loden, based on our investigation, you are not legally responsible for the accident," Officer Reid said. "Although you were on the phone getting directions at the time of the accident, it is not yet against the law in Pennsylvania to talk on a cell phone while driving. The fault lies with Jacob Yoder. The buggy ran the stop sign and he had been drinking. You could sue to recover the costs of your injuries and damages to your car. The Old Order Amish don't usually appear in court—it's against their religion—but they would probably pay."

"Old Order Amish?" Taylor asked.

"One of the most conservative Amish sects," Reid explained. "No cars, no driver's licenses, and obviously, no car insurance."

"You should sue," Connor said. "You've been injured and your car damaged due to this Yoder boy's drunk driving. He should pay for his irresponsibility."

"Maybe if I had been paying more attention, I could have averted the accident," Taylor said. "Maybe I would've seen the buggy coming and realized it wasn't slowing down as it approached the stop sign."

"Don't blame yourself," Connor said. "You weren't just gabbing on the phone. You were lost and legitimately used the phone to ask for directions. You had stopped at your stop sign and were proceeding legally. It wasn't your fault."

Taylor shook her head. "Nevertheless, I won't be suing," Taylor said. "I have insurance to fix my car and I think the Yoders have more than paid for their recklessness. All of them have suffered injuries far worse than mine."

OFFICER REID ASKED Daniel and Sarah and the Lodens to gather in the waiting room on the fourth floor. The group of friends and relatives that had been at the hospital earlier to visit the Yoders had already left and they had the room to themselves.

"I want to brief you all on the results of our investigation of the accident, on the interviews I've had with Taylor Loden, and David, Becca, and Jacob Yoder, as well as interviews other officers have conducted.

"After the singing at the Fisher farm, David initiated the race with Aaron Beiler but Jacob drove the buggy. Both David and Jacob admitted to drinking and we found empty beer cans amid the wreckage of the buggy. We asked the hospital to do a blood alcohol level test when Jacob was in the emergency room. His blood alcohol level was 0.095 percent, which is above the legal limit of 0.08 percent.

"We have concluded that a kerosene lamp Becca Yoder was holding caused the fire at the scene. Most likely the cigarette David smoked during the race ignited the kerosene on the road where the lamp smashed. We were perplexed at the scene Sunday night because there was no sign of the horse that had pulled the buggy. We've since learned the horse returned on its own to the Yoder farm. Jacob said he pulled the reins hard to the left once he saw the car, which caused his side of the buggy to hit the BMW, sparing the horse. Apparently, the horse's reins and the harness snapped from the force of the collision, and though the animal did not hit the car, it did sustain some injuries.

"Mr. and Mrs. Yoder, charges will be filed against Jacob for driving under the influence and for recklessness and he will be fined. He doesn't have a driver's license, but if he did, it would be suspended. Even though this DUI is a first offense for Jacob, he could face jail time because the accident resulted in injuries and property damage. We will be in touch with Jacob about the charges in more detail later. Any questions?" Officer Reid slapped his notebook shut.

The Yoders were silent, heads bowed.

"Thank you, Officer," Connor said. "If we're free to go, we have a conference to attend."

Now I understand, Taylor thought as they left the hospital, why David blamed himself Sunday night for the accident.

TAYLOR SAT IN the center of the panel discussion table, the microphone in front of her, three panelists on either side. She looked out into the audience and saw many familiar faces, including her father's. She paid attention to the remarks made by the panelists, interjected her own comments when necessary, and took questions from the audience, but her mind felt strangely disconnected from her mouth. Uncharacteristically, she couldn't seem to focus completely on the topic at hand, although it was one with which she was intimately familiar. Her mouth mechanically spouted statistics on the number of newspaper acquisitions by large corporations nationwide and how that affected circulation and thus advertising and revenue rates. But flashbacks of the accident kept intruding: the dream-like slow motion spinning of her car after impact, David's crumpled body on the road, Jacob's intense yet frightened eyes in the ambulance.

After her father's luncheon speech, Taylor insisted they both return to Memorial General. Although she had been anxious to leave the hospital that morning, she needed to return and attend to unfinished business.

DAVID'S ROOM WAS sunny but quiet, the TV silent. At first Taylor thought he was asleep and she turned to go but then he said, "Come in."

"I just came to see how you are," Taylor said. "I'm Taylor Loden. I don't know if you remember me but . . . "

"*Ja,* the girl in the car," David said. "Thank God you weren't badly hurt."

"I understand you were racing another buggy. But I don't blame you for what happened and I don't consider myself blameless. If I had been paying attention or in less of a hurry . . . "

"But your car, it was wrecked, *ja?*"

"Yes, but it can be repaired. Don't worry about my car. Just concentrate on getting better." There was an awkward pause.

"My father told me what you did, pulling me away from the fire."

"I was afraid I had hurt you worse by moving you."

"I'll be fine. We Yoders are of strong stock."

TAYLOR FOUND SARAH and Daniel in the lounge waiting for Becca to be discharged. She hadn't spoken to the Yoders during Officer Reid's briefing that morning since she'd been in a hurry to get to the conference. She strode purposefully across the waiting room, her arm outstretched. Sarah shook her hand limply. Daniel merely nodded. Taylor noticed his beefy hands, the dirt under his fingernails, and figured it was just as well he kept his hand to himself.

"I just visited David and I wanted to also visit Jacob but the nurses told me only family can see him for now. Can you tell me how he is?"

"That is not your business," Daniel said brusquely.

Connor watched the exchange from the chair where he had settled to wait for Taylor. He felt no need to come to the aid of his daughter. She stood proud and sure in her black Armani pantsuit, her face hard-edged, so that her cheekbones appeared more prominent than they actually were. Connor eyed Sarah's cotton ankle-length white nightgown, handmade cape, and feet covered by disposable hospital slippers; he cringed at Daniel's dirty trousers, manure splattered boots, and scruffy beard. True farmer hicks, he decided. He was certain Taylor's black patent Louboutin heels cost more than the Yoders made in a month.

"Mr. Yoder," Taylor countered tersely. "I meant no disrespect. I'm merely concerned about your sons."

Sarah rose from her chair. "Forgive us," she said, her voice soft but firm. "We don't mean to be rude. We're a private people. And we're under a lot of strain."

"Sarah, there's no need to apologize," Daniel admonished.

"Daniel, please permit me. Taylor, my husband and I both owe you thanks for saving our David. We saw you drag him from the fire. You'll always be in our prayers."

Connor sat up ramrod straight. He was obviously still out of the loop on accident details. It had been news to him that morning at the police briefing that there had even been a fire.

"As for Jacob," Sarah continued, "more tests need to be done but he can't move his legs yet."

"Mrs. Yoder . . . ," Taylor began contritely.

"Call me Sarah."

A nurse approached and told the Yoders Becca had been discharged and was asking for them. Daniel and Sarah looked at each other. "We'll call a van service," Daniel said.

Connor stood. "I'm Taylor's father, Connor Loden. It would be my pleasure to drive you and Becca home. I assume you're permitted to ride in cars. We could leave right now if you like."

Daniel eyed Connor suspiciously. He didn't know the man and wasn't fond of his daughter, even though she seemed genuinely concerned about his sons. Everything about both of them screamed flashy English folks. But it was nearly midafternoon. Sarah was anxious to get home to the twins and Katie, and the evening milking was fast approaching. To call and wait for a van would take more time. If he accepted Connor's offer, they would get home quicker and he and Levi could do the milking together.

"We don't own cars," Daniel said. "But we can ride in them. We will go with you."

CONNOR PULLED HIS black Mercedes S550 to the front entrance of the hospital. He helped Becca, her left arm in a cast, into the back seat with Sarah and Taylor. Daniel sat in front and stared rigidly out the window. Taylor watched Becca surreptitiously run her hand over the leather seats and the burl walnut wood trim on the inside door panel. Except for Daniel giving Connor directions to the farm, conversation was light.

As the car drove down Stoney Creek Road, Becca began to fidget. When they stopped at the stop sign and began to turn onto Hickory Hill Road, tears trickled down her face. Taylor understood at once; they were passing the accident scene. Becca leaned against her mother and Sarah comforted her in what sounded like German and what Taylor guessed was Pennsylvania Dutch or *Deitsch*. Taylor realized the Amish were bilingual, although all her interaction with them had been in English.

The car pulled into the Yoder's lane and had no sooner stopped at the farm house than the back door flew open and three children came flying out followed by an older couple. Daniel grudgingly introduced the twins and Katie and his parents and retreated into the house.

Taylor and Connor stood awkwardly by while Sarah spoke to her children and in-laws in their language, Katie clinging to Becca's good arm. Taylor heard David and Jacob's names mentioned and assumed Sarah was updating the family on their condition. After a few minutes, Joseph approached Connor.

"Can I sit in your car? *Mamm*, can I sit in the car?" he yelled.

"Me, too!" Emma cried.

Connor laughed. "Of course." He opened the door and they both tumbled in, then listened with rapt attention as he explained the workings of the car, the reclining seats being of particular interest.

Taylor gazed out over the Yoder farm: the expansive two-story stone farmhouse; the furrowed fields as far as the eye could see; the vegetable garden with its dark soil and weed-free orderly rows; the classic red barn; the small pond in the front yard; the two wooden bridges over portions of a creek that meandered through the property, separating the farm from the fields; the wooden rope swing hanging from the oak tree in front of the house. The whole scene evoked an earthy rural beauty, a quiet peacefulness entirely different from the dynamic, often frenetic pace of the city where Taylor lived. Something inside Taylor shifted slightly.

Impulsively, she turned to Sarah. "I'm going to be staying in the area until my car is repaired," she said, ignoring Connor's startled look. "I plan on renting a car. I could take you and your family back and forth to the hospital while I'm here. It would be no trouble." She once again ignored the nagging fear she felt about driving a car.

Sarah hesitated. She wanted to be at the hospital as much as possible. Having access to Taylor and her car would be like having their own personal car service. They wouldn't have to pay a van service or ask neighbors and other acquaintances for rides. Daniel might not be comfortable with the idea but he would certainly understand the money they would save, plus it would only be temporary, until Taylor's car was fixed and she went home.

"I would be most grateful," Sarah said.

"Great. Right now, I need to go check on my car. I can be back here by seven o'clock so we can get to the hospital for evening visiting hours."

CONNOR HELD THE glass of chardonnay up to the light, swirled it, then took a sip. He nodded to the waiter. He and Taylor were dining early at the hotel before she picked up Sarah to return to the hospital. He planned to drive back to Philadelphia after dinner. That afternoon, Taylor had told Connor she had decided to take the rest of the week off from work. She had rented a car and had extended her stay at the Lancaster Hotel. She assured her father she could take care of business from the hotel or the hospital. Connor wasn't concerned about the work, however; plenty of employees at Loden Media could pick up the slack for a few days.

"I don't understand why you want to stay here and play chauffeur for the Amish," he said.

Taylor sighed. "I don't fully understand it either, Dad. I feel compelled to be here. I want to make sure David and Jacob and Becca will be okay. I feel somewhat responsible for the accident"—she held up her hand as Connor started to object—"even though no one else thinks I am."

Connor raised his glass of wine to his daughter. "Whatever you need. Just stay in touch."

He was intrigued. It was the first time in a long while that Taylor took an interest in something other than work.

THE FRONT-PAGE article in the *Lancaster Post* regarding the accident made much of the fact that Amish youngsters had attended a party with alcohol and that the driver of the buggy had been legally drunk. The article even included a picture of the demolished buggy. The story included Taylor's name, of course, but not a picture and did not mention she was a newspaper heiress.

Connor had picked up a copy of the paper before he checked out of the hotel, read it, and had sighed in relief. That had been a necessary phone call, although he had been loath to make it. Only once before had he interfered in his editors' news decisions and that had been when his wife had died; a simple obituary in all his papers had been enough then rather than a splashy news article. So again, with the buggy accident, privacy concerns had overridden his desire for the big, moneymaking story. Best to keep Taylor's identity quiet or she would be hounded unmercifully by the press, perhaps not by the media he owned but by other regional, maybe even national, news outlets. Her hiding out in rural Lancaster would help keep her under the radar, at least, Connor hoped, for the near future.

4

ARON BEILER STEPPED down from his buggy Monday evening and walked across the Yoder's yard and over the creek bridge toward Daniel, who was surveying the tobacco seedbed.

"Evenin,' Aaron," Daniel said. On one knee, he gently handled the tobacco plants, searching for the mature ones ready to be pulled and replanted into the field.

"About a third of the plants are ready to be transplanted. I need to get them from the bed to the field in the next day or so."

"That's why I'm here," Aaron said. "I can help, starting tomorrow, if you'll have me."

With two of his sons in the hospital, Daniel was short-handed in the field. Isaac Fisher, whose farm had hosted the Sunday evening singing, and who also grew tobacco, had already told Levi he and one of his sons would be available that week to help with the transplanting. The police fined Isaac for permitting underage drinking on his property, although he told Daniel he hadn't known about the beer in his barn. He also told Daniel his two offending sons paid the fine out of the small amount of money fathers customarily pay their elder sons from the farm profits.

Daniel looked up at Aaron. He was the second eldest of the three Beiler sons and Daniel had watched him grow up. Since the Beilers ran a large dairy farm, about sixty cows, Aaron wasn't familiar with tobacco fieldwork and would need to be taught. Daniel knew Aaron had offered to help partly because it was the Amish way and partly out of guilt over having been involved in the buggy race that preceded the accident. Daniel disapproved of the racing but placed blame for the accident squarely on the shoulders of his sons. He considered the Beilers a good Amish family, had known them all his life, and was happy David was marrying into the family. He had no grievance against Aaron and was grateful for the offer of help.

"Be here right after breakfast tomorrow," he said.

TAYLOR GRASPED THE steering wheel tightly to stop her shaking hands as she pulled out of the Yoder lane, Sarah in the passenger seat, Mary and Becca in the back. Even though she had driven the family to the hospital the night before, she was still nervous driving, especially in the area where the accident occurred. She saw Sarah glance at her shaking hands, but she made no comment. Taylor had realized the night before that her five-passenger rental car was not sufficient for the chauffeuring she would be doing. The twins and Levi had wanted to go to the hospital too but there hadn't been room. Taylor had offered to make a second trip but Sarah wouldn't hear of it.

Katie and the twins were visiting their aunt and uncle, Rachel and John Esh, who lived in nearby Bird-in-Hand, in a house John, a contractor, had built, and Levi, Daniel, the Fishers, and Aaron Beiler were working on the tobacco, so for the morning the car was fine. But Taylor had decided to drop the Yoders off at the hospital, then return to the car agency and rent a van that could accommodate more passengers.

The women visited Jacob in the morning in the Neuro Unit; they planned to return to the hospital that evening to visit David, since Sarah and Mary wanted to be home within a couple hours to cook the noon meal for the men. If it had just been Daniel and Levi, under the circumstances Sarah would have left them to fend for themselves, but with the Fisher and Beiler visitors, Sarah wanted to make sure they were all fed well as thanks for their help.

Jacob worried Sarah; he had been sullen and uncommunicative since the accident, and had hardly seemed to care whether his family visited him or not. The three women had been in Jacob's room for only a few minutes when Dr. Mayes, the neurosurgeon, arrived.

"I have the results of your MRI," she told Jacob, after Sarah introduced her to the others. "But first, let me explain to you and your family in more detail about the spinal cord." Dr. Mayes lowered the rail on Jacob's bed, sat down, and held up a diagram of the spinal cord.

"The spinal cord is about eighteen inches long and extends from the base of the brain, down the middle of the back, to the waist," she began. "It is the major bundle of nerves that carries nerve impulses to and from the brain to the rest of the body. These nerve impulses tell the brain what parts of the body to move. The spinal cord is surrounded by rings of bone called vertebra, which comprise the spinal column. Specific areas of the vertebra control specific regions of the body.

"The five vertebra in your lower back, between your ribs and your pelvis or hip bone, are called the lumbar vertebra, and they are labeled L1 through L5. According to your MRI, the L3 region of your spinal cord—she pointed to the area on the diagram—has been damaged, resulting in loss of hip and leg functioning. In a permanent injury, no function exists below the level of the injury because the spinal cord nerves cannot send messages between the brain and parts of the body as they did before the injury. In other words, there is no sensation and no voluntary movement below your third lumbar vertebra, and both sides of your body are equally affected. In your case, with an L3 injury, there would also be loss of bowel, bladder, and sexual functioning."

Dr. Mayes rested her hand on Jacob's arm.

"However, since there is still some swelling around the spinal cord, we can't determine yet whether your injury is permanent. There's a possibility of some recovery below the level of the injury but we won't know that until the swelling goes down."

"How long before the swelling goes down?" Jacob asked.

"It could be one or two more days or as long as a week," Dr. Mayes replied.

The silence hung heavy in the room. Becca laid her head on her mother's shoulder.

"I may not walk again," Jacob stated matter-of-factly.

"That is a possibility," Dr. Mayes said. "All we can do right now is take it one day at a time."

After the neurosurgeon left, Sarah, Mary and Becca gathered around Jacob's bed. Sarah's eyes were red-rimmed and she didn't trust herself to speak. Mary spoke instead.

"Whatever happens will be God's will," she said. "And we will pray for the strength to bear His will."

Jacob closed his eyes. "Can you leave now? I want to be alone."

"JOSEPH, PAY ATTENTION to what you're doing," Daniel admonished. "The plant needs to go in the hole, not beside the hole."

"Sorry, *Dat*."

While Katie, Levi, and Sarah took care of the four-thirty milking, Daniel drove the two-row tobacco planter and Emma and Joseph dropped plants. Pulled by two Percheron draft horses, the planter made furrows in the field, one on each side of the planter, as it went along. It had a large water tank mounted on a pair of wheels and a place for two people to sit close to the ground and drop plants into the furrows. The tank's trip mechanism released a small amount of water into the furrow, at which time each twin dropped a plant. With proper spacing—each plant spread about twenty-eight inches apart—Daniel calculated his six acres would yield close to thirty-six thousand tobacco plants.

Daniel figured it would take half the time for he and the twins to transplant what had taken the morning workers four hours to pull from the seedbed. After heavily watering the seedbed that morning, Daniel, Levi, Aaron, Isaac Fisher and his son Jonas had pulled the mature tobacco plants, careful not to damage the root system of each plant. The time consuming part was in determining which of the plants were mature and ready to be pulled since not all the plants matured at the same rate. They had placed the pulled plants in the shade, where they would be ready for transplanting into the field during the cooler early evening, which gave the plants less of a shock. The transplanting ritual needed to be repeated at least twice more as the tobacco plants matured, and Daniel worried about his lack of manpower.

SARAH INVITED TAYLOR to supper Tuesday evening in appreciation of her chauffeuring. Mary prepared the meal, with Becca's one-handed help. Heaping platters of food covered the table: roasted potatoes, meat loaf, gravy, green beans from the garden, pickled beets, homemade bread, butter and apple butter, and for dessert, chocolate cake with peanut butter icing.

Daniel sat at the head of the large pine table that comfortably seated twelve, his sons to his right in order of age—Joseph as the youngest to his immediate right, followed by empty chairs for David and Jacob, then Mary and Levi on the end opposite Daniel. Plates, glasses and silverware sat at David's and Jacob's places, despite the empty chairs, which Taylor learned was an Amish custom. Sarah sat to Daniel's left, then the girls: Emma, Katie and Becca, with Taylor next to Becca. Mary and Levi usually ate supper themselves in their *grossdaadi haus* except on Sundays but since the accident, the whole family had been eating together.

The conversation was sparse and in *Deitsch*. Taylor could pick out a few words here and there but felt left out of the conversation.

She observed the plain yet spacious and airy kitchen: hardwood floors, a wall of maple cabinetry, ample laminate counters, a washing machine in one corner, and off to the side, a walk-in pantry stuffed with canned goods, cereal, bags of snacks, napkins and paper towels, and other staples. The window over the sink sported a dark green shade, partially pulled down, and the walls were plain, no wallpaper, decorated with a battery-run clock, a calendar, and a single framed cross stitch: "Let your life be modest, your manner courteous, your promises true, and share gladly the bounties you receive." Taylor spotted no radio, TV, dishwasher or microwave. However, the oven range, refrigerator, washing machine, and ceiling lights intrigued her.

"I thought the Amish were against modern appliances," Taylor said as she spread apple butter on her bread.

"We aren't against the appliances themselves," Becca explained in English, "only the electricity that comes from public utility lines. Using electricity means you're linked too much to the outside world. Our appliances—the range, the fridge—as well as the lights and our water heater run on propane gas. There's a big above-ground tank behind the barn. The washing machine and our indoor plumbing are run by compressed air, which is powered by a diesel generator."

"What about TV or computers or phones? Are the Amish against all forms of advanced technology?"

"We aren't against technology," Daniel replied with a hint of irritation. "We just don't instantly embrace every form of new technology, like you *Englishers* do, until we decide how and if it will benefit our lifestyle. TV is *verboten* because it's too worldly and full of trash and bad values. Some businesses use computers but don't connect to the whatya call it, the net? Phones we don't keep in the house since we prefer to talk to people in person; we have a phone shed outside which I use only when necessary for farm business." He pointed to the bowl in front of Taylor. "Pass the *dippy*, the gravy."

Taylor stifled the urge to rebuke Daniel by adding *'please'* after his request. The apparent lack of manners irritated her. She had yet to hear anyone in the family say 'please' or 'thank you' when at home. She guessed it just wasn't the Amish way.

Taylor's cell phone rang. She always kept it with her, either in her purse or in a pocket. She glanced at it. "This is from work and I need to take it. Please excuse me." Daniel frowned as she left the table. When she returned, as Sarah sliced the chocolate cake for dessert, Daniel said gruffly, "We'd prefer you turn off your phone when in our home."

"Fine," Taylor said sweetly. "And I would appreciate it if you spoke English while I'm in your home."

ON THE WAY back to the hospital that evening, Taylor's eight-passenger van nicely accommodated Katie, the twins, Becca, Levi, Daniel and Sarah. Mary offered to stay home and clean up after supper.

Sarah had told Taylor the results of Jacob's MRI on the way home from the hospital that morning, the rest of the family informed after dinner, and the twins only told that Jacob was "very sick." Since children under twelve weren't allowed in the Neuro Unit, they couldn't visit him, but they could see David. The ride over was quiet, with just the twins chattering about the van.

"Look, Emma, if you pull this down, there's a place to put cups."

"*Mamm*, why can't they put something like that in a buggy? Then we wouldn't have to worry about spilling soda when we drink in the buggy."

"That would be too worldly," Joseph said with a knowing air. "You're the one always spilling soda in the buggy."

"Am not," Emma said.

"'Member that time you spilled soda on the floor in Jacob's buggy, right after he got it when it was brand new? What are we going to do without Jacob's buggy? *Mamm* and David used it a lot when *Dat* was using ours."

In the rear view mirror, Taylor saw Daniel and Sarah glance at each other. "We'll just have to do without for now," Daniel replied.

DAVID SHUFFLED SLOWLY down the hospital hallway from the elevators, his arms folded carefully against his chest. He winced after every step. But he had practically inhaled breakfast that Wednesday morning so he could visit his brother before any of the family arrived. He had no idea what to say to Jacob, especially after learning from his family of his possibly devastating prognosis.

Jacob was watching "Good Morning America" when David entered his room.

"I'm not surprised you're taking advantage of the TV," David kidded his brother as he slowly lowered himself into the chair beside Jacob's bed. "Are you planning on *rumspringa* forever?"

Jacob managed a slight grin.

"So, how do you like the food here?" David asked.

"I haven't been eating much but I'd give anything for a piece of *Mamm's* shoofly pie," Jacob said, his eyes still on the TV. Pause. "How's your chest?"

David gave a cursory flick of his hand. "I'll be fine." Pause. "What's in your hand?"

"The nurse said it's a remote. It works the TV, turns it on and off and changes channels." He demonstrated to David.

"Let me try." David played with the volume and switched a few channels and then handed the remote back to Jacob.

"Have you seen the *Englisher* yet?" Jacob asked.

"*Ja*. Taylor. She came to see me. She probably saved my life."

"What?"

David explained about the fire and what the police had surmised about its cause. He then looked directly at his older brother and waited until Jacob averted his eyes from the TV and returned his gaze.

"It's all my fault. It was my idea to race . . . ," David began.

"Don't," Jacob interrupted. "I'm to blame, only me. I was the one driving."

"Why didn't you stop at the stop sign?"

"There's no good reason. I was angry we lost the race. I was frustrated about . . .

a lot of things. I wasn't thinking straight."

David opened his mouth to respond but his brother said, "It doesn't matter anymore." Jacob glared at the room and then at his legs. "But I have thanked God that I'm the one in this bed and not you or Becca."

TAYLOR'S TWO VAN passengers Wednesday evening were Anna and Aaron Beiler. While they visited David, Taylor used the fourth floor waiting room as a makeshift office. She bought a cup of coffee from the nearby café, found a table in the corner, set up her laptop, and logged into the hospital's guest Wi-Fi.

"How's the transplanting?" David asked Aaron. "*Dat* told me you're helping out."

Aaron grinned. "My back aches from all that bending. I'll be glad to get back to our cows." He placed his straw hat on the window ledge. "I've heard from many of the Roamers; they send their best," he said.

David nodded.

"There's a singing at Amos Stoltzfus's Sunday night. You going?"

David glanced at Anna. "I should be out of here tomorrow but I don't think I'll be up for it. The whole party thing—the drinking, the cigarettes—is getting old. I'd rather spend a quiet night at home with Anna."

"I know. The barn parties and the beer—we've done it all together for three or four years now. I guess it's time we grow up," Aaron said.

David shifted uncomfortably on the bed. "*Ja,* I think I went to one Roamers party too many."

They chatted a while longer, then Aaron left to give David and Anna some privacy. He took a seat across from Taylor in the waiting room.

Taylor glanced up from her work. Aaron was dressed in typical Amish garb, his straw hat in his hand. But his hairstyle, unlike David's, was not in the traditional bowl cut with bangs, and on his feet were Reebok sneakers. She closed her laptop.

"How do you know David?" she asked.

"We've known each other all our lives. We belong to the same church district since our farms are down the road from each other and we both joined the Roamers at the same time, so we're good friends."

"The Roamers?"

"Our gang."

"Gang?" Taylor was incredulous. "You are *gang* members?"

"Well, we're really just groups of friends but we call them gangs." Aaron explained that several Amish gangs existed in Lancaster County, varying in size and conformity to Amish values. Amish teens join the gang of their choice during *rumspringa*, and these gangs become their social world before they marry.

According to Aaron, members of the most worldly, or sophisticated, groups owned cars and conducted hops, large field parties with Amish rock bands, kegs of beer, and sometimes drugs. On weekends, teens in those worldly gangs traveled to Philadelphia in their cars and attended music concerts, baseball games, or visited the beaches in Maryland or New Jersey. Guys and girls might even have "relations," Aaron said, blushing deeply.

"My sister's old group, the Bluebirds—she left them last year when she turned nineteen and was baptized—are more conservative," Aaron said, participating in singings, group games, and outdoor activities such as volleyball or softball. Other gangs, like the Roamers, fell somewhere in the middle.

"We Roamers do stuff like go to the movies and restaurants and hang out at Walmart. We wear English clothes—some of the girls wear short skirts or jeans and jewelry and makeup—and style our hair different. We buy radios—I have one in my buggy—listen to music, own cell phones and iPads, and a couple of our members own cars. And we do party and drink. I never did drugs, though, and neither did David. And he doesn't have a cell phone, but I do."

"If you can't use electricity, how do you charge the cell phones and iPads?" Taylor asked.

"We charge them at our *Englisher* friends' houses or in cars or with solar chargers, and we use them to take pictures of each other and search the web, even though both are *verboten*, forbidden. Some, not me or David, have Facebook pages with pictures and everything but we only friend each other."

"Interesting," Taylor said, but she was still fixated on the gangs. "What do your parents think about these gangs?" she asked.

"We try not to throw stuff in their face. We don't tell them where we go and they don't ask and we don't use our gadgets in front of them. The girls hide their English clothes under their regular Amish clothes and change once they're out of the house. Even the guys with cars usually park them at an English friend's house so they don't embarrass their parents.

"But it's all going to end for me and David," Aaron said. "We're both getting baptized this fall and I will grow my hair back to the bowl cut and give up all the running around and drinking and the English clothes and my toys—my radio and cell phone." He leaned toward Taylor conspiratorially. "Rumor is that David and Anna will marry this year."

"Really? They seem so young. How old are they?"

"David's same as me, 20. Anna's a year younger."

"But once you baptize, won't you miss your freedom? Won't you miss being part of the real world?"

Aaron raised an eyebrow. "To us, Amish life is the real world.

TAYLOR DROVE SARAH and Becca to the hospital early Thursday since David was being released that morning. Sarah had encouraged Becca to stay home and rest but her eyes had filled with tears. Even Taylor had noticed Becca's clinginess; she didn't want to let Sarah out of her sight since the accident.

When they arrived, David's thoracic surgeon was instructing him.

"For the next three to four weeks, you need to take it easy," the surgeon said. "I understand you live on a farm but no bending, lifting, or moving heavy objects. I want to see you in my office in four weeks. Call to make an appointment. My office number is on this sheet of instructions. Based on your condition in four weeks, you may then be able to resume normal activity. But for now, no milking, no field work. Understand?"

"*Ja,*" David mumbled. His entire life had been filled with hard yet satisfying work. Already, the month stretched long before him.

Sarah brought David clothes to change into since the clothes he had worn the night of the accident were bloody and torn. A male nurse came to help David change from his hospital gown into his clothes.

"Mrs. Yoder, the billing office requested you stop in before you leave today," the nurse said. "It's downstairs on the first floor, near the pharmacy."

"I'll go now, while you're getting David ready," Sarah said.

"I'll come with you," Becca said.

"There's no need for you to come, Becca. You go sit with Taylor in the waiting room."

SARAH SAT IN the hospital chapel, head bowed, hands clasped in her lap. She was accustomed to praying alone in her home or during church in a fellow church member's home, but she found the quiet and beauty of the chapel calming. After her visit to the billing office, she had needed a place to gather her strength and to pray. One wall of the chapel was a water wall; water trickled down the frosted glass and the sound soothed her.

Dear God, she silently prayed *I need you to give me the strength to help my family through this time. And to help Daniel and me figure out how we're going to pay for all this.*

IN JACOB'S HOSPITAL room, Sarah pulled David's tan accident shirt from her sewing bag and began to mend the rip and replace two buttons. She had washed it the night before and what remained of the bloodstains was barely noticeable. Frugal by nature and with more reason than ever to pinch pennies, Sarah had chosen to try and salvage the shirt rather than spend money on the material to make a new one. Her hands were busy but her heart was heavy.

She didn't know what to say to Jacob. He had been withdrawn while in the hospital, understandably so, yet even in the months before the accident, he had been hard to talk to. Sarah knew he had been unhappy and confused about his future and his role in the Amish community but she had hoped the passage of time and the love of his family would help him find his way. But the accident had caused him to withdraw even more.

The uncertainty of his medical condition upset them all and she could only imagine how it affected him. He had a tendency to keep things inside; he rarely asked for help or guidance. She had decided that morning to take her cue from Jacob and let the conversation, if any, go where he directed. She'd be there for him if he decided to reach out, and if not, she'd deal with that, too.

Jacob made small talk for a while; he asked about David and Becca and the rest of the family, he asked about the transplanting. Sarah did not tell him that Becca had to be coaxed that morning to stay home to help Mary and Katie with the twins and David and chores, so anxious was she if away from her mother since the accident. But she did tell him more of the tobacco plants from the seedbed would be replanted in the field that night, if the weather held. He nodded but his mind seemed elsewhere.

"And what of the *Englisher*, Taylor?" he asked.

"Her injuries were minor and she seems fine. She's been kind enough to drive us back and forth to the hospital, as you know. She works in the waiting room while we visit."

"*Ja*, but what is she like?"

Sarah looked up from her darning in surprise. "We don't know much about her," she said. "She's wealthy and works in Philadelphia."

"I want to see her," Jacob said.

Before Sarah could respond, Dr. Mayes, Jacob's neurosurgeon, entered the room, greeted mother and son, and studied Jacob's chart.

"Your last set of CT scans shows the swelling has gone down around your spinal cord and we can now clearly see the damage done," she said. "I'm sorry, Jacob, but your paralysis is permanent. You are paralyzed from the waist down. The medical term is paraplegia. The paralysis is complete, meaning you will experience no function below the waist—no bowel or bladder function, no sexual function, no hip or leg function. However, you will have total muscle and respiratory functioning above the waist. No lasting damage occurred to your upper body.

"Through rehabilitation, you can learn to live with your lower body disability. We can set you up at the Bayard Rehabilitation Hospital in Philadelphia. Bayard has treated thousands of people with spinal cord injuries. You'd stay there approximately eight weeks, maybe more, depending on the pace of your recovery. We'll keep you here for another week, though, to make sure you're stable and then transfer you to Bayard. I know this is a lot to absorb at one time, Jacob, but we'll talk more in the coming week and I will answer all your questions."

There was no sound as Dr. Mayes exited the room. Sarah bent over her sewing, her tears falling in small dark splotches on the tan shirt fabric. Jacob stared unseeing at the ceiling.

JACOB FELL ASLEEP after lunch. Sarah felt disoriented, at a loss as to what she should do next. She thought about having Taylor take her home so she could talk to Daniel, but she knew Daniel needed to finish the tobacco; they couldn't afford to lose the crop. She decided it was better to stay at the hospital and be there for Jacob when he woke up in case he wanted to talk.

Taylor was multi-tasking—talking on her cell phone and reading email on her laptop—when Sarah sat next to her in the waiting room. Taylor took one look at her face and knew something was terribly wrong.

"I'll call you back," she said into the phone. "Sarah, what's the matter? Did something happen to Jacob?"

Sarah had spent a lifetime keeping to herself; any problems had been solved within her own family, and when necessary, as when she had lost her babies, the Amish community had rallied around to support her and her family emotionally and with help around the house and farm. Never had she shared a problem with an outsider, especially someone she had known for only a few days. But Taylor seemed like she wanted to help, and Sarah, overwhelmed with the situation she faced, was in dire need of a sympathetic ear.

"Jacob is paralyzed. From the waist down. He won't walk again."

Taylor moved into action. She turned off her laptop and stuffed it into its bag, and threw her phone into her purse.

"You probably aren't in the least hungry, but let's go down to the cafeteria. I'll get something to eat and we'll talk. You'll tell me exactly what the doctor said."

They settled in a corner of the cafeteria, Sarah with a cup of coffee, Taylor with a salad and a tuna sandwich. Sarah related what Dr. Mayes had said about Jacob's paraplegia and rehabilitation.

"I don't know what to do," Sarah said. "I don't know how to help Jacob, emotionally or physically."

Taylor turned on her laptop and then looked questioningly at Sarah. "I can research paraplegia on my laptop. Is it okay if I use this to help you?"

Sarah thought for a moment. The *Ordnung* prohibited computers but since she didn't own it, the laptop wasn't plugged into an electrical outlet, and the use would be for a medical reason rather than entertainment, she felt only slightly guilty.

She nodded and they spent the next half hour learning the basics about spinal cord injuries.

"It's amazing what useful information you can learn on a computer so quickly," Sarah said. "I understand enough now to ask the doctor questions."

"We're not going to learn too much more because my battery is dying," Taylor said. "But there's one more thing I want to briefly check out."

Taylor found the website for Bayard Rehabilitation Hospital.

"This rehab center is very near to where I live in Philadelphia," Taylor said as she eyed the site. "The center will help patients with bowel and bladder function, wheel chair mobility, learning how to dress and care for themselves, as well as physical therapy to build strength and endurance. The center also provides patient and family education on all medical and psychological aspects of spinal cord injury."

"How much does it cost?" Sarah asked.

"It doesn't say, but I'm sure your medical insurance will cover it," Taylor said, turning off the computer as the battery died.

"We don't have insurance, medical or life," Sarah said. "The Amish don't believe in it. Insurance is seen as not trusting in God's plan."

"You're not required to purchase insurance through the Affordable Care Act because of a religious exemption?"

"*Ja,* just like we're exempt from paying into Social Security and Medicare."

"Then who's going to pay your hospital bills?"

"I don't know," Sarah said, tears welling. "It's so much money."

Taylor remembered that Sarah had gone to the billing office yesterday. She didn't want to pry, but she couldn't help without knowing details. She decided to be blunt.

"How much do you owe the hospital?"

"More than one hundred and twenty thousand dollars. That doesn't include Jacob's rehabilitation or any follow-up care for David or Becca. Daniel said not to worry. We have some money in the bank and Amish Church Aid will help. But I'm not so sure our community can handle that much."

"What's Amish Church Aid?"

"Amish families in our church district make a monthly contribution of one hundred twenty-five dollars. After a three thousand dollar deductible, any family can then receive help from the fund with medical bills. We may also receive donations from individual families in our district and maybe from neighboring ones and there may be some type of fundraiser, like an auction. That's what we've done in the past for other families. Daniel and I have been saving for so long to give David some money, not much, for a wedding gift toward a down payment on a farm. Now, I don't know, I just don't know."

"What did the billing office say? Do they understand your situation?"

"The woman I talked to was very kind. She said they had worked with other Amish families and they would work with us and develop a payment plan."

"Is there anything I can do?" Taylor asked. "I want to help. I feel partly responsible for the accident even though the police said it wasn't my fault. If I hadn't been on the phone asking for directions I might have noticed Jacob and I wouldn't have turned and there wouldn't have been an accident."

Sarah shook her head, but Taylor impulsively rushed on.

"If you'll have me, I could stay with you for the next week until Jacob is transferred to rehab. You are short three people that you count on to help run the farm and your household. Although I can't presume to make up physically for three people, I'm willing to do whatever you need me to do. I could help in the kitchen, in the barn, or in the fields. Plus I can still carpool you back and forth from the hospital and anywhere else you want to go since you're also short a buggy. I can help you find medical information on the computer. Whatever you need."

Sarah looked uncertain. She wasn't accustomed to *Englishers* assertively inviting themselves to stay in her home.

It was true they were shorthanded, and she was grateful to Taylor for the transportation—they had saved a good deal of money by not having to hire someone to take them back and forth to the hospital. But she was sure Daniel wouldn't agree to an outsider living with them. He didn't know Taylor and he didn't trust her. And she lugged the laptop and those cell phones around with her everywhere, and Daniel would definitely disapprove of those devices in the house. She was also dubious about Taylor helping in the barn and the field. She looked at Taylor's clothes, the elegant and rich cut of even the casual outfit she wore that day. She couldn't see Taylor getting dirt under her nails or slopping through shit in the barn.

"I don't think Daniel is ready for you to actually live with us," Sarah said gently. "He is, we all are, very private and normally distrustful of outsiders. But I could use you in the kitchen; I'm sure Mary is exhausted by now. And we are more than grateful for the use of your van. I'll ask Daniel if he could use another pair of hands in the barn or the field. In the meantime, you could pray for us."

"I don't pray," Taylor said, then quickly amended when she saw Sarah's shocked face "That is, I believe in action. I'm a doer. I'll be happy to help wherever you need me."

JACOB PRESSED THE call button near his bed.

"I want to see Taylor, the *Englisher* usually here with my family," he said to the nurse when she entered the room.

"She's not immediate family so she's not permitted in the Neuro trauma unit," the nurse replied.

"I need to see her," Jacob stubbornly responded.

The nurse hesitated. "I'll see what I can do," she said.

SUPPER AT THE Yoder's that night was a quiet affair. By then everyone knew about Jacob's paralysis. Daniel seemed especially gruff, and for most of the meal wore a scowl that made even Taylor wary. The only sounds were the clank of silverware against plates until Emma knocked over her glass of milk and burst into tears.

After supper, Daniel said he needed to repair a harness and retired to the barn, while the others washed dishes and prepared to visit the hospital. Everyone wanted to visit Jacob so Taylor offered to make two trips. Even the twins begged to go even though they understood they weren't old enough to visit.

"We just want to be nearer to Jacob," Joseph explained.

While the family was getting ready, Taylor decided to approach Daniel about helping him for the next week in the barn and the fields. She wanted to plead her case before Sarah had a chance to talk to him.

Taylor entered the barn with some trepidation, given Daniel's foul mood at supper. She wrinkled her nose in disdain at the smell.

She wandered around looking for Daniel but he was nowhere in sight. She walked past the horse stalls and through what she assumed was the tack room because of the harnesses hanging on the wall. She walked down the aisles past the cows, keeping as far from them as she could. She was ready to give up, thinking perhaps she had missed him and he had already returned to the house, when she heard a sound up ahead.

A small doorway stood to her left. She saw Daniel standing with his back to her, leaning against the doorframe, head bent, shoulders shaking. She stood still for a second, then slowly, quietly backed away.

5

THE MORNING LIGHT shone through the white ruffled curtains at the Stoney Creek Bed and Breakfast as Taylor stirred, reluctant to leave the comfy bed with its crisp sheets, fluffy down pillows, and the stunning Amish-made cream quilt with its scalloped edge and appliqúed star of burgundy and blue. The B & B was just a half mile down the road from the Yoder farm and was known for its ambiance, its views of the lush farmland that surrounded it, and its hearty country breakfasts. Tired of the Route 30 traffic and wanting to be closer to the Yoders, Taylor had left the Lancaster Hotel and checked into the B & B the afternoon before.

She snuggled further under the quilt, thinking about the request she'd received at the hospital the previous evening. She'd been sitting in the second floor waiting room working on her laptop while the Yoders visited Jacob when a nurse approached her.

"Are you Taylor?" the nurse asked.

"I am."

"Jacob Yoder would like to see you—alone. I've cleared it with the neurosurgeon since non-family members normally aren't permitted to visit the Neuro Unit."

"Please tell Jacob I'd be happy to visit him. I'll come in the next day or two."

Taylor wondered why Jacob wanted to see her. Was he angry? Did he want to discuss the accident?

The enticing smell of eggs, bacon, and coffee wafted up from the kitchen. She wasn't in the habit of eating a full, sit-down breakfast; usually she grabbed a power bar or a bagel and coffee on her way to work. She hopped out of bed. She decided to visit Jacob that morning, first thing. Right after breakfast.

SARAH STOOD BETWEEN the rows of ripened squash and zucchini and wiped the perspiration off her brow with her arm. She surveyed the garden and her charges.

"Emma and Joseph, stop throwing dirt at each other. Katie, that section of tomatoes isn't ready to pick yet."

Becca and Mary were already handling business at their roadside vegetable stand, a job Becca could usually manage on her own but not with one arm in a cast. Several cars had already stopped at the large stand that stood at the end of their lane alongside Hickory Hill Road and it was only a little after nine in the morning. Sarah wanted to wash the fresh-picked zucchini and squash and take them to the stand so they didn't run out of produce and disappoint customers.

She was grateful for the stand's usual brisk summer business; the extra income it brought to the household was always helpful, and would be even more so with the hospital bills piling up. Every time she thought about those bills, her stomach lurched and she felt rising panic, an emotion she could ill afford. She needed to stay calm for the children and keep the household running smoothly. Daniel exited the barn, the vet due soon to check a sick cow, and Sarah decided to grab him while she could.

"Daniel," she called, lugging a cloth tote filled with vegetables to wash in the kitchen. He stopped and waited for her.

"I want to talk to you about Taylor," she said. "She'd like to help here on the farm for the next week. I'm fine with her helping me with the household chores but she also asked if she could help you with the milking and in the field."

Daniel grunted. "Doesn't seem to me she could handle farm work. I bet her hands have never been dirty. She might be more trouble than a help."

"*Ja*, that's true. But if she could help, that would give Levi a break in the barn, at least for a week. I saw Mary rubbing his back the other night when I brought their finished laundry over to the *grossdaadi*. And another hand in the field would be useful in getting the tobacco transplanted."

"*Mamm*, I'm thinking maybe you just don't want to be constantly tripping over her in your kitchen," Daniel chuckled. "But you make a good point. Another hand, if it's useful, would be welcome. Aaron Beiler is available this week but the Fishers aren't since their own field needs transplanting. I guess I could give her a try. Let's see what she's made of."

"I UNDERSTAND YOU wanted to see me," Taylor said as she stood in the doorway to Jacob's hospital room.

Jacob nodded.

Taylor sat on the chair by the bed and looked expectantly at Jacob.

"I wanted to see you partly about the accident," he said. "I'm sorry. I hope you're okay."

"I'm fine, just some bruises. Don't worry about me. Concentrate on getting yourself ready for rehab."

"What for?" Jacob shrugged. "My stupidity injured my sister and brother and created hardship for my parents and the rest of my family. I got what I deserved. I don't have a life I'm in a hurry to get back to."

Taylor was at a loss for words; she had expected a can-do

attitude, like the rest of his family's. Before she could respond, Jacob continued. "I also wanted to see you because I have a favor to ask. I have two books due at the library in a couple days. Will you return them for me? They're at home in my bedroom in the chest at the foot of my bed. My library card is tucked into my Bible in the top drawer of the nightstand. The library's in Leola, on Hillcrest Avenue."

"Sure, no problem," Taylor said. "You don't want to ask someone in your family to return them?"

"I can't ask Becca or David. Neither is in any shape to drive the buggy. *Mamm* probably would but she has so much else going on right now. And *Dat* doesn't approve of many of my choices, including my reading. He thinks it's a waste of time."

Taylor studied Jacob intently as he spoke; he intrigued her. She figured he had an eighth grade education like most Amish but he seemed more articulate than the rest of his family. "So, you're a reader?" she asked.

"I do read, a lot. I'm not a big talker and I'm somewhat of a loner, especially since everyone I know my age is married. But when I read, I'm not alone. Books help me see things differently, experience the world through someone else's eyes. I lose myself in them."

"Sounds like there's some tension between you and your father. What else does he disapprove of besides your reading?" Taylor asked.

Jacob turned his gaze toward the window. Reserved by nature, he was unaccustomed to talking about himself and had divulged far more to this stranger than he had intended. Yet it felt easy talking to her, almost an unburdening.

"It was always expected I would farm, like my *Dat* and *Daadi*. I never wanted to farm, though. Farming is an important part of Amish culture, but I don't feel the same way about it my father does. He loves feeling the soil in his hands, watching seedlings grow into stalks. Living off the land is deeply satisfying for him. I'm indifferent to it."

"Why is farming so important to the Amish?"

"Farming is the preferred Amish way of life because you work the earth that God created. On a farm, kids learn responsibility and the value of hard work. To work hard is to honor God. Many Amish who work in other professions would farm if they could afford to and even the ones who choose to own other businesses are respectful of the farming life."

"Does your father realize you don't want to farm?"

"He does, but he's impatient with what he calls my 'foot dragging.' He wants me to decide on another livelihood, preferably by yesterday, get baptized, get married, start a family. The usual Amish way."

"If you don't want to farm, what other options do you have?"

"Lots of Amish choose to own small businesses because farmland, especially in Lancaster, is scarce and expensive. I have six relatives who farm, half in Lancaster, half in Indiana or Ohio, where they moved to find affordable farmland. The rest are small business owners. My uncle, John Esh, is a contractor. Another uncle, Samuel Yoder, makes furniture, and a third, Elam Yoder, owns a tree trimming business. I have two aunts, Esther and Ruth, who own a quilt shop together. They've all tried to interest me in their trades—well, except for the quilting—but working with my hands doesn't interest me. And now that I'm paralyzed, farming and many trades are no longer options anyway."

Taylor's phone vibrated in her pocket; normally she would have left the room and taken the call, but instead, she ignored it.

"Jacob, is there any profession you *are* interested in?"

He absently ran his hand through his hair. "Now, since the accident, I don't know." His voice trailed off. Taylor leaned forward in her chair and seemed sincerely interested and he decided to confide in her something only a few other people, none of them his family, knew.

"I overheard my father tell my mother once that I was 'lost' and 'looking for my way.' He paused. "Actually, I'm not lost. I know exactly what I want. I just can't have it if I still want to be Amish."

"What is it you want?"

"I want to learn, beyond the eighth grade. I want to continue my education."

SARAH BUSTLED ABOUT her large sunny kitchen. The noon meal, which the Amish call dinner, was over, and it was time to bake. The Amish attend church services on alternate Sundays, and since the following day was not a church Sunday, she expected many visitors, especially those who hadn't seen Becca or David since the accident. Becca hovered, Katie rolled out pie dough, and Taylor had offered to help although she had never baked in her life.

Sarah had decided to bake two chocolate cakes, two blueberry pies, and two shoofly pies, one to take to the hospital since it was Jacob's favorite.

Becca showed a hesitant Taylor how to operate the battery-powered hand mixer to mix the cake batter. Without air conditioning and with the oven pre-heating and the humid late June air, the kitchen was stifling. Taylor wondered grumpily why, if the Amish had figured out how to run other appliances with air pressure or propane gas, they couldn't figure out how to do it with air conditioning. She decided to verbalize that thought and raised her hand to emphasize the point, forgetting about the still running mixer. Cake batter sprayed the kitchen counter and the walls. Katie giggled and Becca hid her smile behind her good hand while Taylor grabbed a towel to clean up.

In her professional life, Taylor was in the habit of taking charge and being in control; she knew what to do and she excelled. When interacting with the Yoders, though, she felt inadequate and off-balance. She knew nothing about domestic or farm work or children. But she had promised herself she would handle whatever they threw at her.

She resumed mixing the cake, then poured the batter into two pans. Too late, she realized she had poured more batter in one pan than the other.

"Uh-oh," she said to Sarah. "I was in a hurry and now the two cake layers will be uneven."

Sarah finished the latticework on the top of her blueberry pie and wiped her hands on her apron before addressing Taylor.

"We can disguise the unevenness later with the frosting," Sarah said. "But why are you rushing? Do you have somewhere to go?"

"Well, no," Taylor said. "I always hurry through chores or busy work so I can get to the good stuff, you know, the meaningful work." Katie and Becca glanced at each other.

"Here, everything *is* the good stuff," Sarah said. "Chores aren't a burden so much as our way of life, a life that to us is meaningful. All our work is valued as important."

Taylor wasn't sure whether she had just been gently chastised or whether Sarah had merely been explaining their lifestyle. She thought about Sarah's comment and Amish life while the cake baked and she washed dishes. The Yoders, at least based on what she had seen so far, really didn't have anything to rush to. No rushing to get done chores so they could watch TV, or play Xbox or a video game, or go to the movies, or search the Web, or go to the mall, or yak on the phone or Twitter or Facebook. Certainly the Yoders were under a huge strain since the accident, both financially and emotionally, but Taylor had not once heard any member of the family whine or adopt an "oh-woe-is-me" attitude. They coped as best they could, and trusted God and their community for the rest. Taylor thought it a simplistic way to live, but it seemed to be working for them.

THE AROMA OF straight-from-the-oven blueberry and shoofly pies enveloped the kitchen as Daniel came stomping in the back door.

"*Mamm*, that smells wonderful *goot*. Can't wait for supper."

"Only the blueberry pie is for tonight. The rest is for tomorrow's visitors," Sarah said.

Taylor stood at the counter frosting her chocolate cake. The frosting job had started as a gloppy mess until Sarah came to the rescue and showed Taylor the proper technique. Taylor still had vanilla frosting on one cheek, all over her spreading hand, and on her chin, the result of her repeatedly licking her fingers. Daniel shot his wife a sympathetic glance.

"I could use you in the barn to help with the milking, if you're up to it," Daniel said to his guest.

Taylor lifted her vanilla-frosted chin defiantly. "Of course I'm up to it. You just say when."

"In about half an hour. You'll need some boots." He turned on his heel and walked out.

"You can borrow my barn boots," Katie said.

Taylor nodded, and felt her stomach constrict.

A SHORT TIME later, Taylor found herself alone in the house. Sarah and Becca had gone to the market, Katie and the twins were playing down by the pond, and Anna had picked up David in her buggy to take him back to the Beiler farm to visit. Taylor decided it was a perfect time to search for the library books in Jacob's room before she ventured out to the barn to help Daniel.

She climbed the stairs to the second floor. She had gotten a tour of the five-bedroom house on the first night she had stayed for supper. David and Joseph shared a room, as did Katie and Emma. Becca and Jacob, as the eldest boy and girl,

each had their own room. There were two bathrooms upstairs, one for the boys and one for the girls. Sarah and Daniel
occupied the bedroom and bath on the first floor.

Jacob's room was sparingly furnished. A handmade black
quilt with colorful patchwork squares covered the bed. On the
nightstand rested a flashlight and a pair of sunglasses. Nothing adorned the walls except a rack on which hung a black hat
and a pair of suspenders. His closet door stood ajar and Taylor saw
three pairs of black pants and several solid purple, blue, and tan
shirts. She also saw a pair of jeans, two navy long-sleeve shirts,
and several white and grey t-shirts. On the floor were two
pairs of sneakers, one black, one white—Taylor recognized the
white Nikes from the night of the accident—and a pair of
well-worn brown work boots. At the foot of the bed was a
large pine chest. Taylor knelt in front of it and lifted the lid.

Inside were stacks of books, both hardcover and paperback.
On top of the middle stack were two plastic-covered hardback
books. Taylor opened the back cover where each was stamped
Leola Library. One book was *Ethan Frome* by Edith Wharton; the
second was *The Catcher in the Rye* by J.D. Salinger. Next to the
library books were papers folded in half. Taylor hesitated but
curiosity won out and she unfolded them to reveal two lists of
the 100 Best Novels, one compiled by the Radcliffe Publishing
Course, one by The Modern Library. Many book titles were
crossed off both lists.

She glanced through the rest of the books in the trunk.
Almost all were classics: *The Great Gatsby, The Grapes of Wrath,
1984, Great Expectations, Of Mice and Men,* as well as assorted
Cliffs Notes. Also in the trunk were Wharton's *The Age of Innocence,* Sinclair's *Main Street,* Knowle's *A Separate Peace,* Potok's
The Chosen, and two plays, *The Glass Menagerie* and *A Raisin in
the Sun.* At the bottom of the stack of books was a tattered
copy of a Kaplan GED study guide.

Taylor was astonished. Someone with an eighth grade education was reading this level of literature? She studied the

book lists, then took the two library books and closed the trunk.

Taylor opened the nightstand drawer. Inside was a black leather Bible, the King James Version. She flipped through the pages until she found Jacob's library card.

She put the books and the library card in her van. She'd stop at the library Monday and return the books. It was time to join Daniel in the barn.

THE ODOR OF cow dung immediately struck Taylor as she entered the barn. *Will I ever get used to this smell?* She wore a pair of Levis and a grey t-shirt she had bought during a quick stop at the Rockvale outlets on her way back from the hospital that morning, just in case Daniel had asked her to help around the farm. Accustomed to sleek designer heels, she clumped heavily in Katie's boots over to Daniel as he hooked up a cow to the milk machine.

Daniel motioned for her to kneel beside him and the cow. "This here's Sadie."

Taylor swallowed hard. Sadie was *big*. Cows looked much smaller and less intimidating when they stood in a field as you drove by, she thought. Daniel showed her how to slip the rubber suction cups over Sadie's teats. Taylor watched his hands, careful and methodical, dirt under the fingernails, and wondered if the dirt was permanent; it was always there. The milk machine used a pulsating vacuum to cause the rubber sleeve round each teat to simulate the effect of hand milking or of a suckling calf. The vacuum pipe then transported the flowing milk to a stainless steel bucket. The Yoders' milk machine could be hooked up to two cows at a time, but Daniel only instructed Taylor how to milk one. In about five minutes, Sadie provided three and a half gallons of milk.

"When the bucket's full, you dump it into the sputnik, that

stainless container over there with wheels. When the sputknik's full, we pull it into the next room, attach a hose to it, and pump the milk into the refrigerated holding tank," Daniel said.

"What happens to the milk in the holding tank?"

"Every other day, except on the Lord's day, a tractor trailer comes, empties the tank, and takes the milk to the processing plant."

"How are the milk machine and the holding tank powered?" Taylor asked.

"By a diesel generator, and the automatic agitator that stirs the milk in the tank is powered by a twelve-volt battery that's recharged by a small gas generator." Daniel pointed up to the ceiling. "The lanterns are propane. The ceiling fans keep the cows cool and are also run by generator. The generator is kept in a shed outside the barn."

Daniel removed the machine from Sadie. "Your turn to milk Sadie's neighbor, Ellie. If you have any trouble, just yell. I'll be milking in the next aisle over."

Taylor could feel Daniel's eyes on her back as she dragged the milk machine over to Ellie. She sensed this was a test and was determined to pass or at least not humiliate herself. She crouched beside Ellie and grabbed hold of her teats and Ellie mooed, the sound loud and reverberating. Taylor started, lost her balance, and ended on her butt. She quickly scrambled up as she heard Daniel call, "You okay?"

"I'm fine, just fine," she yelled back and resumed hooking up the machine to the cow. She took hold of Ellie's teats more gently, the feel of them soft and squishy in her hand. She giggled, and then she couldn't stop giggling and her whole body shook.

What on earth am I doing in the middle of this aromatic Amish barn on a Saturday evening milking a cow, clodhoppers on my feet, and cow droppings only inches away from where my backside just hit the ground? If my father could see me now!

The next two hours flew by. Taylor got the hang of the milking machine and by the fifteenth cow, half of the herd, she felt somewhat proficient, although slow. Daniel had milked his fifteen cows much sooner than Taylor and had proceeded to scrape the cow droppings from the stalls into the grates which ran down the side of each aisle and led to a large holding tank. Taylor passionately hoped she was never asked to tackle that job.

After completing the milking, Daniel climbed the ladder into the silo and threw corn silage down a chute into a wooden wagon underneath. Taylor then helped Daniel shovel the silage into troughs for the cows. She knew she would be sore the next day. She hadn't exercised since she had left Philadelphia a week ago and she didn't think any of the exercises she usually did worked the muscles she had just used.

When they were done, Daniel merely nodded at her and she followed him out of the barn to supper.

WHEN TAYLOR ARRIVED back at the Stoney Creek B & B, owners Tom and Sally Miller were offering raspberry iced tea and homemade peanut butter cookies to their guests seated on the wide front porch that stretched around the Victorian-style inn. Colorful flower baskets adorned the porch and yellow and white cushions decorated the white wicker settees and wooden rocking chairs that dotted the veranda. Taylor ran up to her room, tore off her smelly barn clothes, took a quick shower, and returned to the porch.

As she sat with the Millers, sipping her tea and nibbling a cookie, she noticed she still had dirt under her fingernails.

The Millers told Taylor they had lived in the area all their lives and had owned the bed and breakfast for more than a decade. Sally was a former middle school teacher and Bill had been a computer technician for a local software company. Taylor told them about her background, the accident, and her current involvement with the Yoder family.

The Millers had read the newspaper article about the accident and Tom mentioned that it was not uncommon for Amish youth to be running wild, or "sowing their oats," during their teen years.

"The police have arrested several Old Order Amish youth in this area for drinking and driving, as well as for drug use and drug sales," Tom said. "Most Amish teens continue to live with their parents during *rumspringa* but some do leave and live on their own in the outside world for a while."

Taylor sipped her tea. "The parents take quite a risk in permitting their teens a *rumspringa*," she said.

"Yes, parents fear that once their kids get a taste of the forbidden, they won't return home," Sally said. "If enough don't return, the Amish community and way of life ends. But the Amish strongly believe in the importance of a freely chosen commitment to be bound by their lifestyle. Most teens do choose to eventually baptize and become members of the Amish church, more than ninety percent in this area."

Taylor wondered why the Amish withdrew from the world. "Why the old-fashioned clothes and the horse and buggies?"

Amish religious doctrine teaches obedience and separation, Sally said. "Members believe if they obey the church's teachings and separate from the modern world they will be pleasing to God and perhaps achieve eternal life. Sacrificing what they call worldly desires—fashion, cars, electricity, technology, higher education—helps them to maintain separateness.

"This separateness they view as a form of suffering, similar to the suffering of both Christ and their Amish ancestors, who were persecuted in Europe during the sixteenth century for their religious beliefs, among them their belief in adult rather than infant baptism. At that time, infant baptism conferred citizenship, which determined taxation. For two centuries, civil and religious authorities branded their ancestors as heretics, and imprisoned, tortured, and burned them at the stake. A few hundred finally escaped to America, landing first in the Lancaster area in the early 1700s. Those few hundred have since multiplied to three hundred thousand plus in thirty-one states, though most settled in Ohio, Indiana, and Pennsylvania."

Taylor finished her iced tea and cookie as she rocked slowly in her chair. The June evening was warm, conversation quiet and scattered throughout the porch, crickets chirped, fireflies flitted in abundance. She looked at her watch; it was a little after nine o'clock on a Saturday evening. If she was in Philadelphia, she realized, she'd probably be working, either at the office or at home. She felt a pinprick of consciousness, and she wondered if her life might be missing something, but in a second it was forgotten.

THE YODER HOUSEHOLD was a flurry of activity when Taylor left on Sunday to visit Jacob. She had helped with the finishing touches on Sarah's food for the visitors. Every inch of her arms, legs, and back moaned in protest from her barn work the previous night, but she suffered in silence, not wanting to appear weak in the Yoders' eyes. There had been a steady stream of visitors since late morning, and the few Taylor had met were certainly not rude to her, yet their greetings had been reserved at best and sometimes downright chilly. Taylor guessed she was eyed with distrust as the *Englisher* whose car had caused injury to the Yoder siblings, even though nearly everyone knew Jacob had been drinking and ran a stop sign. The Amish rally around their own, Taylor understood, and as the outsider, she was therefore suspect and easy to blame. She was glad to leave the house.

She made one stop before the hospital, and when she arrived, Jacob was finishing lunch and seemed pleased to see her. Taylor told him about the visitors at the Yoder home and hinted that he would be getting a food surprise that night when his family visited. She also told him about her experience in the kitchen with her lopsided cake. Jacob grinned. But when she told him about milking Ellie and falling on her butt, Jacob actually laughed. Taylor felt a great sense of accomplishment at cracking Jacob's normal reserve. It was a week ago that day since the accident.

"Jacob, it's been a week since . . . "

"*Ja*, I know, a week since I screwed up my life worse than it already was." He pushed away the movable table on which his lunch tray sat. "Did you find the library books?"

"Yes and I'll return them tomorrow," she said. "I confess I also saw your 100 Best Novels lists. Where did you get them?"

"One of the librarians gave them to me," Jacob said. "Her name's Julia. She helped me pick out books from the list and she showed me how to work the computer to find the books." He told her that while at the library he would also read magazines: *Time, National Geographic, Scientific American,* as well as the Lancaster paper and sometimes *The New York Times.*

"I don't buy the magazines or newspapers because of the cost but I did buy a few of my favorite books, the ones you saw in the chest, most from the bargain tables at Barnes and Noble." He eyed the bag she had placed on the floor by her chair when she first entered his room. She handed it to him with a smile.

Inside were two books she had purchased at the bookstore on her way to the hospital: *The Old Man and the Sea* by Ernest Hemingway and *An American Tragedy* by Theodore Dreiser.

"This one," she said, pointing to the Hemingway book, "wasn't on your list, but I thought you might relate to it. It's about perseverance, determination, and facing a physical and moral challenge. The Dreiser book was on the list but you hadn't crossed it off, so I assumed you hadn't read it yet."

Jacob caressed the book covers with his hand. "Thanks," he said quietly. "Do you like to read?"

"I used to, especially when I was in high school and college. I don't have time to read anymore."

"Why not?"

"You know that Lancaster paper you read in the library, *The Lancaster Post?*" Well, my father owns that newspaper and eighteen more plus eleven radio and television stations, all located in five Mid-Atlantic states and D.C. The company is called Loden Media and we're headquartered in Philadelphia."

"Are you a reporter?" Jacob asked.

"No, not any more. When I first started with the company, I was a reporter for a couple of the smaller papers we own; my father thought it important that I learn all the facets of the business, including the news side. Now I help manage the papers we own."

"Do you miss being a reporter?"

"Well, I don't know, I haven't really thought about it." She paused, thinking back to the days when she used to cover the police beat and local government and also wrote some feature stories.

"I was a reporter during the summers while I attended Yale and also for a year after I received my master's degree in journalism at Columbia. I guess I did enjoy the reporting side, the researching and the writing of the stories, meeting new people. My Mom got such a kick out of the articles I wrote. She'd clip them out of the newspapers and save them in a scrapbook. Then she died. I graduated from Yale, then Columbia, and then got my MBA from Penn and here I am."

"How did your Mom die?"

Taylor stood up and paced the room.

"Cancer, uterine. She was sick most of my junior year at Yale. She died right after spring break, which I spent at home with her, my father, and hospice."

Jacob lowered his head. He was a man of few words and none seemed adequate to the moment.

Taylor had no intention of dwelling on that anguish of seven years ago, and so she chattered on about her job at Loden Media. When she finally stopped and sat down, Jacob homed in on the one detail that had fascinated him most about her story. "You went to *three* colleges?"

"Yes, but they were all for different degrees. My family was very big on education. My Mom believed college broadened you intellectually and socially and taught you to think deeply and critically. My degree at Yale was in English literature with a minor in creative writing. My father wanted me to be prepared to take over the business someday so the Columbia journalism degree and the Wharton MBA from Penn were important to him."

"Those degrees weren't important to you?"

"Well, yes," said Taylor, slightly flustered. "They've clearly been professional assets. But I haven't read any literature since Yale or written anything fun since post-Columbia."

"What would you like to read or write?"

"It doesn't matter. I don't have the time. It's like I'm on auto-pilot. I just keep on cruising at warp speed down the highway.

6

"I'M RETURNING these books for Jacob Yoder," Taylor told the librarian behind the desk.

The librarian quickly looked up from the computer screen on which she was working.

"Is he sick?" she asked.

"Are you Julia?" The librarian nodded.

"Jacob told me about you," Taylor said. "He was in a buggy accident a week ago; he's paralyzed from the waist down."

Julia gasped and motioned for Taylor to follow her. They walked toward the back of the library and sat at a table near the windows.

"I've been helping Jacob select books here in the library for years," Julia said. How do you know him?"

"His buggy hit my car. He ran a stop sign. I've been helping the family on the farm since the accident. I visited Jacob in the hospital and he asked me to return the books. He seems to be an avid reader."

"Yes, his reading tastes are quite diverse," Julia said, "but I've noticed that most of his favorite books have much in common. Many are what I call outsider literature—literature about characters outside of the mainstream, who go against the grain, who don't do what society expects of them—books that discuss the results of unthinking conformity or rigid convention versus personal freedom. He's also drawn to books with themes concerning unfulfilled dreams.

"Jacob has definite intellectual potential but his family and the Amish community are holding him back," she said. "He has a powerful desire to learn; he's curious about everything."

"When I visited Jacob the other day, he said he wanted to continue his education," Taylor said. "Is that prohibited by the Amish?"

"The Amish go to school only through the eighth grade and here in Lancaster they attend Amish-run, one-room schools, not public schools. High school and college are forbidden," Julia explained.

"Why? How do you just shut off a mind at age 14 or 15?"

"The Amish aren't impressed by what they call 'book learning.' They fear it will lead to individual achievement and independence, will entice their youth away from manual labor, and will make it easier to leave the church. They value practical knowledge and learning manual skills, like farming or carpentry, by apprenticeship. To the Amish, it's more important to plow a straight furrow than to understand geometry. Amish children are taught what they need to learn to be successful in an Amish community, either to make a living from farming or from small businesses."

"What do they learn in school?" Taylor asked.

"I have a friend who knows an Amish teacher," Julia said. "Parents pay a fee for each child to attend school. Most of the textbooks are from Amish publishers and the teachers themselves have only an eighth grade education. The children learn spelling, grammar, arithmetic, geography, history, and English, so by the end of eighth grade, they are bilingual. No science is taught, no evolution, no sex education. Although Bible verses are read, religion is not taught. That's left to the family and church. Practical skills are emphasized, not analytical and critical thinking. For example, they don't read passages from literature in order to compare and contrast or to draw conclusions. They aren't intent on developing advanced thought processes."

"Do many of the kids want to go on to high school?"

"Most Amish children don't rebel against the education restrictions. They're content with their lot. Many find satisfaction in the farming life, in manual trades, or as small business owners. But every so often, as in Jacob's case, there is a desire for more. His craving for knowledge is consuming; it is a part of who he is. Jacob needs an outlet for his intelligence."

Taylor sighed. "Jacob has incredible hurdles to overcome," she said. "He not only has to deal with the limits on his education but now he must also deal with the limitations of his body. He faces an intellectual struggle and a physical one."

"He has a strong faith," Julia said, "as well as the love of his family and the support of the Amish community, at least for his physical struggle. And now he has you. Maybe you can help him, too."

"How can I help?" Taylor asked.

Julia hesitated.

"I'm not sure I should be telling you this, but I think it's too important to keep secret. Jacob's been studying for his high school equivalencey degree, the GED."

"Aha," Taylor said, remembering the Kaplan GED study guide she had seen in Jacob's bedroom trunk.

The GED is a series of five tests, Julia explained: math, social studies, science, writing, and reading. In order to pass the GED and receive a high school diploma, each test must be passed separately. For the past three years, Jacob had been studying for the tests. Julia had tutored him, as had several teachers she knew from the local high school. At least twice a week, he would drive his buggy to the library and the tutors would meet him there. His family did not know.

The consensus among the teachers involved had been that given Jacob's eighth grade education, the math and science tests would be the most challenging since he had no foundation in science and needed help with geometry and algebra, Julia said. Therefore, most of the tutoring time had been spent on those two subjects. The strategy had been to try and pass the two most difficult tests first; for the reading and writing tests, his skills were much stronger, due to a great extent to his extensive reading.

"Last December, Jacob passed the science test, and this past March he passed the math and social studies tests," Julia said proudly. "But the GED test will be revised next January and will be offered only on computer. If Jacob doesn't take and pass all five parts of the current test by the end of this year, he'll have to start all over under the new GED standards. So time is of the essense. He's almost there, Taylor. Maybe you can encourage him to go on and take the last two tests so he can receive his diploma."

"What would be the advantage of a high school diploma for Jacob?" Taylor asked. "Would he have to leave the Amish community since higher education is forbidden?"

"Since he hasn't yet been baptized, he hasn't taken an oath to uphold the *Ordnung*, the Amish rules of conduct, and so he wouldn't be officially excommunicated from the community," Julia said. "But with a GED and especially if he decided to go on to college, it would be difficult for him to remain Amish."

"Where would he go if he left his community? How would he survive on his own without his family, especially now that he's paralyzed?"

"Those are valid questions," Julia said. "I'm not sure what Jacob's long-range plans were after the GED or whether now, because of his injury, he intends to follow through with them. He has options outside the Amish community and if he chooses to leave, he will undoubtedly need help. All I know for sure is that his academic potential should not be wasted."

❧

BECCA STOOD NERVOUSLY in front of the house on the sidewalk that led to the pond and watched Taylor push mow the front lawn. Mowing was usually Becca's chore but with her arm in a cast, Taylor had offered at the noon meal to take care of it. With much of the front yard taken up by the pond and several large oak trees, there wasn't much lawn to mow, but Becca was meticulous about the way it was done. She mowed it slowly and carefully, in either a horizontal or vertical direction, leaving the lawn with straight, even lines when she was done. She enjoyed the chore and loved the sweet smell of freshly mown grass. Taylor, however, mowed haphazardly and at breakneck speed, creating crisscross lines all over the lawn, oblivious to everything but completing the task. As she rounded the pond, Taylor looked up, saw Becca, and waved. Becca bit her lip and waved back.

Taylor and the Yoders had settled into a routine for the week. Taylor helped Katie and Daniel at the four-thirty afternoon milking while Daniel and Levi took care of the morning shift; Joseph and Emma also helped at both. By the end of week, Taylor knew her way around the barn, was fast and efficient, and could handle the double milking machine. Even Daniel grudgingly admitted to Sarah one night while getting ready for bed that Taylor was pulling her own weight, at least in the barn.

Taylor drove the family to the hospital to visit Jacob in the evenings after supper or sometimes in the afternoon if chores were light or the weather inclement. She either visited Jacob in the morning after breakfast at the B & B or she worked in her room, then drove to the Yoder farm to help Sarah in the kitchen with lunch and afternoon chores, which usually consisted of laundry, cleaning the house, gardening, or manning the vegetable stand with Katie or Becca.

Sarah found Taylor to be clueless to whatever the domestic chore at hand, yet willing, with a tenacious desire to master the task. She tackled mopping floors or weeding the vegetable garden with the same energy and drive she brought to her professional life. Yet Sarah knew she derived no satisfaction or pleasure from any chore other than finishing it so she could move on to the next. In the kitchen, Taylor tried doubly hard to compensate for her rudimentary cooking skills; she was determined to redeem herself for the earlier lopsided cake.

"How do you feed yourself at home?" Sarah asked one afternoon, not unkindly, as she wrapped a bandage around Taylor's finger after she had cut it while slicing zucchini.

"I usually go out for dinner or order in takeout or throw something in the microwave," Taylor replied. "I never learned to cook. We had a cook at home when I was growing up and I guess I never expressed an interest in cooking so I never learned. It's such a time-consuming chore and I always seem to be short on time."

"Cooking tasty and nutritious food is something good you do for your body, like exercise or taking a rest," Sarah said.

"Yes, nourishment of the body. I get it. But what about nourishment of the mind? The Amish don't seem too keen on that."

Sarah looked taken aback and Taylor, willing to let the point slide for the time being, rushed on.

"I admit there's nothing like the aroma of a pie baking in the oven," Taylor said, "but if I did have free time, baking isn't how I'd choose to spend it."

"How would you spend your free time?"

"I don't know. I don't have any free time to think about that."

Taylor resumed slicing zucchini and didn't notice Sarah's sympathetic look.

DANIEL'S HANDS WERE nearly the size of a child's baseball glove, the muscles enlarged from decades of farming tobacco, the fingers calloused and cracked. It had rained the night before and the dark soil was heavy. Daniel intended to remove the last remaining tobacco from the seedbed that morning and transplant it into the field that evening with the twins' help; he estimated the morning work would take three or four hours to complete. Pleased with Taylor's work in the barn, he had asked her to help with the transplanting, but he bet his father Sadie's next born calf that Taylor wouldn't last to the completion of the back-breaking work, especially as the heat of the day increased.

The Yoders' six acres of tobacco fields were on the opposite end of the property from the barn. Daniel, Levi, Aaron Beiler, and Taylor walked across a small wooden bridge over Stoney Creek, which cut across the Yoder property. The Yoder home, *grossdaadi* house, barn, silo, pond, and cow and horse pastures were on the side of the property adjacent to Hickory Hill Road. The tobacco and cattle corn fields, as well as the curing shed for the tobacco, were on the other side of the meandering S-curved creek.

Daniel showed Taylor how to carefully remove each individual tobacco plant, about the size of a regular adult male hand, from the wet soil of the seedbed so as not to damage the root system.

"How long will it take before the tobacco is ready to harvest?" Taylor asked.

"From removal of the plants in the bed to harvest time is about seventy or eighty days, so we should be harvesting in mid- to late August, if the weather cooperates," Daniel said.

Taylor gently pulled a plant and held it up for Daniel to see then placed it in a rectangular wooden carton, which when full, would be placed in the shade until transplanting.

"What kind of tobacco is this?" she asked.

"It's a genetically modified tobacco to be used in cigarettes that will be nearly nicotine free, so says the tobacco company."

Taylor's eyes widened. "The Amish grow a genetically modified crop?"

"We aren't the backward farmers you might think," Daniel retorted. "We keep up with all the latest farming methods. We're in a lot of ways what you call 'green.' We use manure for fertilizer instead of chemicals, we use drainage trenches and plant trees along streams as buffers"—he pointed to the row of trees lining the crop side of Stoney Creek as it curved through the farm—"to prevent manure runoff from the fields into streams, and there are many farms in the county certified as organic. We pick and choose what is best for the land, our families, and our way of life."

"I didn't mean to offend," Taylor said. "I was just curious. How big will the tobacco plants be when you harvest them?"

Daniel pulled three plants before answering. "When first planted, tobacco seeds are the size of table salt. When the plant matures, it's about three feet high, and the leaves are fifteen inches wide."

They worked in silence for a while. Levi and Aaron toiled a couple rows over.

"Are the Amish permitted to smoke?" Taylor asked hesitantly, not sure if smoking was a sensitive subject considering David's cigarette had started the fire at the accident scene.

"Smoking isn't banned, at least not in our church district," Daniel said. "Some smoke cigars and pipes but commercial, white-wrapped cigarettes are considered worldly." He paused. "But they seem popular among the *die youngie,* the young folks."

"But isn't it hypocritical to grow a crop that will be commercialized into a product you don't believe in? Not to mention the hundreds of thousands of people in this country that die from lung cancer, emphysema, heart disease, and other smoking-related diseases every year."

Daniel stood up. "I'm going to start on the next row. You can finish this one." And he walked away.

Three and a half hours later, sweaty and exhausted, Taylor pulled the last tobacco plant in her row, laid it in the wooden carton, stood up and walked, hunched over due to an aching back, from the seedbed back to the house.

Levi, Daniel, and Aaron finished collecting the cartons filled with plants and placed them in the shade, ready to be transplanted into the field that night.

"You owe me a calf." Levi grinned at Daniel as they followed Taylor across the fields.

JACOB AND TAYLOR passed the week getting to know each other during their hospital visits. He wasn't sullen with her as he sometimes was with his family. He finally had someone he could talk to about books and education and Taylor discovered other things to talk about besides work.

She often read to Jacob as he ate; while reading *The Old Man and the Sea*, Taylor rediscovered the joy of reading. At other times, she worked on her laptop or BlackBerry while he read to himself.

Sometimes they watched TV together and discussed what they saw. Taylor considered bringing up the GED issue but intuition suggested the timing wasn't right; Jacob was still overwhelmed with his disability and his main focus was on dealing with his paralysis.

One morning they looked up Bayard's website. He learned how the rehab center would help him learn to live with his disability, practical things like bowel and bladder management, learning to get dressed, learning to maneuver a wheelchair, physical therapy. Jacob seemed less apprehensive once he understood what he would face at Bayard but still anxious.

"I've never been away from home before, not even for one night," he said. "I'll be there for weeks, alone."

"You can do this, Jacob," Taylor said. "Your family can visit and I live nearby and will help however I can."

One day she introduced him to the *Amazon* website and they ordered two books, which she had delivered to her Philadelphia home, intending to bring them to him after he arrived at Bayard. One was Tolkien's *Lord of the Rings*, which appeared on both 100 Best Novels lists; the other was *The History of the World* by J. M. Roberts and O. A. Westad because Jacob said he wanted to learn more about Middle Eastern, Asian and European history, the World Wars, and how it all tied together to the present.

"It also includes the history of science, art, religion, and technology. Jacob, this book is over a thousand pages," Taylor said before she transferred it to her shopping cart.

"I think I'll have the time to read it," Jacob deadpanned.

Another morning, she looked up genetically modified tobacco on the web and learned it was under attack from public health advocates.

"The tobacco you're growing will be used in cigarettes that will be virtually nicotine free—nicotine being the addictive element in cigarettes—but will still contain nearly all the carcinogens in regular cigarettes that cause cancer and heart disease," Taylor explained to Jacob. "The idea is to help people wean themselves from nicotine while continuing to smoke. But the tobacco company can't market the cigarettes as helping people kick the habit without proving that claim to the FDA, which regulates health claims. So while the company is doing research for the FDA, they're marketing the product in seven states as being nicotine free without claiming it will help people to stop smoking.

"Jacob, your father refused to answer this question, but how can the Amish work so hard to grow a crop that will be used to market a product you believe is worldly?"

"There is some controversy, even among the Amish, about growing tobacco, whether genetically modified or not," Jacob replied. "There's been a growing awareness of the health hazards of smoking and some tobacco farmers have switched to other crops. My father is growing genetically modified tobacco because the tobacco company is paying nearly twice the market rate of standard tobacco and that price is guaranteed for three years. It pays the mortgage on the farm, puts food on the table, and I know my father is trying to save money to help David buy a farm. So you can be as self-righteous as you want but I could argue, based on what I've seen on TV just since I've been in the hospital, that the television industry is focused much more on generating advertising revenue from meaningless and silly reality shows than on programs that inform and educate the public."

Taylor smiled. "Touché," she said.

SARAH MASHED THE potatoes in a large blue stoneware bowl she had received for a wedding gift more than two decades ago. The house was quiet; Becca and the twins were working the vegetable stand and the rest of the family was in the barn for the afternoon milking. She expected Mary shortly to help prepare supper but until then Sarah was alone with her thoughts. She had a decision to make.

Taylor had approached her two nights ago after they had returned home from visiting Jacob. While the others prepared for bed, she and Taylor had lit a kerosene lamp and sat on the couch and talked. Taylor had offered her home in Philadelphia to Sarah and Becca during the eight weeks or so Jacob would be in rehab at Bayard. She included Becca in the invitation because Becca was still dealing with trauma from the accident and couldn't be separated from Sarah for that long. The rehab center was only a few minutes from Taylor's home in Rittenhouse Square, and when Sarah needed to return to Lancaster and the farm, she could catch the nearby bus or train.

Before Taylor's offer, Sarah had wondered how she could afford to stay in a hotel in the city in order to visit Jacob. She couldn't bear the thought of him going through rehab alone without any family nearby. She had prayed to God for a solution; He had answered. If she stayed with Taylor, her only expense would be commuting back and forth to home when necessary, probably for the weekends and maybe a few days here and there during the week: canning needed to be done throughout the summer and Becca needed to return to the hospital in July to have the pins removed from her arm. But someone would have to oversee the household while she was gone and she couldn't expect Mary and Katie to handle that responsibility alone.

The morning after her conversation with Taylor, after a nearly sleepless night, Sarah had hitched up the buggy and visited three of her sisters-in-law—Rachel, Hannah and Susie Esh—and not one of them had hesitated a second before agreeing to help. Rachel said she could take the youngest of her four kids over to the Yoders and help there three days a week. Hannah and Susie, with thirteen kids between them, each agreed to help out a day a week. Sarah's only living sister Ellie—sister Katie was killed at eight when thrown by a horse—who lived in Ohio with her husband, had written right after the accident that she'd be willing to come for a visit and help out, but Sarah knew they had purchased a farm not long ago and money was tight. As much as she missed Ellie, she intended to write back and tell her the household was covered, at least for a while.

She had also discussed the idea with Daniel who, although not overly fond of Taylor, understood the importance of his wife being near Jacob and certainly understood the value of doing so on a cost-effective basis. He had already lined up the six eldest boys of his brother Zach and brothers-in-law Rudy and Eli on a rotating basis for three weeks to help in the barn and the fields. Zach, Rudy, and Eli were all dairy farmers, and so their eldest sons were well versed in farm work. Levi would also help as much as he physically could, and David would be back to work, at least on a limited basis, assuming the doctor's okay, in mid-July.

The whole idea made practical sense yet Sarah was hesitant. She hated to be away from the rest of the children and she was also nervous about living with Taylor in the city. She didn't know Taylor well and they were so different; Taylor was impatient, assertive, and outspoken while Sarah was quiet, calm, and passive. They got along well so far, but would they be compatible long-term?

Plus, she realized she and Becca faced a big adjustment; they'd be living in a home with electricity in the middle of a vibrant city so unlike their peaceful rural existence. Taylor had insisted she would help them navigate Philadelphia, would not work the grueling schedule she usually did, and even promised to show them some of the sights of the city.

Sarah knew Becca would be excited about the opportunity but she worried about the affect on her daughter. She had just started her *rumspringa* and, like many Amish teens, would be susceptible to the lures of the English world. Not only would she be susceptible but she would be living smack in the middle of that world with a woman who represented everything from which the Amish wanted to separate.

But Sarah also had confidence in Becca's upbringing, in the faith they had taught her, and in the loving cocoon of her family. Even if Becca had her head turned for a few weeks, Sarah felt sure the temptations would not be so enticing as to make her daughter seriously question her way of life. As for Bishop Lapp, she believed he would understand, even if he didn't wholeheartedly approve of them living a temporary worldly life in order to be near Jacob. And with that, she recognized she had just rationalized away all her reservations about the move.

She placed the potatoes in the oven as she heard the twins noisily enter the house. She turned to greet them with a smile. She was at peace; the decision was made.

TAYLOR HANDED THE iPhone to Jacob.

"I've already programmed my cell phone number into it so just tap the number one and you'll be able to reach me whenever you want. I thought a phone would be useful, especially when you're at Bayard. Don't worry about the cost. It's on me. Here's the charger, too, and of course I'll give you phone lessons."

Jacob held the sleek black device in his hand. It violated the *Ordnung* in multiple ways: it took pictures, it connected to the Internet, and it required electricity to recharge. It was the epitome of worldliness and forbidden technology. And he wanted it. For the second time in a week, Taylor saw Jacob smile.

7

THE LOBBY OF The Regent, the high-rise building where Taylor owned a penthouse on the twenty-second floor, transfixed Sarah and Becca: black and white tile floor with a round table in the center showcasing a dramatic arrangement of red roses and white lilies, a massive crystal and ruby-colored chandelier, flowing crimson drapes adorning floor-to-ceiling windows that faced Rittenhouse Square across the street.

Taylor had parked the car in the basement garage and they had taken the elevator to the lobby, where Taylor had introduced them to the doorman, Henry, and the concierge, Frederick, both of whom needed to know the comings and goings of every tenant in the building, including long-term visitors.

While Taylor conversed with Frederick, mother and daughter surveyed the lobby. A brawny uniformed security guard sat behind a black marble desk in front of a bank of television screens showing views captured by hidden security cameras. Henry, white-haired and over six feet tall, stood resplendent in his charcoal grey and maroon uniform. Becca thought her eyes would pop.

"Goodness, *Mamm*, we're actually going to live here?"

"I didn't realize she was *this* rich," Sarah whispered.

"Frederick, I want you to keep an eye on them," Taylor said. "They're Amish, in case you're wondering about their dress.

They live on a farm in Lancaster. Neither has ever been to the city and it will certainly be a culture shock. While I'm at work, they'll be here alone. Help them with whatever they need. Also, please reserve the town car and driver for a couple days next week to show them the sights of the city."

"My pleasure, Ms. Loden. Might I also suggest a trip to Longwood Gardens in nearby Kennett Square. This time of year the gardens are magnificent."

"Good idea. Arrange that as well, please. Bill everything to my account."

Taylor then ushered the Yoders to the elevators. "Before we go to my place, I want to show you the pool and fitness center," Taylor said, pushing the button for the twenty-fifth floor.

They had come right from Bayard to The Regent that Friday. An ambulance had transported Jacob from Memorial General to the rehabilitation hospital; Taylor, Sarah, and Becca had followed in the car. Taylor's Z4 BMW convertible was still being repaired so Taylor replaced the rental van she had been driving in Lancaster for a metallic grey Lexus sedan. Sarah had filled out the necessary papers for Jacob's admittance to the hospital and they had joined him for a while in his room on the fifth floor. It had been late afternoon by then and Jacob needed to rest so they left.

The Regent's elevator opened onto the rooftop. At first, Becca was confused. It didn't seem like they were actually standing on the roof of a high-rise building. Shrubberies, flowering bushes, and trees tall enough to provide shade lushly landscaped the area. Round tables with kelly green and white striped market umbrellas and navy blue lounge chairs surrounded a large pool. Taylor pointed out the fitness club at the far end of the roof. Inside, you could see treadmills lined in a row in front of the windows, looking out over the rooftop and the cityscape.

"That's where I exercise," Taylor said. "I'm usually up there three or four mornings a week before I go to work."

Next stop was Taylor's penthouse. The trio exited the elevator; black double doors with long satin nickel handles and beveled glass transom windows opened into the foyer. Their luggage, a motley collection of Taylor's Louis Vuitton monogrammed canvas and the Yoders' recycled white plastic grocery bags and a black American Tourister purchased seven years ago from Walmart when Sarah visited her sister in Ohio, stood on the floor, brought up from the garage by a parking attendant.

"Let me give you a quick tour of the place before you unpack. Then we can either order something in or go out for dinner."

The penthouse décor was sleek and contemporary, with clean-lined dark wood furniture and neutral and earth tone fabrics; its eggshell-colored walls held either original landscape paintings by local artists or eclectic modern art.

Walking from the foyer into the living room was like walking straight into the skyline of the city. Floor-to-ceiling arched windows occupied one entire wall of the spacious room, with no window treatments to detract from the expansive view. A black Steinway baby grand piano stood on an inlay of black and white marble in front of the windows. The seating area—two black leather couches, tan suede armchairs and ottomans, and a black lacquered coffee table—rested on a plush cream carpet. The seating area faced a fireplace cut into the middle of a fieldstone wall. Mounted above the wall was a fifty-inch flat-screen television; stereo equipment, DVD player, and two smaller televisions, usually hidden behind built-in cabinets flanking the fireplace, were on display.

Sarah stared open-mouthed at the wall of TVs. "I know that looks excessive," Taylor explained, "but I actually use the TVs to check our regional stations and to sometimes compare our news with other stations."

The kitchen, with its custom cherry cabinetry, granite counters, and stainless steel appliances led to the dining room, where an eight-seat oval frosted glass-topped table on a bronze metal pedestal stood under a sparkling Murano glass chandelier.

Dazed, Becca and Sarah followed Taylor as she led them from room to room. "I want you to be comfortable here, so please make yourselves at home in any room," Taylor said.

A hallway off the living room led to the library and three bedrooms. Sliding pocket doors opened to Taylor's home office and library. Three walls contained shelves full of books, categorized by type—classics, non-fiction, autobiography, contemporary literature—and arranged alphabetically by author. Taylor's large desk, covered with files and newspapers and her computer, landline phone, and printer, stood in front of another wall of windows.

The two guest bedrooms each had their own bath and walk-in closet. One room was a palate of black and shades of grey, the other of caramel and cream.

"They remind me of licorice and butterscotch," Becca said.

Taylor laughed. "Then we'll call them the Licorice Room and the Butterscotch Room."

In the master bedroom, outfitted in rich chocolate brown and beige fabrics, mahogany cabinetry surrounding the fireplace held books, a few framed family pictures—of Taylor and her father, of her father and mother, and of Taylor as a young girl with her mother—and mounted above the fireplace was a forty-four inch flat screen television.

Becca's jaw dropped as she gazed at Taylor's walk-in closet: shelves with dozens of shoes and handbags, hanging clothes, arranged by season, and sweaters behind glass-paned cabinets lined the walls; tucked in a corner was a thermostatically-controlled closet-within-a-closet, where, Taylor explained, she stored her furs—vests, a short jacket, and one long coat—during the off-season. Another door led to a small laundry room.

The master bath featured a glass block shower with body jets, a whirlpool tub, and a double vanity. A wall niche above the tub held a small television.

Intercoms placed strategically on the walls in each room

carried music from the stereo system or could be used to talk to someone in another room; living alone, Taylor had never used that feature nor did she listen to music.

Mother and daughter politely *oohed* and *aahed* over each room. Yet the penthouse made them both nervous, not just because it was equipped with every electronic device and appliance known to man, but because, although beautifully decorated, it lacked warmth: it seemed sterile and cold, almost unwelcoming.

Taylor had given her decorator free reign and had not been more than marginally involved in choosing furnishings or personalizing the space; as far as she was concerned, the penthouse suited her aesthetically and amply served its purpose. It was close to the offices of Loden Media, convenient to city life, full of amenities that made her life easier—like a housekeeper so she could work without worrying about distractions like dust balls or hand washing her delicates—and was a fine place to be for those few hours a day when she wasn't at the office. And, as her father said when she bought the penthouse two years ago, it was a good investment.

When the tour was complete, Taylor said, "Okay, who wants which bedroom?" "Oh, I want the Butterscotch one!" Becca said.

THE SUN SET over the city as they sat on the wicker-furnished terrace off the kitchen after dinner, their first day in Philadelphia drawing to a close. They had finished their take-out lasagna from D'Angelo's Italian restaurant nearby and Sarah had cleaned up the food cartons and insisted on hand washing the forks and knives rather than putting them in the dishwasher. Becca had suggested they eat on the terrace; she hadn't said so, but she thought the dining room seemed too formal for take-out food.

Taylor wanted to be a good hostess but was itching to get

to her library and check emails. Becca and Sarah seemed content to just sit and chat.

They talked about Bayard and hoped Jacob would make a smooth transition. They agreed to visit him the following afternoon. Taylor told them she was going to the office the next morning and they could spend that time getting settled. They talked about the city and Taylor started to explain about the nearby restaurants and shops but then stopped when it occurred to her Becca and Sarah wouldn't shop, certainly not for clothes, and would also probably not frequent the restaurants because of the cost. She made an instant decision.

"Look, while you're here as my guests, I don't want you to worry about the cost of anything," she said. "Anywhere we go, whether it's to a restaurant or sightseeing, will be my treat. I want to do this for you and I hope you won't be uncomfortable accepting this from me. You're both going through a tough time. I want to make your stay pleasant, as pleasant as possible under the circumstances.

"And I don't want you to worry about helping out around here either. There's really nothing you need to do. Maria, my housekeeper, comes in on Wednesdays and she'll take care of all the cleaning, laundry, grocery shopping, everything. About the most you can do is cook or clean up after meals. If you want to do the dishes by hand, that's fine. But if you just stack everything in the dishwasher, either Maria or I will run it. If you'd rather do your own laundry, feel free.

"We can leave Maria a grocery list. You both can make one, whatever you two want to eat for breakfast, lunch, and dinner. Plus, if you'd like to sample some of the city's restaurants, I'd like to take you. Would you like that?"

"Yes," Becca said quickly, glancing at her mother.

"I guess that would be all right, occasionally," Sarah said.

Taylor made a mental note to call Maria's service and tell them she would be increasing her pay for the next two months while Taylor had houseguests.

"Also, if I'm available, I'll be happy to drive you over to Bayard to visit Jacob; please don't consider it an imposition. If I'm working, then please ask Henry to call you a driver. Okay?"

Sarah had tears in her eyes. "We are so grateful for everything you're doing."

While they had been talking, night had fallen.

"Oh my," Sarah exclaimed, looking out over the skyline. The city was aglow with light, the skyscrapers twinkling in the dark sky, the headlights of the cars on the highways glittering like fireflies. "What a view. You must so enjoy this every night."

Taylor looked out over the city appreciatively, too. She was back in town; she had only been gone two weeks but it seemed much longer and her life seemed different somehow, in an imperceptible way she couldn't quite define. But what she knew for sure was she hadn't eaten on the terrace or enjoyed the view since she couldn't remember when.

TAYLOR'S HOUSE, PENTHOUSE I guess it's called, is more than I ever imagined a home could be. Such fancy furniture and beautiful pictures on the walls, and the fabrics! In my bedroom, the Butterscotch Room, my toes completely sink in the thick carpet, the sheets on the bed are soft yet crisp (when I told Taylor how much I liked them she said they were Frette, whatever that means), my head nestles into the four fluffy pillows, and the comforter on the bed is plump and cozy. I can almost taste butterscotch while I'm lying in it. I've missed writing in you, my journal, and haven't done so since right before the accident. Luckily, I didn't break my right (writing) arm.

Taylor has a couple framed pictures of her mother in her bedroom. She died of cancer several years ago, Taylor said. Her mom and dad look so happy together in the one picture. There's another of Taylor and her mom, standing with their heads together, laughing. Taylor said that was taken when she was eleven or twelve during a family vacation in

Bermuda. I wonder whether those pictures bring Taylor joy or sadness. In the whole house, there are only two pictures of her mom. Did they not take many or did she choose not to display them. If Mamm died, would I forget what she looks like? I know we're not supposed to dwell on what people look like, it's more important what they're like inside, and I know I'll never have a picture of Mamm because photos aren't allowed, but after seeing Taylor's, I can see why it would be nice to have one.

I hope Jacob likes Bayard. I can't get used to seeing him lying in bed. I remember him pitching hay in the barn or driving the horses in the field or playing volleyball with the guys. So tall and strong. He certainly wasn't one to be laughing all the time but when he did smile, it lit up his face. Now he seems to have shrunk, gone inside himself. I don't know what to say to him. He's sometimes grumpy and always so sad. Mamm says Jacob will get through this and God will help him. I want to help him, too. I'm just not sure what to do. Hopefully, just being nearby will help.

When Mamm came to say goodnight tonight, we talked about Taylor's closet. Mamm said she'd never seen so many clothes outside of a store. And my goodness, how can any one person wear that many shoes!? They certainly were pretty, though. All different colors, some with high heels (can she walk in them without falling over?), some with cut-outs for toes, some with straps, some glittery, some plain. What would it feel like to wear shoes like that, for just one day?

JACOB LAY IN the dark on his bed, quietly listening to the sounds from the city streets below, noisy compared to the intensely quiet rural nights he was accustomed to. His head throbbed and he felt anxious. It was Saturday night, his second at the rehab center, and he was overwhelmed from trying to adjust to and absorb life at Bayard.

He heard soft breathing from the adjacent bed. His roommate Eric Richards seemed a nice enough kid, eighteen. Also a paraplegic, he had been in rehab for about three weeks, injured during an ATV accident; the motorbike had hit a field rut and Eric had flown over the handlebars. He had told Jacob the story Friday night at dinner. They had been introduced by Ellen, their case manager, and had sat next to each other in the dining room.

Eric was a talker and Jacob, sullen and scared, was even more reserved than usual, which Eric either didn't notice or chose to ignore. He chatted on about the workings of the center, and Jacob was relieved to let him talk while he listened. He did learn some useful things. There were group outings to museums or sporting events so they could learn to function in wheelchairs in public—"Get used to the stares," Eric had advised—and the center also sponsored its own sporting teams: wheelchair basketball, tennis, and rugby.

Ellen had indeed confirmed all that during his orientation meeting Saturday morning; he had met his occupational therapist, who would teach him how to bathe and dress and manage his bowel movements; his physical therapist, from whom he would learn balance, upper body mobility and flexibility; and the recreational therapist, in charge of leisure and group activities. Classes would be held periodically for family members so they could learn things like proper transfer techniques—for example, helping him out of bed, or up from couches, or out of a car or buggy—and how to recognize physical danger signs, or how to encourage independence.

With Ellen, Jacob toured the gym, the chapel, and his personal favorite, the learning resource center, full of magazines, books, newspapers, and computers with Internet access. Ping pong, a swimming pool, and air hockey were also available, as well as a greenhouse and patio on the roof. He was surrounded by equipment and technology that was new to him and forbidden in his life on the farm, including the flat screen cable TV in his room and the phone on his nightstand.

That Saturday at lunch, Jacob was his usual glum self, and Eric had cheerfully asked, "Are you normally in a crummy mood or have you only been like that since your accident?"

Jacob was so surprised at the forthrightness of the question that he felt emboldened to ask his own.

"How can you be so happy? Are you drugged?"

Eric had laughed, then turned serious.

"For the first few days after my accident, I didn't want to live. Everything had been going my way: I was president of my senior class, dating a hot girl, captain of the lacrosse team, accepted to Penn State, main campus. Then I crashed my motorbike. I figured my life was over. My parents and friends tried everything to snap me out of it. Every cliché you've ever heard about adversity they threw at me: 'You're stronger than you think. Your life's not over, it's just altered. You're still the same person inside. If life hands you lemons, make lemonade. God only tests those who are strong enough to handle it.' I thought it was all crap.

"One day, my nephew Evan came to visit me in the hospital. He's four, my older sister's son. He wasn't allowed in my room because of his age but they snuck him in for like ten minutes because he was driving them crazy asking to see me. He was so excited he ran across my room and hopped on the chair next to my bed. 'I have a surprise for you,' he said, and pulled out of his pocket a bag of peanut M&Ms."

Eric paused to take a bite of pizza and a gulp of milk. "Peanut M&Ms are my favorite. I ate them constantly. I used to stash bags of them in my locker at school. I'd hide them in my bedroom because of course my mother didn't want me to eat so many. Evan knew how much I liked them because whenever we were together I'd always share mine with him.

"He must have been fiddling with that bag of candy in the car all the way over to the hospital. By the time he pulled it out of his pocket, it had ripped, and as he waved it in front of my face, M&Ms flew across the room, on my bed, all over the floor. Evan's lips started to tremble. I hugged him and told everyone to pick up the M&Ms, even the ones on the floor, and put them back in the bag so I could eat them.

"Evan was ecstatic. I looked at his beaming face and started to see things differently. He had found joy in doing a simple thing for me—bringing me candy. His happy face that day was the highlight of my miserable day and every miserable day up to that point. So I decided I would start small. I would try to find pleasure in the little things every day that made me happy or made me smile or at least made me less miserable. Like peanut M&Ms. And that's how I started to come back to life."

ERIC KNEW NOTHING about Jacob except he was from Lancaster—no details of the accident or even that he was Amish—until after lunch that afternoon when Sarah and Becca visited.

When mother and daughter walked into the room, Eric took one look at their clothes, glanced at Jacob in surprise, and said delightedly, "Whoa. No way!"

Taylor came in a few minutes later after parking the car and introduced herself to Eric. Just then a fellow patient showed up to ask Eric to play air hockey, so Eric's curiosity about Taylor could not be immediately satisfied.

The rest of the day, until visiting hours ended at eight-thirty, Taylor and the Yoders spent with Jacob. They toured the rehab center and Sarah and Becca took turns pushing Jacob in the wheelchair. They spent the afternoon sitting on the rooftop patio, enjoying the sun.

Taylor spent most of the time on her laptop and BlackBerry, Sarah had brought her sewing bag, and Becca seemed content to just observe and be with her mother and brother. She inquired about Eric, and Jacob, who seemed slightly more talkative than usual, filled them in on his roommate. They all had dinner together in the dining room, including Eric, who peppered Taylor with questions about her job, since he was considering a journalism major in college.

Sunday was much the same except visiting hours were

longer. Taylor dropped Sarah and Becca off at eleven that morning and went to her office. The two stayed with Jacob all day and ate lunch and dinner with him.

Jacob was grateful for the familiar faces of his sister and mother, everything and everyone else being new and strange. He had never been away from the farm overnight, and was somewhat of a loner; he knew many men in his Amish community but none he would have characterized as a good friend he talked to frequently or that knew his secret.

Lying in bed that night, heart pounding from anxiety, he listened to the cacophony of city sounds below and suddenly felt a faint stirring of excitement. He realized, and this was a welcome revelation to him, that he could choose to view his predicament as an adventure—albeit a difficult and scary one—that he was actually experiencing rather than reading about in a book.

ON MONDAY, TAYLOR'S father took her to the Cascade Restaurant in Logan Square for lunch to welcome her back to work. Taylor drank in the elegant ambiance—the dark wood and contemporary art, and the view of the massive fountain in the courtyard—and was glad to be back in the city. She felt far removed from cows and the smell of the Yoder barn.

"So how are the houseguests?" Connor asked.

"They're settling in. Sarah was making Becca breakfast when I left. I did have some basics in the fridge; Maria must have stocked it with eggs, milk, juice, bagels, bacon. This morning and tomorrow morning Frederick arranged a tour of the city for them—the Liberty Bell, Independence Hall, Penn's Landing, Boathouse Row, the usual."

"And how is Jacob doing at Bayard?"

"As well as can be expected, so far. He seems a little overwhelmed but hanging in there."

"Taylor, you know you don't need to knock yourself out

while they're staying with you. Do what you absolutely need to do at work on a daily basis and let the rest go. I know I'm a fine one to preach but you were just in an accident and I don't want you to take on more than you can handle. Not that you can't handle it, but it's not necessary."

"I know, Dad. I promised Sarah I would be around and I intend to keep that promise. I'm going to try to leave the office around four every evening. Visiting hours start at four during the week, so I can run them over to see Jacob or take them to dinner or both. I can always work while I'm at Bayard or I can come back to the office while they visit or I can work from home. I want to entertain them, too. Thursday is Opera on the Square, right outside my front door, and this Saturday I'm going to take them to the zoo before they visit Jacob."

"I don't think the opera is a permitted activity for the Amish," Connor said.

"Shoot, that didn't occur to me. But Becca's in *rumspringa;* seems like they can do whatever they want during that period. I'll check on that, though. So how's the merger coming?"

"Alan has it under control. Should be a done deal by the end of this month. The Loden Media twentieth newspaper: Erie, Pennsylvania's *Tribune News.* Applause, please."

"You're such a needy mogul," Taylor teased.

WHEN TAYLOR RETURNED to the office after lunch, she called Ben Scott, a reporter for the *Lancaster Post,* a Loden Media paper. She figured he'd know something about Amish culture since he'd covered the Lancaster area for years. She specifically wanted to know what type of culture was permitted or forbidden so she could better plan the Yoders' sightseeing. She informed Ben about her guests and that Becca was in *rumspringa.*

"Can I take them to concerts or the symphony? The Philadelphia Zoo?" Taylor asked.

"Sarah will be cautious and wary. For her, the zoo is okay, as are national parks and historic sites. For Amish youth in *rumspringa*, pretty much anything goes," Ben said. "They do whatever they want, based on the type of gang they join, conservative or liberal. Becca may be willing to try whatever you suggest but will want to be discrete around her mom.

"*Rumspringa* teens are introduced to a wide range of music if they have access to an iPod or cellphone and some install stereos and speakers in their buggies. Teens may also dance to music at parties, but among adults, moving the body to music is considered immodest. Singing in public is considered prideful, and the playing of instruments is forbidden, considered a form of self-expression that focuses unacceptable attention on the individual."

"Can they attend movies or the theatre?" Taylor asked.

"Movies, like television, are considered worldly and sinful, full of violence and sex," Ben said. "The theatre, too, is prohibited."

Plus, the Amish also forbid photography, he said. "The reason usually given is the prohibition against graven images expressed in the Second Commandment, but they also believe that to pose for a photograph is an unacceptable act of pride and vanity. The inner self is important, not the outer shell. The Amish own no family photos, not even wedding pictures.

"But if it's for a government purpose, the Amish will often relent regarding photos. Since many Amish men are avid hunters, some obtain state photo identification cards because they need a photo ID to purchase a gun. Some Amish even have passports. They don't fly but will take trains and buses, for example to Mexico or Canada, and some believe it's acceptable to cruise to ancestral homelands in Europe."

"What about art museums?" Taylor wondered.

Ben explained that Amish artists are rare but a few paint landscapes rather than images of people. "The Amish believe public art exhibits call attention to the artists and therefore encourage vanity rather than humility. Useful creative expressions are encouraged, though, such as quilting, furniture making, and crafts, including those made for the tourist market. These skills are considered practical and useful and are ways to supplement farm incomes."

Taylor thanked Ben for his input. Her goal was to make life easier for the Yoders while Jacob was in rehab and to show them the sights of the city, but she also wanted to culturally educate Becca. A world of opportunity existed beyond the farms of Lancaster and beyond what Taylor viewed as the cloistered life of the Amish, and she wanted to be the one to show it to her young visitor.

8

THE BUILDINGS IN the city are so tall. I look at them and imagine all the people living or working in them, their lives so different from mine. On our tour of Philadelphia yesterday morning and this morning, we saw City Hall where the government is and Society Hill where more rich people live and Penn's Landing near the Delaware River (Mamm reminded me that it was William Penn who offered our ancestors the land in Lancaster so they could escape from persecution in the Old Country) and the Liberty Bell. I bet if an Amishman had made that bell it wouldn't have cracked the first time it was rung!

The city is noisy compared to the quiet on the farm, what with all the cars and trucks and police sirens and horns blowing. When you're in Taylor's penthouse, though, it's so quiet you don't hear the city noise. Taylor says the windows are triple glazed for soundproofing and energy efficiency. Then you go out of the penthouse and all the noise just smacks you in your ears. The other thing I noticed about the city, besides the skyscrapers, was no grass. Not a blade to be found except little patches here and there. Eddie, our driver, said of course there's grass in the city parks. But can you imagine going about your life for days and days without seeing grass? Luckily, I am sitting on grass this very minute. Mamm and I, at Eddie's suggestion, came over here to Rittenhouse Park after our tour. It's right across the street from Taylor's. Soon as I finish writing this I'm going to write to Katie and then I'm *going to start reading a book I found in Taylor's library, "Little Women" by Louisa May Alcott. Mamm is working on the quilt for David and Anna's wedding gift. She's about three-quarters done and it's beautiful, with the wedding ring pattern in mauve and green and white.*

BECCA WOKE ON Thursday morning with a runny nose and scratchy throat and although she took a decongestant Taylor gave her and rested all day, Sarah decided she shouldn't visit Jacob that evening and risk getting him sick. Taylor drove Sarah over to Bayard and then returned to the penthouse to stay with Becca, who had initially been panicked at the thought of being without her mother but understood the necessity of being left behind.

Becca stood at the living room windows watching the activity down on Rittenhouse Square as Taylor walked through the penthouse door.

"What's going on down there?" she asked.

"Opera on the Square. Opera singers from the Academy of Vocal Arts are performing, accompanied by an orchestra and chorus. Would you like to go? We could pack a picnic dinner, bring a blanket, and go listen."

Becca hesitated for a second before enthusiastically nodding yes; her mother wasn't around to disapprove and, after all, this was her *rumspringa*. "I've never heard opera before."

"This will be a real treat for you then. It's been a while since I listened to opera myself."

An hour later, Taylor and Becca spread the blanket on their chosen spot on the square and set the picnic basket in the center. Taylor had found the picnic basket and the blanket in a dark corner of her pantry closet; she had never used them but remembered they had gotten much use by her mother. Taylor had changed out of her business suit into designer jeans and a casual top and Becca decided to forego her *kapp*. They had packed Brie and French bread, both still warm from the oven, as well as chocolate-covered strawberries, and chicken salad with pineapple, mandarin oranges, and cashews, all of which the gourmet deli down the street had delivered. Taylor also brought linen napkins, a chilled bottle of chardonnay, and two crystal wine glasses. She decided Becca could have one sip, in addition to her diet soda.

The square was packed with a mix of ethnicities and ages— a smattering of youth but mostly a thirty plus crowd. Becca, of course, drew the customary stares, which she accepted with her usual equanimity.

As they unpacked their meal, Taylor explained to Becca that opera originated in Italy and was the emotional telling of a story in song, usually in Italian, and accompanied by musical instruments.

From the first strains of *Carmen's* "Toreador Song," to "Figaro, Figaro, Figaro!" from *The Barber of Seville,* to *La Bohème* and *Aida,* and finally through Gershwin's *Porgy and Bess,* Becca sat rapt, at one point her hand suspended in mid-air on the way to her mouth with a chocolate-covered strawberry, as a soprano, backed by chorus and orchestra, hit the high notes gloriously.

As Taylor watched her, she felt a stirring akin to maternal pride, an inner satisfaction in knowing she had brought such pleasure to, of all people, a teenager appreciating opera.

Becca was quiet as they packed up the picnic basket and folded the blanket after the concert. Taylor thought it was perhaps because they were still new to each other, not entirely comfortable together, and because Becca was probably missing her mother—they hadn't been separated from each other since they had arrived in Philadelphia.

But Becca's reserve was actually more contemplative. As they walked through Rittenhouse Square back to The Regent, she said, "I didn't know a human voice could sound like that."

Later that night, she wrote in her journal: *Why would God*

*give someone a gift of a beautiful voice, only to be displeased because
the singer shared that gift in public? Is singing in public prideful, or
simply giving others pleasure with your God-given talent?*

THE COLUMBIAN BLACK spider monkeys swung high above
from tree to tree with their long tails, as if their antics were
part of a show for the onlookers below, and Becca clapped in
delight. For much of the morning, Sarah and her daughter had
gawked in wide-eyed amazement at the animals at the Philadelphia Zoo. Taylor wasn't much of a zoo fan but her visitors'
enthusiasm was infectious. They shivered as they walked
briskly through the reptile house, hardly stopping to even
look at the King Cobra, all three having an aversion to snakes.
In a silly mood, uncharacteristic for Taylor, she and Becca began to mimic the animals: they perched on one leg in front of
the flamingos, then waddled like penguins, and hopped like
kangaroos. They marveled at the size of the rhinos and the
hippos and admired the zebras.

As the trio ambled down the walkway from Big Cat Falls
toward the lake, Taylor began to chant, "Lions and tigers and
bears, oh my! Lion and tigers and . . . " She looked at Becca
and Sarah, expecting a smile of recognition but they stared at
her blankly until she realized they probably never saw *The
Wizard of Oz.* "Never mind," she muttered.

Suddenly, Becca gasped, stopped dead, and pointed upward.
Overhead, a tiger walked across Big Cat Crossing, a mesh net
enclosure fourteen feet above their heads that acted as a trail
for the big cats: tigers, lions, pumas, jaguars, and snow leopards.

"What grand creatures God has created," Sarah said.

"At least in today's zoos," Taylor said, "the animals aren't
stuck in cages like in the past. Now they're kept in enclosures
that resemble their natural habitats, and at this zoo, they've
got these mesh-enclosed overhead paths for the gorillas and

orangutans, too. But I still think they'd all rather live in the wild."

"But then we wouldn't be able learn about and enjoy them," Becca said.

One area of the zoo offered camel rides. Taylor looked at Sarah and Becca with a gleam in her eye. Sarah immediately said, "Oh, no." But Becca was game. The zoo assistant had a tough time helping Becca onto the camel because of her long dress but finally managed. Taylor rode behind her on a second camel and Sarah watched from the sidelines.

"What's the hump for?" Becca asked the young zoo assistant who was leading the camel around the grassy area.

"Most people think the hump is filled with water so the camels can survive in the desert but really the humps are filled with fat. The camels use the fat when food's hard to find.

"Here's another fact I bet you don't know," the assistant continued. "Camels have eyelids like ours but they also have another see-through eyelid that moves from side to side to keep out the desert sand."

Taylor glanced at Sarah to make sure she was looking elsewhere, then snapped a picture with her iPhone of Becca on the camel, quickly slipping the cell back in her jeans pocket. Taylor rarely used her phone's camera feature; she had zero interest in Facebook or Instagram, and until recently, had no one to take a picture of or fun occasions to commemorate.

THE BLACK TEN-PERSON limo pulled away from the Thirtieth Street train station with the Yoder family aboard: Daniel, Mary, Levi, Katie, David, Emma, Joseph, and Sarah's sisters-in law Esther and Ruth Yoder and Hannah Esh. Taylor had hired the limo to take the family to visit Jacob at Bayard; she drove Sarah and Becca, who was disappointed not to ride in the limo. Earlier that morning, the three had gone shopping to purchase items Jacob had requested: toiletries, pens and stationery to write letters home, and shorts and t-shirts—loose clothing for physical therapy since pants with suspenders weren't suitable. Taylor also tucked into the bags of items the two books—*Lord of the Rings* and *The History of the World*—she had previously ordered from Amazon while Jacob had been in the hospital in Lancaster.

The family spent most of the time with Jacob on the rooftop patio; here the twins could move about more freely, although after a few hours they began to get restless. Taylor understood the Amish weren't in the habit of plopping their kids in front of a television as a diversion and although Joseph and Emma had brought some toys to keep them occupied, those resources were exhausted by mid-afternoon. The Sunday visiting hours were long—eleven in the morning until eight-thirty at night. The family wanted to spend as much time with Jacob as possible and had planned to stay all day, going home on the nine o'clock train, but when Emma fell wailing after Joseph ran into her, Taylor could see that even the normally calm Sarah was losing patience. Taylor thought a minute then grabbed her phone and searched the Internet.

"How about if I take Joseph and Emma for a while so your family can visit in peace?" Taylor said to Sarah as she pulled her aside.

"What did you have in mind?" Sarah asked.

"I could take them to the New Jersey Aquarium. It's just over the bridge from here; that should keep them occupied for a few hours."

Sarah look troubled. Taylor went into persuasive mode. "Really, it's not that far and learning about ocean life would be educational."

"It's not that," Sarah said. "The aquarium is fine; it's like the zoo except the animals are underwater. It's Jacob I'm worried about. We thought a big family visit might cheer him up. And he does seem to enjoy having us here but he looks *gabut,* exhausted. I'm afraid all of this might be a bit much for him just yet. Maybe we should leave earlier than we thought, before dinner."

"I could still take the twins and be back by five o'clock. Then I'd love to take your whole family to dinner. Would that be okay?"

"The Amish aren't against eating in restaurants," Sarah said. "We just don't do it often because of the expense."

"Good, then. Do you think they'd like seafood? DiNardo's, in Old City, down by the waterfront, isn't a fancy place but they're famous for their hard-shell crabs."

An attendant came just then to take Jacob to the restroom; during his absence, Sarah discussed Taylor's idea with the family. David, Katie, and Becca beamed at the idea of dinner at a restaurant and the adults seemed grateful, even Daniel.

When the twins were told about the aquarium, they were ecstatic to be going someplace with Taylor in the car.

"What's a 'quarium?" they asked in unison.

AT DINARDO'S, IT was a shell cracking, claw sucking, bib wearing feast, just as its website promised when Taylor had perused it earlier that day. Even Daniel, Levi, and David wore bibs to protect their Sunday-best clothes and attacked their Gulf Coast hard shell crabs with gusto once Taylor demonstrated how to use the crab crackers and the little forks. The group of thirteen ate bowls of New England clam chowder, a bushel and a half of crabs—Sarah, Mary, Becca and Annie Esh had fried crab cakes instead—Old Bay seasoned fries, cole slaw, and pitchers of soda. Trays of crabs sat on the table, along with piles of napkins and picked-clean crabs. David helped Joseph crack crabs and Katie helped Emma.

Taylor sat at one end of table, Daniel at the other. For the most part, the group spoke English out of deference to Taylor, with a few *Deitsch* phrases sprinkled throughout the conversation. Once the family adjusted to the rarity of eating in a restaurant, they settled down to enjoying the food and each other, the men competing to demolish a crab the quickest, the ladies chatting about family life in Lancaster.

Emma was on her second crab when she connected what she was eating to where she had visited that day. She stopped in mid-bite. "Taylor, were these crabs at the 'quarium today?"

"No, I don't think we saw a crab exhibit."

"But do these crabs live in the ocean, like the sharks?"

Joseph interrupted. "We saw sharks with big, huge teeth. They came right up to my face."

Taylor saw Sarah's horrified look. "The sharks were behind glass in a big tank," she explained.

"And then we walked on a rope bridge over water filled with sharks. Emma didn't want to go."

Emma ignored him, still struggling with her dilemma. "But Taylor, are we eating fish from the ocean like we saw today?" Her lips began to quiver as she looked in dismay at the disassembled crab in front of her.

"Yes, we are but it's just like when you eat beef from a cow or pork or chicken. We eat meat from animals that live on the land and we eat meat from fish that live in the ocean. Mostly all the food in this restaurant is from different kinds of fish from the ocean."

"But the fish looked so beautiful swimming in the water. *Mamm*, some of the fish were colors and glowed in the dark."

"Emma, you don't have to eat the crab," Sarah said.

Emma watched her brother suck enthusiastically on a crab leg. She pushed her crab away and took off her bib. "I'll just have some fries and cole slaw."

"Guess what else we saw at the 'quarium?" Joseph said. "A giant specific—he glanced at Taylor—octopus."

"Pacific," Taylor said. "Giant Pacific Octopus."

"With legs everywhere. Emma was scared."

"Was not."

"Was too."

"What was your favorite thing?" Katie asked, diverting an argument between the twins.

"The ride in Taylor's car," Joseph said without hesitation, oblivious to his father's frown.

"My favorite thing," Emma said, "was the waterfall, in the rainforest of Amazon. It was so high up and splashed into a pool filled with all kinds of fish."

Key lime pie and chocolate lava cake topped off the meal. The limo waited to transport the family back to the train station for the trip home. Taylor looked around the table at the satisfied faces and was glad she gave them a brief respite from their problems.

LONGWOOD GARDENS WAS gorgeous. Blooming flowers and colorful gardens and even a conservatory, all belonging to one wealthy person. Our driver Eddie said it was the former estate of somebody named du Pont and used to be land owned by William Penn. I especially loved the Hillside Garden and the Chimes Tower and waterfall. Everywhere we looked were purple petunias, pink roses, and other blossoming flowers I can't even remember the names of, and water lily pools. We ate dinner with Eddie in the café at the Terrace Restaurant. It was more than eighty degrees outside but Eddie said we should try the mushroom soup because Kennett Square, where Longwood Gardens is located, is the "Mushroom Capital of the World." I wasn't too sure about mushrooms but it turns out the soup was delicious. But my absolute favorite thing was yet to come.

Eddie said we had to stay at the gardens until dark because there would be a surprise. Well, I never saw anything like the Fountain Garden in front of the Conservatory, shooting colored jets of water (red, blue, green) high into the air and timed with music Eddie said was controlled by a computer. Mamm and I could hardly breathe it was so beautiful.

Later that night, Taylor called us from her car on her way home. She spent Monday and Tuesday checking things out at the newspaper her company just bought in Erie, Pennsylvania. It was almost eleven o'clock when she called. Mamm and I were getting ready for bed. I heard the phone ring and just kept letting it ring. Taylor said all her business calls go to her cell phone and the only person that calls her at home is her Dad since it's an unlisted number so I figured it was her Dad but then I heard Taylor's voice on the machine asking us to pick up so I ran to answer it.

I wasn't sure which button to push to answer since her phone's fancier than our shed phone and I disconnected the call and she had to call right back. Definitely strange having a phone in the house, will take some getting used to. Anyway, she was calling to tell us she was on her way and not to be alarmed if we heard someone walking around the penthouse very late. I was still so excited about Longwood and I told her all about it. She likes talking on the phone when she drives, says it makes the travel time go faster. It was nice hearing her voice.

Today was another amazing day. Independence Day. Since it was a holiday, the visiting hours at Bayard were all day instead of just four hours on a weekday night, so Mamm spent the day with Jacob. Taylor didn't go to work and asked me if I wanted to take part in some city holiday activities. At first I didn't want to be without Mamm but Mamm said, in that firm voice, that I should go with Taylor. First we took the subway over to Benjamin Franklin Parkway. My first subway ride. It was underground and noisy and a little scary, dozens of people packed in and standing elbow to elbow. Taylor was so afraid we'd get separated she grabbed my apron and wouldn't let go.

On the Parkway were all kinds of food stands. We ate and ate—hot dogs and pizza, fries, water ice, funnel cake (my new favorite thing!!), soda, fresh-squeezed lemonade. Then there was a parade with lots of marching bands (my foot wouldn't stop tapping every time I heard the drums) and girls throwing batons and twirling flags (so this is the kinds of things kids do in Englisher high schools). Taylor said a July 4th parade is a slice of America, happening in other cities and small towns all over the country. I never knew.

Then later, concerts by singers I never heard of and everyone around us was dancing and singing. Of course I didn't know the words but it was hard not to sway to the music, it gets under your skin. I heard somebody in the crowd behind us say, "Look at that Amish girl dancing," but I didn't care. I was having too much fun.

And then came FIREWORKS in the sky over the Philadelphia Art Museum. Taylor said I acted just like a little kid the whole time, squealing and clapping. I could barely stand still. I wish Katie and the twins could have seen them. I felt a little bit guilty since we Amish don't celebrate this holiday because it's based on war and violence, which we are against, but I enjoyed the day anyway.

It's almost midnight now but I wanted to write this all down while I still remembered everything and how it all felt.

There's a whole big world out there I know nothing about.

"WE'LL SAMPLE BOTH and then decide which is best," Taylor said. She and Becca and Sarah were standing on the corner of Ninth, Wharton, and Passyunk in South Philadelphia. In front of them was Pat's King of Steaks and across the street was Geno's. The feud among the locals over which establishment had the best Philly cheese steaks was legendary. It was Friday night and the three had just come from visiting Jacob. They had only stayed for a couple hours because the Bayard patients were encouraged to take part in a group activity on Friday nights. Jacob had planned to watch a wheelchair basketball game.

At Pat's, Becca got a big kick out of ordering according to the four step process outlined on the sign by "I. M. Hungry." She ordered a steak sandwich "wit" onions and cheese whiz while Sarah ordered a sandwich "wit-out" onions and with mushrooms and sweet peppers. Taylor ran over to Geno's and ordered her steak with provolone cheese, put ketchup and hot peppers on it from the condiment stand, then joined Becca and Sarah at one of the outdoor tables at Pat's. They each shared from all three sandwiches.

"Definitely the Geno's steak," Taylor said.

"No, I think Pat's," Becca said. "I love the cheese whiz." They both looked at Sarah.

"Mamm, you're the tie breaker."

Sarah laughed. Ever the diplomat, she said, "I like them all."

At the table directly behind them sat a well-dressed couple, both in business suits, eavesdropping on their conversation.

"What would they know?" Taylor heard the guy say. "It's probably their first time off the farm and out of their shit kickers." The woman laughed.

Not long after, Taylor and company got up from their table, and carried their trash toward the trashcans, Sarah and Becca in the lead, chatting to each other. Suddenly, Taylor tripped, and the trash in her hands ended up on the chest of the well-dressed man who had been sitting behind them; ketchup and onions dripped from his white shirt and tie.

'You freakin' idiot," the man cried.

"So sorry," Taylor gushed, as she grabbed clean napkins off the couple's table and managed to smear the ketchup into his shirt as she tried to wipe it off.

"Get the hell off me," the man said.

Taylor turned away, grinning wickedly as she walked toward Sarah and Becca waiting at the car.

I RODE IN a limousine! The family came down from Lancaster to visit Jacob today since tomorrow is a church Sunday and nobody wants to miss church. Dat, Katie, David and Mammi came with Uncle John and Aunt Rachel, Aunt Susie, Aunt Miriam, Uncle Samuel, and Uncle Elam. The twins stayed home with Aunt Hannah, and Daadi stayed home and rounded up a couple men to help with our milking. Mamm and Mammi rode with Taylor in the car and I rode in the limo. It was black and big and long, 10 passengers, and inside were cushy leather seats, a TV, drinking glasses, and a cabinet on the side filled with ice

and soda and bottles of water. Katie and I had some soda in a glass with ice and we giggled at how hoity-toity we were.

Uncle Elam and Uncle Samuel brought a big black trash bag from Aunt Ruth and Aunt Esther that held Taylor's birthday gift but of course we didn't tell her that. She looked at it strangely as we put it in the trunk of her car when she and the limo met everyone at the train but she didn't ask any questions. I peeked in the bag when she wasn't looking. I sure would love it if it were my present.

It was quite a crowd in Jacob's room. He seemed glad to see everyone. Uncle John talked to Jacob's case manager. He needed information on building a ramp up to the front door of the house for Jacob's wheelchair and he's also going to help renovate the downstairs bathroom. We'll save a lot of money if Uncle John and his crew can do most of the work. Everyone left before dinner to go back to the train. I'm sure David was anxious to get back and see Anna on a Saturday night.

By the time me and Mamm and Taylor got home, we didn't feel like eating out or cooking so we ordered pizza. Taylor asked if we wanted her to take us to a church service tomorrow since it's a church day. She knows we worship at home rather than churches but she thought since we were away from home maybe we'd like to go to a church. There are a couple churches right near Rittenhouse Square, even one with bright red doors, but Mamm said she and I would just pray quietly in our bedrooms tomorrow morning.

9

TAYLOR'S CELL PHONE rang just before noon as she sat at her desk at work. She answered in surprise.

"Hi, Jacob," she said.

"Happy birthday," Jacob replied. "How old are you?"

"Thanks," she laughed. "Boy, you get right to the point. I'm twenty-nine. What are you doing?"

"I just finished my occupational therapy and am getting ready to go down to lunch. Eric just gave me another cell phone lesson since I forgot most of what you taught me. I'm really getting the hang of it now. And he's going to show me how to work the computer in the resource center."

"Great. How was therapy?"

"Inspirational," Jacob deadpanned. "Today I learned how to put my clothes on while still in bed. Also my sneaks and socks. This afternoon in physical therapy we'll be working on keeping my balance while sitting up. Loads of fun. What are you doing?"

"Working on circulation figures for last quarter. Dry stuff but our lifeblood."

"Are you looking forward to dinner tonight?"

"Yes. My father's taking the four of us to my favorite French restaurant, Chez Moi. I hope your Mom and sister enjoy it."

"Should be an experience." Jacob paused.

"I talked to *Mamm* and Becca last night about the frequency of their visits. My case manager, Ellen, talked to me about it earlier. Bayard stresses independence as critical to my being able to deal with my disability. It's important for me to bond with the other patients here in my free time and not just be with my family. *Mamm* doesn't need to be here every day during visiting hours. I'm supposed to learn to function more on my own."

"Yes, your Mom and I did discuss that last night. When she and your sister return to Lancaster on Thursday to get the pins and cast removed from Becca's arm, your mom's leaning towards staying there and just visiting on weekends."

"While *Mamm* talked to Ellen last night, I talked to Becca. She's ambivalent about whether to return to Lancaster or stay with you. She feels obligated to be with the family but she's also drawn to the city and to the experiences you can give her. I told Becca she should continue to stay with you, if that's okay."

"Of course she can stay with me. She seems to be less clingy toward your mom than she was before and I think it would be good for her to stay here. I intend to tell her that before she leaves on Thursday. Is the decision up to her or will your mom decide for her?"

"My mother is a firm believer in *rumpsringa*. She thinks it's a necessary rite of passage and crucial to Becca's decision to eventually return to the Amish community willingly. Restricting *rumspringa* only makes the behavior more enticing, she believes. She has great faith in the power of community and family. She has seen it work with David. I'm a different story but she's still hoping. She also feels it will be good for me if at least one family member is nearby. So the decision will be Becca's."

"I promised Sarah I would look in on you during the week while she's in Lancaster, but I had intended to keep in contact with you anyway. I'll probably stop in some time this weekend, if that's okay."

"Bayard is planning a group outing to a Phillies game on

Saturday afternoon. Families are invited but since mine won't be here, can you come?"

"Sure. Let me know what time."

"Gotta go to lunch now. Eric's starving and is waiting for me. Bye."

Taylor sat quietly at her desk, thinking of Jacob and the way his voice sounded when he talked about his therapy. He certainly wasn't enthusiastic about his recovery; he was just going through the motions. She wondered what she could do to help motivate him.

BECCA EXCITEDLY HANDED Taylor her birthday gift; it was heavy and large and wrapped in a black garbage bag. On top was a Tupperware container filled with homemade brownies Sarah had made that day and several other times during their three-week stay and Taylor was addicted to them. She popped one into her mouth and offered one to her Dad.

"You've got to taste these, Dad. They're delicious."

Connor had arrived a few minutes before and Sarah and Becca had shyly greeted him; they hadn't seen him since the day he drove them home from the hospital in Lancaster. To Taylor, he looked exceptionally handsome in his navy suit, blue and white striped custom dress shirt with white collar and cuffs, gold and diamond cufflinks, and a burgundy silk tie.

Taylor wore a simple black sleeveless knee-length dress, a double row of pearls at her throat that Connor had given her for her twenty-fifth birthday, and gold three-inch Jimmy Choo sandals. Connor thought she looked regal but with an unusual hint of warmth, different than her usual professional yet aloof demeanor. They both provided quite a contrast to Sarah and Becca's Amish clothing.

Connor eyed the garbage bag with disdain as Taylor opened it and pulled out a quilt.

"It's from all our family, in appreciation for all you've done for us since the accident," Sarah said. "Esther and Ruth, my sisters-in law who own the quilt shop, made it, with Katie's help. I know it doesn't match the color scheme in your bedroom but it was started about a week or so after the accident, before we had seen your home, before we even knew when your birthday was. They've been working on it day and night in order to finish it. Happy birthday."

Taylor unfolded the quilt to its full queen size. It was a stunning piece of work, in hues of maroon, navy, and cream. Even Taylor, who knew nothing about Amish quilts, could appreciate the quality of the work, the small, precise stitches, the intricacy of the pattern.

"Here," Becca said pointing, "this small patch is an old shirt of David's, and this is one of Jacob's, and this is one of my dresses."

Taylor swallowed, then swallowed again, working hard to suppress the emotion she felt, due not only to the loveliness of the quilt or the sentimental value of including patches of the three siblings' clothes, but also because Sarah thought its value was lessened since it didn't match her décor.

"It's gorgeous," Taylor finally managed to say. "More beautiful than anything I own. I will treasure it always."

"Yes, it is quite magnificent," Connor said, ashamed of his initial judgment of the bag in which it was wrapped.

Sarah then handed Taylor a smaller package wrapped in plain brown grocery bag paper. "This is from the twins."

Inside was a wooden fish, painted bright blue and yellow. "Levi showed Joseph and Emma how to carve the fish and then they both painted it. It was quite a project," Sarah laughed. "Paint in their hair, on their clothes. But they haven't stopped talking about the aquarium since you took them. They obviously liked the colored fish."

Taylor smiled as she placed the fish on the black lacquered coffee table. "I'll write to the twins myself but please tell them I love the fish. It's a fun reminder of our aquarium trip."

Connor offered Taylor a gorgeously wrapped gift, glossy turquoise paper and matching bow. He was now convinced he had gotten Taylor the right gift. In past years, he had given her jewelry or spa visits or artwork. But recently he had sensed a small change in his daughter that he wanted to encourage with this year's gift. She seemed to be living life a little fuller, getting out and doing things besides work. Even though these activities were done because she was trying to be a good host to the Yoders, he still thought it was a step in the right direction.

Taylor tore at the wrapping paper eagerly. Inside were a box and an envelope.

"Open the box first," Connor said.

Nestled in the box was a hand-blown glass figurine of a hot air balloon. Taylor held it up to the light, where the colors shone like a stained glass window.

"Now open the envelope," he said.

Taylor pulled out a gift certificate for a sunrise hot air balloon ride for two over the Chester County countryside, complete with champagne brunch.

"It's good for anytime up to a year from now," Connor said.

"Dad, neat gift. Thanks."

"I've seen those balloons flying over Lancaster," Becca said. "They're so colorful in the sky."

"Maybe you'd like to come with me when I go," Taylor said.

Becca's shining eyes were answer enough.

"MR. LODEN, YOUR table is ready." Elena, the recently hired hostess at Chez Moi, shot an imperious glance at the Yoders, her eyes slowly travelling down the length of their attire and then back up, resting on the white *kapps*. As Jacques, the long-time maître d', appeared to escort them, Elena said to him in a low but still audible voice, "Perhaps they'd like a table in the back where they could have more privacy." Jacques blanched as he turned toward Connor.

Connor didn't bat an eye at the slight. "Hello, Jacques, good to see you again." Smoothly he shook Jacques' hand, a twenty-dollar bill in his palm. "Our regular table will be fine."

"Of course, sir. Please follow me."

Sarah and Becca, unaware of what had just happened but feeling uncomfortable nonetheless, stared in wonder as they entered the dining room: enormous shimmering crystal chandeliers, plush deep blue and gold carpet, the wait staff in black tuxedos, and flickering candles and a perfect orchid on every round white linen-draped table. Taylor, for once immune to the setting she usually savored, was livid. As soon as they were seated, she excused herself to go to the ladies' room.

She grabbed the first member of the wait staff she encountered on her way and pulled him aside.

"Listen to me," she hissed, "you tell the manager we are outraged. How dare your hostess insult, however subtly, our Amish friends because of their dress. Would she have done the same to an Indian woman in a sari or a Jewish man with a yarmulke or a Muslim woman wearing a headscarf?"

Back at the table, Connor was trying his best to put Sarah and Becca at ease. They gazed bewilderedly at the leather-covered iPad menu, unfamiliar not only with the technology but with French cuisine in general. When Connor explained *escargot* and *Osetra caviar*, Becca looked stricken and said, "Snails and fish eggs? I don't know about that."

"Why don't we order the chef's tasting menu and be adventurous," Connor suggested.

"Whatever you think," Sarah said, and Becca nodded meekly.

They started off with a bottle of Möet & Chandon Imperial Brut champagne to toast Taylor's birthday; Becca was permitted a small sip.

"The bubbles went clean up my nose," she exclaimed.

Three hours and eight courses later, they had feasted on appetizers of caviar ("Salty," Becca said as she relented, closed her eyes, and took a nibble), stuffed snails ("Rubbery"), and foie gras ("I don't like liver, no matter what fancy name it has."), and then moved on to black sea bass, followed by aged beef with black truffle and wine sauce, a selection of cheeses, mint sorbet, and finally banana cake with cream cheese ice cream.

Taylor and Connor shared a bottle of 2012 Altamura Cabernet Sauvignon during the meal. Throughout the feast, in addition to the waiter and the sommelier, they were attended to by a phalanx of servers: one who lit the candles, one who refilled the water glasses, one who replenished the bread basket, one who scraped the crumbs off the table.

"Goodness, I don't think I'll need to eat again for days," Sarah said, as she took a last sip of her coffee. "It was an amazing meal, Connor."

Taylor also had thoroughly enjoyed the meal, not so much for the food—which she always loved when she dined there— but because she delighted in watching Sarah and Becca try and exclaim over each new dish, which, once they got past the appetizers, was enthusiastically enjoyed. She had heard rumors Chez Moi was going to close, a victim of a dining public no longer enamored of the restaurant's pomp and circumstance. She glanced around sadly, already mourning the loss of this small yet special part of her world.

When the waiter placed the bill on the table, he said to Connor, "The manager hopes you enjoyed your meal. The champagne is on the house, in honor of Ms. Loden's birthday." As Taylor, Sarah, and Becca chatted, Gerard Paul, the owner and chef, came to the table in his chef whites and toque.

"*Bonsoir*, Monsieur Loden and *bon anniversaire*, Mademoiselle Loden. I hope you and your guests enjoyed the meal."

"Wonderful meal, Gerard," Connor said, shaking his hand.

"As always," Taylor added.

Gerard bent close to Connor's ear and whispered, "Jacques

and I express our sincere apologies. The hostess has been spoken to."

"No harm done," Connor said. "It's forgotten, and thank you."

I WONDER WHAT it feels like to be confident in who you are and how people react to you. Taylor and Connor let everyone wait on them last night at the restaurant as if they were born to it. I felt so uncomfortable. Who am I that I should be treated like a queen? I also wonder how it feels to be so sophisticated that there are no unfamiliar terms on a menu and to know how to order the right champagne or wine (and the year!). And to know the chef by name! Even on the rare occasion when my family has eaten out, it's usually been fast food or pizza, never in a restaurant that actually serves little tastes of food (called appetizers, I learned) before the real meal. And isn't it funny that liver from a goose or duck and snails and fish eggs would be considered delicacies?

Without Taylor and Connor, Mamm and I would have been lost in that fancy restaurant. I felt like an uneducated country girl. It was nothing that Taylor or her father said or did, they were as nice and helpful as could be. Mamm didn't seem to be bothered at all. She just enjoyed the evening for what it was, one special night out, something out of the ordinary but nothing that would be missed when she goes back to her daily life. She's secure in who she is and the choices she's made. Will I be that certain someday? Did she make the choice to stay Amish because she didn't really understand what she was missing out on? I bet her rumspringa wasn't anything like mine.

Mamm told me the other day Jacob didn't need her at Bayard every day. She said the rehab center wants him to be independent so he can learn to adjust to his disability. Mamm was a little confused at first. The Amish always rally to the cause, we're always there for family and friends. She couldn't understand how Jacob would be better off without our constant support. But after talking to his case manager, she came to realize that, at least for now, he needs to rely on his therapists and other disabled people that fully understand what he's going through. He needs to become strong from within. So Mamm will be going home to Lancaster and she and the family will visit on weekends. She told me she is conflicted. She prefers for me to come home but also wants me to stay in the city for Jacob's sake. She said it was my decision.

I know she's worried about what I will be exposed to here in Philadelphia with Taylor. But she knows my decision to eventually baptize will mean nothing if my rumspringa has not taught me what it is I must truly give up in order to live an Amish life. Some part of her, though, fears she may lose one of her children to the world.

I want to stay with Taylor and explore, even though I so miss Katie and the twins and Dat and my friends at home. But I'm afraid to be here alone without Mamm. Jacob told me that sometimes you have to do things that make you afraid because that's how you grow and become who you really are.

This reminds me of the "Little Women" book I'm reading. I'm like Amy, selfish and focusing on myself right now, not my family. Or maybe I want to be like Jo, who wants something more out of life than being a housewife and mother.

JACOB BALANCED CHEESE fries on his lap, a hot dog in one hand, and a soda in the other. Taylor bought him and Eric Phillies baseball caps and they both wore them with the rim at the back of their heads. Taylor took a cell phone picture of Jacob, and then took one of he and Eric with Eric's phone, which he promptly posted on Facebook. The Phillies were playing the St. Louis Cardinals at Citizens Bank Park. Jacob sat between Taylor and Eric in a section designated for the disabled behind third base.

"By the way, Jacob, Becca called me from the phone shed this morning. She'll be returning to Philadelphia tomorrow. I'll pick her up at the train station late in the afternoon."

"Good. I was hoping she'd decide to come back."

By the seventh inning stretch, the Phillies were up two to one. Throughout the afternoon, Eric had explained the game to Jacob.

"In all your years of *rumspringa*, you never saw a baseball game?" Taylor asked Jacob while the fans stood and stretched.

"My *rumspringa* wasn't . . . isn't typical. A fridge full of beer, an Xbox, and two hundred channels of DirecTV don't interest me. The usual things *rumspringa* youth go crazy for, like watching professional sports teams or toys like PlayStation or fancy cars, were never my things. I drank beer occasionally—it was only in the last few months that I started getting drunk almost every weekend—and I do own some English clothes but my real rebellion was the desire to further my education. And reading. Books took me to places I didn't think I could ever go, not just geographic areas, but places full of new and different ideas. And by the way, I really like *The Lord of the Rings* book you gave me. Talk about a different world . . . "

Rather than standing up to stretch, Taylor shifted slightly in her seat and leaned toward Jacob.

"From what I know of the Amish so far, that's what I disagree with most—they stifle individuality," Taylor said. "For the most part, if you're raised on a farm, you're going to be a farmer. If you father's a carpenter, you'll be a carpenter. And if you're a woman, your choice is marriage and motherhood and maybe teaching for a few years before marriage."

Jacob shook his head. "That's not entirely true. Many married Amish women run small businesses and the choice of occupation for men has moved off the farm due to land prices. Job options are greater than they used to be but certainly not as broad as for you *Englishers*. But if you're going to have a strong community, one that revolves around family and friends and God and takes care of you until you die, then you have to give up some individuality. If more Amish were like me, there would eventually be no Amish."

Taylor sampled a cheese fry as she pondered whether to

broach the subject on her mind. "Jacob, I know you're trying to complete your GED. Julia told me. You only need to pass two more tests. Are you going to continue?"

Jacob watched a Phillies batter foul to left field. "I don't know. I don't see the benefit of it, especially now. If I were to leave the Amish, then the GED would be useful. But if I'm not going to leave—and leaving looks extremely doubtful right now; how could I live by myself?—what good would a diploma be?"

Eric had been quietly listening to the conversation. "No education is ever wasted. That's what my Mom tells me all the time. She says learning broadens your mind, makes you a better citizen, no matter what you do with your life." He sipped his soda.

"You may not be able to imagine it yet since you've only been in rehab a few weeks, but you *will* be able to live independently. Your injury is serious but you have great upper body motion and you're not tied to a breathing tube. You'll be able to function without constant supervision. You'll need a support system, but that could be friends or neighbors, not just your family. Would your family really write you off if you, say, decided to go to college?"

"I'm not baptized yet, so I wouldn't be shunned by my family or community. But it would be impossible to live among the Amish if I went to college. It would be like flaunting the forbidden."

"Let's just take it one step at a time," Taylor said. "First, finish your GED. Then you can decide from there. Maybe you can talk it over with your family at some point. Don't give up on your dream, Jacob, not if it's at the core of who you are."

"I'll think about it," Jacob said, "but I'm not really sure who I am now. I used to be 'that Jacob Yoder boy, the one who refuses to give up *rumspringa*, the one with his nose always in a book.' I felt like I was suffocating in a box. Maybe it's time to outgrow that box."

❧

TAYLOR PICKED ME *up at the train station and we went straight to dinner at an Irish pub called Moriarty's. It was so cute from the outside, a brick building with green awnings, Irish and American flags waving in the breeze, and window boxes filled with ivy. We sat at a round table in the back on the first floor. Flickering candles sat on all the tables and the walls were crammed with Irish knick-knacks. Our waiter, Tim, told us the Pub's first floor mahogany bar was built in 1937 and is 65 feet long.*

We both decided to have chicken wings (Tim said they were a specialty) and fish n' chips with coleslaw and tartar sauce. Delicious. Taylor asked Tim about the beers on tap and she decided on a draft beer from Ireland called Smithwicks. "If we're at an Irish pub," she said, "I might as well have a beer from Ireland." We both thought the beer's name sounded fun. Taylor explained to me what 'beer on tap' and 'draft beer' meant. For dessert, and this was the best part, we had Irish bread pudding with apples and raisins. I thought I'd died and gone to heaven.

After dinner, we walked a couple blocks to the Walnut Street Theatre to see the musical "Peter Pan." Taylor said the theater first opened in 1809 and was the oldest in America and a national historic landmark. She told me all sorts of interesting things about the theater and I wrote notes on my playbill (so I can remember to tell Katie when I get home), which I'm keeping here in my journal. She said some famous stars appeared at the theatre: Katherine and Audrey Hepburn, Marlon Brando, Robert Redford, and Sidney Poitier. Those names meant nothing to me but Taylor seemed excited about them. The theater was also the site of the first presidential debate between Gerald Ford and Jimmy Carter during the 1976 election.

I was thrilled when Taylor told me we were going to see "Peter Pan." One day when we were in her library a couple weeks ago, she showed me the children's book, said it used to be one of her favorites and her mom used to read it to her at night before bed. So I read it. Then last night I saw it come alive in front of my eyes, heard the songs that matched the story, actually saw Peter flying through the air! Taylor said the actor is held up by a nearly invisible wire and harness but I couldn't see anything from where we sat. Captain Hook looked as scary as I pictured him.

It would be fun to be young forever like one of the Lost Boys or Peter, to never grow old and have to make tough decisions. If only life was as simple as pixie dust.

IN A QUIET corner of the rooftop patio, Jacob sat in his wheelchair. He had just eaten lunch and had an hour or so before his physical therapy began. Eric had wanted to tackle another computer lesson but Jacob needed to be alone. He wanted some time to think about what he and Taylor had discussed the day before at the baseball game. And he also wanted to write some letters home; he knew the twins would get a kick out of receiving a letter from him but first he wrote to his brother David.

> *David:*
>
> *Hope all is well on the farm. The worst part of my being here in rehab is knowing how shorthanded you are on the farm and the fact that it's my fault. I don't know that I'll ever come to terms over my role in the family's problems since the accident. I have caused nothing but trouble, from your injuries and Becca's to the loss of working bodies during one of the busiest times on the farm, not to mention the financial burden I have placed on my family and community. I have had a lot of time to think here at Bayard.*
>
> *In the short time I've been here, going on four weeks now, I have learned three important things, two of them from unexpected sources. The first is that I will be physically OK. I have a long row to hoe but I'll be able to live with my paralysis. I'll be able to live my life as I choose as long as I am careful and vigilant. It's no surprise I learned that from my physical therapists and caseworker.*
>
> *The second is that I will be mentally OK. At first I thought the old Jacob (the morose Jacob, the rebellious Jacob, the Jacob struggling to find his place among his people) died the night of*

the accident as I lay on the road, not feeling the weight of my legs. I begged God that night to take me rather than allow my stupidity to harm you and Becca. In a way, God did take my life that night but He replaced it with a new one. I have discovered that although bruised and battered and partially immobile on the outside, who I am on the inside has survived. Not the morose and rebellious Jacob, but the Jacob who still wants to stretch his wings a little. For that insight, I thank my roommate Eric. He's young but his struggles have provided him some wisdom.

And the third thing I've learned is that the help and support I need now and in the future may not come solely from my family or my community. That, surprisingly, I learned from Taylor. Sometimes the greatest lessons come from outside the family. As much as I love my family and value my Amish upbringing, you all may not be able to accompany me on the journey I may take. The Amish community will eventually try to save me from myself, and they will do so in the ways they know best, because they can't understand or accept my choices. So I will need outside help, hopefully from people I have yet to meet as well as from people like Taylor and Julia, the librarian at the Leola Library, and others who have shown me that my goals are worthwhile.

No doubt, some believe my injury was a warning from God to stop trying to be someone I cannot be and to find satisfaction within our own world. But if that were true, I would feel God's urging to go in that direction. In fact, right after the accident, I had resigned myself to life as we know it. But now I believe God is giving me the strength to go my own way, wherever that may lead. I view my physical struggle not as an obstacle to divert my course, but as a challenge to make me stronger and more independent, to find the will and the resolve to follow a different path.

Unfortunately, that path may lead me away from all of you. And if that should happen, I want you to know that I could not hope for a better brother and I will always respect you and the life you have chosen.

Jacob

10

TAYLOR KNOCKED SOFTLY on my bedroom door this morning to tell me she was leaving for work. She said she'd call me throughout the day and to listen for the phone. How could I not hear the phone? There are no other sounds at all. The penthouse is quiet, like a grave. She offered to either take me with her to the office today or to work from home but I told her I'd be okay alone, I'd just putter around the penthouse and read. I'm experiencing something completely new. Being absolutely alone. All my life, my parents, siblings, grand-parents, cousins or friends have always been around me.

I slept in until after nine o'clock this morning!! When Mamm was here, we got up early even though we didn't have to. We fixed breakfast for ourselves and Taylor and then Mamm worked on David and Anna's wedding quilt while I read or wrote letters home or to friends, and some-times we baked. But today I just stayed in bed. The quiet was amazing. It stretched on and on. No banging doors, fighting twins, clanging in the kitchen, mooing cows. Nothing but silence. At first I loved it. Nobody was depending on me to get up and help with anything.

I made myself breakfast (scrambled eggs, toast, sausage) which took me a long time to do myself because now my arm is in a sling, just dur-ing the day for a week or so, which is definitely better than the cast but my skin is so pale and the arm a little sore. The doctor said my range of motion should be fine and to ease into using my arm normally.

135

I read the "Philadelphia Inquirer," the newspaper delivered every day (not one of Taylor's, she doesn't own any TVs or newspapers in the Philly area), took a shower (had to take the sling off, then put it back on after but better than having to wrap the cast in plastic so it wouldn't get wet like before), straightened my room, and watched the city skyline from the terrace awhile. Then the quiet started to get to me and, God forgive me, I turned on the television.

I punched a few buttons on the remote until the TV came on. I watched "The View." At first I felt guilty, but then I liked the sound of people talking so I kept it on all day. Taylor's screen is so big it seems like the people on TV are right in her living room. When she called, she must have heard the TV because she asked me if I was watching it. There was a pause and then she said she'd show me how to work the DVD player and she'd rent "quality" movies I could watch so I wouldn't have to watch daytime or nighttime "crap" on TV.

I don't know what she meant by crap. How do you know which shows are crap? Maybe she meant the commercials, there were hundreds of them. They were interesting at first because I learned about products I never heard of, but then they got tiresome and irritating because they come on right in the middle of good stuff and they go on and on and on and repeat and repeat. I asked her why she owns TV stations if they're full of crap and she said there's some quality shows and educational TV but mostly they own TV stations because they make money and I asked if she liked making money off crap and she sighed and said I didn't understand the world of business.

In the afternoon, I watched "General Hospital." When Taylor called the second time, she told me that show is called a soap opera. In the soap opera, people lie and fight and yell and cry and kiss. Taylor said soap operas represent a "slice of real life." Well, no wonder we Amish are supposed to stay separate from the world if that's how everybody acts in real life. I'm not sure how a soap opera compares to the opera I heard at the park the first week I was here but Taylor said she'd explain that to me when she got home.

She also told me she'd show me how to work the remote so I wouldn't have to watch just one channel all day and she'd choose some *more educational books like "Little Women" ("literary" books she calls them) from her library that I might like to read. Later, I watched "Action News" and got scared hearing all the bad stuff happening in the city (shootings, fires, robberies, car accidents) so I turned it off and read some more of "Little Women." There's just as much lying and fighting in books Taylor calls literary as in a soap opera. Another slice of real life.*

BECCA STOOD HESITANTLY on the corner of Seventeenth and Walnut and surveyed the city blocks before her. The night before, Taylor had asked her if she wanted to venture out of the penthouse during the day, at least for a while. Taylor encouraged her to lounge by the rooftop pool, enjoy the park across the street, or walk a couple of blocks to Rittenhouse Row and the many shops and restaurants that lined Walnut Street and the surrounding area. Taylor had given Becca one of her credit cards and instructed her to use it if anything caught her eye.

"Even if you don't want to buy anything, you could just window shop. At least you'll be out in the fresh air," Taylor said.

Becca had looked dubious. Taylor realized how new this all was for Becca, and how it might be scary to walk the streets of the city alone.

"Okay, maybe that's too much too soon. But I don't want you to be cooped up in the penthouse all day watching TV. How about I meet you for lunch at Pietro's Pizzeria at twelve-thirty? It's on Seventeenth and Walnut. Go straight across Rittenhouse Park to Walnut and then turn right on Walnut and keep walking straight. The restaurant will be on your right. I'll meet you in front. If you're unsure once you get down to the lobby, just ask Henry, the doorman, or Frederick, the concierge. Before you meet me you can walk around and look at the shops."

Both Henry and Frederick had greeted Becca on her way out of the building and Henry had watched her from the doorway of The Regent as she crossed the park until he could no longer see her. Tucked into the small, plain, black shoulder bag Becca carried was an iPhone Taylor had given her the night before. Taylor had shown her how to make a call and answer one and had programmed her cell and penthouse numbers, as well as Jacob's and Frederick's numbers, into the phone.

"I know the phone is a no-no but it's a safety issue, especially if you're going to leave the penthouse. I'll feel better knowing you have it. Keep the phone with you at all times in case you need to reach me. I'll teach you about texting later."

Becca told herself lots of Amish teens acquired cell phones during *rumspringa* and she'd probably only be using this one until she left Philadelphia, and she promised herself she wouldn't use it unless she needed to.

She had about an hour to kill before she met Taylor. She slowly ambled down Walnut Street, gazing into the store windows with names she'd never heard of: Anthropologie, Lagos, Lululemon Athletica, Talbots, Ann Taylor, Michael Kors. She passed the Jacques Ferber store and wondered if that was where Taylor had purchased the furs she kept in the special closet-within-a-closet in her bedroom. Every imaginable form of summer fashion was on display in the store windows: costume and precious jewelry, high-heeled strappy sandals and flip-flops in a rainbow of colors, straw and leather handbags, jeans, shorts, skirts, beaded tank tops, embellished t-shirts, a cornucopia of merchandise beckoning fashion-conscious shoppers.

One upscale clothing boutique, Images, especially caught Becca's eye. As she gazed at the window, her reflection gazed back—purple knee-length dress, black sneaks, black apron, arm in splint, fingers twisting her *kapp* string, brow knit in concentration. The window was full of mannequins wearing various styles of colorful shorts and tank tops and flip-flops.

Becca wondered how it would feel to wear clothes like that, to feel free from the yards of fabric covering her body. She wanted to see the outfits up close, touch the fabrics. She hesitated, then curiosity overcame the fear, and she opened the door and walked in.

Dena was a sales associate of some experience; she had been with Images for several years and counted dozens of well-heeled clients of varying ages as her personal customers. She knew how to read a client, knew what aspects of their bodies they wanted to camouflage or highlight, knew how to pull together an outfit that pleased, knew how to nail the sale. Her clients could be choosy or indecisive or hard to fit but they could all comfortably afford the hefty price tags of much of the merchandise in the store.

When Becca walked in, Dena initially salivated at the challenge of a fashion makeover. That reaction was short-lived as Dena sized up Becca's ability to pay.

"Good morning," she said coolly.

Becca, somewhat emboldened by her success in making it that far on her own, asked to see the outfits in the window.

"Did you have a particular outfit in mind," Dena asked, "or are you expecting me to show you all of the outfits in the window?"

Flustered at Dena's tone, Becca bowed her head and said, "Maybe just the outfit on the far right."

"Yes, that's certainly stylish. But very expensive. Are you sure you want to see that one?"

A savvy, sophisticated teen, or a feistier one, might have managed a retort, but Becca, her cheeks burning, could only mumble, "I should go."

"Yes, that would be best," Dena replied. "Have a nice day."

By the time Becca met Taylor at Pietro's for lunch, her demeanor had returned to normal and she resolved not to tell Taylor about the incident, fearing she would embarrass her.

They ordered two medium pizzas to share, one four cheese

white pizza with ham and asparagus, the other with pork sausage, roasted zucchini, and mozzarella cheese.

Taylor chatted about her work, the new Erie newspaper acquisition and how they hoped to increase the circulation, and how her father was again scouring the region for another media buy.

"Do you like working with your father?" Becca asked.

"Sure. I learn a lot from him."

"Do you think if you had a brother you'd still be working with your father?"

"You mean as opposed to getting married and having children, like Amish women do?"

Becca nodded.

"If I had a brother we'd both be working for our father. English women have many options. We can choose to be housewives and mothers or we can choose to work or we can choose to do both, but it's our choice, not a societal expectation. I'm not defined by what others expect me to do."

"What about the expectations of your father?"

"That's different. He doesn't force me to do anything. I want to do what I do."

"Do you want to get married and have kids?"

"I don't know. That doesn't seem to be in my future for now. There are no husband prospects, if that's what you're asking," Taylor said, laughing. But then she grew serious.

"Becca, you're curious about my life and how it differs from yours. You're looking for answers you can use to evaluate your own life. Well, I don't have any answers.

"What I've learned from meeting you and your family is that even though we're different, we're alike, too. We're all hoping for the same things—people to care about, work that's meaningful, a life that matters. I'm going through something right now I don't fully understand. My foundation is starting to crumble a little.

"Maybe I need to make a course correction, maybe I need

to live more consciously, slow down and smell the roses, as they say. I'm not sure. I'm waiting to see what happens. All I know is that being involved with your family is changing me. Don't look so serious. I didn't mean to dump on you. Let's talk about something fun. Did you enjoy window shopping?"

"*Ja,* there are so many things to buy, so many choices. How do you decide?"

"That's part of the enjoyment of shopping, finding something you love. Did you by any chance notice a store called Images. It's one of my favorites." Taylor took a bite of pizza, glanced at Becca's stricken face, and knew something was wrong.

"What's the matter? What happened?" Although Becca had resolved not to tell Taylor about Images, Taylor had asked and she wasn't going to lie.

"I went in Images. The saleswoman didn't want to help me."

"Tell me exactly what happened."

By the time Becca finished telling Taylor about the incident, Taylor had asked the waiter for the check, threw money on the table, and was hustling Becca out of the restaurant.

"Unbelievable, absolutely unbelievable. Can't believe she did that to you. Totally rude. Inexcusable," she mumbled through gritted teeth as she charged down the street, Becca struggling to keep up. "I bought nearly a thousand dollars worth of clothes in there one afternoon last week after I dropped you and your mother off at Bayard. Work things and some casual clothes to wear when you and I do stuff. I will not stand for this."

Becca tried to make light of the situation. "It's okay. I wouldn't have bought anything anyway. She didn't know I knew you."

"Becca, I know the Amish are passive and don't like conflict. But sometimes passivity is not the way to go. This is one of those times."

Back at the penthouse, Becca watched as Taylor furiously pulled clothes off hangars in her closet, the tags still on them, and stuffed them into a shopping bag.

When the two walked in the door at Images, Becca was winded but Taylor was pure adrenaline.

Dena smiled when she saw Taylor but the instant she saw Becca, she knew she had erred. Taylor slammed the bag full of clothes on the counter.

"I understand you were unwilling to help my friend here today. Very unfortunate. If you're not willing to help her then I'm not willing to do business with you. I'm returning all of these clothes."

"I'm sorry, Ms. Loden. I had no way of knowing she was acquainted with you," Dena said.

"You snubbed her because of the way she was dressed. You assumed she couldn't pay so you dismissed her. Actually, she had my credit card and could have purchased anything she wanted. I want you to credit my card for these purchases and send me the receipt. I will no longer shop here."

As they walked back to The Regent at a more leisurely pace, Taylor began to chuckle. Becca, torn between mortification over the entire incident and admiration for Taylor's boldness, gaped at her in surprise, wondering how the whole mess could be considered even remotely amusing.

"What just happened is similar to a scene in the movie *Pretty Woman*," Taylor said. "Julia Roberts confronts a saleswoman on Rodeo Drive who refuses . . . "

"Who's Julia Roberts?" Becca interrupted.

Taylor sighed. "Never mind. What would you like for dinner tonight? I'll pick it up on my way home from work."

WE WATCHED "PRETTY Woman" tonight on something called On Demand on TV while we ate deli takeout. Taylor said my face was beet red whenever the love scenes came on. Julia Roberts changed her whole look and her clothes and everyone treated her differently. Taylor called it a makeover. Could I do that?

"AREN'T YOU HOT?" The girl standing over Becca was tall and lithe, her highlighted chestnut hair in a ponytail, a bottle of sunscreen in her hand. Her canary yellow bikini showed off her deep tan, and a straw Kate Spade beach tote hung from her shoulder.

Becca had gone to the rooftop pool after lunch. Maria, Taylor's housekeeper, had escorted her, helped her get situated under an umbrella with a bottle of water, her cell phone—with instructions to call if she needed anything—and *Little Women*.

"Not really," Becca replied. She had made a concession to the heat by foregoing her *kapp* and apron and was barefoot, but still in a knee-length, short-sleeve dress, hair up.

"I'm Lauren. Did you just move here?"

"I'm staying with Taylor Loden. I'm Becca."

"Hey, Becca. Mind if I sit next to you?" Lauren plopped down on an adjacent lounge chair.

"Could you put sunscreen on my back? You can use some if you want although you don't have much skin showing."

Becca clumsily began applying sunscreen to Lauren's back as she peppered Becca with questions. "Why are you staying with Taylor and where are you from and what happened to your arm?"

Becca told Lauren about their farm in Lancaster, about the accident, and about Jacob at Bayard while Lauren listened wide-eyed.

"Wow, so you're an honest-to-God Amish person. That explains the dress. Don't you have a bathing suit? I'm dying of heat just looking at you."

"We don't wear bathing suits. We're used to being out in the heat with our dress."

"So it's okay to own a cell phone but not a bathing suit?" Lauren said, gesturing toward Becca's phone.

"Taylor insisted I have the phone. She works a lot and wants to be able to reach me any time."

"Whatever. It's nice having somebody else up here at the pool. Most of the other kids in the building are at camp or traveling in Europe with their parents. My dad's a corporate lawyer working on a big case right now and my mom's at a spa in Arizona trying to lose a few pounds and detoxing her system, as she calls it."

"Who's taking care of you?"

Lauren frowned. "I don't need taken care of. But we have Sylvie, our live-in housekeeper. And Dad's usually home by nine or ten at night." Lauren glanced at Becca's book. "Is that your summer reading for school? I'm supposed to be reading *Age of Innocence* and *The Scarlet Letter* but I have the CliffsNotes. I'll be a junior this fall at The Baldwin School. It's an all-girls school. Where do you go?"

"I'm done school. We only go through the eighth grade. I found *Little Women* in Taylor's library. I like it."

"Why?"

"Because it's about family and four very different sisters and being who you are. I have two sisters so I can relate. What's a CliffsNotes?"

"It's a study aid. Outlines each chapter of the book, gives you the book's theme, the important characters. So you don't have to read the book."

"Why is that a good thing?"

"Duh. So you don't have to read the book."

"But reading the book is the fun part."

"Says you. It's summer. I don't want to talk about school. Do you have a boyfriend back home?"

"No, but there's this guy, John King. We talked a little at the singing, the night of the accident. I haven't seen him since, though."

"Is he a farmer, too?"

"His father makes gazebos. John works there, so do his brothers."

Lauren stared at Becca's face. "You know, with your blond hair and skin color, you'd look great in this new pink Juicy Tubes lip gloss I got yesterday. Want to try it?" Lauren reached for her tote bag.

"I've never worn lip gloss. Amish women don't wear makeup."

"You really are, like, from another world. And I don't mean that in a bad way. You're so different from anyone I know. What are you doing tonight? Want to come to my place for dinner?"

"Taylor's taking me to see a concert at The Mann."

"Amish can go to music concerts?"

"Well, no, but I'm in *rumspringa* so I can do things I wouldn't normally be allowed to do."

"*Rum* what? No, wait. I'm calling Sylvie to bring us up a snack and some lemonade. Then I want to hear all about this *rum* thing. It sounds wicked cool."

LAST NIGHT TAYLOR took me to a Tchaikovsky concert at The Mann. We had seats under the roof but it was such a nice night we decided to bring beach chairs and sit outside on the lawn. Before the concert started, we had dinner at Crescendo, a tent restaurant on the lawn. We had watermelon soup (cold soup!), lemon and rosemary grilled chicken skewers, and strawberries and chocolate chip cookies for dessert. Yummy. Taylor had a Mojito to drink; she let me try a sip. It made my lips pucker. "Stick to your soda," she said.

The night was magic. I saved the program and will keep it here in my journal. The Philadelphia Orchestra played "Piano Concerto No. 1" by Tchaikovsky, accompanied by a pianist. This was my favorite, such beautiful music. I watched the pianist through Taylor's opera glasses. Her hands raced up and down the keys (how do you make your fingers do that?) and her swaying body seemed one with the piano. Taylor said she was a prodigy and had being playing since she was four.

I'm amazed at how all the instruments in the orchestra play separate parts but the sound all comes together. I asked Taylor if she could play that song on her piano and she said a long time ago she had played a shorter version and she was by no means a prodigy. I asked her why she didn't play anymore and she just shrugged and said, "No time, really." I closed my eyes and let the music float around me.

Then came "Romeo and Juliet." Taylor told me the love story the music was based on was written by a famous writer named Shakespeare and was about the fighting between two families and the sad end for their kids, Romeo and Juliet. Parents try so hard to do what they believe is best for their kids but sometimes it turns out all wrong. It made me think of Jacob and his struggle between the pull of the Amish world and whatever is pulling him toward the English world.

In between songs, we talked. I told her about meeting Lauren at the pool and she said she had met Lauren's father and mother once at a holiday party. I said I was at first uncomfortable with what Lauren was wearing, or rather, how little she was wearing, but then I got used to it. It does seem more practical to wear a bathing suit at the pool rather than a knee-length dress.

Taylor looked at me and said, "Becca, do you want some English clothes, just a few things to wear while you're here? Would that make you feel more comfortable or are you okay with your wardrobe?"

I said the outfit in the Images window was so cute, with the shorts and t-shirt and matching flip-flops, and maybe I should have a bathing suit, not a real skimpy one like Lauren's (I'd die of embarrassment) but one I could actually wear in the pool. Taylor seemed excited. She said we could do a makeover and she'd take the day off Friday and we'd go to the mall.

During the "1812 Overture," Taylor said she could actually see the Russian battle in her mind as she listened to the music. I don't know much about war but it was fun to listen to such a big sound, especially at the end with the cannon booming and the bells ringing. The music just grabs hold of you and lifts you up.

I've never heard music like this before. Most of the time when we travel in vans with an English driver, the music on the radio is usually country or pop. Now that I've heard this classical music and also the opera a few weeks ago, I don't understand why it's wrong for us Amish to attend concerts like this. The music is so beautiful it seems as if God created it, or at least gave special gifts to the men and women who created it.

I know we're supposed to be separate from the world, be in the world but not of the world, as the Bible says, but do we have to separate from the really good parts?

I mentioned this to Taylor and she said something about it being a "slippery slope." She said how would the Amish draw the line between this type of concert and other kinds of music with questionable lyrics? Or a wholesome movie versus one with too much sex and violence? Or music versus computer technology? Or one type of technology versus another type of technology? She said maybe it's just easier to ban all cultural and technology stuff in the English world than to try to pick and choose which would be the least offensive.

I also don't understand why it's wrong to play an instrument. I know the Amish believe it's prideful to perform for an audience because it calls attention to yourself, but what about playing with an orchestra? Usually no one player is singled out, they're all performing together. Why did God help us invent instruments if not to be played? Why is playing the piano, or any musical instrument for that matter, different than making furniture or a quilt? All require a skill given by God. There are Amish people who make beautiful pieces of furniture and sell their work. The same with quilts. Those haven't been banned and they haven't been considered prideful. If you play an instrument for your own enjoyment, in your own home, how is that prideful? I guess instruments are expensive and making music could be considered a waste of time, but I don't see how it's any more a waste of time than playing volleyball or softball at school recess or other gatherings except that the sports do encourage group togetherness. Of course, furniture and quilt making are useful because they bring in much-needed money, and quilting can be a group effort, which is good for a sense of community.

I would never be questioning all this if I weren't away from my Amish life. Maybe that's why the Amish elders and ministers don't believe in higher education. They're afraid we may question ourselves right out of being Amish.

The very best part of the night, of course, was the fireworks at the end. They exploded right above our heads. They seemed to be coming out of the sky straight from heaven.

BECCA'S HEAD THROBBED. Since they had arrived at the King of Prussia Mall three hours ago, the sheer number of stores and the dizzying array of merchandise had overwhelmed her.

"Buy whatever you like," Taylor had said. "It's my treat." Becca would have dissolved in a puddle of indecision if Taylor hadn't been there to guide her.

That morning they had purchased three pairs of shorts, five shirts—one polo, two t-shirts and two tanks—and two pairs of flip-flops from J. Crew and Abercrombie & Fitch. Becca's head had started to throb in Abercrombie & Fitch, courtesy of the loud music and dim lights, although the other teens in the store seemed energized by the atmosphere.

Becca felt so self-conscious about the amount of skin show-ing as she tried on the first outfit she refused to come out of the dressing room and Taylor had to go in. Gone were the yards of fabric usually adorning Becca's body. Legs showed, shoulders peeked out from tees, flip-flops bared toes and ankles. Becca felt naked.

They went through several styles of shorts and shirts until they figured out Becca's size. She had ditched the splint early on but still had a hard time getting clothes on and off because her arm was sore, so she abandoned all modesty and asked Taylor to stay in the dressing room and help. Then it was just a matter of Becca choosing what she wanted, which was no easy task.

She was actually fairly clear on what suited her tastes, but she found it difficult to overcome the modesty hump, the internal conflict between what she liked and what a good Amish girl should wear, even though that Amish girl was in *rumspringa*.

The first outfit she chose, although a world apart from her typical Amish wardrobe, was conservative by teen standards—longer shorts, collared polo shirt. As the morning progressed, however, she became bolder—shorter shorts and tank tops.

But all that fashion stress had given her a headache so Taylor suggested they take a break and eat lunch.

They settled into the bright red vinyl booths at Ruby's Diner. Taylor glanced around in amusement at the 1940s décor, and then perused the menu.

"I think I'll have a cheeseburger, onion rings, and a root beer float. How about you?" Taylor glanced at Becca.

Becca stared forlornly at her hands twisting anxiously on top of the white Formica table, her menu untouched.

"My mother and Katie will think I am a vain, vain person when they see these clothes," she said. "*Dat* will have a cow. He'll say I'm *hochmut*, high-minded, full of pride."

"Is it a sin to be proud?"

"The Bible says God resists the proud, but gives grace unto the humble."

"If you only wear the clothes when you're not around your family, when it's just the two of us, then there won't be a problem."

"They'll eventually see them when I go home. I'll disappoint them. And God will know."

"Becca, if you're having buyer's remorse, we can take all the purchases back. But I thought you wanted to branch out a little while you're here in the city. Isn't that what *rumspringa* is for?"

"*Ja*. I'm just a little nervous about actually wearing the clothes. But I'm excited, too. I don't want to be vain, though."

A waitress came to take their order; she eyed Becca curiously. "I'll have whatever you're having," Becca said to Taylor, and Taylor ordered for them both.

"I don't think enjoying clothes or trying to look your best is being vain," Taylor said after the waitress had left. "Vanity is when the clothes and how you look become paramount to everything else, when how you look on the outside is more important than who you are on the inside. Fashion can be a way of showing who you are on the inside, of showcasing your personality. Putting together an outfit is a creative process, like painting a picture or decorating your home. I guess it could be seen as materialistic, but if you can afford what you buy and it makes you happy, what's the harm?"

Becca sat quietly for a few minutes, reflecting. "Besides a bathing suit, I think I would also like a pair of jeans and sandals with heels to wear with them. I've seen so many other girls shopping here in jeans. I've never owned a pair of pants or a pair of shoes other than sneakers or black leather shoes for church. Are heels hard to walk in?"

"It'll take getting used to," Taylor said, smiling.

During the course of the afternoon, they found a bathing suit at Lord & Taylor's—a navy and white nautical striped tankini with matching cover-up and beach towel—a pair of DKNY tortoise sunglasses, and a pink Juicy Tubes lip gloss, the same one Lauren had introduced her to. Becca refused to wear any other makeup—"Makeup is a false mask, a lie that covers up my real face"—or the necklaces and bracelets Taylor had chosen to go with her outfits.

Multiple shopping bags in hand, the duo stopped for a mid-afternoon snack at Auntie Anne's. They sat on a bench and people watched while eating pretzels and drinking lemonade. As she had done all day, Becca stared intently at every female teenager that walked past, trying to picture herself in their outfits. Suddenly, she had an epiphany.

"The teens I've seen here today all look like each other. They have the same type of outfits on, the same style of jeans or shorts, the same style of tops. They look the same just like we Amish look the same with our dress."

"Interesting point," Taylor said. "Teens and the Amish conform to dress for the same reason—group identity."

"*Ja*, but we don't have to worry about what to wear when we wake up in the morning and we never go clothes and shoe shopping unless we absolutely need something. I can't imagine coming to this mall every week and trying to decide what to buy." She took a bite of pretzel.

"I really like this pretzel," she said, "just as much as the ones my friend Amy Fisher makes for the farmer's market."

"Did you know," Taylor asked, "that the founders of Auntie Anne's, Anne and Jonas Beiler, were born Amish in Lancaster?"

"Really?"

"We did a case study on them at Wharton. Eventually the Beilers left the Amish faith but their hand-rolled pretzels started out at a farmer's market in the area in 1988 and then became franchises. Several years ago, they sold the business and there are now more than fifteen hundred Auntie Anne's worldwide with annual revenue over $450 million. The corporate headquarters is in Lancaster."

"Never underestimate the Amish," Becca said.

Their last stop was Nordstrom's, where they found a pair of dark wash 7 For All Mankind jeans and a pair of Tory Burch mid-heel sandals. They brought the sandals and a cream Joie eyelet top with cap sleeves and scalloped hem into the dressing room to try on with the jeans. Becca balked when she saw the price tags. "We could pay the mortgage on the farm for a month." Taylor was nonchalant.

"This is probably a once-in-a-lifetime shopping spree for you," she said. "Just enjoy it."

Becca came out of the dressing room to model the outfit. Taylor hardly recognized the girl standing in front of her. Already taller than average, the three-inch sandals made Becca seem statuesque, the jeans gave her legs a long, lean look, and the top hinted at innocence but with a dash of sophistication.

Becca stood in front of the three-way mirror and slowly removed the bobby pins from her hair bun. Her blond waves fell to the middle of her back. Taylor was dumbstruck at the transformation. "Wow" was all she could utter. Becca no longer looked even remotely Amish; she no longer even looked like a teen. She looked chic and worldly, like she walked straight out of the pages of *Vogue*.

"Who *am* I?" whispered Becca as she gazed at her reflection.

∾

I HUNG MY new clothes in the closet after we got home from the mall. My dresses and aprons, clothes I have worn without thought or complaint for sixteen years, hung dull and dreary next to the bright new stuff. Even the dress colors which I have always liked, the plum and purple, deep blue and green, seemed boring and tired next to the colors and patterns of the shirts and shorts. The cream eyelet top seemed to hang in the closet with an air of worldliness. My black sneaks, a favorite (they were comfortable and, at least for us Amish, a little trendy and pretty much standard on rumspringa teens) seemed clunky and clumsy on the floor next to the colored flip-flops and the sandals.

Taylor suggested we go out to dinner. I wanted to wear a new outfit even though I was anxious. Taylor said we were going to Bellini Grill, a restaurant a short walking distance away from the penthouse, and she thought the jean outfit would be appropriate, so that's what I wore. I let my hair down and put on the lip gloss and felt like a totally different person, which is confusing to me. I know I'm the same person on the inside but why do I feel so different just because I've changed my clothes on the outside? Taylor said it's a "disconnect" from how I've always thought about myself (humble, modest, the same as everyone else) to what I become when I wear the new clothes (independent, aware of my body, stylish).

While Taylor was getting ready, I practiced walking in the sandals around the penthouse. I felt like a giant, about to tip over any second, so I took it slow. I stumbled once and had to grab the back of the couch. I worried I looked like a lame stork but Taylor reassured me.

As we walked through the lobby, Frederick, who was talking to a couple at his desk, stared at me, and gave a little wave. Henry at the door gave me a big smile, tipped his hat, and said, "Well, Miss Becca, don't you look ravishing!" At first I felt guilty (that vanity problem again) but then I figured I'm just getting noticed like I usually do when I'm out in public. No matter which clothes I wear—Amish or English—people stare.

I decided that whenever Taylor and I go out to eat I'm going to try something I haven't eaten before. I want to take advantage of things I'll probably never do (or eat) again after rumspringa. At Bellini Grill, we shared an antipasto of Italian meats and cheeses. Then Taylor had spinach gnocchi with marinara sauce, and I had pappardelle (very wide noodle) with mushrooms, walnuts, and fava beans. We tasted each other's pasta. We were so full after dinner, but still wanted to try a dessert, so we shared profiterole, cream puffs covered with Belgian chocolate. Loved everything.

After dinner, we visited Jacob. We arrived about a half hour before visiting hours were over at eight-thirty and he and Eric were playing scrabble. Both looked shocked when I walked into the room. Finally Jacob said, "Well, aren't you a sight." Now that I think about it, I'm not sure whether he meant I looked good or bad. Eric said, "I'd whistle but I don't want to offend you." We sat around and chatted and Taylor read the newspaper. Mamm and Dat are coming tomorrow to attend Bayard's information session on the warning signs and possible complications of spinal cord injuries and Jacob was looking forward to their visit.

As we left Bayard, Taylor asked how my feet were holding up in the sandals. They had been hurting when we got to Bayard but after resting while we visited, they were fine. She said she saw in the paper there was a free gospel music concert at the Great Plaza at Penn's Landing. I didn't know what gospel music was before we went but I sure do now.

The music is so full of energy that it's hard to stand still and just listen. It gets under your skin and makes your body want to move. People all around us were dancing and clapping and singing with the music. It was the complete opposite of the hymns we sing at church. It takes us fifteen minutes just to sing the Lob Lied, in German, which we chant, in unison, without rhythm. It's more fun when we sing our songs at the Sunday night singings because the tempo is faster and we sing in English, but even those songs can't compare to the enthusiasm of gospel singing. Amish church singing is mournful, representative of Christ's suffering, but Taylor said gospel singing represents the joy of Christ. I couldn't stop myself from swaying along with the music. Even Taylor, who's usually so restrained and formal, was clapping to the music. Afterwards, she bought a music CD from a table where the gospel group was selling them. "Now we can listen to gospel music at home," she said.

All in all, quite a day. I am still Becca Yoder, an Amish farm girl from Lancaster who loves her farm and family. But I also like my flip-flops, designer jeans, sandals with heels, and eating different foods. I like gospel music. I like opera and the symphony. I like limos. I LOVE fireworks. So does that mean I'm just enjoying my rumspringa or am I becoming someone else?

11

BECCA WRIGGLED HER bottom on the wooden bench as she took a bite of her scone. The feel of the bench against the back of her thighs felt strange; she wasn't used to feeling anything but dress fabric on her legs. She wore one of her new shorts outfits and her long hair was down; she felt the weight of it on her bare arms, also a new sensation. She and Taylor had walked to Metropolitan Bakery to pick up breakfast. Becca was self-conscious because "so much leg is showing" but was thrilled with the flapping sound of her flip-flops.

The two settled on a bench in Rittenhouse Square and enjoyed a banana muffin, lemon poppy scone, coffee, and fresh-squeezed orange juice. They were passing the time until Taylor picked up Sarah and Daniel at the train station a little after one o'clock. Taylor planned on taking them and Becca to Bayard for the seminar and then head to her office for a few hours of work since she had taken Friday off to shop with Becca.

"Are you enjoying *Little Women*?" Taylor asked.

"I finished it the other day and loved it."

"Readers have been enjoying *Little Women* since the late 1800s when it was published. Why did you like the book?"

Becca thought for a moment. "I saw myself in each of the

four sisters. Selfish and focusing on pleasure like Amy because I'm here in Philadelphia enjoying my *rumspringa* instead of at home helping *Mamm*, which also makes me a little bit independent and rebellious like Jo. Materialistic like Meg because I like pretty clothes and am enjoying the things your money can buy. And like Beth, I try to please others."

Taylor finished her muffin and took a sip of coffee. "Do you think the author valued rebellion or conformity?"

"I'm not sure. Meg follows the traditional path for women and gets married and has kids. Amy and Jo struggle with their individuality the whole book but then both end up married."

"Yes, but their marriages are equal, which was non-traditional for the times. Amy and Laurie decide on their philanthropy together, and Jo and Mr. Bhaer share the role of headmaster of the school for boys.

"I think Louisa May Alcott was trying to show that women struggle between family duty and personal growth. That's still an issue women, and men too, struggle with today—the obligation to family versus career or the desire for me time."

"Are you struggling with that?" Becca asked. "Do you do what you do just to please your father?"

"If you had asked me that several weeks ago, I would have vehemently denied it. But now, I'm not so sure, to be honest. I don't know what I may have given up, if anything, to be where I am today. I do know that I enjoy my job very much but would I have chosen this path if not for my father? I don't know."

Back at the penthouse, Taylor pulled up the Barnes & Noble website on her laptop. After browsing through the movie selections, the two settled on several Becca could watch the following week while Taylor worked.

"I'm not going to buy anything that would cause your parents anxiety, in other words, nothing with too much sex or violence," Taylor told Becca. "I just want you to enjoy some classic movies I loved when I was younger." She chose *South Pacific, West Side Story, Chariots of Fire, The Sound of Music,* and

Gone With the Wind. Taylor ordered the DVDs and arranged to pick them up at the store across from Rittenhouse Square.

Taylor then chose from her library Jane Austen's *Pride and Prejudice* for Becca to read next. She also showed her how to work the television remote, and the CD and DVD players. Both were going to change clothes before picking up the Yoders but first Becca asked if they could listen to the gospel music CD Taylor had bought the night before.

Taylor turned the volume way up until the gospel music filled the penthouse. She felt the music in every nerve in her body. For the first time in ages, she let go; her reserve broke. She began dancing around the living room, hands clapping, shouting "hallelujah" in time to the music. Becca, astonished, stood still for several seconds, watching Taylor dance. Then she broke into a joyous smile, grabbed Taylor's hand as she passed by, and they both whirled together, Becca's hair flying.

They never heard the phone or the door buzzer.

SARAH AND DANIEL stepped off the train and found a pay phone. The only ride they could get to the train station in Lancaster that morning had necessitated they take the train two hours earlier than planned. So when they arrived in Philadelphia at eleven Saturday morning, Taylor was not waiting to pick them up.

Sarah called Taylor but the phone just rang until the answering machine picked up. Sarah left a message explaining they had arrived early and would take a cab to the penthouse.

Once in the lobby of The Regent, Frederick helped the Yoders buzz up to the penthouse to announce their arrival. No answer.

"I'm fairly certain they're there," Frederick said. "I saw them both come back this morning after breakfast. Perhaps they're both showering or maybe they're up on the roof at the pool." He went over to his desk and retrieved his universal key card. "I'll take you on up and let you in myself. I'm certain Ms. Loden would want me to do that."

The three stood in front of Taylor's black double doors on the twenty-second floor, and despite the thick, expensive insulation and soundproofing in the penthouse, they could hear the gospel music from the hallway. Sarah and Daniel glanced at each other nervously. Frederick knocked on the door. No answer. He inserted the key card into the door and it swung open.

It was Becca's petrified look that made Taylor turn. When she saw the Yoders and Frederick standing in the foyer, she hurried to turn off the CD player.

"We buzzed you and knocked, Ms. Loden," Frederick said, as he backed out of the door and closed it behind him.

No one spoke. Daniel's eyes, dark and hard, traveled the length of Becca's body, noting her disheveled hair and bare arms and legs. Sarah's hand clutched at her throat.

Finally, Daniel barked, "Go get dressed" at Becca in *Deitsch* and she ran to her room. Silently, Sarah followed her.

Taylor found her voice. "Please come in and sit down. We weren't expecting you so soon."

"We entrusted her to your care, "Daniel said angrily once he was seated. "We come here and find her half naked and dancing to music."

"Well, we were dancing to religious music," Taylor began lamely. Daniel glared at her. "It's my understanding she's in *rumspringa* and therefore permitted to be a little freer in her choices. She hasn't been exposed to any of the negative aspects of modern life. No drugs, no cigarettes, no alcohol, no wild parties, no sex, no violence. I want to give her a cultural education. I've tried to introduce her to the good things in life, things she's never experienced and will probably never experience again."

"*You* consider them the good things in life," Daniel said. "We consider them temptations to a world we don't want to be a part of. But *ja*, she is in *rumspringa* and free to explore. I just didn't expect to be slapped in the face with her exploring."

"I would've thought you'd be used to that by now, because of Jacob."

Taylor regretted the mention of Jacob the moment it came out of her mouth. "I'm sorry. That was out of line."

Instead of the retort she expected, Daniel slumped. "For so long I have worried we would lose Jacob to the English world. I have failed my son. I don't want to fail my daughter, too. Maybe she should come home with us. She can do her exploring at home with not quite so willing a teacher. I will discuss this with Sarah."

"Shouldn't that choice be up to Becca?"

"*Neh*. It's my decision and Becca will obey."

While Taylor and Daniel talked in the living room, Sarah eyed Becca's new clothes hanging in the guest room closet. Becca stood by nervously as Sarah ran her hand over the cream silk blouse. "This material is very nice. I can see why you like it."

"*Mamm*, I didn't want you to see me dressed like this. I planned on wearing my real clothes while I was with you today. I wanted to keep the new part of my life separate from my old life."

"It must be easy for you to do that while you're here in the city. Your old life seems far away, *ja*? The new life seems exciting. It tempts you."

Becca began to pace the closet. "I saw *Dat's* face. He'll want me to come home. Don't take me home yet. I'll never get this chance again. Taylor is helping me to better understand the English world and myself. There are things I'm confused about and I want to talk to you about them sometime. But my head is not turned so easily from my faith and my family and my life just because I have a few new clothes or because I danced to music or because I'm living for a bit in Taylor's world. I am not Jacob, *Mamm*. But I do want to be near him while he's here. It's only for another month or so."

"If your father has made up his mind, we must respect that. But I will talk to him."

IN A CONFERENCE room at Bayard, Dr. Reeve, a neurosurgeon, told the families present, with the aid of a power point presentation, to watch for three major potential complications of spinal cord injuries.

"One is the possibility of pressure sores, which are caused by pressure on the skin sitting or lying for too long. When skin is starved of blood, the tissue dies and a pressure sore forms. Normally, nerves send messages to the brain to let you know when you need to change position, but damage to the spinal cord prevents these messages from reaching the brain."

A picture of a skin sore flashed on the screen. "The sore begins as a red area on the skin," Dr. Reeve continued. "If not caught in time, an open sore forms. Such a sore can mean several weeks of hospitalization, possible surgery, or skin grafting, all of which cost thousands of dollars. Sores can be life threatening. An infection can spread to the blood, heart, and bone. Skin sores are preventable with routine inspection and proper equipment such as air or gel chair cushions."

Becca sat quietly between her parents and tried to concentrate but she kept fidgeting. She knew she needed to pay attention because once Jacob returned home, they would all need to know how best to care for him. But she found it hard to focus. She knew she had upset her parents and that caused her anguish but she didn't want to leave Philadelphia, not yet.

She squirmed in her seat, the fabric of her dress enveloping her legs, legs that had been free and unencumbered a couple hours ago. She had worn dresses all her life, had put them on in the morning with hardly a thought, and yet for just a few hours that morning she had felt the sun on her legs and freedom of movement. And she had liked it. She fought to listen to Dr. Reeve.

"A second complication is spasticity, which is rapid muscle spasms, an uncontrollable jerking movement, usually occurring in the legs. Spasticity serves as a warning mechanism to identify pain or other problems that may be occurring below the level of the injury.

"Anything can trigger spasticity, including bladder infections, skin sores, or an injury to the feet or legs. Drug treatment is available for severe spasticity but mostly it comes with the territory for many paralyzed people. Physical therapy, such as muscle stretching and range of motion exercises, can help to reduce the severity of symptoms."

Daniel glanced sideways at his daughter. Her eyes were focused on Dr. Reeve but they were sad eyes. He had seen those eyes before—last spring when they thought they were going to lose Bessie's calf, and just about every day right after the buggy accident. He realized, except for right then, he hadn't seen those unhappy eyes since Becca had been at Taylor's.

"The third risk," Dr. Reeve continued, "is urinary tract infections, when bacteria forms in the bladder. Symptoms include fever, chills, nausea, headache, and spasms. Proper cleaning of catheters or tubes used to empty the bladder can help prevent infection."

Daniel wondered which hurt him more, Becca's eyes or Jacob's expressionless face. He didn't think he could bear to see his daughter gloomy at home, knowing he was the cause. What was the right thing to do? Take Becca away from the temptations of the city, and bring her back home where she could go through *rumspringa* under the watchful eyes of the rest of the family and the community? Or let her follow her heart's desire with the *Englisher* and trust that he and Sarah had taught her well and she'd find her way back to them on her own? He prayed to God for help.

"Lastly," the doctor cautioned, "despite our vigilance and level of care, unexplained heart attacks sometimes occur among young persons who have no previous history of underlying heart disease. Now, let me answer any questions you may have."

After the seminar, the Yoders joined Jacob. He and Eric wanted to watch a wheelchair basketball game before dinner so Sarah and Daniel decided to relax on the rooftop terrace while the boys and Becca watched the game.

The parents sat in silence for a while, each sipping a cup of coffee. Finally Daniel said, "I will not lose Becca, too."

"We haven't lost Jacob yet," Sarah said. "Since the accident, I think he's been rethinking his life and the direction he should go. It would be difficult for him to leave us and live on his own with his injury."

"Maybe if I had come down harder on him over the last few years, he would've come to his senses. I could have insisted he be baptized and become a member of the church."

"Daniel, you know he must baptize of his own free will. Baptism is meaningless if it's forced. If you push Jacob, he'll always have doubts and won't be a strong member of the church or the community."

"I kept thinking he would come around but that didn't happen. I don't want to make the same mistake with Becca."

"It's your decision about Becca, but after talking to her, I believe if she stays with Taylor, her faith will eventually be stronger because she'll know well all the material things she's giving up and will understand better what she's getting in return."

"WHY CAN'T BECCA just refuse to return home?" Taylor asked Sally Miller, the Stoney Creek B & B owner, on the phone from her office. She had dropped the Yoders off at Bayard for the seminar and had called the B & B, hoping to get Sally or her husband Tom on the phone to explain Amish views on obedience.

Sally chuckled. "Speaking from experience, most teens rebel and have stand offs with their parents at some point, but they usually give in to the authority of the parent, especially if the relationship is good. It's similar with the Amish. The pull of the family is strong and although most teens want to explore a little or even a lot during *rumspringa*, very few want to sever ties and leave the Amish community for the modern world. Amish parents do tend to look the other way during the running around years but that's because the years before *rumspringa* are the real grounds of childhood training.

"From the time they are toddlers, Amish children are taught to yield and submit, which prepares them for a life of obedience—obedience to parents, to a husband, to community, to church rules and customs, to ministers and bishops, to God. To disobey is considered a rebellion against God. Disobedience means you're selfish, disrespectful, and headstrong. These are not Amish virtues. Humility is a virtue. Submission is a virtue, or what the Amish call *gelassenheit*, a yielding to a higher authority, resignation to God's will."

"They sound like a flock of sheep," Taylor said.

"They have a different set of values," Sally explained. "The Amish are taught that humility and service to the community are life goals. Sacrificing self-interest and personal achievement for the sake of the community is seen as revering God. They follow the example of Jesus regarding suffering, humility, and simplicity. The Amish believe an individual has a better chance of achieving eternal life in a community of fellow believers."

"So individual identities are stifled."

"No, that's not quite true. An Amish community includes the same range of personalities, talents, and opinions you'd find in any segment of society. The Amish use their talents but not in an ego-driven way. They're not looking for recognition. Among families and the community, strong opinions are voiced and issues are discussed, especially concerning the allowing of technologies, but once a decision is made by an authority figure, the discussion ends. Husbands and wives may discuss issues together but a wife is expected to obey the final decision of her husband. The community obeys the final decision of its bishop. For those who don't toe the line, they're free to leave for a less restrictive order but, if they've been baptized, will be excommunicated and shunned by the community. And they'll face, according to the Old Order Amish belief, eternal damnation."

"What exactly is shunning?"

Sally said that shunning, or *meidung*, and excommunication are ways to control and eventually expel noncomformists from the community. Baptized members who commit a severe offense, such as adultery or purchase of a car, first receive a temporary six-week excommunication, with the hope that the shamed offender will reflect and repent.

"If the offender confesses the sin with humility by the end of the ban, he or she is reinstated into the church," Sally said. "For unrepentant and stubborn members who refuse to confess or submit, full excommunication, or *bann*, occurs by a unanimous vote of the congregation, although every effort is made by church leaders and the community to persuade the offender to cooperate. The excommunicated are then shunned for life by families, friends, and neighbors."

"Shunning is quite a deterrent, then." Taylor glanced at her watch; she needed to pick up the Yoders at Bayard soon. "Are the Amish Christian?"

Sally said the Amish believe in basic Christian doctrine—a divine Jesus, heaven and hell, the Bible as a guide to living—but although they believe obedience and a lifetime of faithful living and good deeds are tied to salvation, they don't believe in guarantees of eternal life. "To them, to be certain of eternal salvation is a prideful attitude. Instead, they obey the church, yield to God's will, and hope for the best."

"How do they feel about faiths other than their own?"

"The Amish are tolerant of other religions and are reluctant to judge or condemn those who practice differently. They don't proselytize."

"Do they know much about other faiths?"

"I would imagine not."

SEATED ON THE gleaming, dark wood pew, Taylor observed the historic grandeur of Old St. Mary's Catholic Church—the two stories of brilliant stained glass windows, the pipe organ on the balcony, the marble Pieta by French sculptor Alfred Boucher. Brass chandeliers from Independence Hall hung from a light blue ceiling, which in the center featured a painting of the Immaculate Conception.

Becca sat next to Taylor, in her Amish Sunday garb, white apron instead of black, *kapp* tied; she had adamantly refused to worship in English clothes. Taylor leaned over and whispered to Becca, "The church was built in 1763 and George Washington worshipped here at least twice, as did John Adams."

Becca had been dubious the night before when Taylor suggested they attend the Catholic service. Taylor had searched online for a church and had discovered that Old St. Mary's, on South Fourth Street, was within walking distance of her father's home in Society Hill. They planned to meet him after the service for Sunday brunch.

They had been sitting in Taylor's kitchen eating Chinese take-out after having returned from dropping the Yoders off at the train station. In the car on the way from Bayard to the train station, Daniel had said quietly to Becca, "Just your mother and I will be returning home—for now." Becca had given her father a grateful look but as soon as her parents had exited the car, she had beamed at Taylor.

"For the past month, you've been getting a cultural education here in the city," Taylor had said as she showed Becca how to hold and maneuver the chopsticks so she could eat her curry chicken without dropping food in her lap. "Exploring different religions, like a Catholic service, can be part of your religious education."

"Are you a Catholic?" Becca asked, struggling with her chopsticks.

"I'm not a follower of any organized religion. But that doesn't mean I can't appreciate the importance it holds for millions of people. At Yale, I took a comparative religion course and studied in depth the three main monotheistic religions: Christianity, Judaism, and Islam. I don't believe the God I studied would disapprove of your choice to attend the service of a faith different than your own. Is that what worries you?"

Becca nodded.

"Have you considered that maybe everyone worships the same God, just in a different way?"

"But the Amish way is supposed to be a light to the world," Becca replied.

"Yes, and both Catholicism and Islam also claim to be the one true way," Taylor said. "It seems to be a required element for a religion to claim a monopoly on truth."

"But the Bible says we should be separate from the world."

"Have you actually read the Bible in its entirety or been to Bible study?"

"We're not supposed to study the Bible. Our faith has been handed down through the generations. We believe what we're told by our church elders."

"Unquestioningly, sounds like," Taylor mumbled. She broke open her fortune cookie and read the slip of paper inside: "*Traveling to a new place can lead to great transformation.*"

Becca read hers: "*A ship in harbor is safe but that's not why ships are built.* That's not really a fortune. Isn't it supposed to say something like, 'You will meet a tall, dark and handsome stranger'?"

Taylor laughed. "Is that what you're hoping for?" Becca blushed.

Becca decided to attend the service, partly out of curiosity and partly because she figured even if God disapproved, He would forgive her since she was in *rumspringa*.

After mass, the two strolled through the church's cemetery, which is higher than street level due to the layering of graves.

"The top layer of graves was added after the 1793 yellow fever epidemic," Taylor said. "Buried here are the remains of Commodore John Barry, Father of the American Navy—the Commodore Barry bridge here in Philly spanning the Delaware River is named after him—as well as Thomas Fitzsimons, a signer of the U.S. Constitution, and Michael Bouvier, great-great-grandfather of Jacqueline Kennedy Onassis."

They walked the tree-lined brick sidewalk toward Connor's home. Quaint street lamps and cobblestone alleyways surrounded brick colonial homes, some with window boxes bursting with flowers and steps with wrought iron railings leading to red or dark green front doors.

"What did you think of the service?" Taylor asked Becca.

"The hymns were beautiful. Very different from our church singing. We use a hymnbook called the *Ausbund*, written by our sixteenth century persecuted ancestors, and the songs contain no music, only words. The tunes have been passed down from generation to generation and we chant them slowly in unison in German with no harmony or rhythm. The *Lob Lied*, or Song of Praise, is always the second song of our service. It's twenty-eight lines long, four verses, and takes us fifteen minutes to sing because we draw out the words so slowly.

"And we don't have an organ at our service. The sound was so . . . ," she searched for the right word. "It made my body vibrate."

"I also liked the comfort of the benches. We don't have kneeling pads at our services. We kneel on the floor and our benches have no backs. I also loved the colorful windows that tell stories from the Bible. And the greeting at the end, when everyone says 'Peace be with you' and shakes hands with the people around them. It made me feel welcome. And the service was short."

"An hour is short?"

"Our service is three hours long."

"Why do you worship in homes instead of a church?"

"A church is a symbol of worldliness, a display of pride," Becca replied. "Worshipping in our homes connects religion with family life, and keeps the size of the congregation small, about a couple hundred people, so we can know everyone."

"Do the Amish have communion?"

"*Ja*, twice a year, in the fall and the spring. Since I'm not baptized and am not a member of the church yet, I've never been to a communion service. But I know that the service starts at eight in the morning and lasts about eight hours. The bishop distributes a small piece of homemade bread to each member and the wine is passed around to the congregation to sip from a single cup. At the end of the service, members wash each other's feet."

"Why?" Taylor asked.

"It's a ritual that symbolizes humility. Members pair off and use tubs of warm water and towels. They stoop, not kneel, to do the washing."

Taylor pointed left and they turned down Pine Street and continued walking. "Isn't it interesting how every religion includes dozens of rituals, different core beliefs, even different books of faith, like the Jewish Torah or the Islamic Quran. Even within Christianity, there are different religious denominations—Catholics, Baptists, Episcopalians, Presbyterians, Lutherans, Methodists, Orthodox—each with big and small ideological differences between them. Did you know Catholics believe that during communion, the wine and bread become the body and blood of Jesus, even though they don't change appearance? It's called transubstantiation."

Becca looked at Taylor blankly. "It's a difficult concept, I know, but my point is that transubstantiation is just one example of a belief that differs among Christians. Other Christians believe communion is merely symbolic of Christ's body and blood.

"Baptism is another example. Some Christians believe in infant baptism, some don't, like the Amish. Some denominations allow women to become pastors or ministers, but Catholics don't nor do they allow their priests to marry, while ministers in other faiths do. Catholics believe in the authority of the pope, others don't. Some believe faith alone is the way to salvation, others believe in faith plus good works. Evangelical Christians believe the Bible is the literal inerrant word of God. Other Christians think of the Bible as an historical document containing God's truths as allegory, metaphor, and parable recorded by fallible men. Issues like evolution, birth control, abortion, homosexuality, and gay marriage have caused dissension, both within and among religions.

"So basically, many believe their own religion is the 'one truth,' the direct path to God and to everlasting life. Is there really only *one* right way to believe? Who's to judge who's right?"

"Should I know the answers to those questions?" Becca asked, rubbing her forehead.

"Of course not. I don't know what the answers are or if there are any so-called *right* answers. But I think it's worthwhile to ponder the questions."

Connor waited for them at his front door; he had seen them walking down the street through his living room window.

"Why do you two look so serious on such a beautiful day?" he said as he hugged his daughter. "Who's ready for brunch?"

12

D AVID FLUFFED THE pillows and leaned back against the headboard of his bed. Knees bent, he propped a tablet of lined paper on his thighs, a Bic pen in hand, both purchased a couple days ago at Target so he could write to his brother and sister. He wasn't one for writing, but he had received letters from Becca and one from Jacob and he wanted to make the effort to write back.

Jacob:

I've been meaning to write you for several days but we've been so busy hoeing the tobacco I haven't had a chance until to-night. I just came back from Anna's. We've been talking about our wedding, which will be this November. You're the first to know officially. I plan on telling Mamm and Dat tomorrow but I think they've already guessed we'd be getting married this year. I don't expect we'll be published to the church district until some-time in October so at least for now, no one else knows except Anna's parents, but of course word will spread by the grapevine soon enough.

Last month I started baptism classes, held a half hour before Sunday church services, and will be baptized this October. Since it looks like you'll be back home by late fall, Anna and I decided to go ahead with our November wedding plans, happy that you'll be able to celebrate with us.

We should be done hoeing in a couple of days. We've got maybe three or four rows left. The weeds seem particularly bad this year. I'm nearly back to normal physically and have felt only slightly sore at the end of the day, nothing a hot shower doesn't help. Had my checkup a couple weeks ago and the doctor said I healed nicely and could resume all activities but that I shouldn't go overboard.

Joseph has kept us entertained in the field. He hoes for maybe five minutes then is distracted by a bug he must rescue or an unusual rock he saves in his pocket to show Emma or he decides to run over to the creek and dunk his head "to cool off my sweating hair," he says. I've even seen Dat crack a smile. I think he's more lenient with Joseph than he was with either of us.

The heat has been getting to Daadi these days so during the afternoon Dat asks him to do something in the barn so he can get him out of the sun. Our Yoder and Esh cousins have been helping out with the hoeing as well as the milking so we're in good shape. Don't worry about the work getting done. As always, it's the Amish way to pull together during tough times.

You won't recognize the house when you get home. Uncle John and his crew have been busy. They built a wheelchair ramp leading to both the back and front doors of the house. Your bedroom will now be on the first floor (Mamm and Dat took your room upstairs) and the downstairs bathroom has been renovated. You have a raised toilet with safety rails, an open shower with grab bars so you can transfer from your wheelchair to a shower chair, and a vanity and sink accessible by wheelchair. We also ordered a special mattress but it hasn't been delivered yet.

David stopped writing. He considered the thoughts he'd omitted from the letter: that although his uncle had done the renovation work for free, his grandparents had paid for the bathroom fixtures and the mattress from their savings; that his grandfather wouldn't be as involved in the backbreaking and grueling work that needed to be done on the farm if they weren't short-handed; that he had seen the fatigue on his mother's face, the strain of traveling back and forth to Philadelphia every weekend in addition to caring for the rest of the family and the anxiety about Jacob and the medical bills; that the furrows on his father's forehead seemed to deepen by the day as he worried about the work getting done, about paying the bills, and about his eldest son's injuries as well as his future.

Those thoughts he couldn't include in the letter. It wouldn't do Jacob any good to know and would only cause him more guilt. He also left out the conversation he had with his father just the other morning, when for a few brief minutes they found themselves alone in the field. David hadn't even eased into the conversation but had just blurted it out as he saw his cousin coming toward them to help with the hoeing.

"*Dat,* I want you to use whatever money you've saved for me for a wedding gift toward medical bills or the upkeep of the farm. I can always get a job working nights and Saturdays at one of the businesses in Lancaster. Anna and I can live with her parents for as long as it takes to save some money toward our own farm."

His father hadn't even stopped hoeing to answer. "We'll get by, with God's help. I won't jeopardize the future of one son to pay for the mistakes of the other."

David took the letter he received from Jacob out of the envelope and read it again. He then continued writing.

You're right, I don't understand your unhappiness during the last few years. I don't understand what "path" away from us you are talking about but I assume it has something to do with the satisfaction you get from reading and learning. I don't understand why you can't find something else that would make you happy within our world or why your "goals," whatever they are, are more important than your God and your family. But it's not for me to judge. God forgive me, but I would rather you not be baptized and go your own way if you must. That way at least we could all still be a part of your life.

We miss you.

David

❧

"YOU BETTER PUT on more sunscreen and get under the umbrella," Lauren told Becca. "Your skin's looking a little red."

When Becca's cell phone rang that Monday morning, she assumed it was Taylor, checking in, but had been delighted when she heard Lauren's voice. The two met at the pool for lunch, which Sylvie provided—tuna sandwiches, banana smoothies, homemade oatmeal and raisin cookies. The mid-afternoon July sun blazed and Becca's uncovered white skin wasn't used to the rays. She had applied sunscreen with a fifty SPF but she and Lauren had spent time in the pool and Becca had started to sizzle. Lauren's jaw had dropped when she first saw Becca arrive at the pool in her tankini and sunglasses.

"Whoa, did you sell your soul to the devil, like Faust?"

"Who?" asked Becca.

"Skip it. You look hot. Love the sunglasses. Taylor take you shopping?"

Becca explained about the trip to the mall and the new clothes and about her parents' visit and the close call with her father.

"Well, at least you had some excitement over the weekend. Mine sucked. My dad took me out driving Sunday. I turned sixteen in May but my dad hasn't had time to take me out driving because of this big case he's working on. He had to work weekends, nights, pretty much all the time. But his case finished Friday so he took me out yesterday."

"That's good. Now your dad can be around more since his case is over."

"Just until the next big case starts. Anyway, he took me out

in the Range Rover but he has no patience. I couldn't do anything right. I ran over a curb making a right turn at the light
and he made me pull over and change places with him so he
could drive home. He said I should take driver's ed at school
before he gets in the car with me again."

Lauren handed Becca the sunscreen and turned over on the
lounge chair onto her stomach. "I guess you don't have to worry about learning to drive." Becca began to reapply sunscreen.

"I can drive our buggy. Jacob and David taught me how but I
didn't really drive it that much anyway. Now I don't know if I
want to drive since the accident. Maybe one of your brothers
can teach you to drive instead of your dad."

"I don't have any brothers—or sisters. There's only me. Do
you miss your family or are you glad to be away from them for a
while?"

"I do miss them. I was never alone until I came to stay
with Taylor. She works a lot like your dad. At home, my family
is always around. Since we all live and work on the farm, we're
together all the time."

"Don't you get sick of each other? What do you do when
you want some privacy or you want to be alone?"

Becca scooted her chair under the shade of the umbrella.
"Sometimes I go sit on the bench under the tree by our pond or
dip my feet in the creek. But it's not long before I go looking for
someone to talk to or play around with. I like being in a group.
My brother Jacob is different, though. He likes to spend time by
himself, usually reading, or he goes off by himself in the buggy."

"So is being with Taylor and being a bad girl during *rum*—
what's the word?—worth missing your family?"

"*Rumspringa.* Because I know it's only temporary, it is
worth it."

A shadow completely blocked the sun on Lauren. Two pairs
of legs appeared in front of her lounge chair. Lauren looked
up. "Hey, Colin and Zoe. You're both back."

"We came up to see if anybody interesting was up here.

Guess you'll do," Colin said. He turned to Zoe. "Want to get wet before we sit?" Both dropped towels at the foot of Lauren's lounge and jumped into the pool.

Lauren watched the two of them romp in the water.

"Are they your friends?" Becca asked.

"Not good friends but we know each other. Zoe is my age. We don't go to school together—she goes to Germantown Academy—but I know her from seeing her around the building plus our moms are friends. Colin is a senior. He goes to boarding school at Phillips Exeter so I don't see much of him except when he's home on vacation. I think he and Zoe have been dating off and on. I'm not sure I like him much but at least now there's somebody else around to hang with."

Colin plopped his wet self down on his towel at the foot of Lauren's chair, while Lauren sat up and made room for Zoe at the end of her chair. Both eyed Becca as she turned over in her chair and sat up.

"This is Becca," Lauren said. She's staying here with Taylor Loden. She's Amish."

Colin eyes traveled over Becca. "Amish, huh? Interesting. Is your buggy parked down in the parking garage?"

"Oh, for God's sake, Colin, give her a break," Zoe said. You just met her this very minute."

Colin held up both hands in mock resignation and grinned. "Okay, okay, just kidding."

"So how was riding camp?" Lauren asked Zoe.

"Same as last year. Do you ride, Becca?"

"Not for pleasure. We use our workhorses in the field and the driving horses to pull buggies. We don't ride horses as a sport; that would be worldly." Becca turned bright red. "I didn't mean . . . " she trailed off.

"Equestrians are worldly?" Colin raised an eyebrow. "More worldly than those DKNY sunglasses on your face?"

"She's trying out the real world while she's here," Lauren tried to explain. "She lives differently at home."

Zoe changed the subject. "Colin, tell Lauren that funny story about the caretaker at the villa where you and your family stayed near Lake Como."

He was halfway through the story before Becca figured out he was talking about Italy. She smiled weakly at the end of the story when the others laughed. The three chatted about school and other friends they had in common but Becca was quiet. Finally, Colin said, "I think Becca needs to loosen up a bit. Let's go down to my place for some libations."

Becca didn't know what libations were. Maybe it was a new kind of food. She didn't like Colin and she didn't think she needed any loosening up but she did like to try new food. She glanced at Lauren. Lauren looked a little uneasy but said, "Well, maybe just one. Becca has to get home before Taylor does."

Colin's family's penthouse was on the seventeenth floor. He led the girls into the library, a strictly masculine enclave— studded leather sofa and chairs, dark wood furniture, heavy draperies. Zoe excused herself to freshen up in the powder room. Becca sat stiffly on the leather couch next to Lauren while Colin went to the kitchen; he came back carrying a liter bottle of Coke, which he placed on the bar cart in the corner of the room amid the crystal decanters filled with various liquids and glasses of varying sizes and shapes.

His back to the girls, he put ice in crystal tumblers, poured in rum and topped it with the Coke, then handed each girl a tumbler. "Cheers," he said, raising his glass. "Cheers," Lauren and Zoe, who had returned, responded.

Becca gulped nearly the whole glass down; she was thirsty from the heat and the sun. Colin pushed a button on the wall and the stereo filled the room with what Colin called "my favorites of the month." Colin left again and returned with baskets filled with pretzels and chips and the group chatted and munched and drank, Colin refilling everyone's tumblers again.

After a while, the voices of Zoe and Lauren became louder and more animated and Becca heard them as if they were far off. She felt woozy, the books on the shelves began to dance, Colin's face became indistinct. Becca turned to Lauren and started to stand up. "I don't feel well," she said as her legs buckled underneath her. Colin jumped up and caught her before she fell, turned to Lauren and said, "First door down the hall on the left" and Lauren led Becca out of the library. As they hurried down the hall, Becca leaning heavily on Lauren, Lauren heard Zoe say, "Colin, what were you thinking?"

"I was bored," he replied, laughing.

"How much did you give her to drink?"

"Not all that much. Don't you think it's funny? She probably never drank before, went right to her head."

"You can be such a jerk."

"Relax, she'll be fine. Wanna go to a party tonight out on the Main Line?"

Lauren's hand rested on Becca's back as she heaved into the toilet. When Becca finished, Lauren wet a white fluffy hand towel and patted it gently over Becca's face, forehead, and neck.

"What happened?" Becca whispered.

"You drank too much."

"Too much Coke?"

"Too much rum and Coke. Didn't you realize you were drinking alcohol?"

"Is that what libations are?"

"Yeah, Colin's a real crack up," Lauren said, rolling her eyes. "I'm going to get our things and take you home."

Back in Taylor's penthouse, Lauren tapped speed dial number one on Becca's cell phone, reached Taylor at work, and told her Becca wasn't feeling well.

"I'll be right home," Taylor said.

TAYLOR PACED BACK and forth in front of Becca's bed, where Becca lay propped up against the pillows, *Pride and Prejudice* on her lap. Her stomach still felt queasy but the worst discomfort came from the sunburn—her nose and cheeks, the tops of her shoulders, her chest, her neck and back, all were on fire—despite the aloe lotion Taylor had rushed to the drugstore to buy and apply.

"Your parents trusted me to keep you safe. Not only do you look like a boiled lobster but you got drunk."

"I now know what libations are," Becca said meekly.

"Oh, for goodness sake. Didn't the Coke taste different to you? You are so naive. Colin set you up and you didn't have a clue. The Amish live in such a vacuum."

Becca had listened to Taylor go on like that for nearly fifteen minutes. She knew Taylor was upset and blamed herself but Becca was tired of hearing it and she was cranky. The crankiness plus the part of her that felt safe with Taylor—safe from the constant expectation of being passive—emboldened her usual conflict-avoidance self. She took Taylor on.

"We Amish may not know or understand all the ways of the English world but I don't think we live in any more of a vacuum than you do."

Taylor stopped pacing in surprise. Becca rushed on before losing her nerve.

"You live in your own little world, too. You go to work, you come home, you work some more, you have your father, and that's it. The places you've taken me to in the city are as new to you as to me. You wouldn't be enjoying them if it weren't for me. You'd just be working. You're not enjoying that big world out there any more than we are. We Amish have intentionally separated from the world because of our religious beliefs. What's your excuse?" Becca clapped her hand over her mouth in horror at her outburst.

But Taylor grinned. "I knew there was a backbone in there somewhere. Try and rest for a while. Enjoy *Pride and Prejudice*.

Later we can watch a movie if you're up for it. If you decide you want to eat something later, come get me in the library. I need to rearrange my schedule. I'm going to be working from home tomorrow and for as many other days as I can while you're here. The rest of the time, I'm taking you to work with me. I'm not letting you out of my sight."

WHILE WORKING IN her study, Taylor received a call from Jacob. He was practicing writing essays for the GED test, with Eric's help.

"Is the past tense of lie, as in to recline, lay or laid?"

"It's lay," Taylor said. "The past tense of lay, as in to put down, is laid."

"Got it. Eric is timing me as I write and checking my grammar and spelling and sentence structure. It's going to his head."

Taylor heard Eric in the background: "I'm helping to corrupt an Amishman."

"I guess this means you're going forward with the GED. Good for you," Taylor said.

"I don't have much else to lose, so I might as well try. What are you and Becca doing?"

Taylor hesitated. She decided not to tell Jacob about Becca's afternoon; he had enough to worry about.

"I'm working for a little bit and Becca is reading *Pride and Prejudice.*"

"I was a little surprised last week when you visited and Becca was wearing English clothes. I know, I know, I wear English clothes but seeing Becca in those jeans and heels . . . According to Eric, I'm being sexist, but she's lost her innocence."

"Believe me, Jacob. She's still just as innocent underneath."

I'VE BEEN CULTURALLY enlightened this week, Taylor says, by movies, TV, a museum and literature. Sometimes it's fun to learn new things and other times it's confusing. Taylor says part of learning is considering different opinions and that's what broadens your views and makes you really think about what you believe or have been taught to believe.

On Monday night, Taylor and I watched "South Pacific." On Tuesday and Thursday, Taylor worked from home and I occupied myself. In the mornings I read "Pride and Prejudice" and in the afternoons I watched "West Side Story" and "Chariots of Fire." I also watched CNN and MSNBC, sometimes both at the same time since she has multiple TVs in the living room. I read the "Inquirer" newspaper and I had long talks with Taylor about current events while we ate lunch and dinner together.

It seems to me that the prejudice I saw in the movies (against Jews in "Chariots" in 1920s England, against Asians in "South Pacific" during World War II, and against Puerto Ricans in "West Side Story" in New York City during the late 1950s) still exists in this country, just against different groups of people. As a country, Taylor says, we always seem to have prejudice or intolerance against some group of people. Today it's prejudice against African Americans, Mexican and Latino immigrants, Muslims, and gays. Taylor said every ethnic group and minority in the more than 200 years of history in this country at one point or another has been discriminated against even though America was founded on principles of equality for all.

Despite so many people believing in religion (well, at least the Christian religions, they're the ones I somewhat understand), there sure is a lot of intolerance among people who supposedly believe in the "turn the other cheek" and "love thy neighbor" teachings of Jesus.

Not to mention what's going on in the rest of the world. Hate between Jews and Muslims in the Middle East and against Americans because of the wars in Iraq and Afghanistan, and also that whole horrible ISIS mess. Taylor said that's a very complex situation of religion and politics all mixed together. But surely God can't be pleased that the humans he created can hardly stand the sight of each other in some parts of the world.

One other thing in "Chariots" that made me think, especially since it was based on a true story, was the way Eric Liddell, the athlete who wanted to be a missionary, believed that his running talent was a gift from God, and to use that talent to the best of his ability was to honor and bring glory to God. For the Amish, to use your talent or skill as a farmer or as a small business owner or craftsperson is considered acceptable as long as you stay humble. So according to one religious belief, God is pleased by your use of the talent he gave you even if you become famous for it. But if you're Amish, He's displeased if you use your talent to attract attention to yourself. Which way is right?

Taylor and I watched the "Sound of Music" Tuesday night (also a movie based on a true story). Taylor said she used to watch it with her mom every year on her birthday until her mom died. She seemed quiet at the beginning of the movie and I saw her eyes water while Maria was singing about the hills being alive with the sound of music. I asked her if she was sad and she said the song was so beautiful it made her cry. I think she was missing her mom.

Maria thought she was going to have a quiet life as a nun and then she ends up with a husband, seven instant kids, and life in another country. As a novice, Maria was forbidden to sing in the abbey but sometimes she forgot and got in trouble. So she sang outside the abbey walls and her music eventually brought the whole Von Trapp family together. So is this an example of a sin (singing) that would displease God if done in the wrong place or an example of "when the Lord closes a door, He opens a window"? Maria had to leave the abbey to test out the real world before committing to becoming a nun, just like I'm experimenting with the world before deciding to be baptized.

I didn't even want to blink my eyes while watching the movie. I will never see in person the gorgeous country of Austria or the Alps, I will never watch this movie with my daughter, and my own "day in the hills" (here with Taylor) will soon come to an end. The Reverend Mother told (I mean sang to) Maria to climb every mountain until she found her dream. And in "South Pacific," one of the characters sang that if you don't have a dream, you can't have a dream come true.

That made me wonder. Do I have a dream? Is it my dream to be baptized, *marry, have kids, and continue my life in the Amish way? Or is that just what's expected of me? Is there supposed to be more to life than that? Do I have a talent not related to family life that I should develop? If so, what is it? How do I find it? Maybe it's enough in life to be loved by your family and contribute to your community. Maybe that's the best dream of all. Or maybe part of my dream is to help Jacob climb his mountain.*

The Reverend Mother also told Maria she had to find her life. I guess that means you shouldn't expect it will just fall in your lap or that it will be easy. Finding your life must be something you learn and piece together gradually, like a quilt.

I asked Taylor how you know if you're living the life you're supposed to. She was quiet for a long time. Finally she said, "I honestly don't know the answer to that question. But I do know that some people go to their graves with their music still inside them." Which I thought was a strange thing to say (maybe she was thinking of her mother?) but she said it was a famous quote that meant some people never discover or use their talents and their dreams are never realized.

WEDNESDAY I WENT to work with Taylor. She only worked about five hours. She knew how boring it was for me to just sit in her office. I watched some TV in the conference room, wrote a letter to Katie, and finished "Pride and Prejudice." We went to the Philadelphia Museum of Art for the rest of the afternoon. We each had the salad bar at the cafeteria for lunch and then spent the next few hours wandering through the galleries.

I saw things I never knew existed. We saw a Japanese teahouse (I should start drinking hot tea, I think it would be soothing). We saw a medieval cloister designed after the courtyard of an abbey in southwestern France. At the center of the courtyard was a pink marble fountain from an actual monastery in the Pyrenees (Taylor said the Pyrenees are older than the Alps). I pictured the monks washing their clothes in the fountain or praying in the courtyard. Taylor said the purpose of some monasteries is mainly for contemplation and prayer. Some people are even more isolated from the world than the Amish.

Taylor gave me what she called a "crash course" in art, both European and contemporary. We saw many religious paintings but I liked the Impressionist landscapes. My favorite was Monet's "Japanese Footbridge and the Water Lily Pool." If you look at the painting up close, you see thick dabs or strokes of colorful paint but when you step back to view the painting, all those bright strokes of color become the bridge and the water lilies and the light reflecting off them. My eyes couldn't get enough.

I also liked Van Gogh's "Sunflowers." So many shades of yellow and gold against a pretty aqua background. It made me happy to look at it. I stood a long time in front of Picasso's "Man with a Guitar." I couldn't see a man or a guitar, only rectangles, triangles, and squares (what Taylor called Cubism). She explained how Picasso used shapes to create the impression of a guitar and how he also repeated the shapes to represent the rhythm of music. Most of the modern paintings were interesting to look at but I didn't like them much.

My cultural enlightenment continued at Tequila's, a Mexican restaurant, where we went for dinner. We ordered tortillas with cheese, chili peppers, and chorizo (a new word for sausage) for starters and I had the carne asada, grilled sliced steak with guacamole, rice, and refried beans. Taylor had enchiladas stuffed with crabmeat, shrimp, and spicy peppers. Mexican food is spicy and tasty. Taylor drank a Cadillac margarita (orange, lime, and cranberry juices) on the rocks, which means with ice, and with salt on the rim. She let me have a sip. Made my tongue twist. After the other day, I had no desire to drink alcohol.

We discussed "Pride and Prejudice" while we ate. Taylor said Jane Austen was writing about prejudice and social status. All I know is I was glad that Elizabeth and Mr. Darcy ended up together and she'd never have to worry about money again. We Amish don't think about social status even though there are some Amish that make more money than most of us. It's just not our way to look down on anyone in our community. But I did see us in the way Austen wrote about how women were expected to behave in the early 1800s. Amish women are also expected to behave in certain ways.

Taylor said she didn't want to hurt my feelings but what did that say about the Amish if women are held to a standard of behavior that was similar to one that existed two hundred years ago. I said women do have a certain place in an Amish community and we are supposed to obey the men, but we're also held in high esteem because we bear and raise children. We also have more freedom than we used to. Amish women a hundred years ago didn't work at all outside the home and now some women own their own small businesses, some away from home.

Even if Amish men make the final decisions, women should have a voice that is listened to and respected, both in the home and in the community, according to Taylor. I said Mamm does that in our family, Dat listens to her all the time, but Taylor is right about women speaking up in the community. Very few women are able to do that in a way that does not cause concern among the men (and other women). Men make the rules and we all follow our bishop and ministers (who are all men). Taylor suggested maybe someday I could be a voice for Amish women. Interesting thought but that scares me to death. I don't think I could be outspoken yet humble at the same time.

What the book also said to me was how people judge each other by first impressions, like how Dat judged Taylor as a too worldly Englisher before he even got to know her (he still doesn't know her well). She does happen to be sophisticated and worldly but I think she's more than that. She's hard to get to know. It's like she's wearing a mask and the mask needs to come off before her real self, hidden deep inside, can come out. Taylor confessed that she too was guilty of judging. When she first met our family, she assumed we were uneducated "hicks." She disagrees with Amish views on education but said she's learning about the good ways in which we live our lives. I wasn't sure what she meant by that but the dinner check came then and she took care of it and our conversation was over.

Taylor and I went on vacation Wednesday night. She calls it "armchair travels." We went to Tuscany, Italy, and saw ancient churches and olive groves and walled towns built on top of rolling hills. The Travel Channel is so much fun. How great it would be to travel but I can't imagine ever having enough money to go that far and I certainly wouldn't be permitted to get there by plane. Maybe someday my husband and family could at least travel by bus and see some of the sights in this country. There's a dream!

Thursday night we watched "Gone With the Wind." Scarlett is unlike any woman I've ever known or ever will know. The things she said and did made me squirm. Taylor said even during the 1860s in the south during the Civil War, as well as during the late 1930s when Margaret Mitchell's book and then the movie came out, Scarlett was considered an unusually outspoken and independent woman. She was feisty but sad in a way, too. For so long, she pursued a dream that was wrong for her (Ashley), all the while refusing to see the right dream (Rhett) under her nose. Taylor said that people pursue the wrong dream all the time in life, not just in a love sense. I asked her if she thought she was pursuing the wrong dream and she said she didn't have much time to dream. But oh, to be kissed like that by someone that looks like Clark Gable!

Tomorrow morning I leave by train to go home and get my sling taken off. I'll be so glad to get rid of it. My arm feels good and I can move it like normal. I'll be back on Sunday with my parents and whatever other family members want to visit Jacob. Taylor and I decided I shouldn't tell my parents about drinking and getting sick at Colin's. It happened once, won't happen again, I'm fine, and it would just worry them and make them want me to leave Philadelphia. And I'm definitely not ready to do that yet.

CONNOR GLANCED SIDEWAYS at Taylor as he drove. She had spent the last half hour emailing on her BlackBerry. One hundred and ten percent focused on her work as usual, but he noticed something different about her. Taylor's edge—the hardness in her face, that blunt, no-nonsense air—was mostly gone, replaced by a softness that made her seem more open and approachable. They were on their way to Lancaster to

pick up Taylor's repaired Z4 BMW convertible. Taylor had decided to drive the two-seater back to Philadelphia and keep it
garaged at The Regent; she'd still use the rental Lexus to
transport the Yoders back and forth from the train station.
The Saturday was sunny with a cloudless blue sky but Taylor
hadn't seemed to notice anything outside the window, so intent was she on her BlackBerry.

"You don't have to feel guilty because you've been working
from home this week," Connor said. "I've been purposefully
eavesdropping at the water cooler and I haven't heard anyone
complain you aren't pulling your weight."

Taylor's fingers flew over the keys. "I know, Dad. I just
want to stay on top of things. I'm almost done. There," she
said, laying the BlackBerry in her lap. "I wanted to get the
monthly circulation figures from the *Tribune News* in Erie.
Since they changed the front-page format and added a weekend supplement, circulation increased five percent. And that's
during the summer with people on vacation. In the fall, circulation should increase even more."

"Good. We're progressing in the right direction. What a
beautiful day for a drive. Let's enjoy the scenery and talk
about something besides work."

From his car's music list, Connor chose Mozart's "Eine
Kleine Nachtmusik," to be followed by Beethoven's Symphony
No. 5, and as the first strains of the violins began, he said,
"Now that you've been through the Incident of the Libations
and have been caught red-handed debasing the morals of a
minor, are you sorry you took on this Amish charity case?"

Taylor laughed. "It *is* a little more than I bargained for. I'm
having a good time, though, most of the time. But Becca said
something to me the other day that stung. She said I lived in
my own little world, just like the Amish. She accused me of
working my life away. Maybe she's right. Maybe I've been
making a living, not a life."

Connor gripped the steering wheel and fought to keep his eyes on the road rather than turning to look at Taylor in surprise. She was actually examining her life instead of just barreling through it full tilt. He kept silent, though, afraid to spoil the moment. Once she started, her thoughts came pouring out in a jumble.

"Since I've taken it upon myself to culturally educate Becca, I've realized how culturally and socially deprived I am. I've lived in the city for years yet I wasn't familiar with all Philadelphia has to offer until I started showing Becca around. I thought my life was full with work and co-workers but my co-workers aren't really my friends. I don't know one single person except you that I would feel comfortable calling at two o'clock in the morning if I had an emergency. And even you and I relate mostly on a work level. Dad, I didn't even know you liked Mozart or Beethoven. I haven't shared my life with anyone until I met Becca and Jacob.

"And what's even more pathetic, I don't know enough about myself to share. I have no hobbies, no favorite TV shows, no travel anecdotes. I haven't read a book in years. I am knowledgeable about current events—obviously, we own newspapers—but I don't have opinions about hot button political issues because I don't think about news in a personal way, only how news affects our bottom line. I know what I used to like but I don't know who I have become."

Taylor closed her eyes and leaned her head back against the car seat. Her cell phone rang; she glanced at the caller ID, saw it was work-related, pressed ignore, and tossed it over her shoulder into the back seat of the Mercedes.

"Dad, I simply drifted into my life. When I was in high school or early on in college, did I ever mention what I wanted to be when I grew up?"

"I remember you talking about wanting to be a newspaper reporter. And you have evolved from that into a budding media mogul." Connor smiled but stopped when he saw Taylor's despondent face. "You should be proud of what you've accomplished. Someday you'll own and run Loden Media. Maybe this angst you're feeling isn't dissatisfaction with what you do but . . ."

"You're going to say I should try to find a balance between work and play. That's a cliché solution. I probably should find a better balance, but it's more than that. I feel unsettled and I don't understand why. I'm not saying I don't appreciate my career. I just don't recall making a conscious decision to be where I am today or to run this company. I'm not blaming you. I also don't recall you pressuring me to pursue this line of work. Somehow my life was just assumed—by both of us."

They drove awhile in silence, then Connor asked, "Well, what happens now?" "I don't know. But I don't want to sleepwalk through my life."

Connor had planned to discuss with Taylor during the drive a phone call he had gotten earlier that week from the Gannett Company offering to buy the Loden Media holdings. He hadn't been surprised by the call; over the last decade, the trend had been for large media companies to gobble up smaller and family-owned media groups and he had turned down several such offers over the years.

He had envisioned Taylor laughing over the offer and him making a quick yet gracious decline by phone the following week. But his daughter had caught him off guard; he would still make that phone call but not with his usual degree of certainty.

THE Z4 ZIPPED down the back roads of Lancaster toward Philadelphia, top down, Taylor's hair whipping in the wind, her iPhone and BlackBerry turned off, Rachmaninoff's Piano Concerto No. 2 in C Minor—from a classical music station on a rarely listened to SiriusXM—booming from the speakers. Before they had parted ways at the car repair shop, Taylor had hugged her father goodbye and, seeing the concern on his face, had told him, "Don't worry. I'll figure it all out."

13

T AYLOR'S FOOT, ADORNED in a black patent Prada slingback, rocked back and forth Monday as she sat anxiously, legs crossed, in the waiting room of the GED test center on the tenth floor of a building on Broad Street while Jacob took the two-hour writing test. She was so nervous for him she didn't even bother to try to work.

Jacob had been studying for the remaining two tests—the writing and the reading comprehension—most evenings since his mother had returned home to Lancaster, encouraged by Eric. Eric had helped Jacob purchase a Kaplan GED study guide online, similar to the one hidden in Jacob's trunk at home, the one he had studied from for three years in order to pass the math, science, and social studies sections of the GED.

Jacob had asked Taylor to drive him to the test center when she had visited him the previous Friday night. She had taken Becca to the train station that morning to return to Lancaster to have her splint removed, had worked a full day, and had then joined Jacob for dinner in Bayard's dining room. Taylor had readily agreed and after dinner had learned from a Bayard therapist how to maneuver Jacob's wheelchair and how to fold it to fit in her car trunk. She also learned how to help Jacob in and out of the wheelchair and the car. Those same wheelchair transfer techniques would be taught in a class at Bayard the following weekend for family members.

All had gone fine that morning. Jacob's newly developed arm and upper body strength, due to his intense physical therapy at Bayard, had enabled him to pull himself in and out of the wheelchair and the car with minimal physical help from Taylor. It was the first time Jacob had been out of Bayard by himself, without a group of other patients and therapists in tow. Taylor was proud of him, both for his courage in taking the GED and his apparent adjustment to his disability, and she had told him so.

In typical Amish fashion, he had dismissed her admiration. "I'm just doing what I need to do," he said.

He appeared less worried than Taylor about the test and explained his nonchalance. "I did all the exercises in the study guide, Eric timed me on the practice tests, and the guide helped me understand the ones I got wrong. I did well on the practice tests so I should be okay. We also practiced writing skills, making sure what I wrote was grammatically correct and flowed coherently. I feel prepared."

Not for the first time, Taylor marveled at Jacob's vocabulary. He sounded like a well-educated twenty-two year old, not an Amish man with an eighth grade education. She decided there was a direct correlation between his verbal ability and his passion for reading.

On Thursday morning, she and Jacob would return to the testing site for the sixty-five minute reading comprehension test. In four to six weeks, Jacob would receive his scores in the mail.

"What will you do if you pass and receive your diploma?" Taylor had asked him that morning on the short drive from Bayard to the GED center.

"I don't know," Jacob had replied. "I'll cross that bridge later."

⌒◡

"YOU'VE NEVER BEEN to the beach?" Taylor asked incredulously as she and Becca watched TV Monday night, after Becca's return from Lancaster. The local evening news featured a story on the popularity of salt water taffy at the beach and Becca had wistfully said, "I've never been to the beach or eaten salt water taffy."

"Well, now that your sling's off, let's go. The crowds and traffic won't be as bad if we go during the week."

Taylor took two days off from work and they drove down to Rehoboth Beach in Delaware early Tuesday morning. Taylor had arranged to stay at the beachfront home of Alan Moore, Loden Media's in-house legal counsel. In her excitement, Becca had chattered non-stop during the two-and-a-half-hour trip ("Will the beach be right outside the house? Like, step out the door and you're in the water? Can we go in the water? But maybe it's too deep. I think I'm a little afraid of the ocean. What's the sand like? Is it soft or prickly? Can we eat salt water taffy? Does it come in flavors?") until Taylor, frantic to distract her, finally played a *Best of the Beach Boys* CD she had discovered in her collection at the penthouse, one she hadn't played in years, and the rest of the way they enjoyed the music.

After their arrival, they hurriedly changed into bathing suits, slathered sunscreen on each other, and gathered their paraphernalia for the beach: umbrella, beach chairs, a large blanket, and a small cooler; Becca's canvas tote bag, borrowed from the Moore family, filled with beach towels, sunscreen, and Harper Lee's *To Kill A Mockingbird*, her latest book selection; and Taylor's work tote stuffed with her laptop, manila files, newspapers, and two cell phones. While Becca searched the kitchen fridge looking for ice packs and water bottles for the cooler, Taylor, in two trips, lugged the umbrella, blanket, and beach chairs the short distance to the beach and set them up, then returned for Becca.

As they rounded the top of the sand dune carrying the rest of their gear,

Becca gasped, dropped the cooler, and sank slowly to her knees in the sand. "Oh!" she exclaimed as she gazed for the first time at the Atlantic Ocean, the waves crashing upon the shore, the sand stretching for miles to the right and to the left, the colorful umbrellas dotting the beach—like a rainbow on sand—already filled with sunbathers.

Taylor glanced down at Becca's rapt amazement and then looked out at the scene. She saw a crowded beach with only a few small plots of sand still available.

"Let's go grab our patch of sand and spread out so nobody sits right on top of us," Taylor urged.

Becca sat in her beach chair, her toes digging into the warm sand, watching the waves, the sunbathers, and the adults and children frolicking in the water. A motorboat sped by in the distance; a plane flew overhead carrying a banner that read, "$1.50 Coors Light Draft, 50 cent wings. Rusty Rudder." Becca wanted to feel the water lap around her feet; she thought she might even brave the waves if Taylor accompanied her. But when she asked Taylor to go with her in the water, Taylor said she wanted to get some work done first; she had been talking on the phone since the moment they had sat down, her laptop on her lap, an Erie newspaper and file folder spread around her on the blanket, held down from the gentle breeze by the tote bags and the cooler.

Suddenly, Becca bolted from her chair. In the distance beyond the breaking waves, she saw fins and then sleek grey bodies as they gracefully arched in and out of the water.

"Taylor!" she yelled. "Look, in the water, something … a big fish … jumped out. What are they?"

Taylor looked up briefly at Becca, annoyed at the disruption. She held her finger up to her lips, and then held up one finger and mouthed, "In a minute" and returned to her phone conversation.

Becca sighed, sat back down, and returned her gaze to the sea.

WE SPENT THE morning on the beach and then took a short break from the sun and the sea and returned to the house for lunch. Taylor suggested we eat on either the deck or the shaded porch but I don't know when I'll ever see the beach again and I didn't want to leave. I wanted to pack a picnic lunch and eat on our little square of sand under the umbrella. So that's what we did.

The Moore kitchen was well stocked since Taylor says the family spends nearly every weekend and most of August at the beach, so I made chicken salad pitas with apples and raisins, found carrots and nectarines in the fridge and what looked like homemade peanut butter cookies in the pantry, and filled a jug with peach iced tea. I even found a wicker picnic basket with silverware and colorful plastic dishes, all while Taylor answered several emails and faxed a report with numbers, I think she called it a spreadsheet, to her father from Alan's home office.

As I bit into my nectarine, juice running down my chin, I watched Taylor who, tired of fighting the ocean breeze, had folded the front news section of the "Inquirer" into a manageable square and was reading on her lap while munching a carrot.

"When you're done reading, can we go in the water?" I asked, as I wiped the juice from my chin with the back of my hand and put the nectarine core in a plastic bag in the picnic basket.

"Sure," Taylor said. "I'm done work for now. Just let me check my BlackBerry and make sure nothing has come up."

I'm ashamed of what I said next but it just popped out of my mouth. That seems to happen when I'm around Taylor but never at home. I'm much more aware of what I say and how I say it when I'm around my family and friends. For the most part, I loved our morning at the beach. I read "To Kill A Mockingbird" and just sat and enjoyed the sights and sounds. But part of me felt abandoned. Taylor worked the whole morning, either talking on the phone or typing on her laptop. I'm not used to sitting right next to a breathing body who pays no attention to me at all. We Amish love to socialize. It's what we live for. I can't imagine sitting by my friend Lizzie and ignoring her while husking corn or darning clothes.

"If you didn't check your phone every ten minutes, you wouldn't feel forced to deal with the messages," I said. "Don't you want to have fun on your days off? Is the work you do really so important?" How rude was that?

Taylor frowned but put the phone back into her tote. "Well, I did take off work at the last minute to bring you down here. I have responsibilities I need to take care of." She removed her sunglasses, tossed them into her tote, and stood up.

"Do you know how to swim?" she asked.

"Some. Jacob and David taught me how to float and tread water and hold my breath underwater in our pond."

"Race you to the water," she said and off she ran. She can be fun when she lets go a little.

At first we just stood at the edge of the water, and the ocean and the sand swirled around our feet. It was so hot but the water felt cold as it splashed my legs. Then we walked out until the water came to our waists, then to our chests, and then we were right where the waves break and we were laughing and jumping up over the waves and Taylor yelled at me to keep my mouth shut and never turn my back on the waves which I immediately forgot when I turned to look back at the beach to see how far we had come. I heard Taylor's "Watch out!" at the same time as I felt the force of the wave as it hit and broke over me and I went down, down under the water, my back scraping against the sand, and then I felt my arm grabbed and I was out of the water, gasping and gagging, tasting the salt water in my mouth and trying to snort it out of my nose and feeling the weight of a clump of sand in my bathing suit bottom. I lost several bobby pins and my hair was loose and stringy around my face.

"Are you okay?" Taylor asked, half laughing, half concerned. "Do you want to go back on the beach?"

"No, but my, you know, is filled with sand," I whispered. We waded

out into the deeper water, beyond the break of the waves, and I wriggled most of the sand out of my suit, never taking my eyes off the waves.

That evening, after we had showered and changed (I wore my jeans and silk top), we went to dinner at the Blue Moon, a restaurant recommended by Alan Moore. We had to drive around for a while looking for a parking space in downtown Rehoboth but we finally found one. The Blue Moon is a cute little blue and yellow cottage about two blocks from the beach. We sat in the glassed-in front porch. Whenever I eat out with Taylor I try to burn the meal into my memory because I don't think I'll ever taste fancy food again.

For appetizers, we had crispy squid (wait until I tell Katie I ate squid!) and fried green tomatoes (!!), and for the entrée (fancy word for main course) we both had Maine lobster spaghetti, which was chunks of lobster over black (squid ink, said the menu) cappellini with peas in a cream sauce (heavenly). Taylor also had a mango mojito and of course I tried a sip and it was probably my favorite of all her drinks I've tried.

For dessert we walked over to Rehoboth Avenue and The Ice Cream Store, which had more than 100 flavors of ice cream, many unusual and with silly names. We giggled as we tried to choose. How about Bacon ice cream? Booger? (Joseph would want to try that.) Dirt? Motor Oil? Thunder and Lightning? I finally decided on Ooey Gooey, cake batter ice cream with crushed Oreo cookies and caramel and fudge swirls. Taylor tried Holy Purple Cow, raspberry ice cream with white and milk chocolate chips. We sat on a bench on the boardwalk and people-watched as we enjoyed our waffle cones.

On the way home we stopped at Jungle Jim's and played miniature golf. The course has waterfalls and streams and Taylor got a hole-in-one on hole seven. So much fun. Joseph and Emma would love it.

It occurred to me as I was getting ready for bed that I've been having such a good time in the city and at the beach that I nearly forgot why I'm really here. Jacob is sitting in a wheelchair only a few blocks from Taylor's, struggling to put his life back together, and here I am having the time of my life. Shame on me.

"BECCA, YOU NEED to find your center of balance," Taylor said. "Don't hunch over the handle bars. Sit up straight."

"I'm trying. But I keep feeling like I'm going to tip right over."

Taylor had noticed the cherry red tandem bike with the white basket in the Moore's garage when they arrived home the night before and had suggested they ride into Rehoboth the next morning for breakfast at an outdoor café she had noticed just off Rehoboth Avenue.

"I don't know how to ride a bike," Becca had said. "We Amish can use rollerblades or scooters, but bicycles are banned."

"Why?" asked Taylor, exasperated. "What's the difference between a scooter and a bike?"

"I'm not sure. It's just always been that way. But Jacob once told me that when bikes were first banned in the early 1900s, they were considered a status symbol. And now some bikes can go faster than a horse and buggy, which makes them too modern."

After another half hour of riding up and down the driveway, Becca finally was able to balance herself behind Taylor and off they went into Rehoboth, keeping to the back roads.

Once they reached town, Becca noticed other bikers on the boardwalk. "Can we?" she asked Taylor.

"The sign says we can ride on the boardwalk until ten o'clock this morning, so let's go."

They rode from one end of the boardwalk to the other, the only mishap occurring when Becca saw the salt water taffy displayed in the window of Dolle's. In her excitement, she lost her balance, but Taylor managed to skid to a halt without the bike tipping over.

"We'll come back for the taffy after breakfast," Taylor promised.

They ate at Café Papillon on Penny Lane, seated outside at a table for two, the bike parked a short distance away at a designated spot on the Avenue. They shared a raspberry and cheese croissant—"So flaky and fluffy," marveled Becca, the seasoned baker—and two crepes, one strawberry with whipped cream, and one with egg, cheese, salmon, and tomato.

"I love the beach," Becca said contentedly as she finished the last of the strawberry crepe. "I hope I can come again someday."

"Do the Amish take vacations?" Taylor asked.

"We do travel. We visit friends and family in other communities and if there are tourist attractions near those communities, we visit them. We take buses or hire vans to get there. We're not opposed to vacations but especially for the farmers, it's hard to get away from the farm. Someone still has to milk the cows and take care of the horses while we're gone.

"My family has never taken a vacation. We can't afford to. But maybe one day, when I'm married and have my own family . . . "

AFTER BREAKFAST, WE shopped the Avenue. So many stores (and restaurants) lining both sides of Rehoboth Avenue for blocks. Items for the home, clothes, jewelry, shoes, books, beach stuff. Not to mention the dozens of outlets we passed out on the highway as we drove in yesterday. How do Englishers choose what to buy? I started to feel anxious and overwhelmed, just like when we shopped at King of Prussia.

Taylor noticed my distress and said, "Don't hyperventilate. You don't have to buy anything. We can't fit that much in the bike basket anyway. Just window shop."

I stopped in front of one store. In the window I saw a small figurine of a fish leaping out of the water, like the one I saw swimming the day before. Taylor said it was a dolphin. The next thing I knew we were walking out of the store carrying a bag with my dolphin figure in a box inside.

"It's a souvenir you can always keep to remember your days at the beach," Taylor said.

By then we had worked up an appetite for lunch. Grotto Pizza seems to be everywhere, three of them on the Avenue and the boardwalk within a short walk of each other. We ordered the Baker's Choice pizza, with pepperoni, mushrooms, sweet peppers, sausage, and extra cheese, and we each had a garden salad.

Finally, Dolle's for dessert. The place is full of all kinds of candies, not just salt water taffy. There are chocolates and homemade fudge and licorice and gummy candy and caramel popcorn. The twins would go nuts in there. Of course, I couldn't decide between the twelve taffy flavors, including chocolate, strawberry, peppermint, licorice, lemon. I chose assorted one pound boxes for Jacob and my family, and finally picked out my own assortment: orange, cherry, and lime. Taylor doesn't like salt water taffy so she bought a small tin of caramel corn instead. I ate a few pieces of taffy as we walked back to the bike (it gets stuck in your teeth!) and loved them all but lime was my favorite.

We biked back to the house, our purchases piled in the bike basket, changed into our suits, and went for a walk on the beach. I picked up several seashells as souvenirs for the twins and Katie and me, too. Then we sat on our beach chairs right at the edge of the water, the breaking waves sometimes rushing under our chairs and we had to hold on, laughing.

In the late afternoon, we packed up our chairs and towels (Taylor actually didn't bring any work down to the beach this time so we didn't have much to carry back) in silence. I was sad to leave and as we walked slowly back to the house, I turned around for one last look at the sand and the sea, trying to memorize the scene in my mind, hoping that when I'm back in my bed on the farm and I close my eyes at night, I'll still be able to hear the sound of the waves crashing on the shore.

We stopped at the Big Fish Grill for dinner on the way home. I wanted to try as many kinds of fish as I could at one sitting. For starters, we had roasted red pepper lobster bisque (fancy word for soup). Then I had linguini with shrimp, scallops, clams, and mussels with a lobster sauce, and Taylor had fried scallops with creamed spinach and corn on the cob. For dessert, we shared warm apple cobbler with cinnamon ice cream. Everything was delish. I have always enjoyed the food we ate at home (Taylor calls it "comfort food," lots of meat and potatoes and veggies), but I never realized how many different foods there are out there in the world to try.

On the way home, we blasted the Beach Boys again and I ate more salt water taffy. I thanked Taylor for bringing me to the beach and told her how much fun I had. For a few seconds she was quiet and then she said, "Don't thank me. I should be thanking you. I had fun, too." I'm not sure I understand why she should thank me.

I'm looking forward to Mamm's visit this Saturday. She's coming alone and staying overnight at Taylor's because Dat and David and Daadi are helping at the Zook's barn raising over in Leola, and Katie and Mammi are taking care of the twins, who are a little under the weather with summer colds. We're going to a class at Bayard to learn how to help Jacob in and out of his wheelchair and about the different kinds of wheelchairs. I guess he needs to get one before he comes home. I've seen Jacob for weeks in his wheelchair at the rehab center, but I can't picture him in a wheelchair at the farm. I still see him healthy and strong, milking cows, working the fields. But I wonder if there's a tiny part of him that's glad he can no longer do the work that he has for so long merely tolerated for the sake of our family.

ERIC SHOVED THE last of his possessions into his duffle bag and zipped it closed. It was Friday morning and he was leaving the hospital for good.

"I guess that's everything," he said. My parents should be here any minute."

Jacob sat silently in his wheelchair by his bed, watching his roommate with mixed emotions. Part of him was happy for Eric, who was finally going home, returning to his life, finishing high school, then on to college. The rest of him was unhappy to be losing his personal cheering section, his real world tutor, his friend.

"I'll keep in touch," Eric said. "I'll text and call you on your cell, at least while you're still here. I don't know that I'd dare call you once you get back to the farm."

"*Ja, Dat* might end up tossing my cell into the manure gutter," Jacob joked.

Jacob wanted to tell Eric he would miss him, wanted to thank Eric for his support, for his pep talks, for making him laugh.

"I . . . , " he began. "Thanks . . . " The words stuck in his throat. Finally he just shook his head.

"Forget it," Eric said. "I know. Me, too." His parents arrived, said goodbye to Jacob, and wished him luck. His dad shook Jacob's hand and grabbed Eric's bag. Jacob and Eric locked eyes, then Eric grinned, and gave a thumb's up. His mom wheeled Eric out of the room and he was gone.

THE SATURDAY MORNING service began with the blessing over and lighting of the *Shabbat* candles. Becca and Taylor sat among the Rittenhouse Synagogue congregation. Becca had agreed, again out of curiosity, to attend the synagogue service a few blocks away from Rittenhouse Square as a continuation of her "religious education." A friend of her father's and a member of the congregation, Evan Mayer, would meet them after the service. Connor had explained to Evan that Becca was Amish and was exploring other faiths.

"Why do some men wear those small hats?" Becca asked, reflexively touching the strings of her *kapp*.

"They're called *yarmulkas*," Taylor said. "They're worn as a sign of respect and reverence, to show that God is above them."

"I don't understand the language," Becca said.

"It's Hebrew, one of the world's oldest living languages. Unlike English, it's written and read from right to left."

Becca's eyes widened when she realized the rabbi was a woman and she watched engrossed as the rabbi took the ornate Torah parchment scroll from the Ark and read the weekly prayer.

Taylor whispered to Becca that the Ark, or *Aron Kodesh*, was a holy cabinet usually located on a wall facing Jerusalem, and the Torah was the first five books of the Hebrew Bible, or what is considered the Old Testament in the Christian Bible. The rabbi offered the *D'var Torah*, the sermon on the Torah passage just read, then put the Torah away. The congregation sang hymns, led by the cantor, and the rabbi offered concluding prayers.

A social hour followed the service. Evan approached the two, Becca's Amish clothing making her easy to spot in the crowd, and explained that the social hour, or *Oneg Shabbat*, involved the *kiddush*, the blessing over wine, and the *hamotzi*, the blessing over bread. Evan then introduced them to Rabbi Weiss and left to rejoin his family.

"*Shalom*," Rabbi Weiss said. "Welcome to our synagogue." She led the two over to a corner where they sat down. "Did you enjoy the service?"

"It was beautiful," Becca said, "even if I didn't understand most of it."

"Can I answer any questions for you?" Rabbi Weiss asked.

"Rabbi, could you explain to Becca the difference between Christianity and Judaism."

"Of course," she said. "Christianity evolved out of Judaism and the two have much in common. Both believe in the same God and share the Old Testament. Jesus and his early followers were Jews. A major difference between the two religions is that Jews don't believe Jesus was the Messiah or the Son of God or that he rose from the dead. Jews don't believe people are born with original, or inherent, sin whereas Christians believe Jesus' death absolved mankind's original sin.

"Jews also don't believe in God as a holy trinity—the Father, the Son, and the Holy Spirit. We believe God is only One. Even among the Jewish faith, there are many differences in rituals and traditions. There are conservative congregations such as ours, as well as reform and orthodox Jews. For example, the orthodox Hasidim, like your Amish brethren, dress apart from the norm and wear head coverings, and the men sport beards and *payos*, which are long twisted side curls."

Taylor glanced at Becca's puzzled face. "I think one issue Becca is struggling with is whether there is only one true faith, whether only one religious group will be chosen by God to enjoy salvation or an afterlife."

The rabbi nodded. "That is certainly what many organized religious groups believe," she answered. "Many followers believe their particular religion is *the* one favored by God, and there is only one path to salvation. Obviously, if that's correct, if there can be only one 'right' religion, so to speak, then hundreds of millions of other followers must be wrong."

Becca shifted uncomfortably in her chair. "I've been taught to believe that if I'm not baptized and don't follow the Amish faith and non-conforming ways, I won't get to heaven, I'll go to hell. I'll lose my values and morals if I leave the Amish."

Rabbi Weiss smiled kindly at Becca.

"I understand you've visited a Catholic church as well as this synagogue. Do you think the people you've seen worshipping these two different faiths have no values or morals? Do you believe that because they live in the modern world, they are necessarily bad or immoral people? Do only the Amish have morals and values that are pleasing to God?"

"I don't know," Becca mumbled. "I never thought of it that way."

"Becca, I'm in no way trying to talk you out of your beliefs or your adherence to the Amish lifestyle. From what I understand, there is much to be admired in the Amish way of life. But I also think much is to be admired in many faiths."

THE LATE MORNING August heat sucked the air out of their lungs as they exited the air-conditioned synagogue and headed toward South Street for lunch.

"South Street is one of Philadelphia's main tourist attractions," Taylor told Becca. "It's eclectic and bohemian, tacky and seedy. There's something for everyone."

Taylor pointed out some of the more interesting shops as they walked down the street, toward Penn's Landing: Cheesesteaktees, for Philly slogan graphic t-shirts in a bubble gum-scented store; a Brazilian rainforest mural on the entire side of a former McDonald's; Hats In the Belfry, for all things hats; and various bars, restaurants, tattoo parlors, coffee houses, bookstores, antiques, and of course, the requisite Starbucks and Subway. Becca especially enjoyed the places with cow references—the Moo Tattoo shop and The Cow and the Curd food truck parked on the street, offering battered fried cheese curds.

They chose the long-standing South Street Diner for lunch because of its extensive menu and classic diner atmosphere. They sat in front of a large arched window, perfect for people watching, in a booth with a Tiffany-style lamp overhead. Becca's mouth watered as she eyed the bakery case filled with fruit pies, cakes, cream and meringue pies, cheesecakes, and cookies.

In a nod to Becca's sense of food adventure, they decided to try the Greek specialties on the menu. Becca ordered moussaka, a three-layered casserole of eggplant, ground beef, and potatoes topped with a béchamel sauce. Taylor tried the spanakopita, a pie with spinach, onion, and feta cheese. Later, for dessert, they both shared baklava, phyllo dough stacked with honey and nuts.

Becca had just taken a mouthful of moussaka when Taylor said, "Here's some food for thought: Should any one religious group have a lock on the afterlife?"

Becca slowly lowered her fork to her plate, her hand shaking slightly.

"God has a grand plan we may never understand. That's why we have faith and live a life that honors Him."

Taylor shook her head. "Organized religion doesn't necessarily require blind faith or rigid certainty or discourage critical thinking and dissent."

Becca thought for a moment. "I'm not sure what you mean by organized religion, but my Amish community helps us live our beliefs, is there for support when we need help. It's the group that helps us live the way we want to live to best honor God and to have a hope for eternity in heaven."

Taylor nodded. "But what if there is no afterlife? What if all we have is this one life here on earth? Shouldn't we then be concentrating on living this life instead of competing over who's going to be admitted to the next one? If there's no heaven, then there's no need to be intolerant of faiths other than our own. Then maybe we wouldn't need to kill each other in the name of religion as we have done for centuries. Can't this one life we have be enough? Why do we need an afterlife?"

"Because," Becca said, "I couldn't stand to think I'd never see my parents or grandparents or other family again in heaven after they die. Don't you want to see your mom again?"

"Yes, I would like to see her . . . alive, right now, in this world. Belief in an afterlife is attractive because to think that nothing exists after death is frightening. But heaven is not a certainty. You hope, you have faith, but you do not *know*."

"Well, I do believe," Becca said, her voice quavering.

"I'm sorry if I've upset you. You've probably never talked to anyone in your life that questioned your faith or faith in general. Enough talk for now about religion. Let's just eat and enjoy our meal."

TAYLOR YAWNED AS she ambled down the hall from her bedroom to the kitchen. It was early but she wanted to make coffee and breakfast for Sarah and Becca, perhaps scrambled eggs and fresh fruit, and she could run down to Metropolitan Bakery and pick up a loaf of raisin nut bread.

She stopped as she saw Sarah sitting alone on the terrace, head bent, hands folded, a Bible opened on the table. Taylor knew it was a church Sunday for Sarah at home and she was hesitant to disturb her.

The coffee had just finished brewing when Sarah looked up, smiled wanly at Taylor, and closed her Bible. Taylor poured two mugs of steaming French roast coffee, added a dash of milk, and joined Sarah on the terrace.

"Becca still sleeping?"

"*Ja*, I didn't want to wake her, she looked so peaceful. She can pray herself later."

Sarah and Becca had stayed with Jacob until evening hours were over the night before and by the time Taylor had picked them up and brought them home, both had been tired and went right to bed. There had been no chance to talk.

"How did the wheelchair class go yesterday?" Taylor asked.

"Jacob gets in and out of the wheelchair, and in and out of bed, by himself fine. Getting from the wheelchair into and out of a buggy may be another thing. We obviously weren't able to practice that yesterday. Jacob isn't comfortable asking for help; he likes to be independent."

"What will you do about a wheelchair for Jacob?"

"Jacob chose a manual model from a catalog with the help of his occupational therapist. He wanted to discuss it with me first but plans to order it on Monday and pay for it from his savings. He believes the accident was entirely his fault and he knows we're struggling financially, although I haven't told him so. I told him his bank savings are for his future and he said, '*Mamm*, this *is* my future.'" A tear rolled down Sarah's cheek.

"I've noticed a change in Jacob," she said. "Before, he was depressed and short with us and didn't talk much. Yesterday, he seemed more open and upbeat and his attitude about his disability is better. His case manager told us early on that it was normal for paralyzed patients to go through a range of emotions, most of them negative in the beginning, but that the majority eventually come around and learn to live with their disability and enjoy life. I wish that for Jacob and have prayed to God to help him accept his life. But I know my son still feels sad and frustrated. He doesn't know what to do with his life. I ache for him and I don't know how to help him."

Taylor felt a pang of guilt. She had no intention of telling Sarah about Jacob's GED quest and his dream of college. That was Jacob's story to tell.

"Jacob will deal with his future in due time," Taylor said. "Right now, he needs to finish his physical therapy and learn to cope at home on the farm. Then he can tackle the rest of his life."

JACOB HEARD THE distant sound of car horns and sirens on the streets below as he began a letter to David:

David:

I'm sitting in the atrium by myself. It's nice and quiet here on Sunday nights. Visiting hours are over and everyone's in their rooms watching TV. When I look out the windows and see the vast black sky and the stars, it makes me think of home, when you and I were younger and used to lay on the hay bales in back of the barn on summer nights, looking up at the sky and just talking about stuff, nothing important. I miss that.

I order my wheelchair tomorrow. Not quite as exciting as ordering a buggy but since I'm paying for it, I spent a lot of time choosing. You wouldn't believe how many models there are, a whole catalog of them, with different colors and all kinds of optional features. I chose a simple black rigid manual chair, instead of a folding or a power chair. The power chairs are too expensive and obviously the power source would be problematic for us. The rigid chair is stronger, lighter, and easier to maneuver than a folding chair. The back folds down and the wheels pop off for when I need to get it in a buggy or van.

Good news! I should be coming home in a couple weeks. I'm getting around well, my upper body strength is good, and I'm able to transfer myself from the bed or a couch to the wheelchair and back. I'm learning to be independent again.

The hardest thing is dealing with my bladder and bowel movements. Instead of being intermittently catheterized (every six hours) by the staff in order to empty my bladder, I can now wear an external condom catheter and a leg bag, which enables me to urinate on my own. I trigger urination by tapping over my bladder area with my fingers for a minute or so until I go and then I periodically empty the bag into the toilet throughout the day.

The bowel process is a little more difficult. Every other day, about 30 minutes after supper is my scheduled time for a bowel movement. I'm training my bowel to empty at a planned time so I can avoid accidents and leakage. I sit on the toilet and begin digital rectal stimulation, which is a fancy way of saying I stick a lubricated gloved finger up my butt and rotate it until I begin to poop. I then manually remove the stool with my finger. The whole process usually takes about a half hour. I now know how our cows must feel when we artificially inseminate them.

Remember when Joseph was learning how to dress himself and he'd put his pants on backwards? I've done that a couple times myself while learning how to dress and undress. I wear mostly shorts and t-shirts since it's easier to move during physical therapy but the other day I tried on a pair of my farm pants and suspenders and I managed just fine.

On a good day, I'm thankful I'm only paralyzed from the waist down and I've adjusted to not being able to feel or use my legs. But on an off day—mostly every day until recently—I hate how my legs hang useless and weak and am full of self-loathing *and regret for what my future may have been. My therapists and Eric (before he went home) and Taylor have been on a mission to convince me that my future can still be whatever I want it to be. Sometimes I believe them and sometimes I don't.*

How are your plans for the wedding coming? Mamm said you and Anna are thinking of traveling out to Ohio after the wedding for a couple weeks to see some of our Yoder clan. Mamm's eyes light up when she talks about your wedding. She needs something fun to look forward to, a diversion from sadness and stress, as we all do. Anna is first-rate. I couldn't be happier for you.

See you soon.

Jacob

❧

THE BABY GRAND piano stood elegantly in front of the floor-to-ceiling windows in Taylor's living room, bathed in a soft ray of light from the full moon. Taylor stood beside it for a moment, listening to the water running as Becca showered. It was Sunday evening and she had just returned from dropping Sarah off at the train station.

Taylor's right hand casually played a G major scale, then a C major, then a C sharp minor. She sat down on the bench and ran through those scales with both hands, up three octaves and back down. *Not bad*, she thought. *A little rusty.*

She stood up, opened the piano bench, and rummaged through the stacks of sheet music. She searched for a minute and pulled out Beethoven's "Moonlight Sonata." She began to play the first of the three movements, hesitantly at first, then with more confidence. The movement is played slowly and quietly, yet Taylor didn't hear the shower stop and didn't realize Becca stood transfixed in the bathroom, wrapped in a towel, listening. Taylor played to the end of the first movement, the last chord soft, *piano pianissimo*. She removed her hands from the keyboard, lifted her head, and saw her mom standing in the living room, smiling.

"I love hearing you play," she said, before she transformed into Becca, in her white nightgown, hair wet from the shower.

Taylor jumped up, the second movement forgotten. "I should answer my emails and get a head start on my Monday morning," she said, and hurried to her study.

14

I WALKED THROUGH a two-story model of a giant heart at The Franklin Institute, the heart thumping as the valves opened and closed and the blood whooshing as it circulated. At Sir Isaac's Loft, I sat in a chair and lifted myself with The Giant Lever, and screeched in fright as the Bowling Ball of Doom swung within inches of my face. I met Benjamin Franklin for the first time. I now know that Franklin invented the bifocals Daadi wears. He also invented a flexible urinary catheter, which probably led the way to the various catheters that doctors have told us Jacob has used. And although we Amish have always avoided the use of electricity in our lives, I never thought of lightning as nature's electrical current.

Taylor and I left her office in the middle of the afternoon on Monday because she wanted to take me to the Franklin Institute to see a special traveling exhibit about a man named Charles Darwin.

At the Darwin exhibit, I saw two live tortoises, fifty pounds each, from the Galapagos Islands, an iguana five feet long, and horned frogs. I had trouble with this exhibit and Taylor had to explain evolution to me. I always thought God made all the creatures of the world at the same time but Taylor said Darwin showed that all life happened over a huge period of time according to a process called evolution by natural selection, which means that over time, changes happened to a species that allowed it to better adapt to the environment and survive. She said all life, including humans, evolved from earlier species.

For instance, boa constrictors have tiny hind bones, a clue that snakes evolved from lizards. Some fish live in caves with eyes that don't work, which is an example of them adapting to their environment, a dark cave where fish don't need to see to live (Makes sense, because why would God make fish with eyes that don't work?). In the Galapagos Islands, animals live that appear nowhere else on earth, which Taylor said means those animals evolved solely to adapt to life on those islands. More than 350,000 kinds of beetles exist in the world, an example of lots of adaptation (or God really liked beetles!).

She explained to me about fossils and how fossils have left a history of evolution that goes back millions of years and shows how different species have evolved. A 375 million-year-old fish's bones found in the Canadian Arctic showed a neck, shoulders, primitive lungs, and arm-like front fins, the beginnings of features later found in land animals. Scientists think the fish was able to prop itself up in shallow water and for short periods on land to hunt for prey.

Taylor said the majority of the scientific community, hundreds of thousands of scientists, supports evolution. But despite that, some religious groups don't believe in evolution (she called them creationists) and want their intelligent design beliefs (that everything was created by a God Designer) taught in public schools, but our courts have struck down those efforts due to separation of church and state.

I must have looked troubled because she said, "Becca, plenty of religious people, including the pope, understand and accept evolution and still believe in God. They believe God created beings that evolve."

Taylor also said that scientists studying human DNA, which she explained to me is hereditary information stored in living cells, like a recipe, believe that modern humans are descendants of people who lived in Africa 200,000 years ago. This was fascinating to me. There has been so much prejudice against African Americans, yet we all came from the same place. And not only that, Taylor said, but humans share a common ancestor with gorillas and chimpanzees. I found this hard to believe.

But doesn't the Bible say God created man in His image? I asked.

Taylor thought for a minute, then said, "If I had to choose between believing in scientific learning based on observation and experimental investigation and validated by some of the best minds on earth versus believing in conflicting interpretations of a book written nearly two thousand years ago by fallible human beings, and retranslated with many flaws and disparities from Greek and Hebrew, and with much debate concerning its historical accuracy and whether it's the literal word of God or parable and allegory and metaphor, I would pick science."

So I wouldn't forget, I made her write on a napkin what she said while we took a break and had a snack in the cafeteria. I've since read what she wrote over and over and am still not sure if she answered my question. I think she's saying she believes the scientists over the Bible when it comes to how man came to be. But seems to me if God created evolution then he still had a hand in creating man and that's what the Bible verse means.

At Fels Planetarium, I learned the Earth formed about 4.5 billion years ago. I had no idea the earth was so old. I also had no idea about our solar system or what a small blip we are in the vastness of our universe. Our galaxy is only one of billions in the universe (with only a few thousand visible by telescope) and the universe is about 14 billion years old. God is certainly a patient being. Taylor said creationists believe the earth is less than 10,000 years old based on their interpretation of the Bible's Genesis and opened a multi-million dollar museum in Kentucky based on that belief, which Taylor said was "far outside the bounds of worldwide scientific consensus."

Before I met Taylor, I never gave a thought to what I didn't know because what I did know was enough. Now I realize that what I don't know is huge and overwhelming. We aren't taught many things in our schools. Taylor said, and I don't think she was trying to be unkind, "What if everyone in the world was Amish? Look at the discoveries that would never have been made in science and medicine, not to mention the contributions to art, music, and literature."

That may be true, but when all is said and done, would all the things I don't know help me to live a better life as an Amish person or to be truer to God? I said this to Taylor and she looked at me long and hard, gave a big sigh, muttered something about "the extreme difficulty of overcoming ingrained provincial ideas" (whatever that means) and suggested we go to dinner.

I am now a fan of Indian food. At Karma in Old City, we sat on shiny black chairs surrounded by yellow and orange walls that held colorful artwork. Taylor said it was "vibrant and eclectic." I always learn neat new words from her.

I had tandoori chicken and a side of spicy eggplant and Taylor had a lamb dish with fried coconut and hot red peppers. We both had basmati rice and naan bread, plain and stuffed with raisins and almonds. So good, I must have had a half dozen pieces myself. For dessert, we both had kulfi, Indian ice cream in mango and pistachio.

TAYLOR AND BECCA gazed at the vibrantly colorful mosaic front of the two-story sprawling Islamic Center of Philadelphia and then entered the front door. Taylor had called ahead and explained Becca's religious exploration to Imam Hadi, who had graciously agreed to meet with them before the noon prayers.

Once again, Becca refused to appear in a place of worship in *Englisher* clothes and so wore her Amish church clothes and *kapp*. Taylor wore a conservative black pantsuit. Imam Hadi was waiting for them at the appointed time in the lounge inside the main entrance.

"*Assalamu alaikum*," he said. "Peace be upon you." He took them on a brief tour of the first floor *masjid*—mosque or main prayer hall—and the separate prayer area for women, as well as the *wudu*, or ablutions, area, where Muslims wash parts of the body with water before prayer. They also toured the rest of the building, which included a school for kindergarten through grade eight, a library, and a small grocery store. Back in the lounge, the imam motioned for them to sit in the black leather chairs.

"Do you know much about Islam?" Iman Hadi asked Becca. She shook her head.

"Islam is the second largest religion in the world, after Christianity," the imam began. "About 1.6 billion Muslims from all walks of life across the globe—in the Middle East, in Asia and Africa, as well as the Americas and Europe—share the faith. Islam tends to be equated with the Arab world, but a majority of the world's Muslims live in Asia, especially Indonesia and India, and Africa. Over 3 million live in the U.S.

"In Arabic, Islam means 'submission,' as in complete submission to the will of God. Muslims believe Muhammad, peace and blessings be upon him, was the final messenger and prophet of God. In the year 610, at age 40, Muhammad received his first revelation from God through the angel Gabriel. Muhammad is a role model for Muslims, much like Jesus is for Christians, except Muhammad is solely human. Islam is based on both the Quran, which is the holy text in Arabic of God's revelations to Muhammad, and the *hadith*, a collection of the actions and sayings of Muhammad, compiled after his death."

Imam Hadi explained that Muslims believe in one God, called *Allah*, and in life after death. Muslims believe Islam, Christianity, and Judaism all originated from Abraham. "Like Christians and Jews, Muslims see themselves as children of Abraham, and we also believe in other prophets such as Noah, Moses, and Jesus. Muslims respect and revere Jesus, peace be upon him, and consider him one of the greatest of God's messengers to mankind, and the Quran confirms his virgin birth. But we don't believe Jesus is the Son of God."

Becca, forehead creased, fidgeted, and the imam stopped. "You look confused," he said. "Do you have a question?"

Becca glanced at Taylor, who nodded her encouragement, then said, "Well, isn't the Bible also the word of God and the Bible says Jesus is the Son of God."

Taylor smiled. "This is exactly the reason why we are visiting other places of worship, Becca. To show you that other people believe just as passionately, but differently. Please continue, Imam Hadi."

The imam then explained the various obligations of Islamic life: to pray in Arabic toward Mecca, Islam's holiest city, five times a day in a mosque or wherever they happen to be; to fast from dawn until sunset during the holy month of Ramadan; to make a pilgrimage to Mecca, in Saudi Arabia at least once in a lifetime if physically and financially able to go.

"Thank you for giving us a glimpse behind your religion," Taylor said, "but pardon me, Imam Hadi, and with all due respect, I'd like to ask a tough question. Please keep in mind that I'm in the media business and expected to address controversial issues. My only goal is education, to understand your point of view."

The imam nodded. "I will do my best to answer your question."

Taylor took a moment to gather her thoughts. "Since 9/11 and the rise of terrorist groups like ISIS, there has been widespread anti-Muslim sentiment and controversy about Islam. Many people believe Islam to be a religion of the sword, spread by the sword. In many passages throughout the Quran, God instructs Muslims to violently defeat the infidels, or nonbelievers of Islam, which for the most part are seen as Jews, Christians, Hindus, and even other warring Muslim sects, such as the Sunni and Shiites. Because the Quran is considered by its followers to be the actual and final word of God, critics claim a literal reading of the Quran helps fuel terrorism in the name of Islam. Of course, many factors other than religion—economic, political, geographic, educational, as well as hostility toward Western foreign policy—complicate the issue of Islamic terrorists. That being said, how do you respond to this criticism?"

The imam shook his head but spoke calmly. "The Quran, like the Old Testament of the Bible, does contain passages that advocate fighting and killing and war but these passages refer to the violent period in which Muhammad, peace and blessings be upon him, lived. Radicals quote such passages out of context to support their political agenda and justify their violence. Many other passages in the Quran encourage peace, mercy, tolerance, and compassion. This is the Islam that the great majority of Muslims all over the world practice.

"And frankly, we Muslims are horrified by the atrocities committed in the name of Islam and frustrated by the often uneducated commentary against our religion by media personalities, which in turn gives rise to the Islamaphobia we are tired of defending against."

Taylor agreed that yes, plenty of people fear Islam out of ignorance. But, she added, to question the contents of a holy book, whether it be the Quran or the Bible, is a legitimate intellectual exercise and not meant to be a personal criticism of Muslims, Christians or Jews. And such questioning and commentary is also, she continued, a First Amendment free speech and free press right that has long endured in U.S. history, and to which she, of course, was partial.

"So let me be a devil's advocate," she said, "on behalf of the many well-intentioned non-Muslims who don't want to scapegoat Islam and who whole-heartedly believe that most Muslims are good, tolerant, and peace-loving people, but who are nevertheless confused about the Quran. They wonder about these numerous blatantly violent passages whose meaning seems clear: kill nonbelievers unless they submit to Islam.

"How do you defend the literal meaning of these violent passages, the very passages terrorists quote to justify a beheading or a suicide bombing, which you then condemn as horrific? Is it inconsistent to say the Quran is the inerrant word of God but then claim a literal meaning of its problematic passages is taking them out of context?"

Becca twisted nervously in her seat. She was uncomfortable with Taylor confronting a religious authority, something she could not conceive of doing under any circumstances in her Amish world. On the other hand, she was enthralled by the conversation.

Taylor smiled at Imam Hadi. "Again, please forgive my outspokenness. I believe this type of conversation is beneficial to

Becca's understanding of religion, and how other religions compare to her own."

"I appreciate your interest in Islam," the imam said. "To answer your question, there is a literalist meaning of certain verses but that doesn't necessarily lead to the correct interpretation when you consider the totality of the Quran—the context of the passages, the historical time in which Muhammad lived—and the *hadith*. In the Bible as well, a literal reading of some verses may be considered problematic but critics don't discredit the entire Bible or the Christian religion because of them. So too, Islam should not be the victim of violent militants who believe their interpretation to be the only one possible, who believe they alone speak for God."

"What is the way forward, then, Imam Hadi?" Taylor asked. "How do you refute ISIS and this type of scriptural extremism?

"I do not deny that this is a serious challenge for Muslims to address. ISIS and its ilk must be militarily defeated, with the help of Muslim countries. But that is not enough. The ideology that breeds these terrorist groups—the radical version of Islam they believe should be forced on the rest of society—must be discredited. That is a difficult and long process that requires a dialog among all Muslims."

Iman Hadi glanced at his watch. "I have a few more minutes before the noon prayers. Anything else you'd like to discuss?"

"Yes," Taylor said. "What are your thoughts on the restriction on Muslim girls' education and the corresponding high rates of illiteracy among women throughout the non-Western Muslim world?"

First of all, Imam Hadi explained, Islam encourages the pursuit of knowledge, for both men and women. He acknowledged the difficulty in educating young Muslim women in rural areas. "But," he insisted, "this is not due to Islam but stems from cultural dogma, which proposes that girls don't need education because they're supposed to stay at home and take care of the family."

Becca asked, "What's wrong with staying home and taking care of the family?"

"Nothing, of course," Taylor said, "if it's a choice. And you have had eight years of education, which is eight years more than many Muslim girls experience."

Taylor then asked, "What about the practice of separating women from men in mosques, such as this one, when they pray?"

"Not all mosques in this country separate men and women. Here in our mosque, we believe the focus is on prayer and God, not gender mingling. We also pray in a prostrate position and women feel uncomfortable in that position with strange men behind them. And we aren't the only religion that practices that. Orthodox Jews also pray separately."

"So do the Amish," Becca said. "The men and women sit separately during our service but we are all in the same room."

Becca had been wondering about something since she saw the women entering the *masjid*.

"Muslim women also wear a head covering," she said, touching her *kapp*. "What is it called?"

"The covering is called a *hijab* and it's a sign of respect in the house of God," the imam said. "Here, it's worn like a headscarf with the face uncovered. Throughout the world, when Muslim women appear in public, they wear different traditions of female dress, not because the Quran requires it, but based on the country and expressions of local custom. Sometimes the dress is compulsory. Often it's a voluntary choice. For example, some wear a *niqab*, a veil covering the face except for the eyes, or the *burqa*, a loose outer robe that covers the whole body and face, with a mesh screen over the eyes. Here in the Philly area, many women wear a loose, body-covering garment, called the *abaya*, which can be fashionable and colorful, with modern clothing layered underneath."

"Critics, including some outspoken Muslim women, say such dress is a sign of oppression and subservience to men," Taylor said.

Imam Hadi turned toward Becca and gently asked, "Do you feel that your dress oppresses you?"

"Well, no. It's the clothing we have chosen, both men and women, to make a statement about our way of life. I'm not sure how I'd feel, though, if I were only able to see the world through two eye slits. If I grew up that way, I guess I'd be okay with it."

Imam Hadi explained that head and body coverings for Muslim women can be political, cultural, or religious statements, or a combination. "Muslim women, as well as men, prefer to dress modestly, as instructed by the Quran. They believe their modest dress encourages society to focus on their intellect and their character rather than their looks, and they're unhappy about being judged by others on the basis of what they wear as opposed to their beliefs and actions."

Becca said nothing but nodded her head in agreement.

Taylor had one last question for the imam. "It's the same question I could ask a Christian or a Jew. If the three major monotheistic faiths are interrelated, why not teach that God's message was sent equally to all cultures and all nations? Why concentrate on the merit of one faith over another? Can't a good Muslim, a good Christian, and a good Jew all be acceptable to God?"

The imam sighed. "Can religions be separate but equal? I don't have the answer. There are verses in the Quran some scholars interpret to mean that the diversity of people and religions is according to God's plan and there should be tolerance of other God-loving faiths. That discussion must be left for another day."

Imam Hadi stood. "I'm afraid we are out of time. Ms. Loden, Ms. Yoder, I have found our conversation stimulating but now I must leave you and go lead the noon prayer. You are welcome to stay and watch, if you desire."

Taylor and Becca took off their shoes and watched the prayer session from the back of the *masjid*. The men prayed with Imam Hadi in person, while the women watched closed circuit TVs with a live video feed of the prayers. Both men and women lay prostrate on the ground in submission during the prayers. At the end, they turned to each other and said, "Peace be with you."

❧

"I PLANNED A treat for you," Taylor said to Becca in the car after the mosque. "We're going to afternoon tea. Scones, finger sandwiches, pastries . . . "

Becca looked pensive.

"What's the matter?" Taylor asked. "You don't want to go?"

"No, it's not that. Tea sounds great. I was just thinking about what you said to the imam, about religions being equal. Does that mean being Amish is just one way to follow God?"

"Becca, I am certainly no expert. Numerous religious authorities would claim that perspective dilutes real commitment to any faith. But many people do view religion that way. They believe any faith is just one expression of following God, is one of any number of different paths to the same end. And that people of all religions are children of God and therefore equal before God.

"Does God really care whether we are Amish, Baptists, Methodists, Catholics, Jews, or Muslims? Or whether we read the Torah, the Bible, or the Quran? Or whether we celebrate Yom Kippur, Christmas, or Ramadan? I have no idea. But for the sake of argument, maybe to believe is the important thing to God, not how we believe. How we believe—the rituals and traditions, the way we eat, or pray, or dress—is merely personal preference."

❧

A HARPIST PLAYED in a corner of the Mary Cassatt Tea Room at The Rittenhouse Hotel, the usual stares accompanying Becca as she and Taylor sat at a table in front of large arched windows overlooking a garden terrace, where they had come for afternoon tea after their trip to the mosque.

Although outwardly Becca appeared calm as she sat quietly, her hands clasped together in her lap, inside her stomach fluttered. She was able to appreciate the elegance of the room and the novelty of having afternoon tea but at the same time she felt the familiar strain between the world of luxury she temporarily inhabited and the plain world of her upbringing.

She studied the menu, bewildered at the wide selection of teas offered and finally chose Duchess' First Love, an Earl Grey blended with rooibos, which she learned was a South African red tea. Taylor ordered the house blend.

The waiter brought the tea in delicate white china pots with matching gold-rimmed tea cups. The afternoon tea included crustless finger sandwiches—egg salad, chicken salad, smoked salmon, prosciutto and avocado—and raisin and buttermilk scones with whipped butter, preserves, and clotted cream, as well as an assortment of miniature pastries.

Becca sipped her tea and slathered her scones with butter and strawberry preserves. As she ate, Becca thought of the church, synagogue, and mosque visits and the time she had spent with Taylor so far. Having just finished reading *To Kill A Mockingbird*, she decided she could relate to Scout Finch.

"In *To Kill A Mockingbird*, Scout learns how to look at things from another person's point of view," she said, "like we've been learning other perspectives concerning religion and how I've been sort of living in your shoes these past weeks."

"Yes," Taylor said, surprised that Becca had initiated a literary discussion. "The novel does address the theme of tolerance. In the U.S. South in the 1930s, racial and class prejudice was common. What do you think the title means?"

Becca poured herself another cup of tea. "Miss Maudie says

it's a sin to kill a mockingbird because they just sing and do no harm. Scout and Jem learn that bad things happen to good people and those good people are like mockingbirds."

"Yes, both Scout and Jem lose their childhood innocence, and to kill a mockingbird is to harm an innocent. Who else in the book could be considered mockingbirds?"

Becca thought for a minute. "Boo Radley and Tom Robinson were both good and innocent people harmed in different ways— Tom wrongly convicted because of the town's racial prejudice and Boo by his cruel father."

"Would you like to see the movie tonight? It's the last of the ones we bought at the bookstore. Gregory Peck is a perfect Atticus Finch."

"Gregory who?" Becca grinned.

WE ALL WORSHIP the same God, in different and similar ways. We all pray, but in different places: churches, mosques, synagogues, our homes. We all have our holy books: the Bible, the Torah, the Quran, and the rules and rituals based on those books. Jerusalem has been a holy city for three religions, and all three religions revere Abraham. And Taylor said there are even more religions, like Hinduism and Mormonism and others, which I know nothing about.

Religious people sometimes judge each other on their faith. Isn't God the only judge of faith? Maybe He intended for there to be different paths to the same end. Maybe not. I don't know. I have such a headache from thinking about all this. If it weren't for Taylor, I would never think of any religion but my own. I don't know whether to be thankful or upset that I now have a bigger view of things.

I asked Taylor last night if she believed in God. I've hesitated to ask her, mostly because I was afraid of the answer. What if she said no? How would I feel about hanging out with someone with no faith, some-one I like and admire very much? But my curiosity won out. She said she strongly believes in the secular foundation of our government, the separation of church and state, which means keeping religion out of politics and public policy. Everybody has a right to choose the religion that's right for them, she explained, as well as the freedom to not believe in any religion or Supreme Being. She believes you can disagree with or question someone's faith choice but, in the end, should be tolerant of it, as long as they do no harm to others who believe differently. So she didn't really answer the question. And I didn't press it further.

Taylor thinks if I know more about other religions, I will see mine in a different light and that will expand my thinking and my choices. Well, that is true. I am no longer sure that if I left the Amish, I would lose God and go to hell. I now understand there are many ways to believe in and honor God and I can't judge which is right or which is wrong. For now, though, I still must live what I have learned in my church. To do otherwise would disrespect my family and my community.

I can't wait until tomorrow. Mamm and Katie are coming to stay with Taylor for a few days. The Pennsylvania Dutch Festival starts Thursday at the Reading Terminal Market and ends Saturday and us Yoders will be working a booth selling produce and quilts with the Rueben Stoltzfus and Abner Zook families. This is the first time in several years we've done the Festival. We did it once five years ago, but it was such a hassle traveling back and forth from Lancaster to Philadelphia. I'm guessing we're doing it this year because we need the money. Mamm and Katie are coming down with the other families in a rented van early tomorrow morning to set up at the market and I'll meet them there.

Even though it's only been two weeks since I was home and saw everyone, I feel like a different person. I've seen and done so much I think it's changed me but I'm not quite sure how. I'd love to talk to Mamm about the religious stuff but she might be concerned that I attended other religious services and she'd tell Dat, who I'm sure wouldn't be happy and might even make me come home for good.

Taylor and I did watch the "Mockingbird" movie and Taylor was right, the actor who played Atticus was just how I pictured him in my mind as I read the book. There's something so wonderful about reading a book and then seeing it come alive with all the characters and the scenery. We ate popcorn and drank strawberry smoothies and I was

having such fun even though I knew I should feel guilty. I mentioned
this to Taylor and she said, "That which is forbidden always brings
guilty pleasure." She sounded like a fortune cookie.

AFTER THE DEMISE of the Reading Railroad, the old train shed
at Twelfth and Arch Streets was transformed into the Reading
Terminal Market, Taylor told Becca. On an ordinary day, the Terminal, across from the Pennsylvania Convention Center, is one
of the city's best farmers' markets, she said, known for its fresh
meat, cheeses, produce, and seafood, an eclectic array of flowers,
unusual spices and ethnic foods, and is also a popular lunch
spot, with stands featuring everything from cheese steaks and
hoagies to pizza, gyros, Peking duck, and sushi.

As they walked into the market, the Amish were preparing
stands offering an abundance of fare for the annual three-day
Pennsylvania Dutch Festival: shoofly pie and other homemade
pies, breads, and cakes; jams, jellies and preserves; chicken
pot pie; homemade ice cream; pretzels and donuts made while
you wait; farm-fresh produce and cheeses; handmade crafts,
including quilts, braided rugs, wooden toys, cedar chests, all
offered by Amish women and men, young and old, some using large hand-held calculators to add customers' orders.

Taylor noticed all the market stands had phones on the
back walls and she asked Becca about this.

"We lease the stands so technically we don't own the
phones, so it's okay."

Taylor learned from Becca that on Saturday, the Festival
would move outdoors in order to create a country fair in the
city, including a farm animal petting zoo, buggy rides, canning
and quilt-making demonstrations, and a dunk-your-favorite-
Amish-merchant tank.

Taylor said hello to Sarah and Katie, told them she'd be
back to pick them up that evening, bought an apple fritter at

Beiler's Bakery, and left for work.

That night, the three Yoder women and Taylor enjoyed take-home food from the festival: chicken pot pies and a streusel cake with chopped walnuts. Sarah said she couldn't wait to take a hot shower and get off her feet and Katie and Becca, sharing the Butterscotch room, offered to help clean up after dinner, but Taylor shooed them out of the kitchen.

"I'll clean up. You go rest. You have another early day tomorrow."

Taylor sat at the kitchen island afterward, ate another piece of cake, and thought about the next day with Jacob, a day about which she dared not tell Sarah or even Becca.

"STOP FOR A minute," Jacob requested as Taylor pushed his wheelchair down the brick path of Locust Walk. Jacob's hands gripped the wheelchair's arms as he eyed the formidable gothic buildings, some covered in ivy, on both sides of the tree-lined walk which cut across the campus of the University of Pennsylvania.

After she had dropped the Yoder women off at Reading Terminal, she had picked up Jacob at Bayard and brought him to Penn. They had already attended an information session at College Hall, which housed the undergraduate admissions office. Jacob had heard about the approximately twenty-one thousand full-time students at the three hundred-acre West Philadelphia campus, had learned about the highly selective admissions process, and to him, the staggering cost for tuition, room, and board.

They had crossed The Green, the center of campus in front of College Hall, with its lush lawns and trees and the bronze statue of Penn founder Benjamin Franklin. They had toured the Van Pelt-Dietrich Library, a modern, box-like building, site of the University's main book collection and filled with lounges, study carrels, computer labs, and more books than Jacob had ever seen in his life. They had visited 'Main Street,' or Perelman Quad, had eaten lunch at one of the eateries in Houston Hall, and had also seen The Quadrangle, home to three college houses, each with its own coat of arms, and with summer students lounging on the lawns and throwing Frisbees and footballs. They had checked out Kelly Writers House, a favorite of Jacob's, one of the oldest buildings on campus, which sponsored readings by poets, fiction writers and journalists, and offered writing courses and workshops.

As they toured the campus, Taylor had explained to Jacob about taking the SAT college entrance exams, how difficult it would be to get in—but not impossible; he'd be a poster child for the adversity and diversity all universities looked for—how financial aid was available to students in need, how the campus was handicap accessible, how it was her alma mater due to graduate school at Wharton, and how she could help him if he matriculated there.

Taylor waited quietly as he observed Locust Walk. It hardly seemed like an urban campus so idyllic was its insulation from the noisy city surrounding it. The castle-like architecture of its buildings was beautiful, yet formidable and intimidating, a perfect metaphor for how he viewed the university and his chances of ever seeing it again.

"We should go," Taylor said. "The class starts in a few minutes." They had arranged to attend a summer class, "Sociology of Media and Popular Culture," which, according to the on-line class description, examined the relationship between the media and culture, including the significance of reality TV and TV talk shows, and the growing obsession with celebrities. Taylor had chosen the class because it fit into the timing of their day and because she knew Jacob had been watching TV at Bayard and thought it might be of interest to him.

Jacob introduced himself to the professor and Taylor wheeled him to a spot at the back of the class. The open windows caught the slight breeze in an otherwise sultry day and the room was filled with about a dozen students taking the six-week class. Taylor used the time to respond to e-mails on her BlackBerry. When she was done, she glanced at Jacob.

He sat upright in his wheelchair, bent slightly forward, listening attentively to the professor. His face held a look of longing so great Taylor was immediately envious. She wondered how it felt to want something so passionately and yet doubt it was attainable.

She then wondered if perhaps she had done Jacob a disservice. She knew of his desire to continue his education and thought he would enjoy visiting a college campus. Penn had seemed a good choice because she knew her way around but realistically his chances of being admitted were slim at best. His SAT scores would need to be extraordinarily high, necessitating a prep course and countless hours of study. She didn't doubt he had the intelligence and the drive to excel but his lack of secondary schooling was a disadvantage, even if he did pass the GED.

He would also need to overcome social obstacles: learning to live on his own with a disability, learning to interact with non-Amish people, learning how the modern world worked. He had the motivation to overcome such obstacles, but given his limited interaction with the world so far, he faced an uphill climb.

She realized she should have waited until he left Bayard and taken him instead to a small community college near his farm in Lancaster, a more likely choice since he would have a better chance at admission and would be closer to his family. She vowed to do that after he returned to Lancaster. She didn't want to be responsible for a dream dashed.

FROM THE TIME Taylor and Jacob left the sociology class through the car ride back to Bayard, Jacob hadn't said a word.

Normally taciturn, he seemed almost brooding as he stared out the window. Taylor was reluctant to interrupt his mood, so they made the trip in silence. When they arrived back at the hospital, he surprised her by inviting her up to his room.

Jacob stored his Penn information packet in his bedside drawer and then turned to Taylor.

"I want you to come live with us," he said quietly. Taylor stared at him blankly.

"In Lancaster, at the farm, I want you there to help out, to help me."

"But Jacob, I have to work."

"Don't say no yet. Just listen." He paused to summon the courage for a request he knew was a huge imposition. The idea had occurred to him a couple weeks ago and he had thought of nothing else since. He had bided his time until an opportunity arose to speak with Taylor alone.

"Ellen, my case manager, said I could probably go home a week from today, barring anything unforeseen."

"Jacob, that's terrific news."

"She said I've made great progress. She'll talk to *Mamm* this weekend but feels confident my family can handle my physical needs and can ease me back into normal daily life."

"Then why do you need me?" Taylor asked.

"My family will help me adjust physically to being at home and in the community with a wheelchair. What they can't help me with is the way I feel inside. I know what my family will try to do, especially *Dat*. They're going to try to encourage me to baptize, join the church, make peace with being Amish. Even though we have never discussed it, they suspect I'm conflicted about staying in the community. They will see my disability as even more reason why I can never leave. They'll be terrified for my health, my safety, and my soul."

Jacob stared down into his lap. "I don't know if I can fight them alone any longer. I've been fighting them for years and look how that turned out. I'm afraid I'll give in. I'm afraid I'll forget about school. If you were there, you would remind me of what is possible."

"Jacob, why on earth would your family consider my living with you—even for a short time—if they knew my role was to encourage you to leave?"

"Because I'm going to tell them you are the reason I'm dealing with my disability better. *Mamm* has been worried about my attitude. I know I've been sullen and uncommunicative, even before the accident, but more so after. The last time she visited, she noticed I was more upbeat and I could tell she was pleased. I'm going to tell her you helped me see that being in a wheelchair is not the end of my world. I'm going to tell her you can help me explore different trades. I'm going to tell her that if you aren't nearby I could lose the momentum. All that is true."

"Why can't you just tell them you want to continue with school?"

"If I tell them now, the entire weight of my family and my community will come down on me. The pressure will be relentless. My parents, grandparents, aunts, uncles, ministers, all will try to dissuade me. If I definitely decide school is what I want to do, I promise I will tell them and deal with the consequences. It's just for a few weeks, Taylor, just until you can help me figure out about school and what may or may not be possible."

Taylor was silent. She had never heard Jacob talk for so long at one time. He usually conserved his words and his feelings but when he did speak, the emotion knocked you over. A part of her felt uncomfortable about not being forthright with Jacob's family about school but she understood his reasoning.

She began to mentally plan the transition. She could work out of the *Lancaster Post* office and from the Yoder farm as long as she had her BlackBerry and laptop. Philadelphia was only an hour and a half away if she needed to be at the home office. She'd have to deal with her father but felt confident she could convince him her mission was worthwhile. Surely he'd agree no one should be denied an education that truly wanted one.

"Okay. I need to talk to my dad, but if your parents agree, I'll come."

Jacob rewarded her with a rare smile.

DANIEL WATCHED HIS wife brush her long blond hair as she sat on the edge of their bed. He smelled the fresh outdoorsy smell of her nightgown, which Katie had taken off the clothesline late that afternoon. Daniel lay under the covers and knew his wife had something to say to him.

He had known as soon as she had walked in the door last night from Philadelphia; the worry showed in her eyes, in the slight downturn around her mouth. But it had been late, she had been tired from travel, and was in no mood to talk. She briefly told him the Festival had gone well, they made nearly a thousand dollars, and Jacob was well, would in fact be coming home soon.

Throughout the day, when he had seen her in between working the barn and the fields, she had seemed distracted. The subject must be serious if she was having trouble discussing it. He decided to give her a hand.

"Is something the matter, Sarah?"

Sarah brushed a few more strokes, laid her brush on the bureau, and climbed into bed.

"Jacob wants Taylor to come stay with us for a while when he comes home from Bayard," she blurted.

Sarah watched Daniel's face tighten and he began to shake his head no.

"Before you decide, listen to his reasons." Sarah relayed her conversation with Jacob, how he was convinced Taylor could help him put his life back together.

"Taylor could help him find a trade, something he can do in a wheelchair. Daniel, she seems able to get through to him, something we haven't been able to do no matter how hard we've tried. If she can help him find a purpose to his life, then maybe everything else would fall into place—the baptism, the settling down.

"I talked to Taylor yesterday before we left the city. She's willing to help in whatever way she can, both with Jacob and on the farm. She can take him around to talk to other Amish tradesmen. We wouldn't have time to do that with him, what with the harvest coming soon, David's wedding to prepare for, and the demands of Jacob's at-home physical therapy."

"Doesn't she have to work at her newspaper business?" Daniel asked gruffly.

"*Ja*, but she can work out of their Lancaster office and from our farm, if we would permit her to use her computer and phone in our home."

"Absolutely not. I will not tolerate her ringing phone all hours of the day and night and will not permit her computer use out in the open where our children can see it."

Sarah had anticipated her husband's objection to Taylor's technology and she had thought of a solution during the train ride home yesterday.

"If we opened up a corner of the attic for her, she could work there, away from the rest of the family, and we could tell her she couldn't use her cell phone in front of us, she'd have to go to our phone shed or the attic."

"How would we explain all that to Bishop Lapp?"

"We would explain the reasons, how we think it will help Jacob, and that it's only temporary. He'll understand and will also be able to explain it to others in our community who might not be so understanding."

Daniel was quiet for several minutes and Sarah knew better than to pressure him. Finally, he said, "Do you think the disruption of having her here is worth the good she could possibly do for Jacob?"

"I think God sent Taylor to Jacob for a reason," Sarah answered.

"We'll try it for a month and then we'll see," Daniel said, and turned onto his side, but his eyes did not close, not for a long time.

15

CONNOR RAN HIS hand through his hair, trying to decide how to respond. Taylor had just told him she wanted to live with the Yoders and work out of the Lancaster office for a month or two, maybe more. They were alone in his office and his assistant had been instructed to hold all calls. What had started as a quiet Tuesday morning had just turned into a headache. He should have known something was up when Taylor came into the office that morning without Becca.

Since the Libations Incident, Taylor had insisted on either bringing Becca to work or working from home to maintain oversight. Becca had asked to spend the day with Lauren at the pool; once Taylor had determined Sylvie would be around to keep an eye on the two of them, she told Connor, she had relented. Now he knew why. She had wanted to talk to him alone.

Lancaster was only ninety minutes from their home office; Connor could drive up or Taylor could drive down at any time and she could certainly be connected to everyone by email and cell phone and Skype. But the idea unsettled him and he wasn't sure why, apart from the obvious—he would miss her.

"Why can't you just visit them? Is it necessary to actually live there?" he asked.

"Jacob wants me around for moral support, and maybe I can help him get into college if that's what he decides to do."

"But his future is not your responsibility. From what I understand, you and he are attempting to buck hundreds of years of cultural tradition. The Amish don't want their children to attend high school or college. Why get in the middle of what could ultimately become a family and community crisis?"

"He asked me to help. He's desperate."

"Okay, for the sake of argument, let's say he passes his GED, decides to go to college, and even gets admitted somewhere. What do you think his parents are going to say when they realize you have facilitated the leaving of their son? I don't see this ending pleasantly."

Taylor hadn't expected her father to object so strenuously to her plan. She was thrown a little off guard but was determined to make him understand her reasoning.

"Dad, you didn't see his face when he was sitting in the classroom at Penn. He wants to learn, he craves it. How can it be right to deny him something he desires so badly? You've always told me to accept challenges outside my comfort zone, to do what makes me uncomfortable because that's how I'll grow. So that's what I'm doing and so is Jacob.

"I'm obviously not looking forward to angering his parents but maybe the end justifies the means. They're okay with *rumspringa* and they let their children choose whether to be baptized. Jacob is exercising his right to choose. Or maybe it won't get ugly. Maybe they'll realize how important school is to Jacob, that it would make him happy, and they'll decide to give him their blessing or at least not actively try to thwart him."

Connor frowned. "You need a reality check. They don't care whether he's happy. They care whether he will dishonor their God and how that will affect his eternal life and theirs. They would gladly sacrifice his happiness for the chance to save his soul. And I'm not sure their children really do have a choice.

They're indoctrinated from birth. They know they're going to lose their cocoon of safety and security as well as their family and friends if they leave the community. A couple years of *rumspringa* is not a choice, it's an illusion of a choice."

Taylor took a deep breath. "You may be right. But I have to try. I have to do this."

Connor mentally debated what he should say next, hesitant to bring up a subject that had long vexed him. He decided to plunge ahead.

"Taylor, for God's sake, what is your attraction to these people? Yes, I understand they are humble, honest, frugal, and live their beliefs. But they're like a cult—they reject individuality in favor of community."

"Well, how individual are we as a society, Dad? We follow the same fashion and music trends, pursue whatever celebrities do, adopt the next technology gadget, whether it suits our lifestyle or not, and endless advertising pitches dictate our choices.

"But think what the Amish do have. They're content with living off the land and with little materialism. They're not slaves to the next big thing. They don't take Social Security or Medicare or medical insurance or food stamps or welfare checks, because they genuinely care about and look after each other. Kids are raised at home, work alongside their families, and actually see their parents every day, all through the day. There is little violent crime, no alcohol or drug abuse among adults, no divorce. Their lives don't revolve around shopping or fame or technology or on making piles of money. They find meaning in faith, community, and hard work."

Connor leaned back in his chair and locked eyes with his daughter. "Granted, you've reached out to a group you initially didn't understand and found common ground. But despite your rationalizations, aren't you trying to change what makes the Amish unique, at least for two of the Yoders? You want more education for Jacob and you want to modernize Becca." He rushed on before Taylor could respond.

"Is something else going on here, Taylor? Is your real motive to help Jacob or are you running away from your own life? You mentioned before that you're rethinking your future. If you focus your energy on helping someone else, you don't have time to concentrate on what, if anything, needs fixing in your own life."

Taylor was quiet for a few moments. "I don't know, Dad. But maybe helping Jacob will, in the end, help me, too."

TAYLOR WANTED TO make dinner tonight with no help from me. I was skeptical since she hasn't had much practice in the kitchen. I went with her to the office this morning and while she worked getting things wrapped up to come live with us, I read "Jane Eyre" in the conference room. Around noon, Taylor suggested we have lunch at the Italian Market. I can now add spizzato sandwiches to my list of new favorite foods. The sandwich was so good, filled with veal chunks and mushrooms and green peppers, I had two. We sat outside on Ninth Street at a table with an umbrella and I could smell all the different food—the bread and pastries from the bakeries and fish and cheeses and pizza and herbs. Taylor said it was like watching a real-life slice of immigrant life a hundred years ago. The closest I'll ever get to Italy. Something about the atmosphere must've inspired Taylor because she decided to buy some homemade pasta and make dinner.

She bought big round cheese ravioli and tomato sauce from Talluto's and a right-out-of-the-oven crusty loaf of Italian bread, and then she bought cannoli from Isgro Pastries for dessert. We spent the rest of the afternoon back at the office, where she stored the cannoli and ravioli in the office fridge.

I sat and watched her from the kitchen counter as she made dinner tonight. "How hard can this be?" she asked. "I boil water for the ravioli and microwave the sauce." She did great until she tried to pour the pot of water and ravioli into the colander in the sink. Water splashed out of the sink and down the cabinets and a little onto her bare foot. She screamed and jumped up and down and the rest of the ravioli flew out of the pot onto the counter and a few on the floor. "Maria cleaned today," she reassured me as she picked the ravioli off the floor, "so five second rule applies."

After she cleaned up, she put the tomato sauce in the microwave but didn't cover the bowl so sauce splattered all over the inside of her microwave. Once she cleaned that up and made the salad, we were ready to eat. We had taken a couple of bites (so good) when she remembered the bread and jumped up to cut the loaf. She seemed a little frazzled after all that, but I assured her the dinner was delicious. I wonder if she'll ever cook again.

Cannoli, which originated in Sicily, are the most scrumptious food! The crispy tube-shaped pastry shells are filled with ricotta cheese. Melts in your mouth. There's a few left and we're taking them home. We'll probably have to hide them from the twins or nobody else will get to eat them.

After dinner, we called Jacob. We talked to him on speakerphone and then Taylor left to take a shower so Jacob and I talked alone.

I asked him how he felt about going home and he said he missed everyone and was glad to be leaving the hospital. But he said he felt guilty, too, because he would need help with his physical therapy and that would be another chore for the family. Therapists will come to our home a couple times to show us how to help him with his stretching exercises. Ordinarily, he would go to a therapy place two to three times a week but since we have no insurance and can't afford the expense, the family will handle his therapy.

He said he'll also feel guilty hanging out in his wheelchair while everyone milks cows or works the fields. He hopes he can find a way to be useful. I tried to tell him how happy we were simply because he was alive and that helping with his therapy was in no way a chore. But he didn't want to hear it. He has already made up his mind to live with the burden of guilt.

⌒〜

THE MID-AUGUST HEAT in the city was oppressive, even in the late afternoon, but Becca was reluctant to leave the pool.

She and Lauren had spent most of the day relaxing by the water. Lauren was leaving the next day to vacation at her parents' second home in the Berkshires and Becca was leaving Saturday. Their time together was over.

Becca had learned much about *Englisher* teens by spending time with Lauren. On those days when Taylor had worked from home, she and Lauren had picnicked in Rittenhouse Park, lazed by the pool, or chatted and laughed in each other's bedrooms. For Becca, it was nice to have someone her age to talk to and although Lauren came from a different world, she didn't judge Becca and seemed genuinely interested in her life. For Lauren, it was a relief to not be expected to shop constantly, or drink and party, like her other friends from school. Being with Becca was refreshing and easy and they enjoyed talking about boys and their families and their dreams for the future.

"I guess today's the last time you'll wear your tankini," Lauren said. "Can you imagine your father seeing you in that?"

Becca laughed. "He'd have a stroke. But I'm going to keep it. Maybe someday when I get married, I can wear it if my husband and I go to the beach."

"Will it be hard going back to Amish life after all this freedom you've had and all the things you've seen and experienced?" Lauren asked.

"I'll still be in *rumspringa* when I go home, but it will seem tame compared to what I've done in the city. I can't wait to see Katie and the twins and the rest of my family. I hope Taylor and I can keep on reading and maybe she'll take me to different restaurants in Lancaster. But I think my life will be mostly the same as when I left."

"What about John King?"

Becca blushed. "We'll have to see about that."

They fell quiet, then, watching the pool area get more crowded as folks came home from work. Becca gathered her sunscreen, sunglasses, and towel and stuffed them into her tote bag. "I guess I should go in," she said as she put on her cover-up. "Taylor will be home soon."

"I'm going to miss you, Becca." Lauren said. "You are so . . . real."

Becca looked down, embarrassed. "Have a good vacation and good luck when you go back to school." They hugged.

"Bye." Lauren watched Becca walk away, then turned onto her stomach on the lounge chair, rested her head on her arms, and closed her eyes.

"I BOUGHT SOME clothes today suitable for the farm," Taylor told Becca as they ate take-out cheese steaks on the terrace. "I shopped at lunch. Now I have boots for the barn and sneaks and another pair of jeans and t-shirts and shorts ... long shorts," she said as she saw Becca's concerned look. "It's the middle of August. I can't cover myself up like you do. It's too hot. I can't imagine living without air conditioning but I guess if you all can do it, so can I. I'm also packing a few work out-fits for when I go to the Lancaster office."

Becca looked out over the city, savoring her last Philly cheese steak and trying to glue the view into her memory.

"There are ways to keep cool in the summer," Becca said. "The barn is cool since we run fans for the cows. We can splash in the creek and it's nice and shady under the big oak tree in the front yard."

They watched the Travel Channel after dinner, both aware it was their last night alone at home together. They had plans in the city the next night and then they were leaving on Saturday.

"I guess we won't watch any more TV together," Taylor said as they sat next to each other on the couch, a bowl of popcorn between them.

"Well, if we do, it won't be at my house," Becca joked. "I'll miss watching movies with you and our armchair travels. Isn't

Greece beautiful? Look at that sunset on Santorini and those white buildings built right on the cliffs leading down to the sea."

Taylor got up from the couch, left the room, and came back carrying a wrapped box, which she handed to Becca. "So you can travel all over the world without a TV," she said.

"Oh!" Becca said as she opened the box filled with several coffee table books with beautiful photographs of Italy, Greece, France, the Far East, Egypt, and India.

"These will take the place of our armchair travels," Becca said, as she caressed the cover of the books, one at a time.

THE GRASSY FIELD lay misty and quiet in the pre-dawn morning; the crew had unfurled and inflated the brilliant rainbow-colored hot air balloon and it stood ready for passengers.

"I've just decided I'm scared," Becca whispered to Taylor as the pilot helped each passenger climb into the wicker basket. The roar of the propane burners shattered the quiet as the three-story nylon balloon began to lift. The pilot explained how the burners warm the air in the balloon, enabling it to climb. Longer burns provide lift, she said, and shorter burns maintain altitude or allow the balloon to descend. As the air temperature cools, gravity pulls the balloon down. She told her passengers the ride would be about an hour, the distance four miles. The balloon would then land in a field and the chase crew would deflate the balloon and pack up the burners and the basket on the trailer. They would then enjoy a champagne toast, or Mimosas if preferred, as well as croissants, pastries, and bagels.

Becca had been wide awake and excited from the moment her alarm had gone off at four o'clock that morning, an hour Taylor had called "insane."

"I'm used to getting up early in the morning," Becca had said. She grinned. "Pretty soon, so will you."

Taylor had decided to redeem the birthday gift certificate for the sunrise champagne hot air balloon ride from her father as a farewell to her and Becca's time in the city.

Becca watched as the ground receded, the chase crew became a mere speck, and the balloon lifted above the trees. In the east, the sun peeked over the horizon and the sky glowed gold, the early morning haze evaporating as the balloon climbed to a thousand feet. The rolling hills and streams of southern Chester County spread beneath them, as did historic stone estates and sprawling horse farms, with the cityscape of Philadelphia in the distance.

"How adventurous do you feel?" the pilot asked her passengers. "Who's up for a pond splash and dash?" The other passengers nodded enthusiastically. Becca glanced warily at Taylor, who shrugged; she wasn't sure what a pond splash and dash was either.

The balloon descended slowly, down, down. Below the balloon lay what looked like a puddle, but the puddle soon became a large pond and the balloon was heading straight for it. Becca moved closer to Taylor and watched anxiously; the other passengers chatted excitedly. The pilot turned on the burners and just as the corner of the basket splashed into the pond, the balloon began to rise again, heading toward a grove of trees, where a group of deer stood. The passengers cheered, the deer scattered.

"How about a tree grab?" the pilot asked, and within minutes, the balloon itself had cleared the trees but the basket hovered near the branches. Taylor reached out and grabbed at the leaves. "Becca, hurry before we lift," Taylor cried, and Becca, laughing, swatted at the tree branch as the balloon continued to climb.

"Are you still scared?" Taylor asked Becca.

"I was so busy looking at the view, I forgot to be scared."

Once the balloon had risen again and the roar of the burners had ceased, the silence was total, as the balloon floated, drifting with the wind. Taylor thought if she closed her eyes, she wouldn't even realize they were moving. She observed the picturesque landscape below and realized she should feel on top of the world. She was part of a thriving business she would one day own and every material thing she desired was attainable. But she didn't feel like she owned a piece of the world; she felt more like it owned her.

The landscape below also inspired Becca to consider her place in the world. Her life was like a speck seen from high above, a tiny corner of the world, though a somewhat larger corner than three months ago. Her life would always be small yet rich in its own way. She wondered if she could be content, even happy, in her small plot of life. Or should she grab a bigger piece of the world now opening up for her?

THE TAMARIND TREE in Asia grows up to seventy feet tall and its fruit makes a sauce popular in Thai food. How do they harvest fruit from a tree that tall? Taylor and I ate dinner tonight at Tamarind, a restaurant on South Street. I can now add Thai food to my list of new food.

For appetizers, we had tofu (which is made from soybeans) stuffed with shredded carrots and diced cucumbers, deep fried, with peanut sauce. Taylor had chicken woonsen soup, which is noodle soup with chicken, vegetables, mushrooms, and tofu. I had chicken tom khah, coconut milk soup with chicken, fresh lemon grass, and kaffer leaf. Our waiter told us kaffer leaf was from a Thai lime plant. Herbs and spices like lemon grass and kaffer, cilantro, coriander, and cumin give Thai food its special flavor, he said. For dinner, we each had tasty flat noodles (mine with chicken, hers with pork) with Thai red chiles and tamarind sauce.

Then another music treat. We walked over to the Great Plaza at Penn's Landing for a Smooth Jazz Summer Nights concert by a saxophonist and his band. I was sad about leaving the city, but this jazz music perked me right up. Jazz, gospel, classical, piano, religious hymns, opera, the modern music we hear on the radio in Taylor's car, movie music, it all makes you feel good. Going to a Sunday singing at home now will seem a little boring but I guess I'll get used to it once I get back to the routine.

I'm worried that I'll forget everything I've been exposed to: the taste of all the unusual foods, the different moods of music, the energy of crowds, the high rise views of the city, the scene of fields and valleys from a basket in the sky, the richness of Taylor's penthouse, the feel of silk and denim clothes, how tall I am in heels, the sun on my body in a bathing suit, the sand between my toes, Monet's water lilies, stained glass windows in a Catholic Church, Jewish men in yarmulkes, Muslims laying face down to pray. Now that I've experienced all this, can I give it up forever?

I finished packing when we got home from the jazz concert. I threw the rest of my lip gloss away since the tube was almost finished anyway. I wrapped some shorts and tees around my leaping dolphin figure and the seashells. My jeans and silk shirt, sandals, and bathing suit I will keep in my hope chest at home. The flip flops I can wear around the farm or even out in the community during the rest of the summer. I'm bringing "Jane Eyre" home to finish reading and Taylor gave me her copies of "To Kill A Mockingbird," "Pride and Prejudice" and "Little Women," which I'll share with Katie and maybe even read to Emma when she gets a little older. The coffee table books I'll keep on my bureau so I can look through them and "travel" whenever I want. Taylor said I can keep my cell phone as long as I want, so I'll use it (cautiously and not in front of Dat) until Dat finds out and makes me give it up.

I'm now lying in bed as I finish this. Tomorrow, I'll ride back to Lancaster with Taylor while Mamm and Dat bring Jacob home in a van. I look around my Butterscotch Room, snuggle into the pillows, and wonder if I'll be back.

❧

JACOB SAT PATIENTLY in his wheelchair looking out the window of his room. He was dressed in Amish pants, shirt, and suspenders, an outfit his mother had brought with her last week when she visited. His new wheelchair had been delivered earlier that week and he had spent time adjusting to it.

He expected his parents soon and was ready to go. After one last gaze at the city below, he turned away from the window and wheeled himself over to the bed. His bag was packed, full of his rehab shorts and sweats and t-shirts, as well as books and magazines he had read during his stay and letters from his family. His Phillies hat lay on top; he placed his cell phone under it then zipped the bag closed. He had already said good-bye to his therapists and his case manager, who had wished him luck and told him to keep in touch. He would see everyone again in about six months, when he returned for a check-up.

He had mixed feelings about leaving. He hadn't made many close friends during his stay, except for Eric, but he had enjoyed the people he met, and there had been rules, routines, and hard work, which he had appreciated, not only because he was learning to manage his disability, but because being absorbed took his mind off the nagging question that had been dogging him for months, even years: What to do with his life?

What he would miss most about Bayard was the sense that his future was his own, that whatever direction he wanted to go was under his control, as long as he was cautious and took care of himself. He dreaded the hopelessness he had felt at home before the accident, when he had rebelled, with disastrous results, against succumbing to the future mapped out for him. He felt more certain about what he didn't want to do than what he did. Life on a farm was out of the question. He wanted more than anything to further his education but was realistic about the odds. He had decided to depend on Taylor to help him figure it out. So for a while, at least, he would still have one foot stuck in Amish soil, the other pointed in a different direction.

16

"**E**MMA, I NEED to rinse the wheel. Move out of the way," Joseph demanded.

"I'm not done washing the door, just hold your horses," Emma said, then squealed as Joseph turned the hose on the buggy's right front wheel, spraying the bottom of Emma's dress and bare legs and feet in the process. She turned toward her brother, arm raised to throw the sudsy sponge at him.

"Hey, knock it off, you two," Jacob said, as he supervised the twins washing of the family buggy. "Joseph, I will take over the hose if you can't handle it responsibly. Emma, you missed a spot on the door window, top right corner."

The twins immediately turned their full attention to the task at hand. They were excited to have Jacob home again, and as typical eight-year-olds, they idolized their eldest brother and wanted to please him.

"If you do a good job on our buggy, maybe *Daadi* and *Mammi* will let you wash theirs."

"We will, Jacob, you'll see," Joseph responded. "And we could've washed yours, too, 'cept now it's all wrecked."

"Thanks for reminding me," Jacob murmured, then stifled a grin as Joseph tripped over the wash bucket and forlornly watched the soapy water soak into the ground as Emma called him a "lunk head."

Taylor watched the scene from the open window of the bedroom she shared with Becca as she changed the two twin beds with linens she had just pulled off the clothesline. To an outsider watching from a distance, the buggy washing appeared a normal family scene, but Taylor knew the behind-the-scenes story.

Jacob had been home only a few days, everyone walking on eggshells around him. The day before, a physical therapist had visited and had taught Sarah, Becca, and Katie Jacob's therapy routine. Taylor busied herself in the kitchen, but Jacob's bedroom door was open, and Taylor saw Katie nervously wringing her hands and Jacob seemed embarrassed by the attention.

David and Daniel had headed off to the fields right after breakfast, David looking backward at Jacob still seated at the table in his wheelchair. Jacob got up for breakfast but not in time to milk the cows. Taylor sensed he was unsure of his place, what he should do, and his brother and father weren't yet certain what he was capable of physically and didn't want to rush him. Things were awkward and off balance, but everyone tried to be pleasant and upbeat and maintain the normal routine.

Right after breakfast, Taylor had helped Sarah with the laundry, learned how to use the air pressure-powered washing machine, and had hung the laundry on a clothesline connected by a pulley system from the back porch of the main house to the buggy garage.

All morning, as she had performed her various duties—cleaning up the kitchen after breakfast, sweeping the back porch, shaking the dirt out of the numerous throw rugs covering the hardwood floors—she caught sight of the laundry flapping high overhead in the breeze, organized by garment so all the men's shirts hung together, as did all the women's dresses, all the trousers, all the socks, and she had a hard time reconciling the self she was in her other life with the self that hung laundry by hand.

She had completed her assigned chores quickly and efficiently but without one hundred percent focus—she thought about the phone calls she needed to make for work—yet she couldn't help but notice the clean, fresh outdoorsy smell of the linens as she made the beds. Maybe it's worth sacrificing a clothes dryer to enjoy this, Taylor thought as she breathed in deeply the smell from the pillowcase. But then she pictured hanging and removing the clothes in the middle of February, winter winds howling, and decided a dryer also had its good points.

Becca's second floor room was sparsely furnished: twin beds covered with brightly colored quilts Becca and her mother had made, a bureau, an end table between the two beds, a worn round braided rug on the hardwood floor, a hope chest at the foot of the bed her Uncle Esh had made for her sixteenth birthday, and a small closet. On the end table sat a battery alarm clock, a flashlight—"In case we have to go to the bathroom in the middle of the night," Becca had explained—and a Bible. On the bureau top rested a small hand mirror, a wooden hairbrush, and the travel books Taylor had given her before they left Philadelphia. The walls were bare and the open windows had dark green shades raised to let the breeze and sunshine in.

Also on the second floor were David and Joseph's bedroom, Katie and Emma's, and Daniel and Sarah's, which used to be Jacob's, as well as two bathrooms, one for each gender, which Sarah and Daniel also shared.

As soon as she finished the beds, Taylor planned to head to her "office" in the attic, which she reached by pull-down stairs in the second floor hallway. Daniel had helped her set up a makeshift desk using an old pine table and rocking chair gathering dust in a corner of the attic. He had repaired a missing spoke from the chair and Sarah had given her an old chair pad.

The first time Taylor entered the attic, she nearly melted from the mid-August heat and so had gone out and bought two battery-operated fans, which did little more than blow around the stifling air. But she was determined not to complain, mostly because she had no choice. Daniel forbid her to talk on the phone in front of the family, but she carried at least one of her phones set on vibrate with her at all times. She charged her iPhone and BlackBerry in her car and her laptop at the *Lancaster Post* office. In order to enable email and Internet use in the attic, she set up her phones as Wi-Fi hotspots and also used a MiFi device for her laptop.

A half hour later, Taylor reached up on tiptoes and pulled down the attic stairs. The rest of the family knew when they saw the stairs down not to disturb Taylor. The first thing she did after turning on her laptop was peel off her clothes. Around the Yoder family, despite the August heat, Taylor wore long walking shorts and a polo shirt, her concession to their sense of modesty; she walked around in bare feet, unless working in the barn, as did the rest of the women and the twins. Taylor had yet to see David or Daniel without boots. But in the attic, she changed into short shorts and a tank top, and turned on the fans.

She picked up her phone and settled into the rocking chair, ready to do her *real* work.

"*MAMM SAID* WE need twelve pounds of blackberries for preserving and to sell at our stand," Becca said.

"I love blackberry jam," Emma said, skipping along, her bucket banging against her legs. "*Mamm* said I can help preserve this year."

The early morning sun peaked out of the clouds as Katie and Taylor, walking briskly behind Emma and Becca, crossed the footbridge over Stoney Creek and made their way to the woods behind the tobacco fields, where a large blackberry batch grew wild. Each carried a plastic bucket and Becca instructed Taylor to pull only the deep black plump berries and to reach in between the stems to find the hidden fruit.

"Taylor, I want to pick near you," Emma said, as Becca and Katie ventured further into the patch. "Do you like blackberries? They're my favorite, but I also like cherries and strawberries, too. Do you like blackberry jam? Wait 'til you taste *Mamm's*, she makes the best jam."

For the past several days, Emma had been Taylor's shadow, following her everywhere except to the attic, chattering incessantly.

For every handful of berries Emma picked, several went into her mouth. In a short while, her lips and teeth were stained black. Taylor furtively snapped a picture of a smiling Emma with her cell phone; she had no future plans for the pictures she took of the Yoders, nor did she occasionally glance at them on her phone, yet she nonetheless felt the desire to take them. At the end of an hour, they all sat under the shade of the trees to rest. Becca and Katie talked quietly together, and Emma, leaning against Taylor, almost nodded off in the warm summer air.

From where she sat, Taylor looked out over the Yoder farmland—the rows of ripening golden tobacco leaves and beyond that the tall stalks of cattle corn—and the meandering Stoney Creek. She reached into her bucket, popped a couple blackberries into her mouth, closed her eyes, and savored the sweet burst of flavor.

Later that morning, as they walked back to the house, Taylor looked down at her hands and quipped, "My other BlackBerry never stains my hands."

❧

SARAH RAN HER kitchen during preserve time like a drill sergeant on a mission. She had already frozen a batch of blackberries for her family's future use in fruit salads or on cereal or in pancakes or muffins. Emma helped Mary put the blackberries in containers to sell at the vegetable stand. The rest of that morning's pickings were to be "put up" as blackberry jam.

Becca and Katie had mashed the berries through a sieve to remove the seeds and were simmering them on the stove with lemon juice, fruit pectin, and sugar.

"Now girls, stir the berries until the sugar completely dissolves and then increase the heat and boil the mixture for five or six minutes," Sarah instructed. In the meantime, she and Taylor had sterilized a half dozen quart mason jars in boiling water.

When the mixture was ready, they formed an assembly line at the kitchen table. Sarah carefully poured the jam into the sterilized jars with a small funnel. Becca wiped the rims with a cloth and Katie used a narrow, rubber spatula to remove any trapped air bubbles in the jars. Emma, with Mary's help, screwed the lids on tightly. Taylor then placed the jars back into a large pot of boiling water for another five minutes. "To be sure we kill all the organisms that cause food to spoil," Sarah explained.

After the allotted time, Sarah removed each quart jar from the pot with tongs and placed it on dishtowels on the counter to cool for the rest of the day. Later, Sarah would label the jars and store them in the large pantry off the kitchen, saving one jar to slather on toast the next morning, the rest to be used throughout the winter.

As they all helped clean up the kitchen, Taylor heard popping sounds coming from the jars.

"Uh-oh," she said, taking the washed pot lid from Sarah to dry.

"That's actually a good sound," Sarah said. "It means the vacuum effect has taken place, which causes the lids to pop down and seal."

"I know preserving is the epitome of going green," Taylor said, "but it took us all morning to pick the blackberries and preserve them. Wouldn't it be easier to just buy jam when you go to the grocery store?"

Sarah smiled. "You tell me tomorrow after you taste the jam whether it was worth the trouble."

"Well, at least that's the end of the preserving," Taylor said.

"Oh, no. Next week we're preserving tomato sauce, with tomatoes from our garden. And now we have just enough time to prepare lunch before the men come in."

WEEDS PEEKED OUT of the moist dark soil and Taylor hated them. No matter how many she pulled, dozens remained. Up and down the rows of the vegetable garden she crawled, her fingernails encrusted with dirt—"I need to trim my damn nails and be done with it," Taylor mumbled to herself—her knees dirty, the sweat trickling down her back. She was cranky and hot.

Next to her, Becca hummed quietly, her fingers moving deftly; it irritated Taylor that neither the heat nor the chore bothered Becca. She consoled herself with the thought that as soon as she finished weeding, she could escape to her attic office, where even though it was just as hot, at least it wasn't full of dirt.

As Taylor rounded the last row, she saw at the edge of the garden several staked plants that didn't look like the tomato, cucumber, zucchini, carrot or basil plants in the rest of the garden.

"What're these?" she asked Becca.

"They're sunflowers. I planted the seeds when I came home in late July to get my cast off, right after I saw Van Gogh's painting in the museum. There are ten of them and they should grow to about eight feet. I can't wait to see them bloom."

"I'm glad you were inspired by art but I'm outta here," Taylor said as she pulled one final weed. "I'll be in the attic. Yell up the stairs when you need my help with milking or supper."

THE SINGSONG VOICE of the auctioneer rang out over the front lawn of the Abram Miller farm. The crowd, most of which had been in attendance since the pancake breakfast that morning, knew the proceeds of the auction would benefit the Daniel Yoder family, and many of them, as well as Amish from other church districts, had generously donated food, crafts, furniture, and quilts. The Miller family lived on the northeast edge of the same church district as the Yoders and had offered their farm for the auction.

As was the custom, the Yoder family was not in attendance because, Becca told Taylor, their presence should not influence anyone to buy. Taylor, however, had no such inhibition. As she walked the grounds she drew some stares and whisper but no one was sure of her identity. The mainly Amish crowd included a fair number of *Englishers*, mostly neighbors of the Amish who had learned of the benefit auction by word-of-mouth.

Taylor was curious to see an Amish auction, but she also intended to contribute to the fundraising in a way that would not embarrass the Yoders, who assumed she was working at the *Lancaster Post* office that Saturday morning.

Tables laden with homemade baked goods—pies, cakes, cupcakes, bread, and donuts—and crafts such as table runners, potholders, decorative pillows, and baskets dotted the lawn. Food stands sold barbeque chicken, hamburgers, hotdogs, and soda. Dozens of colorful quilts in various sizes hung on display, with names like Penn Dutch Star, Heart and Nine Patch, Log Cabin Dahlia, and Double Wedding Ring, all tagged with prices starting at three hundred dollars, some significantly more. Taylor noticed the *Englishers* seemed more than willing to spend to own one or more of the beautifully made quilts.

She sat in the audience with her bid number and in quick succession placed winning bids on an oak high back rocking chair, a cedar chest, a porch glider, and three quilts, all of which she paid for, then donated back to be re-auctioned. She then headed off to work.

A week later, as Taylor folded laundry on the Yoder's back porch, she overheard through the open kitchen window Sarah tell Mary the auction had raised a significant amount of money but even with the community Church Aid they had previously received, it still wasn't enough to retire the hospital and rehab bills. Daniel and Sarah had paid several thousand dollars from their own savings and also made monthly payments to the hospital and Bayard. Taylor gathered from the conversation that Mary and Levi had insisted on paying a portion of the bills, although Daniel had initially refused their help.

"We still have a little money in savings," Sarah said, "but Daniel wants to give it to David for a wedding gift. I'm not sure that's what we should do with the money but he is adamant."

"The district will probably organize another fundraiser, maybe later in the year after the harvest," Mary said. "All you can do for now is pay what you can and pray. God will provide."

Out on the porch, Taylor wondered what more she could do to help.

EMMA STOOD AT the bottom of the attic stairs and yelled, "Taylor, *bischt du faddich?*"

"What?" Taylor yelled back.

"*Bischt du faddich?* Are you finished? Is your work done? We're going to have a picnic under the oak tree by the pond and wade in the creek. Come with us."

"Emma, I can't. I still have work to do. Maybe later."

"All right," Emma said, her disappointment apparent in her voice. "But we only have a little while before milking time so you may be too late."

"Okay, fine," Taylor said, turning off her laptop. "I'll come down for a few minutes." Since she'd return to the attic shortly, Taylor didn't bother changing out of her shorts and tank.

In the kitchen, Sarah was making a lemon pound cake for supper. Becca and Katie had packed a picnic basket with brownies, pretzel sticks, seedless watermelon cut in chunks, homemade bread, a jar of blackberry jam, and plastic cups, paper plates, a knife, and that week's *Die Botschaft* newspaper. Emma carried a jug of lemonade and Joseph had blankets under his arm for sitting on the grass. Katie blushed when she saw Taylor's outfit and quickly looked away. Becca, memories of her own skimpy city summer still fresh, hardly noticed, but Joseph's eyes widened and Emma said, "You have lots of leg."

"*Dat* and David are in the field but said they'd walk over for some nice cold lemonade in a little while," Joseph said. "*Mamm*, are you coming?"

"I'm going to finish this cake and then I have some sewing to do," Sarah said. "Katie and Becca, make sure you watch the twins around the pond."

As they walked out the front door and down the lawn towards the pond, Taylor noticed Jacob sitting under the oak tree reading. He looked up as he saw them approaching, closed his book, and set it on the ground beside his wheelchair.

They spread the blankets under the shade of the oak and chaos reigned as the twins and Katie dived into the picnic basket at once.

"Hold on! Hold on!" Jacob said. "Let Becca spread everything out on the blanket, then you can dig in." While the others were focused on the food, Jacob eyed Taylor sitting next to him, bent over and whispered, "Looks like I'm not the only rebel around here."

Taylor grinned. "It's so darn hot in the attic. Your dad will probably give me a hard time if he comes over. Here, have a brownie and some watermelon," she said, handing him a plate.

Taylor slathered blackberry jam on a piece of bread, leaned back against the tree, and took a bite.

"Delicious," she said, slowly chewing and relishing each bite. "I now understand why you make your own jam."

After she finished the bread, she ate several chunks of watermelon, the juice dribbling down her chin. For once, she wasn't eating merely for nutrition and sustenance or as an excuse to get together with someone to discuss work. She concentrated on the flavors exploding in her mouth, thinking in that moment only of the food and her enjoyment of it.

Katie picked up *Die Botschaft* and riffled through it.

"Is that an Amish newspaper?" Taylor asked. "What does the title mean?"

"It means 'The Message,'" Katie said. "It's a weekly newspaper written by unpaid Old Order Amish and Mennonite scribes who write letters about everyday stuff that happens in their communities. We've subscribed to it for as long as I can remember."

Taylor scanned the sixty or so pages of the paper with interest. "It's like chatting with a neighbor over a fence," she said, reading some of the letters. "Here's one about shelling peas under the shade of oak trees in nearby Ephrata, a pitchfork accident in Ohio, an appendectomy in Minnesota, the birth of twins in Missouri. There are lots of ads but no photos."

"To the best of my *kenn*, knowledge, no photos are allowed," Katie said.

"It's like a local newspaper without news—no politics, no murders or other crime, no sports. Just human interest stories. And I bet this paper has no problem with declining subscription revenue." She folded the paper and returned it to Katie. "There's something familiar about this paper, but I'm not sure where I would've come across it."

Joseph jammed several pretzel sticks in his mouth, gulped the rest of his lemonade, then rolled up his pant legs.

"Beat you in the water," he yelled, and Emma close behind, dashed into the creek. Katie and Becca hiked their dresses above their knees with their hands and followed, laughing and splashing each other without regard to their clothes. Jacob wheeled himself over to the creek to keep an eye on things and Taylor sat on the edge and dipped her feet in.

"Why don't they swim in the pond?" Taylor asked.

"It's probably six or seven feet deep," Jacob answered. "The twins don't know how to swim yet."

Taylor noticed the wistfulness in Jacob's eyes as he watched his siblings romp.

"This can't be easy for you," she said.

He didn't answer right away, then said, "This part of our life makes my insides knot when I think about leaving."

The lazy summer afternoon, the easy camaraderie, the antics of the twins, all made Taylor forget about returning to work, until she saw Daniel and David in the distance, walking toward them. She wasn't in the mood for a confrontation with Daniel about her dress or lack thereof.

She jumped up, muttered "back to work," and quickly walked back to the house and her attic oven.

MAMM ASKED ME yesterday morning while we baked bread how I felt about being back home. I told her I was getting back into the routine and everything was fine. But that wasn't quite the truth. I am getting used to being back on the farm, what with all the chores and the animals and the noise, and it is so good to see Katie and David and my parents and the twins and Mammi and Daadi, but if I want to be honest with myself, I do miss the city. With Taylor, there was always something new to experience. A new food, a new activity, a new place to visit, things I had never seen or done before. And once I got used to

it, it was great having some quiet time, either by myself or alone with Taylor. Here, there's somebody around all the time. I love my family and I love working the farm and contributing to our life together. It's just that I feel like I spent the summer learning new things and "broadening my horizons," as Taylor would say, and now I'm back here and things are the same, not necessarily boring, but the same. One thing that's different. I don't have as much time to write in this journal. Katie's calling me to help with dinner.

"THE FIELDS ARE alive with the sound of shearing," Becca sang loudly to the tune of "The Hills Are Alive" from *The Sound of Music*, as she cut a four-foot tobacco stalk, its broad leaves slightly yellowish, with long-handled shears, "the stalks they have grown for a thousand years." Taylor, working one row over with a hatchet, laughed out loud.

"The fields fill my heart with the sound of shearing, my hatchet wants to shear every stalk it sees," she continued the tune.

The Yoder family, with the exception of Mary, Emma, and Jacob, were harvesting the six acres of tobacco. Once cut, the stalks and leaves would lie in the sun for a couple days to wilt, the start of the curing process where the moisture in the leaves begins to dry out. The wilted stalks would then be spudded, or speared, onto a lath, a wooden stick topped by a metal spear, and carted to the tobacco shed to hang for a few months to finish curing.

Taylor stopped for a minute to rest, her arm tired from the hacking, and she was hot in her long shorts. She didn't know how the Yoder women tolerated working that energetically in the heat wearing long dresses and aprons. Taylor could hear both David and Daniel several rows over chastising Joseph for cutting the stalk too high. She heard Sarah and Katie discussing what Mary and Emma were preparing for the noon meal.

"When's your Dad coming?" Becca asked Taylor.

"He'll be here at the farm on Monday but will come up Sunday night and stay at the Stoney Creek B & B. I'm looking forward to seeing him."

Daniel had told the family at supper two nights ago the tobacco was ready to harvest and all hands were required on deck for the next three weeks. Taylor had hastily talked to her father by phone right after the meal and had then cornered Daniel later that night and asked him if he could use another pair of hands to help with the harvest.

Daniel, reluctant to take on an inexperienced worker, had remembered how Taylor had pulled her weight during the transplanting. Perhaps her father was just as helpful. The more help, the faster the work went. The weather forecast called for clear skies, at least through the next five days, and it was always desirable to haul the speared tobacco into the curing shed before it rained.

"I won't need him 'til Monday when we start to spud the stalks on the lath. If he can work three or four days, I've got Hickory Sam Stoltzfus and Boom John Zook from over Intercourse way coming to help after that."

Later, Taylor had asked Becca about the unusual Amish names and she had explained that because so many Amish families had the same first and last names, nicknames based on geography or personal traits were common in order to differentiate between them all.

"Hickory Sam is from the Stoltzfus family who live further down Hickory Hill Road," Becca said. "Boom John is the Zook who talks in a loud voice."

Taylor hadn't seen her Dad for two weeks, since she had left the city to stay with the Yoders. Connor missed his daughter and so agreed to take a few days of vacation to help the Yoders. He wasn't eager to cut tobacco but how hard could the work be if the women did it?

CONNOR CLUMSILY SLID the stem of the wilted tobacco plant onto the wooden lath, making sure, as Daniel had instructed, not to damage the leaves. Slowly he speared four more plants onto the lath, then stuck it into the ground and moved down the row with another lath to repeat the process. David and Levi, each driving horse-drawn carts, traveled down the rows, picked up the laths, weighing forty pounds each, and stacked them in the cart.

Connor looked out over the field and saw Taylor and Becca spearing in the far right corner, Sarah and Katie in the far left, and Daniel and Joseph several rows over from him.

"Looks like you got the gist of it," Daniel said to Connor about an hour later, as they worked opposite each other but three rows apart.

"You've got a nice spread here," Connor said. "Taylor said you have a three-year deal with a tobacco company to grow genetically modified tobacco."

"*Ja.*"

"Why don't you increase your acreage, hire people to help, and really take advantage of the price you're getting for this contract?"

Daniel speared two more plants onto his lath and stuck it into the ground before answering. Earlier that morning he had watched Connor struggle to reach competency in the tobacco field; he hadn't been above asking questions and he'd exhibited an impressive level of persistence and determination to get the job done right. Daniel decided Connor was an acceptable *Englisher*, despite his line of work in the media.

He had had misgivings the night before, however, when Connor had arrived at the house to see Taylor after checking into the B & B. He had stepped out of his black Mercedes sedan dressed impeccably, not a hair out of place, with the air of a successful businessman who never got his hands dirty, and

Daniel had thought right then he'd last maybe an hour in the fields. But he'd been proved wrong—again. Daniel grudgingly admitted to himself that Taylor and her father were more solid than they appeared.

"Making more money isn't always the goal," Daniel said. "The Amish way is to work the land as a family, teach kids responsibility and work ethic. I've got about as much acreage as we can handle right now. Probably too much since I'm down a pair of hands—Jacob's—and will be losing David, too, in a few months when he marries."

"What will you do then?"

"Haven't decided." Daniel, watching his youngest son a row over out of the corner of his eye, said sternly, "Joseph, slow down. You speared too fast and ripped that tobacco leaf.

"Once the contract's up, I could try another crop, maybe soybeans, or add more cows, labor I can handle with the family I have left and still make enough to live on."

"I've been worrying about the future, too," Connor said. "Newspaper circulation and revenue are decreasing. People are getting their news online so advertisers are fleeing to the Internet. The media is consolidating into publicly-held companies, and private owners, like me, are becoming fewer and fewer as we sell out to the mega-companies."

"That so?" Daniel, half listening, gestured to David to drive the cart over to pick up his row of speared plants.

"I realize the fate of the media, especially television, is not one of your primary concerns," Connor said. "I know you believe the media to be one of the roots of all evil, full of violence and sex and useless programming, and I'll grant you, there is that. But a properly functioning media providing news and vital information to a voting public is one of the cornerstones of the democracy in which we live, a democracy whose constitutional protection of freedom of religion has supported your desire to live separate from the world, particularly in how you educate your children. I am as passionate about providing news to the public as you are about providing wholesome milk to consumers or farming your land with respect so it continues to sustain the markets you serve, as well as your family."

Daniel looked at Connor and nodded, two businessmen agreeing to disagree but sharing regard for the accomplishments of the other.

"You gonna sell out, too?"

"Don't know," Connor said, spearing the last of the plants in his row. "That depends on Taylor."

MARY OBSERVED JACOB from the kitchen window. He sat in his wheelchair on the back porch, watching his family and the Lodens in the tobacco field. On his lap was a large envelope, which he had kept, Mary noticed, after placing the rest of the mail for the day on the kitchen counter.

Mary and Emma were preparing chow chow—a mixture of carrots, beans, asparagus, cauliflower, and peas pickled and served cold—for supper that night. They had already made potato salad and two dozen hamburger patties; hot dogs would also be served, and for dessert, carrot cake with cream cheese icing and ice cream. The supper menu had been discussed at noon, when they had all devoured a quick meal of lunchmeat sandwiches, tomato salad, a zucchini casserole, and fruit, and at that time Connor had been invited to supper. Propane grills, he had learned, were not considered too modern for the Amish, and he had promptly offered to man the modest grill on the back porch while the rest of the family took care of the evening milking.

INSIDE THE WOODEN gable-roofed tobacco shed were varying tiers of horizontal support beams on which the laths were hung, spaced far enough apart so the tobacco leaves would not "shed burn," or smother. The doors to the shed were wide enough to accommodate the horse-drawn cart loaded with the laths. Ventilation panels with hinges built into the side of the shed could be open to the air and breezes, which helped to dry the moisture out of the tobacco leaves.

Levi told Connor the tobacco hung to cure in the shed for two months. Before curing, the leaves contained eighty-five percent water. Curing dried out the moisture and brought out the aroma and flavor of the tobacco. After curing, the crop would be taken down and stripped—the leaves pulled from the stalk—and bundled to sell.

David maneuvered the cart laden with laths into the shed. He then climbed a ladder and joined Daniel on the second highest tier in the shed, twelve feet off the ground, and turning slightly, yelled down to Connor, "Ready!"

Connor, standing in the cart, lifted a lath and handed it to David, who grasped it, maintaining his balance on the thin beam of wood, and hung it from the tier above him.

Up to that point, Connor had felt he was keeping up fairly well with the Yoders, despite the ninety-degree August heat in the field which, he now realized, was nothing compared to the stifling heat in the tobacco shed up close to the roof where Daniel and David worked. He also quickly realized as he lifted over and over again each forty-pound lath that for the long haul he was no physical match for the endurance of the Amish men.

Joseph and Levi were still out in the field driving the other cart and picking up laths from Taylor and the Yoder women. As the men emptied one cart, Joseph would drive it out of the shed, hop out, drive the full one in to be unloaded, and then take the empty cart back into the field for he and Levi to fill. When one area of the tier was full, David and Daniel moved to another section. With the entire tier across the shed full, they moved to the beam below.

For the next ten hours, with a break for lunch and a short mid-afternoon break for water and rest, Connor worked. When his energy flagged and his back ached, he had only to look up at David, who less than three months ago had suffered three broken ribs and a collapsed lung, or watch sixty-seven-year-old Levi, and he kept going, his shirt soaked to the skin with sweat, his arms leaden with fatigue. At the beginning of his three days of work, he told himself he just needed to get through another day, and then just through the rest of the afternoon, and finally, he begged himself to just get through the next hour. The Yoders, though, would stick with the job for another ten days, until the entire tobacco crop hung in the curing shed.

TAYLOR HAD TROUBLE putting one foot in front of the other, so exhausted was she after another day in the tobacco field. She decided if she so much as saw a single pack of cigarettes, she would smash them to pieces on the spot.

Sarah and the girls had completed the evening milking and returned to the house for supper while the men finished up for the day in the curing shed. Only Taylor and Emma remained in the barn; they had just finished feeding the cows. Lulu lay in her stall and Emma was lying on top of her, talking softly and rubbing her side. Emma unaware, Taylor pulled out her phone and took a quick picture.

"Emma, let's feed the horses so we can go in and eat. I'm starving."

"Coming," she said, running toward the horses' stalls, still full of energy even after a full day of housekeeping and meal preparation with Mary.

"Hello, my Sandy and Molly," Emma said, wrapping her arms around each draft horse's neck and feeding them a carrot while Taylor raked fresh hay into their stalls. "I bet you're hungry tonight after carting all that tobacco."

In the next stall over was Chestnut, and Taylor took a moment to watch him eat, a faint scar from the accident visible on his right flank. She finished feeding the rest of the horses and shooed Emma out. She wanted five minutes alone. She wasn't used to having people around her every minute of the day. She leaned on the rake, closed her eyes, and reveled in the relative quiet of the barn.

"Wake up. I have some news," Jacob said, and she whirled around.

"I wasn't sleeping. Well, maybe I was, standing up."

"This came in the mail yesterday but I couldn't find a chance to speak to you alone." He handed her an envelope. Taylor hung the rake in its spot on the wall and opened the envelope.

After a minute, she looked up, her eyes shining. "Jacob, you did it. You passed the GED. Here's the diploma and according to the transcript, you aced every test. Congratulations!" She placed the papers back in the envelope and handed it to Jacob. "Now what?"

"I've been thinking. I want to take the SAT test. Depending on my scores, I'll decide about college, although I'm not sure I can even afford to go. Will you help me with the test?"

"Of course I'll help you with the test. I will also help you apply to colleges, if that's what you decide to do. You might be eligible for grants or scholarships to help with the tuition." Suddenly, she knew without a doubt what she wanted to do. "I'll tell you what. If you're accepted to a college, I will help pay for your tuition and room and board for the whole four years or however long it takes."

Jacob's eyes widened. "I can't accept that kind of money from you. How would I ever repay you?"

"Look, you accept money from your community in an emergency. To me, this is the same idea except that instead of hospital bills, the emergency here is your future, the fulfillment of a dream. The only repayment I would expect is that you get the education you want and find a way to put it to good use."

They talked for a few more minutes. Taylor told him she would purchase SAT prep materials and would call Julia, the librarian, to help round up some teachers who could help him study. They'd register for the test and aim to take it in November, again in December, if necessary.

"It's going to be difficult," Taylor said. "I don't want to get your hopes up. I've personally never known anyone who's taken the SATs without attending high school, although I'm sure it's been done. You're going to have to study day and night and even then it might not be enough." She paused. "Maybe you should tell your parents now. Aren't they going to wonder what you're doing in your room all the time or where you're going if you have to meet a teacher?"

"No, not yet. I want to see how the test goes and I still want you to take me to visit some area businesses. I'm not going to tell *Mamm* and *Dat* until I make a decision."

They heard Sarah yelling from the house. "*Cum Essa!* Come eat!"

"Okay. It's your call. I'll support you any way I can." Taylor pushed Jacob out of the barn and into the house for supper.

CHAPTER

17

THE SLIGHT BUT warm breeze, the rhythmic clip-clop of horses' hooves, the gentle motion of the buggy lulled Taylor; from the open window she watched a cornfield pass by, could actually see the ripening stalks, could almost reach out and grab one, could hear children's shouts and cows mooing, in the distance.

"Wow, it's an entirely different perspective riding in a buggy," Taylor said to Becca, who was driving. "In a car, everything zips by, and you hear no noise from outside because the air conditioner or the radio is on. On the other hand, if we had taken my car, we'd have been there by now."

Becca's hands tightly gripped the reins; she nodded as Taylor spoke but her eyes never left the road. Since the accident, she'd ridden in a buggy but had not driven one. Taylor had offered to drive her car to run the errands Sarah had asked them to do, but Jacob had been encouraging Becca to "get back on the horse" so she had decided to face her fears. Katie sat in the back, oblivious to Becca's anxiety, and scanned the grocery list.

"Let's make the bank deposit first," she said. "*Mamm* said we can get ice cream at the store. It'll melt if we go to the bank after the store."

"*Ja,*" Becca said.

"Looks like the Beiler celery is coming up *goot,*" Katie said as she eyed the plot alongside the road as they passed their neighbor's farm. "They sure did plant a lot."

"*Ja,*" Becca said.

"'Course, they'll need a lot. It'll be a big wedding. Anna says lots of folks are coming from out-of-state."

"*Ja.*"

"Why is celery so important at a wedding?" Taylor asked.

"A larger than normal celery patch is a clue that someone in that family is getting married soon," Katie answered. "The wedding dinner includes the traditional creamed celery dish and celery sticks, and celery is used in the stuffing that's served with chicken or turkey, and the table centerpieces are made with celery."

Twenty minutes later Becca turned into the bank and amused Taylor by pulling up to the drive-through window. The teller didn't seem at all surprised to see a horse and buggy. Becca deposited the monthly milk check from their dairy business and a thick wad of dollar bills from their vegetable stand, setting aside a twenty for groceries.

When doing the regular twice-a-month grocery run, the Yoders shopped at a large Amish-owned grocery store or sometimes at one of Lancaster's chain stores, but when they needed just a few items, they shopped at a small Amish country store.

Sarah needed two dozen eggs, flour, and a bag of bulk cereal, and had acquiesced to the request for ice cream. While the sisters shopped, Taylor browsed the Amish-made crafts for sale in the store. She eyed small watercolor prints and note cards of farm landscapes, buggies, gardens and flowers, quilts, and scenes of Amish life by an artist named Susie Riehl. The rare individuals depicted in the prints were faceless.

Taylor pulled out her iPhone and Googled the artist. She learned Riehl had painted at her kitchen table in the rare free time she had while raising six children, two of them adopted, on an Old Order Amish farm in Lancaster County, was self-taught, and had come to the conclusion that her artistic talent was a God-given gift, not to be ignored. She first began to sell her paintings in order to pay the hospital bills for her cesarean deliveries.

Taylor was drawn to a print of a window, the top covered by the traditional green shade, from which could be seen in the distance a farm and a road with a buggy passing by; in the foreground, a straw hat and jacket hung on the wall and the top half of a wooden chair sat in front of the window. She liked the simplicity of the painting; it made her feel peaceful and calm. She purchased the print and then went in search of Katie and Becca.

She found the sisters in the freezer section trying to decide between mint chocolate chip or butter pecan ice cream; they decided to buy both. As they stood in line, searching their purses for the extra change they needed since the total came to more than twenty dollars, Taylor watched a woman customer at the next register.

She was definitely Amish. She wore a deep violet blue dress in the typical style but the drape of the dress hung beautifully and the material seemed richer than the standard polyester; her black apron had a subtle sheen to it and her shoes were black leather pumps. The black handbag she carried was also plain, but to Taylor's practiced eye the leather was expensive, unlike the cheap bags the Yoder girls carried. The woman paid by credit card and on her way out, she noticed Becca.

"Hello, Becca," she said. Becca, slightly flustered, said, "Hi. It's good to see you."

The woman left the store and Taylor watched her get into her carriage, a regular gray buggy, but the horse—and Taylor realized she had no experience in judging horses—looked like a thoroughbred.

"Who is she?" Taylor asked Becca.

"She's the mother of a boy I know, John King. Their family owns a gazebo business."

"Becca is sweet on him," Katie said.

"Am not. You just shush."

"I saw you staring at him after church Sunday. You could hardly take your eyes off him."

"Oh, for Pete's sake," Becca retorted, not willing to admit anything.

Taylor changed the subject. "This Mrs. King, she looked the same but different. Is she Old Order Amish?"

"*Ja*," Becca said. "But word is they make a lot of money in the business so can afford better stuff. But they don't act like nose high people, or snobby. They're not *hochmut*, or high-minded. They're just plain ol' Amish but with more money than most of us."

I LIKE THE way John King carries himself. He stands straight and sure, and he walks with confidence, like he knows exactly what he wants, but not in a prideful way. But he scares me a little, too. He's a couple years older than me, well into his rumspringa, and certainly seems to be enjoying it. He drives a car, something black and sporty-looking, and he uses a cell phone, doesn't even bother trying to hide it, except at church, of course. Am I attracted to him because he seems so worldly (and is that really a good thing)?

He nodded at me at church on Sunday as we were walking in and my stomach did a little flip flop. It was the first time I'd seen him since right before the accident. After church, I sort of lagged behind the rest of my family as we walked to the buggy and he came up to me. We chatted for just a minute and then he asked me if I had a cell phone (how did he know??) and what my number was. My face must have looked stricken because he said, "Don't worry, I won't call, just text. Keep it on vibrate." Seeing his mamm today at the store just made me think about John again. I hope I see him at the next singing. My phone is hidden in my room but now I'm going to have to keep it in my dress pocket, just in case.

THE HOUSE WAS quiet and dark as Taylor tiptoed down the stairs, wincing as they creaked. Her alarm clock had read one thirty in the morning and she was unsure at first what had woken her. She had sleepily turned over and then realized she wasn't hearing the quiet *whirr* of the battery-operated fan in her and Becca's room.

Batteries must be dead, she thought. She couldn't fall back asleep without the breeze, even though sultry, from the fan. While up, she checked her phones for messages, responded to a few emails, and then headed to the kitchen for batteries.

Through Jacob's slightly ajar bedroom door, Taylor saw him in his wheelchair, books spread on the bed, studying by the light of the gas fixture overhead. She decided not to interrupt him.

Taylor had called Julia the day after Jacob told her he passed the GED and the librarian had been ecstatic. In no time, she found Jacob a math tutor and a teacher from the local high school who also taught an SAT prep course, as well as both an English literature and a U.S. history teacher in case he decided to apply to colleges requiring two SAT subject tests in addition to the regular SAT test.

Taylor offered to pay all the teachers for their time, but according to Julia, the teachers were willing to help Jacob regardless of payment in order to "further the education dreams of a student with huge potential." Taylor, however, insisted on paying them.

Jacob had met the teachers and began studying; Taylor saw the bedroom door closed at various times throughout the day and night. Jacob ate meals with the family, did what he could to help in the barn or around the house, assisted the women with his physical therapy, and the rest of the time disappeared into his room, the door closed. The family thought he was reading or brooding or resting. When he needed to meet a teacher, Taylor drove him, and Sarah nodded approvingly to herself, assuming they were visiting local businesses in search of a job.

The previous week, Jacob and Taylor had visited three local colleges within an hour of the farm: Franklin & Marshall, a small private liberal arts college; Millersville, a medium-size public university; and Elizabethtown, a small private college.

While perusing the bookstore at Franklin & Marshall, Taylor turned from flipping through a physics book and saw Jacob, eyes closed, inhaling the smell of the philosophy book in his hands. He glanced up, saw her looking at him, hastily closed the book, and put it back on the shelf.

"I like the smell of new books," he said simply.

They had also visited the Lancaster branch of the Harrisburg Area Community College, a commuter school about six miles from Jacob's home offering two-year associate degrees, which Jacob was willing to consider if he wasn't admitted to a four-year college, though he thought the daily back and forth commute would be "too in-your-face" for his parents to handle; a clean break to a live-in college would be a better option, if possible.

Taylor found batteries in a kitchen drawer and returned to her room, the light still on in Jacob's room.

IT WASN'T LIKE Taylor to pause during farm chores and savor the moment, but before she started the gas-powered trimmer and it roared to life, she inhaled deeply the sweet smell of the grass that Becca had just mown. Taylor trimmed the grass in the yard that Becca's push mower missed, around the base of the oak trees and the sidewalk, and as she trimmed around the edge of the vegetable garden, she noticed something different about the sunflowers.

That morning, on her way back to the house from milking the cows, Taylor had noticed the faces of the sunflowers, still in their bud stage, turned toward the east as the sun rose. As she trimmed around the garden that afternoon, the sunflowers had turned westward, their faces tracking the sun.

She stopped trimming and gazed at the sunflowers, their faces stretched toward the sun, their roots embedded in the moist and fertilized soil, receiving the sustenance they needed to bloom, and then she resumed her trimming.

"WE'RE THIRD GRADERS now," Joseph said indignantly. "We can walk ourselves."

Taylor had offered to walk the twins on the first day of school since the Yoder family, as well as Hickory Sam and Boom John, were rushing to spear the last of the tobacco and get it into the curing shed before rain that night. Taylor was curious about the school but Joseph had been somewhat offended by her offer.

"It's just for today, Joseph. Don't you want to show me your school?"

Both Joseph and Emma nodded eagerly.

Taylor and the twins, each carrying a small Igloo lunch cooler that had been to school with their brothers and sisters—Emma's was pink and Joseph's red—walked over the footbridge across Stoney Creek, past the tobacco fields already alive with activity, to the far end of the Yoder farm, past the blackberry patch, where they picked up a well-worn path through the woods that bordered Stoney Creek Road. The school was a half mile from the Yoder farm and rather than walk along the road, all the Yoder children had taken the route across their property and through the woods on the path that came out onto the road right across the street from the one-room schoolhouse.

"Are you excited to start back to school?" Taylor asked as they trudged through the fields.

"*Ja,*" Emma said. "I can't wait to see my friends Lizzie and Ruth and . . . "

Joseph rolled his eyes. "'Cause you haven't seen them since last week at church."

"It's not the same at church," Emma retorted. "Anyway, I love Teacher Rose and this year we're going to learn cursive writing and read chapter books and the school will be safe, *Mamm* said."

"I'm not scared, either," Joseph said.

"Scared? What could you possibly be scared of?" Taylor asked.

Both Emma and Joseph looked at her with solemn eyes and then Taylor realized they were referring to the Nickel Mines Amish school shooting, in which a milk truck driver had killed five girls and gravely injured five others as they stood in front of the blackboard before killing himself.

"Yes, that was a big news story. Are you worried about that happening again?"

Emma shrugged. The footpath ended and they crossed the road, Emma skipping into the schoolyard, Joseph running ahead.

Taylor entered the school and inside the door in a small outer room were rows of hooks for coats but which contained lunchboxes of all colors and sizes, while others rested on the floor. A bin in a corner held jump ropes, softballs and bats, and volleyballs. Children of various ages crowded into the room, shouting to friends and chatting excitedly to each other.

In the main room, which housed grades one through eight, five rows of five desks faced a blackboard, above which were showcased letters of the alphabet, both capital and lower case. Above the alphabet were the names of all the students: a cutout of a tractor for the boys' names, a flower for the girls. Colorful artwork adorned the walls, as well as maps of different continents and a map of the U.S. with state capitals, and a clock that read twenty minutes past eight. A world globe sat on top of a bookcase crammed with books. On the blackboard were arithmetic problems—different problems for each grade—and a list of twenty spelling words.

Emma grabbed Taylor's hand. "Want to see our teddy bear? Nice people from all over the country sent so many bears they shared one of them with us."

A small black bear sat on a corner of the teacher's desk, next to a Bible and a framed hand-drawn picture of a quilt. Also on the desk were flash cards, a phonics book, McGuffey Readers, a U.S. history textbook, German and English grammar books, and a songbook.

"Scholars, attention please," Teacher Rose said, clapping her hands to silence the chattering children. "We have a visitor today. Let's use our inside voices. We begin class in ten minutes."

Taylor introduced herself to Teacher Rose, who looked to be in her early twenties. "Emma wanted to show me the bear," Taylor said.

"The public sent so many bears to the surviving children of Nickel Mines that many of them were given to other area schools." Teacher Rose pointed to the framed picture of a quilt. "And this is a drawing one of my former scholars made of the Comfort Quilt."

Taylor remembered reading about the Comfort Quilt. Hurricane Katrina victims from a school in Mississippi had presented it to the Amish after the shooting. The Mississippi students had received the quilt from a school in New Jersey, who in turn had received it after the tragedy of September 11 from Catholic school children in Ohio, who had created the quilt.

"The quilt was passed on to Virginia Tech after the shootings there," Teacher Rose explained, "by an Amish delegation made up of several family members of the ten families whose children were killed or wounded in the Nickel Mines attack."

Taylor remembered the day of the shooting and the media explosion as reporters from all over the world descended on the Amish community—the phone calls back and forth between her father, the *Lancaster Post's* editor, and their TV stations, the authorization to go over budget for reporters' overtime and to print more newspapers, frantic calls from their staff to acquire more ads to fill increased pages and TV time. In the days following, Taylor's job had been to crunch numbers based on increased newspaper sales and TV viewers. She never stopped to read the stories in depth and certainly had not reflected on them. At the time, she had felt a detached sympathy for the victims but the story hadn't touched her in a visceral way. She had been concerned only about how the story affected Loden Media.

Taylor recalled then why *Die Botschaft* had seemed familiar to her a couple weeks ago when Katie had showed her a copy during the picnic by the pond. A few weeks after the schoolhouse shooting, their paper in Harrisburg had received a copy of the Amish newspaper; a headline at the top read "Thank You." For the first time in thirty years, *Die Botschaft,* usually written by and for the Amish only, had printed a message aimed at *Englishers.* The Amish paper thanked the state police and emergency crews for their handling of the Amish school shootings, and also thanked people around the world for their kind acts, donations, and prayers on behalf of the victims and their families. According to the *Die Botschaft* editor at the time, an exception had been made, approved by an Amish bishop, to contact the media in order to get the thank you message out to the non-Amish world. The Harrisburg paper obligingly wrote a news story about *Die Botschaft's* message, which other newspapers as well as TV stations picked up. Message received.

Taylor watched the scholars seat themselves at their desks, their innocent faces turned expectantly toward Teacher Rose, and saw Emma's dear face and the faces of all the girls. She flashed on an image of the Nickel Mines girls standing terrified in front of the blackboard with the gunman and it all became more than just a lucrative news story from the past.

For Taylor, it wasn't just a matter of remaining objective about the news in order to present a fair and balanced news story. She had not let emotions of any kind—not the messy emotions inherent in personal relationships, not emotional reactions to news events, not the everyday emotions related to being a citizen of life—interfere with the way she did her job or the way she lived her life since her mother's death. If an incident didn't touch her personally, she wasn't affected by it at all. She didn't lack compassion; she merely refused to feel it. She had been living a detached life.

She suddenly felt light headed and nauseous. She told the teacher she didn't want to interrupt the start of the school day, said goodbye to Joseph and Emma, and hastily left the schoolroom.

On the path through the woods, Taylor vomited, wiped her mouth on the back of her hand, and walked quickly back to the Yoder farm, ready to throw herself into farm work to forget the images in her mind and to stop the feeling of delayed grief.

JACOB BREATHED DEEPLY and smelled the earth, the soil he could no longer feel with his hands unless someone helped him to the ground. The smell and the feel he had disdained for so long now seemed to enrich his senses.

It was a half hour before sunset and he had wheeled himself over the creek bridge and into the cornfield. He sat in the middle of a row, surrounded on both sides by six-foot high cattle corn stalks that would be harvested in a couple weeks. For the first time in almost two decades, he wouldn't be a part of that harvest, as he hadn't been a part of the tobacco spearing.

To his surprise, he had mixed feelings about this. It wasn't work he had ever enjoyed but a sense of satisfaction had accompanied the completion of the work. Learning to manage his disability should provide some pride, but he was disabled due to an act of bad judgment for which he was not proud. Coping with his disability was a necessity; a real sense of accomplishment would come from working hard to reach another goal that would define his future.

He was valiantly trying to master the SAT test. He felt good on some days and frustrated on others. The night before he had studied quadratic equations, hadn't made good progress, and consequently felt as if his whole effort was an exercise in futility. But then Taylor had worked with him that morning and the algebra had become clearer and he would meet with his math tutor the following day. He knew he needed to fight the sense of futility and hang on to the hope. Even though he didn't yet know what he would do with a college degree, if he were fortunate enough to acquire one, he knew from a place deep within that he wanted to further his education, and that would most likely mean his future would not include sitting in a cornfield again.

The sun was setting, the household preparing for bed. Time to head back to the house. He attempted to turn the chair around in the row but the front wheels had become embedded in the soil and wouldn't move forward. So he pushed himself backward and managed to travel a few feet before the wheels again became stuck in the soil. He could not move forward or backward and dark was fast approaching.

He hadn't told anyone where he was going and he wondered how long before he was missed. He couldn't remember whether he had closed his bedroom door before leaving the house. If shut, his family would assume he had already gone to bed and wouldn't miss him until morning.

He hated to ask for help but didn't relish spending the night in the cornfield. Taylor had urged him to always carry his cell phone with him, in case of an emergency in which he would need to dial 911. He was sure this was not a 911 emergency. He considered calling the phone shed but doubted anyone would hear the phone since they were all in the house. No one in his family knew he had a cell phone except Becca and she used her phone infrequently and kept it hidden. But he knew the one person virtually certain to have instant access to a phone.

"You're where?" Taylor asked. "Okay, let me think. Becca's in the shower and I'm in my pajamas. Wait, I hear Katie in the hall. I'll throw on a pair of jeans and we'll both be down to get you in a few minutes. Sit tight."

Katie and Taylor were able to drag the chair and Jacob to firmer ground and then wheel him back to the house. As they exited the cornfield, Katie began to chuckle. Jacob swatted at her with an arm but the chuckle turned into a bend-over-at-the-waist laugh. Taylor joined in and even Jacob grinned. Katie and Taylor promised him they wouldn't tell the men he had gotten stuck in the cornfield. And Katie never asked Taylor how she knew Jacob had been in trouble.

TAYLOR PLOPPED THE stack of books on the library desk and Julia began to check them out.

"*Bridge to Terabithia, Charlie and the Chocolate Factory, Harry Potter and the Sorcerer's Stone,*" Julia read, smiling. "These can't be for Jacob."

"They're for his younger twin brother and sister," Taylor said. "I promised Joseph and Emma I would read to them before bed."

"Good for you. I understand Jacob is doing well at his SAT prep," Julia said. "His teachers told me he has laser beam focus and is a quick learner, and his SAT prep teacher said he has an affinity for taking standardized tests, based on the results he's getting on the practice tests.

"According to his math tutor, he's having some difficulty with math but should be able to muscle through with hard work. His previous math tutor, the one that helped him pass the math portion of the GED, apparently taught him well beyond the level needed for the GED, so Jacob actually has a pretty good foundation."

"He's working around the clock. And he's determined," Taylor said. "I don't know if he'll score high enough to impress most college admissions, but he should do well enough to at least get into a community college. Then he could transfer to a four-year college later."

"I'm sure Jacob is grateful for your help."

"I do feel like I'm on a personal mission to help him. Yet I'm also caught in the middle. His parents don't know and I wish he'd tell them, but when he does, it won't be pretty."

"Hang in there," Julia said. "All this hard work will pay off somehow."

JACOB RAN HIS hand through his hair. "What are my options?" he asked the attorney.

"You could request a trial or plead guilty."

Jacob, Taylor, and the defense attorney specializing in DUI matters, Steven Burke, sat at the Yoder kitchen table. The Yoder elders, part of a culture hesitant to interact with the court system and unfamiliar with the world of law and lawyers, had gratefully ceded the matter to Taylor to handle. She had insisted on hiring the attorney after Jacob had received in the mail a notice of the filing of a criminal complaint regarding his DUI and reckless driving charges. Jacob had protested that he couldn't afford an attorney and vowed he would absolutely not ask his parents to foot the bill.

"We can't afford *not* to hire an attorney," Taylor had argued. "You need legal advice. These charges could affect your future."

Taylor had offered to pay for everything but Jacob had refused.

"I will pay for my mistakes. I've been saving money all my life from the small share of the farm income my father has paid us boys and what I've earned working for other farmers when needed. It's not a lot of money but it paid for my wheelchair and it'll cover this, I hope. I had intended to use the money someday for my future, whatever that future turned out to be, but this mess is my fault, and my fault only, and I will take care of it."

They had finally agreed that Jacob would pay all the fines and costs associated with the charges and Taylor would pay the attorney's fees.

"What happens if I plead guilty?" Jacob asked his attorney. "I did drive after drinking, I did race, I did run a stop sign. I'll plead guilty, pay the fines, and save my family the embarrassment of a trial."

Steven shook his head. "I don't advise that approach. A guilty plea would involve a minimum of forty-eight hours in jail, as well as criminal convictions—misdemeanors—on your record."

"Jail?" exclaimed Taylor. "For a first offense?"

Steven nodded. "Even though this was Jacob's first DUI offense and his blood alcohol level was below .10 percent, the accident involved injuries and property damage—to his siblings and to your car—which make the penalties higher."

Instead of a trial or pleading guilty, Steven suggested Jacob apply for, and most likely would be accepted into, a first offender program offered by the Lancaster District Attorney's Office. The program would be in lieu of jail time but would require probation and alcohol highway safety school, as well as counseling or treatment for alcohol abuse, if needed.

"I haven't had a beer since the night of the accident," Jacob said quietly, "and I don't plan on drinking and driving again."

"Good. That's one of the goals of the program. The total cost would be two thousand dollars, including the program fee, the fines, the highway safety school, and probation supervision. However, if you successfully complete the program, the DUI and reckless driving charges will be dismissed and expunged, or erased, from your record. In other words, you would no longer have a criminal record."

Taylor, who had been taking notes, paused. "Jacob, having a criminal record would affect future employment and possibly even your education plans."

Jacob bowed his head and closed his eyes. In the silence, Taylor heard the ticking of the battery-operated wall clock.

"I'll do the program. I'll do whatever it takes."

Steven Burke placed his yellow legal pad in his briefcase, stood up, and shook Jacob's hand. "I'll make it happen for you, Jacob. You just concentrate on your future."

THE WOODEN TREE swing creaked as Taylor shifted position. Jacob sat nearby in his wheelchair as they both sipped iced tea and ate chocolate chip cookies Becca had baked that morning.

"Thanks for taking me around today," Jacob said. "It was revealing."

"You didn't seem particularly excited about anything you saw," Taylor said.

"It reaffirmed what I'm not interested in."

That morning after chores, Taylor and Jacob had gone "job scouting," as Taylor called it. She had compiled a list of Amish businesses after talking to David and scanning the Lancaster County Business Directory at the library, and immediately Jacob had nixed more than half of them.

"Let me make sure I understand," Taylor had said. "You don't want to work with your hands, so home-based businesses like craft shops, or horseshoeing, or furniture or cabinet making, like your Uncle Samuel, are out. You're also not interested in small retail shops, like shoes or hats or hardware stores. Machine repair or welding shops and carpentry or construction trades, like your Uncle John's, are impractical because of your disability. But you are willing to consider a larger business, where there might be a possibility of administrative or management-type work."

"Somewhere where I can use my mind, not just my hands."

"Small business owners need to be skilled in the running of a business, not just in the making of the product," Taylor said.

"I know, but I don't want to run a small business."

So they had visited a large local Amish-owned retail store that sold bulk foods and what they called "bent and dent" groceries in two locations, and a moderate-sized silo manufacturer that shipped silos locally as well as throughout the region.

While waiting for the bulk foods owner to see them, Taylor watched a gentlemen dressed similar to the Amish approach the register with a basket full of groceries. He placed the basket on the counter, and instead of taking the groceries out of the basket, he stepped back. The cashier emptied the basket, totaled the groceries, and told the man what he owed. The man then placed the money on the counter and the cashier returned the change to the counter, the man picked it up, and left with his groceries.

"What just happened there?" Taylor asked Jacob.

"That's Abner Graber. Our church excommunicated him several years ago. After his first wife died, he remarried out of the faith and joined his new wife's slightly more liberal Mennonite church. So now he's shunned by the Old Order Amish."

"But he's still permitted to do business here?"

"Church members can talk to a shunned person but can't accept anything directly from their hands."

"Are you going to be shunned if you go to college?"

"Since I haven't formally joined the church, I won't be shunned because I haven't broken a baptismal vow. But I won't be exactly welcomed either."

Both of the owners expressed eagerness to employ Jacob when he was ready and able. The bulk foods owner needed a bookkeeper; he currently outsourced the job but was willing to "bring the job in-house" if Jacob was willing to learn. Jacob had no desire to work with numbers all day. The silo owner, who was not from Jacob's church district but knew the Yoder family, said he had just lost one of his office assistants and "am going crazy doing all the paperwork myself so the job's yours if you want it."

"Paperwork?" Jacob had asked.

"Keeping track of all the invoices and bills."

Jacob's eyes glazed over on the spot.

"Jacob, you have to start somewhere," Taylor said as she sipped her tea. "Your first job doesn't have to be the one you stay with the rest of your life."

"Yours is," Jacob retorted.

"That's different. It's a family-owned business, like many of the Amish family-owned businesses."

"I know, I know. I just want to go to college. Nothing seems to measure up to that. But I'm well aware that if college doesn't happen, I need to find a job. We'll just keep looking."

TAYLOR POURED MILK from the bucket into the sputnik and then hooked up the milking machine to the next two cows. Becca worked around her, feeding the cows.

"I finished *Jane Eyre* last night," Becca said. "Jane had to go through so much before she could finally be with Mr. Rochester."

"What do you think Jane learned from her hardships?"

"She wanted to belong somewhere, to have a family that cared about her. But she also wanted freedom and independence."

"Did she find what she was looking for or did she compromise?"

"At first I thought she gave up her freedom to marry Mr. Rochester, but I think maybe she found freedom by being in an equal relationship. She had her own money and someone who loved her, and she did it all on her terms."

Daniel walked up behind them.

"Stop filling your head with useless things you read in a book." Becca jumped at the sound of her father's voice. "What's important is what you give to your family, your community, and your God. Sadie's hungry. Is your book learning more important than feeding her?"

Taylor stood, the milk bucket in her hand. "Books can be windows into our lives," she said to Daniel. "We read them to understand ourselves better or get a different perspective on how other people live. That's important, too."

"Bah!" Daniel said, and he strode across the barn.

18

THE WIND HOWLED, the rain fell in torrents. Taylor and the twins sat on the couch in the family room while she read *Charlie and the Chocolate Factory*; Joseph held the flashlight because "it's more fun reading by flashlight in a storm."

Earlier that evening, before the weather had turned bad, the entire family had gathered around the kitchen table for a lively game of Yahtzee, followed by the card game Uno. Even Daniel had enjoyed himself. But that had ended as the storm worsened.

The tropical storm force winds from Hurricane Isabel lashed the Yoder farm and the entire Lancaster area. As the family prepared for bed upstairs, Daniel paced from one window to another downstairs, eyeing the field of cattle corn, periodically shaking his head, so intent on his worry he hardly noticed Taylor and the twins. Taylor had been reading to Emma and Joseph before bed for several nights. She had come to realize that Daniel didn't mind the simple reading of a story; it was analyzing the story that was a waste of time to him.

The twins fidgeted as Taylor read. Before Daniel entered the room they had been absorbed in the story but they soon became distracted by his pacing. They didn't dare ask him what was wrong, deterred by the grim look on his face.

Two days ago, the Yoders had started harvesting the silage corn, used through the year as feed for the cows. Down each row, Levi drove the horse-drawn, gasoline-powered corn binder, which cut the corn and bundled it. Close behind, Daniel followed in a horse-drawn wagon, while Joseph walked alongside, tossing the bundles into the wagon.

When full, Daniel drove the wagon to the barn, where both corn and stalks were ground by a chopper machine, also run by gas, and equipped with a large fan to blow the silage into the silo. While Daniel unloaded the bundles from the wagon and fed them into the chopper machine, David, having already unloaded a second wagon, drove back to the field to follow Levi. Taylor had watched this display of teamwork that afternoon from the attic window while she worked, as the sky grew increasingly dark and the wind picked up.

Daniel knocked on Jacob's bedroom door and after a pause, during which Taylor imagined Jacob concealing his study materials, Jacob invited his father to enter. After a few minutes, Daniel reappeared and called David down from his room. The door once again closed and Taylor could hear the three of them talking in *Deitsch* in low, urgent voices.

THE NEXT MORNING, Daniel and Levi surveyed the mangled rows of corn. The hurricane's winds had blown through the fields like a scythe, leaving the acres of corn flat and twisted.

"We can't steer the wagon or the binder down the rows," Levi said.

Daniel nodded. "If the corn's on the ground too long, it'll get dried out or moldy. We're going to lose the crop."

"Don't panic, yet," Levi said.

"I can't afford to buy feed for the cows this year," Daniel said as they turned to walk back to the house for breakfast.

"I know. But our farmers all over the county are facing the

same problem. We'll get everyone together and figure out something."

"Last night, Jacob suggested we hire a harvester to get the job done. That would cost me a couple thousand but way less than the cost of feed."

"Let's go talk to Bishop Lapp after we eat."

TAYLOR WATCHED THE three Amish men, one of them Jacob, work the phones in the small room set up as an emergency center at the Gordonville Fire Company near Paradise, not far from the Yoder farm. During the drive over, Jacob had told Taylor that the area bishops had met and had given their blessing to allow farmers to hire chopper operators to harvest the corn by combine.

"These huge combines—they can cost up to five hundred thousand dollars apiece—not only can get through the tangled fields but they can cut and grind the corn into grain at the same time," Jacob had explained. "What would take five days using our corn binder and wagon method they can do in six hours. And unlike horses, they can go day and night and are equipped with lights."

"What if a farmer can't afford to rent these machines?"

"Then the community will help pay."

"Why is it okay to break the rules and use modern machinery?" Taylor had asked. "Are the bishops usually in the habit of changing the rules when circumstances require?"

"It was a rare rule breaking, a one-time only decision, based on a crisis situation," Jacob said. "The bishops knew many farmers could lose their crops. The crops need to be harvested to feed the cows. The cows need to survive or the livelihood of the farmers is gone."

"But what's the difference between using a combine and using farm equipment powered by gas engines?" Taylor asked.

"We can use farm equipment powered by gas engines as long as we pull them with horses but we're forbidden from using self-propelled equipment. That's where the line is drawn."

"Why not let farmers rent the combines if they need them," Taylor argued as she parked her car in the fire company lot, "like the policy on using, but not owning, cars?"

"Because if you allow modern farm machines," Jacob responded, "you defeat the whole purpose of the Amish way of life, which is to limit the size of the farm so it's affordable and manageable, teach children a work ethic, and keep the community separate from the outside world."

Taylor lifted Jacob's wheelchair out of the trunk, popped the wheels on, and helped him out of the front seat of the car.

"But you're not really separate from the outside world. You use phones, you interact and do business with *Englishers*, and you use hospitals and vets."

"Any concession we've made has been to try to preserve as much of our lifestyle as possible and still survive in the world around us. We continually balance lifestyle with survival."

The small room was set up with a desk, three chairs, and three multi-line phones; Jacob had dubbed it the "Harvest Aid Hotline." The two other bearded men were both retired farmers who, like Jacob, had volunteered to man the phones. He hadn't said as much, but Taylor knew Jacob's involvement made him feel useful, a way to give back, a way to atone, in some small measure, for the damage he had caused both his family and his community.

Taylor moved one of the chairs into the corner to make room for Jacob's wheelchair. She sat on the chair for a few minutes before she left and watched the three men talking at once as they juggled the phones, switching between English on the phone and then *Deitsch* as they conferred with each other, trying to hire operators locally and throughout the region. Taylor gathered from the English conversations that operators were willing to come and help but needed a couple days to finish harvesting the crops of their regular non-Amish customers.

As she watched Jacob meld his Amish heritage with the resources of the modern world, she wondered which world, in the end, he would choose.

I WANT TO know the difference between making an exception to use Englishers' heavy equipment to clear the cornfields and making an exception for Jacob to go on for more schooling. I know he's studying for something school-related. I saw all his books in his nightstand yesterday when I was helping him with his therapy. His nightstand drawer was slightly open and I looked in and saw the books. He saw me looking but he didn't say anything and neither did I. I'm torn between wanting him to be happy and not wanting him to leave us. Why can't Dat be as open-minded about Jacob as he is about farming? Why is it more important to make an exception for a farming reason than for your own son? Dat would probably say because farming is our livelihood and we have to survive and Jacob's survival doesn't depend on him going to school. But maybe Jacob's survival, in a way, does depend on him doing something he so wants to do.

By the way, the hurricane also flattened my sunflowers. I'm so disappointed I won't get to see them bloom.

THREE DAYS AFTER the Harvest Aid Hotline, Jacob sat on one of the wooden footbridges straddling Stoney Creek that connected the Yoder farm to the fields and watched the combine save his family's harvest. The combine had started late that afternoon, having come directly from another Amish farm, and would work hours into the night, until the job was done.

As the sun set, the sky blending from grey blue to dusky pink, the massive machine powered through the battered fields. When darkness came, the combine's lights eerily pierced the night, the sound of the rumbling machine and the grinding stalks a stranger to the normal evening stillness.

"THE DEVICE IS called ReWalk and it underwent clinical trials locally at Moss Rehab. Initially developed in Israel, it was designed to help paraplegics walk," said Dr. Collins. He had just completed Jacob's follow-up exam at Bayard and had told him he was doing "remarkably well" with his physical therapy and bladder and bowel management. Taylor had driven him down that afternoon, after he had finished his first highway safety school class that morning in Lancaster.

"How does it do that?" asked Jacob.

"It's basically a wearable robot. You strap on motorized leg braces and carry a battery fanny pack. A keypad worn on the wrist like a watch allows you to command the braces to perform motions, like standing up from a wheelchair, walking, climbing and descending stars, and sitting down. You also use crutches for balance and stability."

"Is it available for personal use and how much does it cost?" Taylor asked.

"The FDA has approved it for home use. The cost now is about seventy-seven thousand dollars."

"Well, that's the end of that," Jacob said.

"Don't rule it out yet," Taylor said. "You never know what money may be available for patients through foundations or donors and as it becomes more widely used, the price will come down."

Dr. Collins said exciting results had occurred from another technology tested called an epidural spinal cord stimulator. "An electrical device implanted in the spine of persons with complete paralysis from the waist down stimulated the spinal cord. Participants were then able to voluntarily move their legs, hips, knees, and feet, and were also able to stand. The technology as of yet can't cause walking, but the fact that a spinal cord injury may not necessarily be permanent is groundbreaking."

"Something else to keep in mind for the future," Taylor said to Jacob.

⁓

SARAH PLACED JACOB'S clean laundry in his dresser drawer and then stood and watched him lift his free weights, exercising his upper body. His muscles bulged under his white t-shirt but something didn't seem right.

"Jacob, do you feel okay?"

"I have a wicked headache and I'm hot. Other than that, I'm fine."

He finished with the weights, leaned over, and placed them on the floor. He attributed the headache to his relentless studying.

Sarah felt his forehead. "You do feel warm. I'm going to take your temperature." The thermometer confirmed a fever and Sarah knew, because of her Bayard training, that a fever was not a good sign. She helped Jacob into bed and encouraged him to rest. She grabbed her address book from the kitchen, headed to the phone shed, and called the local family doctor and made an appointment for Jacob for the next day.

After Jacob woke from a nap, Becca asked him if he felt like doing his range of motion exercises. Katie and Sarah had gone to the grocery store and took the twins so Jacob wouldn't be disturbed. The men and Taylor were in the fields, picking up residue corn cobs left on the ground from the combine and throwing them into the wagon, to be ground later for feed.

"Not really, but I need to do it, so let's go."

About fifteen minutes into the routine, as Becca helped Jacob with leg bends, his leg began to twitch and tremble. Jacob had spasms periodically; they were like mini seizures, an overactive muscle response resulting in uncontrollable jerking movements, and usually lasted only a few moments. His spastic leg cuffed Becca on the side of her head.

"Oops," Jacob said.

"It's okay. Let's change positions. That usually works." She helped Jacob roll over on his side but the spasm continued. Jacob's legs straightened and became rigid and his entire body began to shake.

"Something's wrong," Jacob said.

Becca froze. She needed help but no one was around. She didn't dare leave Jacob to run to the field for help or even to run to the phone shed to call 911. She reached into the pocket of her dress and hesitated for just a second, then pulled out her cell phone.

TAYLOR'S PHONE VIBRATED in her pocket. She glanced over at Daniel, just ahead of her in the corn row. She knew he'd probably admonish her for answering but none of the younger kids were around and since it was Becca, she decided to risk it, but she bent down behind the wagon to talk.

"Jacob needs help," Becca said, her voice frantic. "Tell *Dat*. Come quick!"

By the time Daniel, David, and Taylor ran into the house, Jacob's legs were wildly scissoring; Becca leaned on the top half of his body to keep him from rolling off the bed.

"This isn't normal. The spasms have never been this bad," she said.

"I'll call 911," David said and ran out to the phone shed.

Taylor turned to Daniel. "I can get him to the ER faster in the car."

Daniel locked eyes with Taylor, struggled internally for a moment, then scooped Jacob up in his arms, legs swinging, and headed out the door, Taylor right behind.

"Becca, tell David to tell the 911 dispatcher to alert the hospital we're coming," she yelled over her shoulder as she flew out the door.

Daniel placed Jacob in the back seat of the car and firmly held his legs on his lap as Taylor roared out of the driveway.

"TELL ME EXACTLY what the ER doctor said." Sarah and Daniel sat at the kitchen table that evening, the rest of the house asleep.

"He said Jacob had a UTI, a urinary tract infection," Daniel explained. "Some bacteria probably got into his catheter. Bad muscle spasms occur when something, like an infection, irritates the body below the spinal cord injury. It's a very common thing. We were at the ER for a couple hours, they started him on antibiotics, did some tests, then sent us home. Jacob needs to continue taking antibiotics, be very careful with his bladder routine, and drink a couple quarts of water a day. He's going to be fine."

"Thanks be to God."

"*Ja,* but I've been stewing on another problem since we got home from the hospital. Where did Becca get a cell phone and who's paying for it? Let me guess."

"I asked her that this afternoon when she told me what happened. She's had the phone since the summer. Taylor bought it for her and is paying the bill."

"We need to take it and tell Taylor a thing or two."

"That was my first reaction, too, but I held my tongue. As much as we may hate to admit it, it's a good thing she had that cell phone. It came in handy in an emergency. Becca says she keeps the phone hidden, Katie doesn't know she has it, and the twins have never seen her use it."

"But Taylor is mocking our authority. She prances around here in her English clothes, she's got the car parked in our driveway, and that computer in the attic. She's everything we don't believe in."

"That's not quite true. From the outside, she's everything we don't believe in. But Taylor's been good to us as a family and to Jacob. She and her car got Jacob to the hospital quickly today, and she's helping him find a job. She's useful around the farm. She spends a lot of time reading to the twins and Becca is very fond of her."

"Hummph. Wonder why."

"I don't think it's just because of Becca's access to Taylor's worldly life. She likes to talk to her. She's working through things by talking to Taylor. That's a good thing."

"The community's starting to talk about our *Englisher*. Chickie Abram Glick asked me the other day how long she'd be staying. We need to take action before we get a visit from the minister."

Sarah waved her hand dismissively. "The community talks about everyone all the time. So far, there's not much to say about Taylor. Other than her car, she's kept to the shadows. She's polite and she's careful to keep her gadgets away when she's around our family and other Amish."

"She's a problem waiting to happen, I tell you."

"Her stay is only temporary. She'll help Jacob and then her work will call her back to the city. In the meantime, let Becca keep her phone. It's part of her *rumspringa* and it's useful in case we need it for Jacob. She'll put it away eventually, of that I'm sure. And besides, I heard the other day that over in Bishop Studer's district, they approved electricity in a house for a paralyzed man who needs a breathing machine. Wouldn't a cell phone used for Jacob's safety fall in the same category?"

"Against my better judgment, I'll be patient and wait—but only a little longer."

FLIES BUZZED AROUND the barn during the Sunday service, the early October day warm, the barn doors open to admit the slight breeze; bales of hay stacked high around the perimeter made room for the rows of wooden benches, and the men's black hats hung from pegs on the wall.

David sat on the front row bench, head bowed, hand over his face, signifying his submission to God and his church. To his left sat Aaron, to his right another male ready to take the baptism vows. Across the aisle sat Anna and three other girls, all eighteen or nineteen years old, heads also bowed with hands over faces. The seven had attended instruction classes together through the summer, meeting separately with a minister during the first half hour of Sunday church services. Behind the candidates' two front benches sat the rest of the silent congregation; all had heard two hours of sermons before the baptism part of the service.

Bishop Lapp requested the candidates kneel; a deacon stood beside the bishop with a pail of water and a cup. The bishop asked each candidate whether he or she was ready to commit to the authority of Christ and his church and to promise obedience to the *Ordnung*. Each candidate answered yes.

The bishop laid his hand on David's head and said, "You are baptized in the name of the Father, the Son, and the Holy Spirit. Amen." He cupped his hands over David's head and the deacon poured water into the bishop's hands and it dripped over David's head and face. For the girls, the bishop's wife untied the ribbon of each black organdy *kapp* and removed it so the water could drip over an unadorned head.

Bishop Lapp then took the hand of each member and told him or her to stand. "In the name of the Lord, we extend to you the hand of fellowship. Rise up and be a faithful member of the church." He greeted each new male member with a holy kiss; the bishop's wife kissed each female.

David watched as Anna brushed away a tear as she replaced her *kapp*. He and Anna and the others were as of then full-fledged adult members of the church for the rest of their lives. David's *rumpsringa* past was behind him and the future excited him; he and Anna could finally be married.

Behind them in the congregation, Jacob and Becca had watched the service, both with a mixture of pride and ambivalence.

TAYLOR AND JACOB pulled into the parking lot of King's Gazebos in an industrial park in New Holland. Jacob had seen a
help wanted ad in *Die Botschaft*, the Amish weekly newspaper,
and the owner had agreed to see him. When Taylor saw the size
of the building and the tractor trailers waiting to be loaded, with
license plates from California, Georgia, and Colorado, she realized this business was not in the same league as the bulk food
store and silo manufacturer they had previously visited.

Tobias King lived in Jacob's church district, although his
company was located outside of it. He took them on a quick
tour of the site, his booming voice matter-of-fact rather than
boastful. As they walked, Taylor eyed the flecks of sawdust in his
beard, his deep blue shirt, sleeves rolled up, and black pants
with suspenders; with the exception of his pricey scuffed Timberland boots, nothing about his work clothes differed from the
dress of other Amish men, unlike the impression she remembered his wife's clothes made that day at the country store.
She guessed him to be in his early forties.

Tobias pointed out that a combination of solar panels on
the roof and hanging propane gas lamps lit the ten thousand
square foot building. Air compressors powered by diesel engines
ran table saws and other machinery. Generators fueled a copy
machine, and battery packs ran the small kitchen's microwave
and coffee maker. Taylor noticed multi-line phones and computers on a few office desks.

"You're permitted to use landlines and computers?" she asked.

"They're stripped down versions, good for word processing, accounting, and spreadsheets only. No Internet. The
church bishop was wary of them at first, too much like a TV
screen. But without the web, they're really no different than
typewriters or calculators, which we're allowed to use as long
as they aren't run by electricity. And as for the phones, since
we're off the electric grid here for everything else, the bishop

decided not to make a fuss about them, especially since the few computers and phones we have are mostly used by my non-Amish employees."

"You don't have a company website then or sell through the Internet?"

"We do, but the website is maintained and run by an outside media firm."

Taylor looked skeptical.

"I know it seems like a contradiction," Tobias said, "but we can't be competitive in today's business world without Internet technology. Since we try to operate within the *Ordnung,* we outsource that technology, so it's separate from us, but granted, the business does benefit from access to computer services provided offsite. It's like how we deal with cars—can't own them but can ride in them. It's a compromise."

"How big is the company?" Jacob asked.

"We ship thousands of various size gazebos throughout the country every year with thirty-eight employees, thirty of them Amish. Our annual sales are about nine million."

"This is a larger than normal Amish business," Taylor observed.

"*Ja,* most Amish businesses are the small mom-and-pop variety but there are many who do reach annual sales of a million or more. There's a wood lawn furniture outfit right down the street that sells to WalMart and a storage shed business across town so big he got in trouble with the church and had to sell to an outside buyer. Some business owners refuse to downsize or sell and leave the church instead."

The tour ended in Tobias's office. Seated behind his large oak desk, on which rested piles of paper, a hand-held calculator, and copies of the *Wall Street Journal, Time* magazine, and the *Lancaster Post,* Tobias asked about Jacob's family. "I hear your brother's getting married soon."

"It's not official yet but I expect there will be a church announcement sometime this month."

"Is he going to continue to farm?"

"He'd like to. He's got some money saved and I'm sure our father will contribute what he can as part of his wedding gift, but with the price of farmland these days, it'll be a while before he can save enough for the down payment."

"What'll he do in the meantime?"

"He'll live at the Beiler's after they marry and help work their farm, which is larger than ours. He and Anna are considering starting a small retail business of some kind or he may take a factory job. He hasn't decided yet but he really wants his own farm, eventually."

"I see. Well, here's what I need. An assistant office manager, someone to work with my full-time office manager and assist with her overflow. You'd need to keep track of my schedule, help oversee the billing and payroll departments, keep track of order fulfillment, and also be the go-between with the outside media firm that runs the company website. It's a part-time job, two, occasionally three days a week. You'd be paid on an hourly basis.

"Also, I rent three vans to pick up my Amish employees, so you'd have a ride to work. I know you may sometimes have physical issues and I'm willing to work around that if you think you can handle the job physically. Sound like something you'd be interested in?"

Jacob was spared from answering by the ring of a cell phone. Tobias pulled his cell out of his pocket, not a smartphone, Taylor noticed, and said, "I need to take this," and left the office, standing a short way down the hall. His booming voice still carried.

"*Ja*, that's right. I want to sell a thousand shares. There's some land I want to buy."

Taylor, astonished, turned to Jacob. "He's talking to his stock broker?" Jacob shrugged.

"Tobias King has been known to buy land and then resell it, with no or low interest, to a fellow church member who wants to farm. He also loans money to people who want to start businesses. He and other wealthy Amish businessmen try to spread the money throughout their communities."

As Tobias returned to his office, Taylor didn't even wait until he seated himself at his desk.

"Excuse me, sir, but how can you own this large of a business and consider yourself Old Order Amish and separate from the world?"

Tobias took no offense to Taylor's blunt question. "It's a definite balancing act between Amish culture and operating a profitable business. I am both respected and criticized in my community. Some look at the size of the business as greed. Others, who have benefited because of me, either through loans or jobs, are appreciative and don't complain. The Amish way of life is important to my family and me. But being a businessman is also a part of who I am. It's a constant struggle but worth it so far.

"I saw you eyeing my cell phone. I only use it for business, and I turn it off and lock it in my desk drawer at the end of the workday, even though technically the church has not yet banned cell phones. So, Jacob, what do you think about being my assistant office manager?"

"I appreciate the offer and yes, I am interested. When would you want me to start?"

"My current assistant office manager will be leaving in about six weeks. She's pregnant and wants to return home to raise a family. I was hoping the new hire could train with her at least a week or so before she leaves. How about I touch base with you in a couple weeks and we'll work out the details and the timing."

"Sounds good."

"Here's something else for you to think about. I know you're struggling with your future. I've talked to your father briefly and well, you know how church members talk. If you need to get away and clear your head, I own a small cottage in Pinecraft. You're welcome to use it for a week or two whenever you want. You'll probably need to take someone with you and that's okay, too."

Taylor interrupted. "Pinecraft?"

"It's an Amish village in Florida, near Sarasota," Tobias explained. "Many retirees from Amish communities around the country winter there and it's a vacation spot for families of all ages. Buses run down there from Lancaster all winter. We usually go for a couple weeks in February and in the summer. We rent it out the rest of the year but for you, Jacob, just ask."

"THERE'S AN EXTRAORDINARY amount of wealth generated by Amish businesses," Ben Scott said. "With only two job options—farming or business—some of the brightest Amish become successful entrepreneurs, not just of home-based businesses but of multimillion dollar retailing or manufacturing enterprises, despite only an eighth grade education."

Taylor, still amazed by what she had seen at King's Gazebos, had dropped Jacob off at his final highway safety school class and had made a beeline for her reporter source on all things Amish at the *Lancaster Post* office.

"Amish farmers may be wealthy in land but not in cash," Ben said. "It's the business owners who are making the real money. Here's an example: Smucker's Harness Shop over in Churchtown. Started by an Amish man named Moses, a former dairy farmer. The company made hand-cut fine leather harnesses and sleigh bells. In the late nineties, *Forbes* magazine estimated sales at six million a year.

"The shop outfitted the Budweiser Clydesdale team, the horses of Ringling Bros. and Barnum & Bailey Circus, and at one time, the pets of Michael Jackson and a Saudi prince. He was a big giver in the community, lived modestly, and managed to avoid a showdown with the church. Moses has since retired but his son Daniel and a former employee both took over portions of the business and still craft harnesses and other leather goods."

"But there are consequences to getting too big."

When Amish businesses get too successful, Ben said, the owners may voluntarily leave the church or are excommunicated, or they sell the entire business to non-Amish buyers or break the business into parts to sell to different owners, then use the profits to buy land or invest in new businesses.

"Who determines what's too big?"

"The individual church districts; some are more flexible than others. If an owner is low-key, provides jobs to fellow Amish, and loans or donates money for mutual aid throughout the community, the bishop is reluctant to say much. But if an owner becomes publicly prideful or flaunts his wealth or uses a technology in a forbidden way, then the community complains and the church reacts."

"But Ben, stockbrokers? They have stockbrokers?"

"Most don't have stockbrokers but many do invest in mutual funds. They certainly don't spend ostentatiously like many wealthy non-Amish business owners, but their houses are becoming larger, have brick or stone exteriors, are beautifully landscaped, and of course, are built with the attached horse barn. Some wealthier business owners also buy rental properties and hunting cabins in the mountains. Vacation trips are more common—they take trains or buses or hire drivers. But you still don't see them spending lavishly."

"They're not really separate from the world, Ben, as they claim."

"I guess you could look at it that way, but the Amish see it as a concession to business survival. The Lancaster area *Ordnung* is one of the most flexible in the country. The business class grew so fast in the Lancaster area that the church was caught off-guard. So the *Ordnung* for business seems more flexible than the one for farming, which grew in the traditional way over decades. Some farmers do complain that church leaders are more forgiving when it comes to business technology."

Taylor said it seemed unfair that the church would be forgiving of businessmen who venture into the modern world, but not of those who want to further their education. "What happens to the kids who can't farm or whose fathers don't have their own workshop or business to train them in? What kind of future do they have? Hard to find a decent job if they're hampered by their lack of education."

Ben nodded. "The ban on education, for the majority of the Amish," he said, "has kept them from leaving the community for other career opportunities, has kept them segregated from the world to a large extent, and has thus preserved their way of life."

I JOINED THE Pilgrims last night. I went back and forth between them and the Bluebirds, which my best friend Lizzie joined. I decided to go with the Pilgrims not just because John King is a member (that, of course, was a big factor) but because they're not quite as conservative. Spending the summer in the city gave me a taste of what's out there and I didn't want to totally give up that sense of discovery, not just yet, any-way. Anna Beiler's younger sister Rachel also joined and Mattie and several of my other friends. Lizzie, I think, is a little bit mad at me for not joining the Bluebirds so I'll try to smooth that over.

John was at the gang meeting last night at Spud Smucker's barn. Rachel's older brother Ben dropped us off in his buggy and later brought us home. John said hi to me when Rachel and I walked in. He was standing over in a corner of the barn with a group of guys and he had on faded blue jeans and a white tee shirt and a black leather jacket. I swear to you my heart turned over in my chest when I saw him. He later texted me and said, "Glad u joined." Made my night.

Rachel asked me later if I was into him. I guess she saw my eyes fol-low his every move the whole night. I told her he was okay. I'm not ready to share my feelings yet. She then showed me her cell phone (one of Ben's English friends gave her his old one), and she taught me how to use those smiley face things, she called them emoticons, and we gig-gled about how naughty we are.

It was after eleven when I got home so I was groggy this morning when I helped Mamm with breakfast. She didn't say anything at first but right before everyone came in from milking, she asked me if I had a good time last night. I haven't told her about John King but she knows I was going to join a gang since most everyone does. Then she told me something surprising.

She said when she was my age, maybe a little older, she went with some friends in a van to a carnival near Harrisburg and rode the Ferris wheel and bumper cars, blew money on whac-a-mole and skeeball, and threw up eating too much cotton candy. As she was telling me this, Dat came in from the barn and heard us. As he washed his hands, he said that was nothing. He and Big Red Beiler and some other guys used to hook up a CD player and boom box speakers to a car battery and blare them in the buggy all over town and one time they had the bad luck of passing the minister and his wife in their buggy. They traded stories like that all through breakfast. Even David said he and Aaron went to a Coldplay concert at the Wells Fargo Center in Philadelphia. They didn't know much about Coldplay but went with a bunch of people in a couple of guys' cars.

You never think of your parents as having lives other than being parents, but I guess they did. I was surprised because they had never talked about their rumspringas before. I thought about that while I scrubbed the kitchen floor. I decided they're trying to tell me rumspringas are okay as long as you don't go too far, like David and Jacob did with the drinking and racing. What would they think of all the things I did in Philadelphia? I'm not brave enough to tell them.

OMG, OMG, John just texted me and asked me to go to the movies. Mamm and Dat cannot know this. If Dat found out I was in a car with a boy he'd hit the roof, even though David's probably been in cars with girls (before Anna). It's okay for guys to do stuff during rumspringa that girls can't do without a lot of fuss and bother. That's just the way it is.

Should I wear Amish clothes or the English clothes packed in my hope chest? I need to talk to Taylor.

PILES OF NEATLY stacked clothes adorned the kitchen table, shirts separated from pants separated from dresses and further sorted according to whom the clothes belonged, all eventually carried to bedrooms and placed in closets and dresser drawers. Taylor pulled a purple dress from the laundry basket, folded it, and placed it on top of Becca's pile, smoothing it with her hand and giving it a pat before pulling a pair of black men's pants from the basket. She glanced at Sarah. "David's or Jacob's?"

"Those are David's," Sarah said, biting off the thread from a hem she was repairing on Emma's dress. "If you have news work to do Taylor, I can finish up here."

"I do, but I'll get to it in a bit. I want to see how my pie turned out. It smells scrumptious, if I say so myself."

Much to Sarah's surprise that Saturday morning, Taylor had asked for help baking an apple pie, and to Sarah's further surprise, Taylor had slowly and patiently, unlike her usual fling with chores, rolled out the dough for the crust, chopped Granny Smith apples, and fashioned the lattice crust top.

"I want to thank you for helping Jacob find the job at King's," Sarah said. "He told me it's not something he wants to do forever, but he seems pleased."

"He's relieved he will now be able to help pay for his hospital and rehab bills."

"*Ja*, that will be a help, but more important is his future. He said he's still searching for a trade and you are helping him with that."

Taylor paused before answering. She felt uncomfortable keeping the secret of Jacob's college dream but it wasn't her secret to tell.

"He's conflicted but is working hard to figure out what he wants to do," she finally said.

"I pray every day God will help him find his way."

As she folded clothes, Taylor, nervous about keeping yet another Yoder sibling secret, was tempted to tell Sarah what was going on with her eldest daughter. Becca had told Taylor the night before as they got ready for bed about her "date" with John King.

"But what should I wear? My silk shirt has short sleeves. I'll freeze."

Taylor lent her an ivory cashmere cardigan sweater and a pair of black platform pumps to wear with her jeans.

"How will you pull this off, Becca? Are you going to just wear these clothes out of the house in front of your parents?"

"Goodness, no. I'm going to wear everything under my usual dress and apron. I'll roll up my jeans so you can't see them and I'll carry the shoes in my purse."

"Your mom trusts me not to overstep her authority with you."

"Not to worry. No one tells parents anything during *rumspringa*. What the parents don't know they can't get *kerflommixed*, excited, about. *Mamm* knows I joined a gang, and once you join, you go out on the weekends."

"But what about the car? John's going to pull in the driveway and hop out to get you?"

"Of course not. He's going to meet me at the end of our lane, so no one sees the car."

"And where will you change your clothes?"

"I've been thinking about that. I'll change in our vegetable stand. It's at the end of the lane right by Hickory Road and it's empty this time of year. I'll leave my regular clothes in there and change again when I come home. I think I'll even let down my hair." Becca beamed, pleased with her plan.

Taylor thought back to her teenage years. She didn't remember sneaking out of the house but maybe she had. What would her mother have done? She stopped the thought; she didn't need to go there.

"Are you all right?" Sarah asked as Taylor hastily folded the last of the clothes and threw them on top of the piles.

"I'm fine. I'm going to check on my pie and then head to the attic to work."

DAVID SOPPED THE gravy on his plate with his biscuit, took a bite, and continued talking.

"It's bad enough here with the fuel prices up and milk prices down, but it's even worse in northern Indiana. Anna and I were going to visit the Grabers—Gideon and Mary Beth—after the wedding but now I'm not so sure. Gideon was laid off from his factory job and things are tight, not just with him but the whole community."

"What factories do the Amish work in?" Taylor asked

"More than half of the Amish in the Elkhart-LaGrange settlement work in the RV and mobile home factories. Hundreds were laid off when the economy tanked. The church districts can't help make up the lost wages because so many in the community are unemployed. Several of the bishops are allowing them to collect unemployment, but only if they've exhausted all other options. Some are resisting it but others figure they paid into the state unemployment system, they need to feed their kids, so they're taking it."

"Is Gideon taking unemployment?" Jacob asked.

"He didn't say in his letter. Mary Beth is cleaning houses for *Englishers* to help make ends meet. Gideon's hoping to get called back to the RV factory but in the meantime he's doing odd jobs around town."

"Why do the Amish work in factories?" Taylor asked.

"Same reason as here," David said. "Land prices are high and property is scarce. Instead of starting small businesses or learning construction trades, like we did in the Lancaster area, they went into the factories."

Daniel took another helping of pot roast. "Maybe more Amish will return to their roots—small shops, crafts, and woodworking—instead of working in factories," Daniel said. "You rely too much on a single industry and look what happens."

Becca, waiting for a break in the conversation, jumped up and began clearing the table.

"You in a hurry? Got someplace to go?" Daniel asked.

"I'm meeting some friends later," Becca mumbled.

"Katie, while Becca's clearing, bring in Taylor's pie, the vanilla ice cream, and some plates and forks," Sarah said.

"Taylor, I'll have some of your pie later," Becca said. "I need to go get ready."

The family praised Taylor's pie. Joseph called it "yummy *goot*," Jacob joked that she had "redeemed" herself, and even Daniel ate two large helpings.

A short while later, as Sarah, Katie, and Taylor cleaned up from dinner, Becca hurried through the kitchen, head down, said a curt goodbye, and bolted out the door.

"Have fun. Don't be too late," Sarah called after her.

Taylor was the only one who noticed the hint of jean peeking out from under Becca's dress.

LATER THAT NIGHT, Taylor and Jacob sat by the pond, talking quietly.

"*Dat's* not saying much, but things are rough. Milk prices are ten or eleven dollars a hundredweight, down from twenty-four dollars a year ago."

"That's like getting half a paycheck," Taylor said.

"It's a good thing we have the tobacco crop. That will help carry us through. *Dat* has some savings but he's using it to pay hospital and rehab bills, thanks to me. He's got a credit line at the bank, based on equity in the farm, but I know he won't tap that unless things are desperate. I picked a fine time to have an identity crisis and bang myself up."

"I wish there was something I could do to help." Taylor

leaned back on the bench and looked up at the stars in the black sky; in the city, she hardly noticed the night sky but in the country everything seemed clearer. "What's that smell?"

"It's the tobacco curing," Jacob said. "As the leaves lose moisture, the aroma kicks in."

"What a sweet smell, like walking through a humidor. The smell of cigarette smoke is vile but the smell of tobacco curing is pleasant."

They sat in silence for a while, heard the distant clip-clop of horses hooves on a country road, the soft lowing of a cow in the barn.

"If you hadn't had the accident, would you still be here on the farm?" Taylor asked.

"I would never leave my father and David when times are tough. No matter how much I dislike farming. I'm trying to do what I can now, even though it isn't much. I'll start work at King's in a few weeks and will feel useful again. In the meantime, I need to study hard, take the SATs, wait for the scores, and then we'll go from there."

Taylor asked how the SAT studying was coming along.

"I'm working on math—scatter-plot and bar graphs. Not too bad."

Taylor pulled the shawl she borrowed from Sarah tighter around her shoulders as she shivered slightly in the chilly fall air.

I AM REALLY sweet on John King. Last night, he took me to dinner at the Olive Garden (he had lasagna and I had five cheese ziti) and then right down the street to the "Moses" show at the Sight & Sound Theatre. I've heard about this theater before but never been. It does live religious shows based on stories from the Bible. The theater is huge and the show was all about the life of Moses, the parting of the Red Sea, the burning bush, the Ten Commandments. Even real camels and horses and sheep on the stage!

We talked a lot all night, except during the show, of course. I told him about Jacob and his struggles and about Taylor. He was very interested in her and her business and asked a lot of questions about that.

He told me I looked pretty. He looked amazing. Black jeans, a dark grey v-neck sweater, and that black leather jacket that makes him seem so worldly. And sooo cute.

I know this was just our first date but he seems so nice. And responsible. And a good listener. And did I mention cute?!

After the show we had ice cream at the Strasburg Country Store. We both had mint chocolate chip in a waffle cone. Yummy. They make the best waffle cones there, thick and crispy.

At the end of the night, which by the way, I didn't want to end, he dropped me off in front of our vegetable stand and said, "I'll text you soon."

I picked up my regular clothes from the stand and didn't bother getting changed. For one reason, it was chilly. Plus I figured everyone would be asleep since it was late and no one would see me.

When I got to my room, I tried to be quiet and not disturb Taylor but she woke up and wanted to know all about my date. So I told her everything.

She smiled and asked me if I wanted to see him again.

What a silly question!

19

DANIEL RIPPED THE rotted wooden board off the horse stall wall, threw it in a pile, and fitted a new piece in its place. Now that the fall harvest was over, he could attend to the numerous maintenance projects around the farm. David and Levi had taken the horses over to the blacksmith to be shod, and Daniel intended to replace the decayed boards from their stalls before they returned.

He nailed the board in place, his back to the entrance of the stall, unaware that Taylor stood behind him.

"Daniel?"

Daniel continued hammering until he had nailed the board in place. *"Ja?"* he said as he moved to the side of the stall and used the hammer claw to loosen another rotted board.

"I wanted to talk to you about the auction, the one held the other day on your family's behalf. I asked Sarah and she told me the auction had raised some money, not as much as the first auction and not enough to pay the rest of the hospital bills."

"Why is that any of your business?"

Taylor had thought about financially helping the Yoders for weeks now. She had a trust fund established by her father, a third of which she had received at age twenty-five, of which she used a portion to buy her penthouse, a third she would receive when she hit thirty the following year, and the rest at thirty-five. She couldn't think of a better way to spend some of it than on the Yoder family. She hadn't expected the conversation with Daniel to be easy and she pressed on.

"Please don't think I'm trying to invade your privacy but I want to help you and the family. You've all been so kind to me since I've been here and I know I'm helping around the house and the farm, but I want to do more."

"Not necessary," Daniel said, as he tugged with both hands to remove the stubborn board.

"I know. But it would give me great pleasure to do more. I'd like to pay for some of the hospital bills."

Daniel grunted and the board finally gave; he tossed it on the pile and walked around Taylor to pick up a new board.

"We can't take your charity," he said.

"But why not? What's the difference between taking my charity or taking charity from your community?"

"We don't want to rely on handouts from *Englishers*. That's why we don't take Social Security or Medicare. We take care of our own people. And besides, you make part of your money from the television industry. We don't believe in it and I won't take any money made from that."

"What if I paid for a buggy for Jacob? I've done some research and there's a carriage maker in Bird-in-Hand that can outfit a buggy to be wheelchair accessible."

Taylor noted with some satisfaction that that news made Daniel pause, hammer in mid-air for a moment before it again found its mark.

"If Jacob wants a buggy, he can save from his new job and get one."

Taylor knew this argument was lost. "Okay, fine. But if you change your mind, either offer will always stand."

"I won't," Daniel said, as he hammered another board in place.

FATHER AND DAUGHTER relaxed on the couch in Connor's office before they headed off to a late Friday dinner, each sipping a pinot noir from a collection housed in the wine fridge in the built-in bar. From the windows, the city lights sparkled but the rest of the offices were dark and quiet, everyone else gone for the night.

"Tough day," Connor said, running his hand through his hair. Taylor noticed a few more strands of white at her father's temples and his face looked tired. She was glad she had come home for the weekend. Over the last several weeks, they had spent a lot of time on the phone with each other but it was good to see him in person.

"Bad news on circulation figures for the newspapers. Twelve of twenty papers down," Taylor said. "At least the radio and TV stations' numbers were good."

"Yeah, that makes up for some of the hemorrhage we're experiencing on the print side."

"The economy is bouncing back. That should help some."

Connor poured more wine in both of their glasses. "Maybe a little. But the shift from advertising in newspapers to ads on the Internet seems like a trend that's here to stay. We need a long-term strategy or our business will bleed to death. We've either got to cut costs or build a money-making news presence online or a combination of the two."

"We'll do whatever it takes."

"I'm glad to hear you say that. I wasn't sure how invested you still were in the business."

"Dad, how can you say that? Of course I am."

Connor reminded her of their drive in late July to Lancaster to retrieve her repaired Z4 and her comment then about feeling as if her involvement in Loden Media was assumed rather than a conscious decision.

Taylor wanted to reassure her father, but she also wanted to be honest with him. "I can't imagine doing anything other than working here with you. But I do feel like I'm going through something that may lead to some changes, but I don't know what yet."

Connor nodded. "You've been rather distracted lately. Don't get me wrong, your work isn't suffering, but you do seem focused on things other than work, the Yoders mainly. I'm curious. What are you getting out of this arrangement?"

"Well, I haven't stopped to really think about that. I just know I need to stay involved. We found Jacob a job and now I want to get him through the SATs and help him make a decision about college."

Connor placed his wine glass on the coffee table and leaned forward in his chair. "Taylor, I think it's good that you're sharing your life with people outside of work, that you are being a mentor, even a friend, to Becca and Jacob."

Taylor glanced at her father in surprise. "I never considered it that way." She thought for a moment. "Maybe that's a change I'm going through, making room in my life for something other than work."

Connor smiled. "That's a good change. How much longer will you split your time between the Yoders, the Lancaster office, and here?"

"Maybe another month to six weeks or so. The SAT test is in a couple weeks, and I also want to stick around to help with David's wedding in November."

"It'll be good for the family to have something to celebrate. Do you interact much with the rest of the Amish community?"

"Not much. I'm trying to keep a low profile. I don't want to jeopardize anything for Jacob or embarrass the Yoders with my so-called excess of technology and worldly ways."

Connor chuckled. "Luckily, we've kept you under the radar since the accident in June. Imagine what a circus it would have been at the time if the media had played up your identity."

"You think my identity would have caused more publicity for the story?"

"Absolutely. Much more could have been made of the story with the media heiress angle, but the *Lancaster Post*, in deference to me, ignored that slant, and as a result, the story remained a local one and wasn't picked up by the *AP* or the national media."

Taylor sipped the last of her wine. "I never realized that ... until now."

ON MONDAY MORNING, Taylor decided to start with one large local paper and a news service. Once the story hit the newsstands and the web, she hoped to hear from the *New York Times*, the *Washington Post*, maybe *Good Morning America* and the *Today Show*, perhaps even *CNN*. She had thought about her idea all weekend but hadn't discussed it with her father; she had no intention of being dissuaded. She would contact the media, use her identity to publicize the story, talk about the Yoders and how the accident had hurt them financially, and wait for the compassionate public to send donations. Daniel couldn't refuse charity from dozens, maybe even hundreds, of sympathetic readers and viewers, Taylor thought.

Two hours later, working from her attic office, Taylor had done phone interviews with reporters from the *Philadelphia Inquirer* and the *Associated Press*. Not long after that, she saw the first *AP* online stories on *Yahoo* and *AOL*, with headlines that read: MEDIA HEIRESS HELPS STRUGGLING AMISH AFTER BUGGY CRASH.

And we're off and running, she thought. She figured she could set up photo ops with the media from a distant location; photographers could shoot the Yoder farm with a telephoto lens, the family wouldn't be disturbed, and their ban on appearing in photos wouldn't be compromised.

She figured wrong.

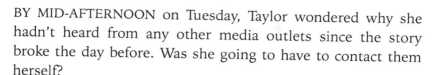

BY MID-AFTERNOON on Tuesday, Taylor wondered why she hadn't heard from any other media outlets since the story broke the day before. Was she going to have to contact them herself?

In the attic, she concentrated on a stack of paperwork until the sound of cars traveling down Hickory Hill Road and doors slamming finally intruded on her focus. *Awful lot of traffic out there this afternoon.* She glanced out the window.

It took only a second for the horror to register. "Oh, no, no, no!"

JACOB WHEELED HIMSELF down the ramp from the kitchen door on his way to the tobacco curing shed to check on progress. The news photographer's wide-angle lens took several shots of him before Jacob noticed the commotion on Yoder Lane.

Daniel and David walked out of the barn, having finished the afternoon's chores and intending to join Jacob on the walk to the tobacco shed.

"What the hay?" Daniel asked, looking at the numerous television vans and the crowd of reporters with cameras heading down Yoder Lane.

"Get inside, go!" Daniel ordered both David and Jacob. Just then Taylor came running out of the house.

"What have you done?" Daniel spit out between clenched teeth.

"I'll handle it. Don't worry."

From the window inside the family room, Sarah and Becca watched the gathering crowd with dismay and confusion. Katie, who had been watching from upstairs, flew down the stairs and out the front door, Sarah yelling, "Stop!" to no avail. Almost immediately, though, she realized what Katie was doing. Emma and Joseph, on their way home from school, stood frozen in a panic on the bridge over Stoney Creek; several of the reporters had spotted them and started toward them with cameras. Katie grabbed the twins by the hand and ran with them to the front door, which Sarah opened and then closed quickly behind them.

Taylor reached the crowd, introduced herself, and ordered the reporters back down the lane.

"I'm sorry, you can't be here. It's an invasion of the Yoders' privacy. They didn't ask for this. I'll answer all your questions, but please, leave their property."

The media formed a crush around Taylor, the questions rapid fire.

"How is Jacob doing?"

"Will the Yoders lose their farm?"

"Why are you living here?"

"Miss Loden, how can you say our being here is an invasion of the Yoder's privacy when you initiated the story about them?" one ABC reporter asked, microphone in Taylor's face. "What did you think was going to happen?"

TAYLOR SAT IN her car in the Wawa gas station parking lot, looking through the *New York Times* and the *Philadelphia Inquirer*. Several photos accompanied both papers' stories: Jacob in his wheelchair, the twins on the bridge, Sarah and Becca looking out the window, Daniel and David outside the barn. The story had also made the morning shows, *MSNBC* and *CNN*, and a dozen papers throughout the country had run the *AP* story and photos. Taylor sighed deeply. The whole idea had been a disaster. Her father had questioned her news judgment, Daniel had been apoplectic, and if it hadn't been for Jacob's plea to his parents, she'd be on her way back to Philadelphia.

After the media had finally left, Daniel had demanded an explanation from Taylor. Sarah banished the kids to their rooms. David took the buggy and fled to Anna's, and Jacob retired to his room, door closed. Daniel had paced the kitchen, as Sarah and Taylor sat at the table.

"What were you thinking?" Daniel asked with quiet fury, then launched into a tirade in Deitsch. Sarah waited until he was finished.

"I know you must've had a reason," Sarah said, her voice calm yet disappointed.

"I did. I am so, so sorry. I thought I had it all figured out. I never thought the media would just show up here, but in retrospect, I should have known better. I was trying to help."

"Help how?" Daniel choked. "How was that mess supposed to help?"

"I thought publicizing the story through my name would draw attention to your situation. I thought people would learn about the family's physical and financial hardships and would want to help by sending donations. I thought you would be more willing to take their charity since you wouldn't take mine. I was trying to help you pay off your hospital and rehab debt."

Daniel stopped pacing and glared at Taylor. "We don't want or need that kind of help. We don't want to rely on outsiders for help. We can handle it on our own, and among our people, with God's help."

"Well, if you want to believe that, then maybe God was trying to help you through me."

"Taylor, we appreciate your wanting to help," Sarah said, "but this was not the way to do it. Begging for help from outsiders, especially through media publicity, is against everything we believe in. It's prideful, it's . . . ," she hung her head, "humiliating."

"Now we'll have to go make this right with Bishop Lapp," Daniel said. "I just don't think we can have you here . . . "

"*Dat*," Jacob interrupted. They all turned in surprise; Jacob had quietly approached from his room.

"Taylor did wrong but she had good intentions. I think we can forgive that. We'll talk to Bishop Lapp. He'll understand we did nothing wrong. The story came out in the paper and on TV, but if Taylor promises to stay out of the limelight in the future, it will all blow over, and that'll be the end of it."

Sarah nodded to Jacob and looked at Daniel. He sat down heavily on a kitchen chair and held Jacob's eyes. He knew Jacob was asking him not to send Taylor away. He also knew his eldest son was struggling to right his life and although he did not quite know how to help him, he was scared to death of losing him.

"We'll go talk to the bishop," he agreed.

WE SHOULDN'T HAVE, but we did. We told Emma and Joseph to play checkers in my room and then Katie and I sat on the top step and listened to Dat grill Taylor. My heart beat so fast I could hardly breathe. Taylor is so brave. I know she was upset but despite that she still dealt with Dat, stood up to him right to his face, but in a respectful way. I wish I could do that. I rely on Mamm to be the go between for me, like that time in Philadelphia when they caught Taylor and me dancing to gospel music.

When I heard Jacob's voice, I was surprised and proud of him for speaking up too, although it's different for the men. As a daughter, I am expected to be obedient, to my parents, to my elders, and one day to my husband. I see how Mamm defers to Dat but she also has her say, too, in a quiet way. Mamm is heard by Dat. I want to have my say. I want to be heard, too.

DANIEL SLAPPED THE rubber-banded, eight-inch stack of checks and cash on Bishop Lapp's kitchen table.

"I don't know what to do with all this," he said. "There's

checks for twenty dollars, fifty, some for a hundred and five hundred, a few for a thousand, one for five thousand. And there's cash; people sent in a couple dollars, fives, tens. It amounts to a little over thirty-nine thousand dollars." He spread his hands helplessly.

"These donations came in for several days after the story appeared in the newspapers and on TV," Jacob explained. "My father believes we can't accept this money. He's appalled by the story and ashamed."

"*Ja*, an unfortunate incident," Bishop Lapp agreed, "but you got caught in something not under your control. What could we do with the money if you don't accept it?"

"We talked about donating it to local fire companies or the Mennonite Disaster Service," Jacob said.

"Worthwhile causes, to be sure. But these good people who donated wanted to specifically help your family. To not accept would be to reject their kindness in giving."

"Didn't think of that," Daniel muttered. "But it still doesn't sit right with me."

"Maybe your annoyance should be directed at the source of the problem rather than the folks trying to help by donating."

"Taylor was trying to help, too." Jacob said. "Her judgment was poor, I agree."

"You defend her. That's understandable. She's been good for your family in many ways," the bishop said. "I trust your opinion of her."

He picked up the stack of donations and placed it in front of Daniel on the table.

"I have known you for many years, Daniel. You are a man of integrity, a man who honors God and church, your family, and our community. Some among us talk negatively about this incident but most in the community know you as I do. Take the money in the spirit in which it was intended. Use it to pay your debts or for whatever need you have. God would expect no less."

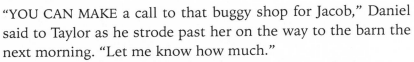

"YOU CAN MAKE a call to that buggy shop for Jacob," Daniel said to Taylor as he strode past her on the way to the barn the next morning. "Let me know how much."

Taylor smiled to herself and followed him into the barn.

SARAH DRIED THE last plate from breakfast and put it away. She watched Daniel speak briefly to Taylor on his way to the barn and she thought about their discussion last night. Daniel had decided to use the bulk of the thirty-nine thousand in donation money—about thirty-two thousand, after deducting the cost of a new buggy for Jacob—to pay the Bayard rehab bill; with what they had already paid thanks to Amish Church Aid and the auction money and their own savings, that would leave about twenty-three thousand they still owed. Plus they also owed nearly sixty thousand to Memorial General. Sarah sighed. They would be making medical payments for a long, long time.

TAYLOR WAITED ANXIOUSLY on the sofa in the high school guidance office while Jacob took the SATs; she glanced at the bulletin board with notices of college recruiter visits, at a table stacked with packets containing helpful information on the college application process, next to copies of the school's newspaper. Once again, Taylor was nervous for Jacob, even more nervous than when she had waited for him to take the GED tests in Philadelphia in July, so nervous that although she brought a briefcase of work, she couldn't focus on it and ended up mindlessly phone surfing.

She had been permitted to wait there for Jacob because of

his disability, in case he needed physical help at any time during the nearly four-hour test. She didn't doubt he had the stamina required to take the test; she saw what he did every day in the barn or around the farm, despite the wheelchair, but after his muscle spasm incident, she wasn't taking any chances.

Only Sarah had been in the kitchen early that morning when she and Jacob left to take the test at a local high school. Her eyes had been curious but she hadn't asked where they were heading, for which Taylor was grateful; she didn't want to lie and Jacob's sharpened number two pencils and his graphing calculator felt heavy in her purse.

She didn't know whether she'd ever have kids, hadn't in any meaningful way contemplated it, yet she thought she knew the anxiety and pride parents must feel for their children at this time in their lives, anxiety about the stress endured not only in studying for and taking the admissions tests but in selecting the colleges to apply to, and the pride in seeing children work hard to reach a goal. It occurred to her that her parents must have felt that way about her own college process many years ago. But she couldn't compare her situation to Jacob's; his struggle—the academic catch-up on top of his disability—was staggering and no matter how it turned out, she was so proud of his effort and perseverance her eyes welled up.

She wished Jacob's own parents could feel such pride for their son.

DAVID HAD JUST dipped his finger in the bowl from which Katie had finished icing the double layer German chocolate cake topped with flaked coconut and toasted pecans, made especially for his twenty-first birthday, and licked it when Emma yelled, "We have a visitor!" Excited about the upcoming birthday festivities, Emma hopped up and down on one foot in front of the family room windows as the buggy drove down the lane. A modest pile of birthday packages for David sat on a corner of the kitchen counter, the cake was nearly done, and as soon as the rest of the family and Taylor came in from the evening's milking, supper would be eaten and then the party would begin. The family had decided to exempt David from the evening's farm chores and Anna, visiting to celebrate with him, had just finished setting the table.

Jacob, the first to come out of the barn, greeted Tobias King as he stepped out of his buggy.

"We'll be ready for you at work week after next, if you can be there," he said. "It'll be Susie's last week and she can train you before she leaves."

"I can be there," Jacob said. "First thing Monday morning?"

"*Ja*, that'd be fine. It'll be good to have you, Jacob." As they started toward the house, Tobias said, "I know it's near supper time and I won't stay long, but I'd also like to talk to David, if he's around."

"He's inside, lazing around the house. Seems to think it's a big deal 'cause it's his birthday," Jacob joked.

"Ah, then I've come at a good time."

Once David and Tobias were seated in the family room—and Sarah, Katie, Anna, Emma and Jacob, more than a little curious, tried to occupy themselves in the kitchen—Tobias came right to the point.

"I recently bought a small farm, about forty acres, not far from here. The man who owned it died and his family is moving out to Ohio to be with relatives. I'd like you to farm it, if you're willing. You can rent the land from me, with an option to buy in five years."

David swallowed a couple times and it took him several seconds to find his tongue and even then he was at a loss for words. "I . . . *ja*, I would . . . I accept," he finally stammered.

In the kitchen, the others hadn't meant to eavesdrop, but Tobias' hearty voice had carried. Anna's hand flew to her mouth and she turned to Sarah with wide eyes.

"Good. Some repairs need to be done to the barn and farmhouse but they're both in pretty decent shape. How 'bout I come by for you Saturday morning, say around ten, and we can go take a look at your farm."

"MY FAMILY IS *redding up* the house for the wedding," Anna said as Taylor drove her and David to the Lancaster County courthouse to get their marriage license. "When you picked me up, *Mamm* and my sisters Anne Marie and Rachel were washing windows and *Dat* and the boys were painting the living room." Anna brushed a stray piece of hair back under her *kapp* and sighed. "There's so many last minute things to do before the wedding next Tuesday. Everything needs to be in apple pie order."

"It's been crazy over at the Yoder's, too," Taylor said. "All the women, even me, are baking up a storm—cakes and cookies and pies. I just do whatever they tell me to do and try not to get in the way."

"Before we get too far down the road Anna, did you bring your ID with you?" David asked from the back seat.

"*Ja*, I have my Pennsylvania non-driver's license," Anna said rummaging through her purse, "and my social security exemption number and my birth certificate."

"*Goot*," David said. "One less thing to worry about."

"Is your wedding dress ready?" Taylor asked.

"I finished sewing it last night. And my two *newehockers'*, my attendants', dresses I finished last week."

"Will you wear your dress again after the wedding, or is it a one-time dress like in an *Englisher* wedding?"

"Oh, no. I'll wear it again after the wedding on Sundays for church."

"I have a board meeting in Philadelphia Tuesday morning but I plan on coming to the wedding right after. Becca told me the service is in the morning. What will I miss?"

"The service, like a regular church service, starts at eight-thirty and is about three hours long," David said. "There's singing and scripture reading and sermons having to do with bible references to marriage and relationships."

Anna continued. "The first song is 378, that's the page in the *Ausbund,* our hymn book, and David and I enter to the second song, the *Lob Lied.* At the end of the service, we take our vows, the minister blesses us, and then the celebration begins with the noon meal."

"How many guests are you expecting?"

"Probably around three hundred," Anna said.

"Wow. They'll all fit in your home?"

"The furniture in the living room and kitchen will be moved out on Monday," David explained, "and the bench wagon from our church district and also one from a neighbor district will bring the benches we use for church. They'll be set up to sit on and also converted into tables."

"Does your family make the food for all those people?"

"*Neh.* The parents help organize the wedding and the helpers but don't do any work that day," Anna explained. "The cooks, lots of them, are folks from our church district. They'll prepare most of the meal beforehand but for the wedding day cooking, we'll use our *grossdaadi* kitchen since guests will be seated in our kitchen. There are so many people, we'll eat in shifts.

"The waiters who help serve the food at the tables are my aunts and uncles. The *forgeher,* or ushers, seat the guests according to age and how they're related to David or me, and the *hostlers,* teenage boys, take care of the buggy horses in the barn. And there's dishwashers and table setters, too."

"It's quite the production," David said. "We've been running around like chickens with our heads cut off, which by the way, is one of my jobs, to cut the heads off the chickens that will be cooked for the noon meal."

"What will you both do after the wedding? Is there a honeymoon?"

"We'll spend our first married night at my home," Anna said. "The next morning, we'll get up at four in the morning to clean up. After that, we start visiting friends and relatives, off and on, for several weeks."

"The first thing I'll be doing is changing my look," David said, grinning. "I've got some serious beard growing to do. We're also planning a trip to Indiana to visit relatives in December for about ten days, after I help *Dat* strip the tobacco. And then we come back here, live with the Beilers, and Anna's going to work for my aunts Esther and Ruth in their quilt shop and I'm going to lend myself out as a farm hand to make some money and work toward setting up our new farm, hopefully by next spring." He beamed.

"You both seem excited and happy," Taylor said.

"And grateful," Anna added.

"*Ja*, grateful," David agreed. "I'm grateful to have lived to see my wedding day."

WHEN TAYLOR ARRIVED at the Beiler farm Tuesday, it was nearly noon, the yard already packed with gray-topped buggies, a few black carriages belonging to Old Order Mennonites, and a handful of cars and vans hired by the Amish traveling long-distance. Inside was a whirlwind of activity, men setting up tables in a u-shape around the living room, one corner reserved for the bridal party, and unpacking chests filled with dinnerware and utensils, only brought out for weddings and funerals.

Becca noticed Taylor standing awkwardly by the front door and rushed to escort her to the kitchen, where the Yoder and Beiler families were seated, the fathers at the head of the table. As they ate—"roast," a mix of shredded chicken and bread stuffing, along with mashed potatoes, gravy, creamed celery, cole slaw, applesauce, cherry pie, donuts, fruit salad, tapioca pudding, bread, butter, jelly—Becca introduced Taylor to Anna's parents, grandparents and siblings, and pointed out to her the wedding cake she and Katie had made, one of several elaborate cakes decorating the corner of the table where the bridal party sat in the living room.

After each seating, washtubs were brought to the living room to wash dishes. From where she sat, Taylor could see the bride and groom. Anna, simply attired in a mid-calf length navy dress with white apron and *kapp*, seemed to glow, despite the absence of a wedding train or veil, flowers or rings. And for the groom and his attendants, not a wedding tux in sight, just black suits, vests with hooks and eyes rather than buttons, white shirts and black bow ties, which Becca explained were not worn for a regular church service.

After they ate, Becca took Taylor upstairs to Anna's bedroom to view the display of wedding gifts received so far: dinnerware, pots and pans, casserole dishes, kitchen utensils, and tools, such as hammers, screwdrivers, a wheelbarrow, wrenches, shovels, rakes.

"They'll get other gifts as they visit friends and relatives over the coming weeks," Becca said, nearly knocking over a mop leaning against a bucket. "Anna's parents gave them a bed, chest of drawers and night stands, a fridge and stove, and a kitchen table and six chairs. Her grandparents gave them a kitchen hutch, and a sofa and coffee table for the family room. All the furniture and appliances are stored for now in a relative's barn. 'Course, she'll also have all the things she's accumulated over the years in her hope chest, like quilts, sheets, towels, tablecloths."

Becca also told Taylor that Anna's oldest brother had contributed a used buggy to the couple since his family had recently bought a new one. From the Yoder family, David had so far received a rocking chair from his furniture maker uncle Samuel Yoder, and from his uncle John Esh, the contractor, an offer to make whatever repairs might be needed at the new barn and farmhouse. Mary and Levi had bought the couple a horse for the buggy.

In the corner of the room, rolled up and standing upright, was the oval braided rug Taylor had bought them for the family room; Becca had told Taylor Anna had seen the rug in a local shop, had loved it, but thought it too expensive. When the rug had been delivered to the Beiler farm the day before the wedding, David had been there, and told Taylor that Anna had jumped up and down with excitement.

"David will use the money our parents gave him to buy farm equipment and a few cows and a work horse," Becca said, tripping over a set of small throw rugs on the floor.

"Are you okay?" Taylor asked. "You seem anxious."

"I am a little nervous. One of our wedding traditions is for the bride to play matchmaker. She decides which couples sixteen and older sit together at the evening meal. Right now, she's asking the guys who they want to sit with." She lowered her voice and leaned closer to Taylor. "I'm hoping John King chooses me. If he does, that means we're a couple."

The rest of the afternoon, the wedding guests visited and the younger ones gathered to sing, mostly religious songs with a faster tempo than those sung in church. As the waiters served the evening meal—stewed chicken, fried sweet potatoes, macaroni and cheese, platters of cheese and cold cuts—Taylor watched Sarah and Daniel eye Becca seated happily next to John King; as of that moment, they and everyone else were made publicly aware of the two seeing each other. Jacob, to the right of Taylor, also pensively watched his sister as he ate.

"What are you thinking?" Taylor asked.

"That David is settled and Becca, for now at least, is happy. All is as it should be."

"Is it?"

"For them it is."

"Don't you at least want for Becca what you desire for yourself? The freedom to make her own choices?"

"Becca will find her own way, in time."

Peanut butter and oatmeal cookies, candy, nuts, mints, ice cream, and the cutting of the various wedding cakes followed the meal. It was nearly midnight as the last of the guests prepared to leave. As Taylor headed through the yard to her car, Bishop Lapp appeared by her side. Not having spoken to him privately before, yet nonplussed, Taylor kept on walking, waiting for him to speak.

The bishop exchanged no pleasantries about the wedding, no small talk about the weather. Instead, he quietly said, "No more surprises up your sleeve, I hope." Then he turned and walked to his buggy, a *hostler* waiting there with his horse.

20

ILOVED DAVID'S wedding. I had such fun, and now everyone knows about me and John King. There's been a lot of teasing. Emma and Joseph smack their lips whenever they see me and Lizzie said, "Oooh, when's the wedding?" Mattie said she knew I was stuck on him and Anna's younger sister Rachel said he was cute and joked they had celery seeds left over if we wanted them.

One thing about the wedding. I remember sitting in the kitchen and watching Taylor walk in the front door right before the noon meal. She's been living with us for weeks but for some reason it was strange to see my rumspringa friend in the midst of such a traditional Amish gathering, like two branches of my life intersecting. She stood by the door before she saw us, but in those few seconds she seemed different. Usually she seems hurried and stressed and is already thinking about the next place she needs to be or the next thing she must do, but just then she seemed calm and steady.

When we milked this morning, she asked me whether dating John would impact my rumspringa. I said I really liked him but had no idea about my future, with or without him. She said my rumspringa time in Philadelphia wasn't long or deep enough to make a decision whether to stay separate from the world. She said I've only "grazed the surface" and if I wanted to experience a serious "mind expanding" rumspringa, I could travel more, to New York City or California or even Europe *(wow!!), or take an art class or get tutored in any subject I might have an interest in.* "How do you know you won't find something that sets you on fire if you don't explore more?" she asked.

I wondered how we could do all that right under Mamm and Dat's noses and she said once she gets Jacob settled, she'll go back to the city and I could come visit her any time and we could do whatever I wanted. I said I would definitely like that and in the end, what I do with my life is my choice. And then she said something that really made me think.

"Do you really have a choice? Your elders lead you to believe you do by allowing this rumspringa period, but you really don't because your lack of education and your socialization have taught you to fear and distrust the world, instead of embracing its choices and challenges." She asked me how many people I knew who left the Amish for good. I said none. She said my 'choice' is actually an illusion of choice with my only option being to return to the fold and all that is familiar and safe because it's too scary to join the outside world. "You never get to experience independence or individuality."

We were so focused on our conversation that we didn't notice Katie throwing hay in the stall next door. She overheard us and was upset.

"What good is the whole big world without your family?" Katie asked. "Isn't our way of life and our family more important than independence or individuality? How could you hurt and disrespect Mamm and Dat by leaving? They can hardly bear what's happening with Jacob."

Taylor looked down at her feet at the mention of Jacob. Something is going on with the two of them. I don't feel like I can ask either one of them what it is, though.

It's true that we Amish are taught that the importance of our way of life is as a group of faithful believers, working together toward salvation. If I stay Amish, my life will be predictable. I'll marry, have kids, follow the rules and routines. In return, I'll belong to a large and loving extended family and group of friends, and be supported all the days of my life by my community, especially in my time of need. I'll never be alone. I'll always know who I am and where I'm going (and what I'm wearing). Mamm and Dat seem satisfied and content. Is there more to life than all of that? Is community and security worth more than my

individual freedom? I don't know yet. I guess that's what I need to figure
out and what Taylor is trying to help me with.

ELI, ONE OF Jacob's co-workers from King's Gazebos, hoisted
the wheelchair from the back of the van, then helped Jacob
into it.

"See you tomorrow," Jacob said, and watched the van pull
out of the driveway.

He thought about joining whoever was in the barn for the
evening milking but decided instead to head inside and change
for supper. He wanted to be by himself, at least for a little
while, and reflect on his first day at work.

He wheeled himself up the ramp and into the kitchen,
greeted his mother and handed her his lunch pail. She wanted
to know about his day but he didn't want to talk about it yet;
he had talked all day, on the phone and to new co-workers,
and he wasn't accustomed to talking that much. He wanted to
enjoy a bit of silence.

"I'll tell you all about it at supper," he promised.

In his room, using the rehab techniques he had learned at
Bayard that were by then routine to him, he changed out of
his Amish work clothes—new black pants, green shirt, and
suspenders he had bought specifically for work —and emptied
his bladder catheter and leg bag. He then changed into the
grey sweats he felt most comfortable in. He threw his shirt in
the laundry basket and hung his pants in the closet, on the
clothes bar his uncle had lowered so he could reach.

Then he just sat and closed his eyes. It had been a hectic day,
full of the noise of saws and men's shouts, and new people, and
unfamiliar things to learn, like the phone system and the copy
machine and co-workers' names and the different types of gazebos. Part of him was exhilarated by the challenges, part of
him missed the daily quiet of the farm and being able to see

his family throughout the day, and part of him knew that once he mastered the tasks assigned to him, the rhythm of the work would become routine and unsatisfying and he would feel the desire for substance once again.

He needed the job to help pay his medical expenses, and the work ethic he was raised by also motivated him to perform well. But he also realized this job represented the calm before the storm; his parents thought he was getting on with his life, his Amish life, and he wasn't looking forward to telling them what he wanted to do with his real life, should he have the opportunity.

So he was waiting, like the quiet lull between seasons of farming, the down time after the fall corn harvest and before winter's tobacco stripping or the next spring's planting. He was waiting for his next season to begin.

THE SMELL OF turkey wafted through the living room of Taylor's penthouse as Connor watched Thanksgiving Day football on TV. Taylor had insisted on cooking everything but the pumpkin pie, which she had ordered from a local bakery, and Connor had initially stared at her aghast. The Taylor he knew had no interest in cooking, with culinary skills hardly capable of microwaving a bag of frozen peas. Usually they dined at one of the city's restaurants for Thanksgiving, but Taylor said Sarah had given her a turkey-with-all-the-fixing's tutorial and she felt up for the challenge.

"Dad, you can carve now. The turkey's been out of the oven for a half hour. It actually looks like it's supposed to. Skin's a nice golden brown."

Connor stood at the entrance to the kitchen and nervously surveyed the scene before him. The mixer whirred as Taylor whipped up the mashed potatoes; bowls and cooking utensils littered the counters, along with remnants of chopped onion and bread cubes and unidentified puddles of liquid. Yet Connor had to admit she had pulled it off. Sweet potatoes bubbled on one stove burner, green beans steamed on another, gravy warmed on a third, and the stuffing scooped into a serving dish. She looked a little frayed, though; cheeks flushed, she suddenly dropped the mixer, grabbed an oven mitt, and pulled the dinner rolls out of the oven.

"Well, they're just a little burned on the bottom, but edible."

Twenty minutes later, they sat at the dining room table, the feast spread before them on the good china, candles glowing. Taylor looked at her father triumphantly, and Connor raised his glass of cabernet to his daughter.

"To talents you never knew you had," he said. "What are the Yoders doing today?"

"Other than milking the cows, same as us, except more people and more food."

Throughout the meal, father and daughter, who hadn't spent much time together over the last several weeks, chatted amiably. They talked about the news industry and the status of their media portfolio. They talked about the Yoders and Taylor brought her father up to speed on the family, including David's wedding and Jacob's recent SAT test taking.

"Don't get your hopes up about his scores," Connor warned. "He doesn't have the academic foundation. Really, it's an uphill battle."

"I know, but he's so bright and has worked so hard. Even if they're not great scores, I think he could do well at a community college."

"Would he really leave his family and buck his roots and way of life so he could go to college?"

Taylor had also wondered about that. Despite his protestations to the contrary, would Jacob really leave if he had the opportunity?

"I don't know. But I want to help him any way I can if he does decide to follow through."

The two cleared the table, cleaned the kitchen, loaded the dishwasher, and then returned to the table with plates of pumpkin pie and vanilla ice cream.

For months, Connor had pondered his daughter's attraction to the Yoder family. He understood Taylor's stated goals—to help Jacob continue his education, to help Becca enjoy a meaningful *rumspringa*, to physically aid a family short on manpower due to an accident she believed was partially her fault—but for what was she really searching?

He had finally decided that at least part of the Yoder's appeal was his daughter's desire for a sense of connection to an extended family, something he obviously—and this stung him—hadn't been able to provide for her since her mother died. Both sets of Taylor's grandparents had died years ago and he, too, was an only child.

He had thought meaningful work would provide a structure for her to heal. It wasn't uncommon for people to bury themselves in their work to survive grief; he had done it himself. But she had used her job instead as a long-term means of isolation, diving into work to the exclusion of everything else. He felt guilty he hadn't noticed her loneliness sooner and done something about it, although what he could have done, other than encourage her to branch out and open up—a feat easier said than done—he didn't know. Connor shifted uncomfortably in his seat.

"Honey, when are you coming home? When will your time with the Yoders be finished?"

Taylor took a bite of pie and slowly chewed before answering.

"Who am I outside of my job? If you take away my role as media heiress or vice president of Loden Media, what's left that reflects the core of me?"

Connor lowered his fork. That wasn't the direction he had anticipated the conversation going but he sensed she wasn't just waxing philosophical.

"Uh . . . "

"I have defined myself solely by what I do. There's no *me* left if you take away the career role I play."

"Who do you want to be?"

"Something more than I am."

"Well, people have grappled with self-esteem angst for ages."

"I mean, what are my values? What are my passions or do I even have any? Who are the people, besides you, necessary to my life?"

Connor cleared his throat and tried to gather his thoughts. He owed his daughter more than mere platitudes.

"Defining who we are is a slow process involving much trial and error. It often takes a lifetime."

"That may be, Dad, but I think by now in my life I should have more than one interest and one significant other. I'm one-dimensional."

"Something's holding you back from living a fuller life. What are you afraid of? If you reflect on that and come up with an answer, then you can go about redefining yourself."

"I've wasted so many years."

"No time is ever wasted if in the end you discover something about yourself that helps you move forward."

Later that night in his home, as Connor reflected on the conversation with his daughter, he realized two things: he still didn't know when Taylor was coming home, and his life was a mirror image of hers.

TAYLOR PUTTERED AROUND the penthouse that long weekend; she cleaned out her clothes closet and readied a large bag of items to donate to charity, she watched old movies on cable, ate leftover turkey, searched her library for a classic to read—she decided on *Howard's End* by E. M. Forster—and when Connor called Saturday to see when she was coming into the office—

"No hurry, I just thought we could have lunch together."—he was surprised to hear her say, "I'm not coming in today, Dad. I won't be in 'til Monday morning and that afternoon I'm heading back to Lancaster. But let's go to brunch tomorrow."

Late that Sunday night, as Taylor passed through the living room, turning off lights before retiring, she stopped by the piano. One hand caressed the polished wood; she sat on the bench, both hands resting lightly on the keys. She saw herself playing in the living room of her childhood home, felt her mother's hand on her shoulder, heard her say, "What a beautiful passage." She continued to sit, willing her hands to play, but she couldn't overcome the past, so she stood, and went to bed.

DANIEL WALKED SLOWLY into the kitchen, tossed the day's mail on the kitchen counter, and sat down uneasily at the kitchen table, an unopened white envelope in his hand. The house was unusually quiet; Sarah, the twins and Becca were running errands, Taylor was in Philadelphia, and David was working odd jobs at a couple farms down the road. Jacob and Katie had just finished his physical therapy and he wheeled himself into the kitchen to grab a class of milk while Katie ambled over to the *grossdaadi* to visit with her grandparents before it was time to start supper.

"Is something the matter?" Jacob asked his father.

Daniel turned over the envelope and slit it open with his finger. "There's been a rumor among some of the other tobacco farmers but I was hoping it wasn't true," he said as he pulled out a letter and read it.

"The company is putting a hold on the last year of our contract to grow genetically modified tobacco. They say they have a huge inventory. They're going to pay us for this year's crop but want us to skip next year's. If we farmers don't want to wait out the year to see what happens next, we can go back to growing burley tobacco."

"They must be having trouble selling those nearly nicotine-free cigarettes," Jacob surmised.

"Well, we'll have had two good years, thank God for that."

"Do you want to go back to growing burley?"

Daniel folded the letter and put it back in the envelope. He looked into his son's face, feeling a momentary spark of anger. *What do you care? You never liked farming tobacco anyway.* He felt instant shame, thinking of the work his son had done during the hurricane and how hard he tried to help around the farm.

"I don't know," he said. "I just don't know."

"DAT SAYS YOUR brother's doing well at the job," John told Becca, as he shifted the black mustang into third gear. "He's a fast learner."

"*Goot,*" Becca said as she leaned back in the leather passenger seat and smiled. "Everything's *goot.*"

All was right with the world. She was with John, who she thought looked better than fine in his jeans and navy crew neck sweater and what looked like new Timberland boots. She noticed he kept glancing at her sideways as he drove and was glad she and Taylor had gone to the outlets and purchased a few "date clothes," as Taylor called them. She wore a cream merino wool turtleneck sweater and ankle boots. She liked wearing high-heeled shoes but had to admit she felt more stable walking in a lower heeled boot. She had brought her black cape in case she needed it and had thrown it on the back seat, next to John's leather jacket.

It was chilly outside but her sweater was warm. Taylor had offered to buy her a coat but Becca reasoned she could hide English clothes better under a cape; wearing a new coat would just be too glaring for her parents. She had again left her regular clothes and sneakers in the vegetable stand and John had picked her up at the end of the Yoder driveway. They were on their way to Red Robin, a burger place Becca had never been to but John said was one of his favorites.

"I try to keep an eye out for him during the days he's there," John said. "Of course everyone helps him get around in the chair, though he doesn't seem to have much trouble on his own."

Becca wondered whether to tell John about the books she saw in Jacob's room and her suspicion that her brother and Taylor were up to something, but she decided not to say anything that might jeopardize Jacob's job. But choices were on her mind.

"Do you like working at the factory? Do you want to work there always?"

"I do. It's my family's business and my two younger brothers are involved, too. Someday *Dat* will retire and then we'll take over. I'm still learning but I like the business end of it; my brothers seem to enjoy the actual building of the gazebos more than running the business, but they are still young, yet."

"I think I want a business, someday," Becca said, surprising herself. She hadn't realized that idea had been percolating in her mind and she certainly hadn't meant to divulge that to John. She feared he might be interested in a more traditional Amish woman.

"What kind of business?"

"I don't know yet, but something that's all mine that I can do outside of the home. Not something craftsy, I don't really have skills like that, but something useful."

"Do you have anything in mind?"

Becca relaxed. John didn't seem perturbed at all, just interested.

"*Neh*, but I'm definitely going to think on it."

◠⌣

DAVID'S BLACKENED FINGERS tore the tobacco leaves off the stalk at a breakneck pace. Joseph and Emma stood next to him at the ten-foot long wooden table in the stripping room attached to the tobacco shed, their faces scrunched in concentration, their fingers moving at a considerably slower pace. Last year they had only been permitted to run errands and help pile the stripped stalks in a corner of the room; this year their father had pronounced them old enough to strip, and after school and on Saturdays, they attacked the chore with great pride.

"David, slow down your hands. I can't see what you're doing, "Joseph said.

"What pile do these leaves here go in?" Emma asked. "I'm so *ferhoodled*, mixed up."

"Don't worry about separating the leaves into the piles yet. You just strip the leaves off and I'll sort them. But just so you both know, the leaves are graded by the tobacco company according to quality, or position on the stalk. The tip leaves, here on the top of the stalk, are the most valuable. They go in one pile. The lugs, or the leaves in the middle of the stalk, are another pile, and the bottom leaves, the flyings, go in the third pile."

Levi stood at the end of table, stripping the tips. Jacob, on a day off from the gazebo plant, sat beside Levi in his wheelchair; he couldn't reach the table, so had fashioned a board across his wheelchair to use as a table. Levi handed him the stalk, Jacob stripped the lugs, placed the leaves in a box on the floor, and tossed the stalk up on the table for Taylor to strip the flyings. At the end of the table, David was in charge of apprenticing the twins. Taking a break from organizing his farm, he came over every day to help strip and usually also helped with the milking.

Daniel worked the baler, a wooden box about three feet long and two feet deep, with notches to feed twine to tie the bale. He collected the boxes of stripped leaves, made sure only the same grade leaves went into the bale, and dumped the leaves into the baler. He pushed the wooden lid down to compress the leaf. When the box was full, he pulled the front off, tied the twine, and removed the eighty-pound bale from the box and stored it in the tobacco shed.

Three days ago, the men had started to take down the laths of tobacco from the tobacco shed in preparation for the stripping. For the next couple weeks, every waking hour would be spent in the stripping room, except on Sundays and during the time spent milking. Throughout the afternoon and evening, non-tobacco farmers would drop by to help, as would friends and relatives, men and women, the room filled with chatter about farming, local news, neighbors.

Taylor spent the morning at the Lancaster office, then joined the family for lunch in the stripping room, followed by an afternoon of stripping. She wore gloves, unlike the men, to keep her fingers from staining. Despite the wood-burning stove in the corner, she borrowed a hooded sweatshirt from David to offset the chill in the room. Propane gas lamps hung from the ceiling and provided light at night.

She enjoyed the monotony of the work, letting her fingers take over while her mind focused on the sounds of the stripping room: the rustle of stripped leaves, the crackle of kindling in the stove, the crunch under foot of the flakes of tobacco leaves covering the floor, the buzz of conversation and community, the swishing of stalks dumped in the corner.

"David, how much tobacco are we stripping?" Taylor asked as she eyed the growing pile of stalks.

"We'll probably harvest about two thousand pounds of tobacco an acre, or twelve thousand pounds from our six acres. At eighty pounds a bale, that's one hundred fifty bales of tobacco."

"Is that a lot? Are you actually making enough money to justify all this work?"

"Emma, you ripped that leaf. Slow down. It's better to go slower and do careful work than go faster and do a poor job."

"Okay, okay," Emma muttered.

David turned back to Taylor. "With the contract price at a dollar fifty a pound, we make about eighteen thousand dollars for the crop."

Taylor sighed. "Farming is hard work with low pay."

"Most farmers aren't wealthy, but farming is satisfying, meaningful work."

"I didn't mean to disparage the work. If just seems like so much work for not much money."

"You have to remember, what the tobacco company is paying us per pound is twice what we would have made at auction for burley tobacco," David explained. "And you take the tobacco earnings along with what we make on the milk and our vegetable stand, and we're doing okay. It pays the bills, puts food on the table, and it's work you can pass down from generation to generation."

"What happens to the tobacco once it leaves here?"

"It's taken by wagon to the tobacco company's New Holland warehouse, where it's loaded onto eighteen-wheelers and taken to North Carolina for processing. The stalks, which are high in potassium, are loaded in our wagon and spread over the field to fertilize the soil for next season's crops."

At noon, they sat on bales of hay and ate hearty vegetable and beef soup and homemade bread. David sopped up the last of his soup with his bread, devoured it, then said to Jacob, "How's it going at King's? They still putting up with you over there?"

"I'm getting the hang of things. I feel like I'm starting to pull my weight and earn my pay."

"That's *goot*, very *goot*," Daniel said. "Now that you're getting settled, have you thought about your future, what you plan to do next?"

Taylor froze as she and Becca stacked bowls to cart back to the kitchen. Jacob popped the last morsel of chocolate chip cookie in his mouth and locked eyes briefly with Taylor as he handed her his soup bowl.

"I know this job isn't where you want to end up," Daniel continued, "but it's a start. Taylor's supposed to be helping you find a trade. Do you have any ideas?"

"I'm working on it, *Dat*."

"What about baptism?" Daniel pressed. "You'll be ready by next fall?"

"I don't know. That depends."

"Depends on what?" Daniel sputtered.

Jacob lowered his head and stared into his lap.

Daniel rose abruptly. "Let's go. We've got work to do."

DAVID MADE SURE the fire was out in the stripping room's stove, caught up with Jacob on his way back to the house that evening, and offered to push him the rest of the way. Daniel and Levi were already in the barn milking, and the women were in the kitchen preparing dinner.

"I know you're capable of getting yourself around in the chair but it's the least I can do after giving Dad an opening to grill you at lunch."

"It was bound to happen sooner or later. I wish I had an answer for him."

"Don't tell me if you don't want to, but do you have a plan?"

"*Ya*, I do but I'm not sure if it's achievable."

"It must be something you're afraid is going to set *Dat* off. And upset *Mamm*."

Jacob looked at the farmhouse in the distance, the light on in the kitchen. He imagined the warmth and the enticing smells that would soon greet him, and felt his stomach constrict.

"I don't know if I can do this to them. And I don't know how to go on if I don't."

David waited, hoping his brother would explain.

Jacob took a deep breath. "I've gotten my GED and now I want to go to college. I took the entrance exam and am waiting for the scores. If they're good enough, I'm going to apply. Taylor's been helping me."

"Whoa. That won't go over well with the family, or anyone else." They walked in silence until they came to the bridge over Stoney Creek and David stopped pushing. He leaned over the bridge railing and stared into the dark at the rolling hills of farmland in the distance.

"There must be another choice besides college."

"Who am I choosing for—my family, my community, or myself?"

"What about your God?"

"How can I honor Him with the work I do if I don't honor the work itself?"

"You could honor Him with the life you lead, with the life we've been taught."

"But is that life the only life that would honor Him?"

David began pushing again.

"Maybe you're thinking too much."

TAYLOR RUBBED HER hands together and watched her breath vaporize in the chill of the stripping room as Jacob added wood to the dying embers in the stove. At chores that morning and at breakfast, Jacob had been unusually quiet and she hadn't seen him the rest of the day. She had spent the time working in the attic and had planned to strip tobacco a couple hours before dinner and then again until bedtime. Sarah and the girls were preparing dinner and as she walked to the tobacco shed she met the men heading the opposite way to the barn for the evening milking. Jacob was alone in the stripping room when she arrived.

For a while they worked in amiable silence. "Looks like you guys made good progress today," Taylor said, nodding toward the four-foot high stack of stripped stalks in the corner.

"*Ja,* with the exception of Joseph tripping over a bale of hay and flying into that stack, scattering it everywhere. *Dat* yelled at him and made him straighten the pile again before he could strip anymore."

"Your dad seems a little irritable these days."

"The end of the tobacco contract is weighing on him. Plus he's frustrated with me. Things are tense between us."

"It may be time to tell your parents about college. I feel uneasy hiding your plans from them."

"So do I. But I don't have anything concrete to tell them yet. I need to know my SAT scores so I know if I even have a shot at college. And even if I do have a chance, I don't know what I want to do with a degree."

"Most college students don't know what they want to major in or do with their life when they start college. It's a process."

"But I feel like I need to have a solid plan, a good reason to upend my family."

"The scores will be posted online in a few days."

"Part of me wants to know the scores and part of me doesn't, especially if they're bad."

"No matter what, we'll figure it out."

The room started to warm and the propane lights cast a cozy glow as Jacob and Taylor stripped again in silence.

"I think I need to get away for a few days, go somewhere where I can think, after the tobacco is done and I get the SAT results," Jacob said.

"Where do you have in mind?"

"Pinecraft. Remember, Tobias said I could use his place in Florida." He wheeled around and tossed more wood on the fire. "But I need someone to travel with, just in case something happens. Would you consider going with me? Just for a few days, maybe a long weekend."

"But the trip by bus would probably take a day each way."

"Not by bus, by plane."

Taylor looked at him in surprise.

"I know, planes are forbidden, but so is education. I'm already way over the line."

Taylor thought for a moment. "We'd have to see the doctor first about you traveling. But a plane does make more sense. Shorter travel time."

"And less to worry about with my catheter and we can schedule flights around my bowel move . . . my other issues. Will you go?"

"It would be nice to get away from the cold, spend some time in sunny Florida." Taylor grabbed an armful of stripped stalks and threw them on the pile. "If the doctor okays it, I'm in."

"I'll talk to Tobias at work tomorrow and then we can work out the details."

THE VAN STOOD idling in the Yoder driveway while David and Anna said their goodbyes to the family in the kitchen.

"Give Gideon and Mary Beth and everyone else our best," Sarah said as she hugged her son.

"We'll miss you more than we already do," Emma said as she and Joseph clung to their brother.

"Can't I come with you to Indiana? I'll be good, I promise."

David smiled as he tousled Joseph's hair. "Not this visit. Maybe next time."

Taylor, Katie, Becca, Levi and Mary took turns hugging the newlyweds. Daniel clapped his son on the back and said, "Safe trip, son."

Jacob sat a little apart from the family crowd. Anna hugged him and told him to take care. David slapped his older brother lightly on the head and said, "Try to stay out of trouble." But then he bent down and whispered in Jacob's ear, "I will pray for you and the decision you must make."

The van pulled slowly out of the driveway, David and Anna waving out the window.

"DANG IT! THAT does it!" Daniel finally yelled after the third time Joseph dropped a box of stripped stalks as he carried them to the baler, which happened right after Emma slid into Hickory Sam Riehl, who was helping strip at the table, as she skipped to throw a bundle of stalks on the pile in the corner.

"Okay, you two antsy pants," Sarah interjected. "I need you to go run around the house five times as fast as you can. Then you can come back here but only if you're serious and ready to work."

The twins, chastened, left the stripping room.

"Should've done that sooner," Sarah said to Katie and Becca, stripping beside her. "They spent all day in school and then came straight here. No time to blow off steam."

"Race you to the house," Joseph said as they sprinted across the bridge over Stoney Creek.

They were into the third leg of their trip around the house, Joseph in a tizzy because his sister was slightly ahead of him, when Emma glanced into Jacob's bedroom window in the front of the house and immediately came to a halt, Joseph nearly running into the back of her.

"Look," Emma said breathlessly. "Jacob's home from work."

"Taylor's looking at the computer with him," Joseph said. "So what? But *Dat* better not see the computer, he'd be mad."

"If we're real quiet, we can sneak up and surprise them. Then maybe they'll come back to the stripping room with us."

"We're supposed to be running."

"We can finish running after we surprise them and say hi."

"All right."

In the bedroom, Jacob stared at Taylor's laptop screen.

"You're looking at the College Board website," Taylor explained. "I've been waiting for you to get home so we could look up your SAT results online. Now's a good time since everyone's in the stripping room."

Taylor had placed her laptop on Jacob's bed. Jacob moved his wheelchair closer so he could see the screen.

"I set up an account when you registered for the SATs," Taylor said, "and now I'm entering your user name and password."

Jacob's score report page filled the screen. Silence filled the room as they absorbed the numbers on the screen.

Outside the closed bedroom door, Joseph and Emma stood quietly, proud for having come this far without making their presence known. They had been about to burst through the door when they realized how quiet Jacob's room had become, and they looked at each other in surprise.

"Taylor, what am I seeing?" Jacob's voice caught.

Taylor threw her arms around Jacob. "You are seeing the numbers of a man who is going to college. These scores are amazing: Reading 720, Math 610, Writing 750. Your total SAT score is 2080, out of a possible 2400. That's well above average. And your subject tests scores: you got a 690 on English Literature and a 640 on U.S. History, also solid scores out of 800. A 2080 score would be better than good for a typical high school senior. But to consider your academic background, and what you had to do to catch up . . . Just look what you have done, Jacob," Taylor said, tears in her eyes.

Jacob's face was white. "These scores are good enough to get into college?"

"Yes, yes, yes! They are good enough to apply to all of the colleges we looked at. I'm optimistic you'll get into a least one of them. We also should find a keyboarding class for you so you can become proficient on the computer. You'll definitely need that skill in college.

"Now, we've got to call Julia and all the teachers that helped you study for the tests and tell them the results. They're going to be ecstatic. And while we're at it, we're also going to need a couple teacher recommendations for the applications." Taylor took charge, as Jacob sat dazed.

Outside the closed door, Emma covered her mouth with her hands and Joseph's eyes widened as they backed away from the bedroom. They knew that "going to college," no matter how excited Taylor sounded, was not a good thing.

When the twins walked quietly back into the stripping room, Sarah noticed with satisfaction that they were properly subdued.

~

"ANOTHER DAY AND we should be done stripping," Daniel said at supper that night.

"Just in time," Sarah said. "It's our turn to hold Sunday services this week. And the evening singing will be at our house, too. We've got a lot of cleaning and cooking to do in the next couple days, starting after supper." She addressed her daughters. "We're going to bake bread tonight and move out the living room furniture. Tomorrow we'll scrub the living room floor, bake more bread, help Mary make schnitz pie, and then clean the kitchen."

"Schnitz pie?" Taylor asked.

"It's made with dried apples, apple butter, apple sauce, and brown sugar," Sarah said.

"I'll help, too, of course," Taylor said. "How many people are you expecting?"

"There are twenty-seven families in our church district so that's about a hundred and fifty or so people, adults and children."

Sarah glanced at Daniel and then over at the twins, who had been unusually quiet throughout the meal.

"Why the long faces?" Daniel asked.

"We're just sad," Emma said.

"Sad? Why?" Sarah asked.

"We're going to miss Jacob," Emma said.

"When he goes to college," Joseph said.

"College?" Sarah looked confused.

Taylor felt dizzy for a moment and one look at her face told Daniel all he needed to know. His fork clattered to his plate and he turned to Jacob.

"Jacob, what's going on?"

"*Dat*, I . . . "

Jacob stared down at his plate, then looked up at his father.

"I want to go to college. I passed the GED tests and I did well enough on the college admissions test to apply."

Daniel turned in a fury to Taylor. "You are behind this. How dare you . . . "

Emma began to cry. "We thought you knew," Joseph said, stricken.

"Daniel, wait," Sarah said. "Becca, Katie, take the twins and go up to your rooms, now."

They left the table, Emma's cries intensifying as Katie tried to console her. Sarah sat back down, and with trembling voice, said to her son, "How long have you been planning this? We thought you were trying to find a future within the community."

"I'll tell you how long this has been going on," Daniel said red-faced, turning toward Taylor. "As long as she's been here."

"I'm sorry," Taylor began but Jacob interrupted.

"Don't blame Taylor. It was all my idea."

"We trusted you to help us, Taylor," Sarah said in a small voice, "not tear us apart."

"I . . . " Taylor had dreaded this scene for months, had fervently hoped it would go better than the worst-case-scenario, but it hadn't and in her distress, she found herself, uncharacteristically, at a loss for words.

"Taylor advised me more than once to tell you of my plans," Jacob said. "I didn't want to until I was sure of what I intended to do. I didn't even know college was a possibility until we got the scores today."

Daniel raked his hand through his beard. "She's tempting you with the modern world. She's tempted you from the first day she met you," he said. "She's been living in our house, tempting our children, right under our noses and against our wishes. I knew she was trouble from the beginning."

"No! That's not it. It's me, *me*! I'm the one who's straying because there's nothing for me here."

Jacob watched his mother's face crumble.

"No, that didn't come out right." The normally reticent Jacob struggled to articulate his anguish. "It's because of how I feel about my family that I'm having such a hard time deciding my future. I don't want to cause you pain or embarrassment but I want to learn so much more than you're willing to teach me. I can't explain it. I *need* to do this."

"If everybody got further education," Sarah said, "it would draw people away from the community. We would no longer be separate from the world."

Taylor's distress turned to anger. "What kind of rationale is that? You deny your son his dream because you don't want to break up the community? As a community, you limit the education of your children so they can't succeed in the outside world and have no choice but to stay Amish."

"Taylor, stop," Jacob said.

"No, Jacob. They need to hear this. You're depriving their minds. That's like depriving them of food. You're arguing that it's better to have unfulfilled adult members who sublimate their talents and potential just so you can keep the group together."

"It's not just that," Sarah said. "If we don't separate as a community from the world, as the Bible commands, then God will be displeased and there will be no hope of salvation for Jacob, no hope of heaven for him since he isn't baptized."

"Is there really only *one* way to please God?"

"It's the only way we know."

Daniel had heard enough. The years of pent-up frustration with his eldest son, his rage at the *Englisher* interloper who had schemed behind his back, his worry about the loss of the tobacco deal and the medical bills, all coalesced into a reckless abandon, and he said to his son, "If we aren't good enough for you, then maybe you should leave."

"Daniel, no!" Sarah cried.

Jacob stared at his father, his eyes flashed, his hands gripped the arms of the wheelchair, and then suddenly he went limp, the fight gone.

"I've already thought of that," he said quietly. "I could join a less restrictive, more progressive community, a Mennonite group. I don't want to leave, but if you want me to I will."

Taylor struggled to control her emotions and her voice. "As a community, you make exceptions all the time. Your businessmen use computers and phones at work, your carpenters use cell phones on the job, you used combines after the hurricane. Why can't you make an exception for Jacob?"

"We make exceptions in order for the community to survive financially," Daniel responded. "We don't make exceptions to our religious beliefs. And we don't raise our children to put themselves first, before God. We raise our sons and daughters for the Lord. The occupation is secondary."

Sarah put her head in her hands for a few seconds then looked up. "Our community is our roots, our way of belonging to something bigger than our individual selves. It's what gives our lives meaning. Jacob, your wanting more schooling is a rejection of our values and the way you were brought up. What message does that send to your brothers and sisters?"

"You should thank God you wake up every morning," Daniel said to Jacob.

"Waking up in the morning is the easy part. I have tried so hard, but I can't be who you want me to be. I have not forsaken my God. I just don't believe there is only one way—your way, the Amish way—to serve Him."

"Don't you see?" Taylor said. "The way he coped with trying to do it your way was to smoke, drink, withdraw. He nearly killed himself in the process. Is that the kind of life you want for your son?"

"He is Amish. He needs to take responsibility for who he is, not for who he thinks he wants to be," Daniel said.

Sarah rose from the table, her face pale, hands shaking. "Daniel, we have so much to get done before Sunday. Can we talk about this later?"

Daniel nodded, glared at Taylor, and stomped out of the kitchen into the night.

JUST BEFORE EIGHT o'clock Sunday morning, buggies filled the Yoder lane and the congregants began to enter the home, Minister Stoltzfus first, then elder church members. Men and women sat on the tightly packed, backless benches in separate sections, according to age. Single women wore white aprons, married women wore black, and the men wore black vests and white shirts.

Taylor watched from the back of the family room, ready to escape upstairs when the service started, returning later to help serve the light lunch. She noticed the simplicity of the service; other than the *Ausbund*, a hymnbook with words but no music, there were no religious props: no altar, no pulpit, no flowers, no candles, no choir, no organ. According to Becca, during the service, a deacon read the scripture for the day from the New Testament, and the minister then preached for an hour without a prepared sermon or notes. Singing, including the fifteen-minute *Lob Lied*, silent kneeling prayer, and at the end, a meeting to discuss district business, rounded out the service.

"How do the kids sit still for a three-hour service?" Taylor had asked Becca as they got ready for bed the night before.

"The toddlers are allowed to wander around quietly within reason and mothers bring snacks for them," Becca said. "If they become too loud or restless, they're taken out of the room. The older kids are taught to sit patiently and be quiet and that's what they do."

A man toward the front of the room began to slowly chant the first hymn, signaling the start of the service. The congregation joined in and Taylor walked up the stairs to her room.

She sat on the bed for a long while, thinking, the melancholy chanting in German of the *Lob Lied* wafting from below, and then began to pack her clothes, in deference to the decision she was certain was coming.

TAYLOR LOST COUNT of the number of seatings it took to feed all the church members. The turnover from the table—spread with homemade bread, jelly, peanut butter, cheese cubes, pickles, schnitz pie, and coffee—was constant, yet orderly. She had just replenished baskets of bread when she felt a gentle tug on her elbow.

"A moment of your time, if I may," said Minister Stoltzfus, as he led the way to the back corner of the living room.

"Daniel spoke to me yesterday about Jacob's problem and your involvement," he said. "I know you mean well, but Jacob's place is with his family and his community. We will help him find his way."

"With all due respect, Minister, much as you may want to guide Jacob, you aren't helping him. Trying to pressure him to fit within your narrow set of beliefs is stifling him. Your religious and cultural dogma is pushing him away."

"We as a people have survived for hundreds of years, against religious persecution, against intolerance, against the impulses of the modern world, because we stick together and live our beliefs. To do otherwise, to make exceptions for wayward members, to give in to temptations, jeopardizes our very survival."

Taylor's took a deep breath to steady herself. She could feel dozens of Amish eyes watching her, judging, but she felt she owed it to Jacob to fight on his behalf, knowing that it was probably futile. "The Amish as a society have benefitted from this country's constitutionally protected religious freedom and tolerance for your beliefs. Yet Jacob is a victim of intolerance by the Amish, his own people, because of his desire for education. The intolerance and persecution you have fought against from the modern world you have now inflicted on Jacob."

The minister looked sadly at Taylor and shook his head. "You can't project your priorities onto us. We need to do what is best for all our members, not just the one."

"What does that mean? You're going to ask him to leave?"

"We take seriously our obligation to our members, especially the aged and disabled. It is not your concern what we will decide to do, but we will decide together as a community."

BECCA WRAPPED HER arms around her black wool cape and shivered slightly as she and John King swung slowly on the wooden tree swing, the rest of their friends enjoying the Sunday evening singing inside the Yoder home.

Becca had spent the weekend, throughout the vigorous house cleaning, in a high state of anxiety. The twins were glum, Katie was red-eyed from crying, Sarah was tense and unusually curt, and Daniel was just plain grumpy. Even Levi and Mary, once they had been told of Jacob's plans, seemed solemn and sad. Everyone went about their business and no one talked about it. Becca had tried discussing the issue with her mother, but Sarah had said, "Now's not a good time," and all Taylor would say, when she and Becca managed to find themselves alone, was "I just wanted to help Jacob." Jacob, other than helping with routine farm chores and at meals, stayed in his room.

Becca had first alerted John Friday night in a text that read, "FAMILY CRISIS," and then had told him in more detail what had happened once they snuck outside during the singing.

"I knew he and Taylor were up to something," Becca said. "Jacob's been through so much, most of it his doing, but is it really so bad he wants to go to college?"

"My father is deep into the modern world as a business-man but is still Amish," John said. "But Jacob can't go to college and still be Amish. It does seem unfair. He may leave us in the future but maybe he won't. Lots of *Englisher* kids go to college but come back home to their families and use what they've learned to benefit their communities."

"But many also go to college and leave their families to get jobs in other states. If all the Amish did that, we wouldn't have an Amish community anymore."

John shrugged. "It wouldn't be the end of the world if Jacob left. You and your family could still see him. He won't be shunned since he's not baptized."

"I know, but there would always be a cloud over his head and ours. Everyone would look at us differently. And what about his afterlife? Doesn't the Bible say we need to be sepa-rate from the world? If Jacob joins the world, will God be angry? We're taught to obey, and our lifestyle is based on, His teachings. But I learned this summer that different religions believe different things about God's teachings. So does getting to heaven depend on which teachings we follow or does getting to heaven depend more on how we live our lives, not just that we're Amish. We are Amish because we were born to it, raised that way, and that's all we know."

John did not immediately respond. It was one of the traits Becca liked most about him, his quiet way of thinking things through before he spoke. She realized with a start that he reminded her of Jacob in that regard.

"If Jacob joined a more liberal Amish or Mennonite group," John said, "all things would be forgiven in time by our community. Life would go on. You and your family could still have a relationship with him, even if he didn't live as Old Order Amish. All our lives, we've been taught how to live. Our church elders decide on stuff to believe in and we stick with it, full of good intentions. But really, only God knows what he wants from us."

"Tell that to my father," Becca said. She leaned against John and rested her head on his shoulder, and they sat in silence in the cold.

"JUST FOR THE sake of argument, Jacob, what would you do with a college education?" Bishop Lapp asked. He sat with Jacob in Mary and Levi's *grossdaadi* house, away from the crowded Sunday evening gathering in the main house. Once he had heard about the family crisis from Minister Stoltzfus that morning, a visit to the Yoders was necessary.

"I don't know. I haven't thought that far yet."

"Do you want to leave our community?"

"I don't know that yet either."

"But you do know you want to turn your family's lives upside down in the meantime."

Jacob's jaw clenched. "I don't want to cause pain to my family. I just want to learn more about God's world. Why is that bad?"

Bishop Lapp stroked his beard.

"Think of it this way, Jacob. A herd of horses is grazing contentedly in a pasture. But then one horse tries to reach across the fence and graze on the other side. That horse must be reined in and returned to the herd. If not, other horses will follow. They may knock down the fence and run off, opening the way for the rest to leave, too."

Jacob remained silent.

"You are still young," the bishop said. "Our way is not yet clear to you, but I have hope that someday it will be and you will take your place here with us."

He rose to his feet. "You are strong and capable and have managed your disability well, but even for you, it will be difficult on your own. Think long and hard, Jacob, about your future, physically and spiritually. May God be with you."

As Jacob wheeled himself back to the main house, he passed Sarah and Daniel on their way to speak with the bishop.

The three sat together in the family room. "We do have a problem here," Bishop Lapp began, "one which deeply concerns me. But the solution is not so clear. Dealing with a wayward member is always difficult, but in this case, even more so.

"If Jacob were baptized and insisted on attending college, I would need to bring the matter to the church members, and although excommunication and shunning would be an option, probably many wouldn't be comfortable with that outcome because of his disability. Of course, since he's not baptized, the *bann* is not an option. As a community, we could ask him to leave voluntarily, but at this point, I don't think that's a solution, either. He's recently handicapped, and no matter how well he thinks he's doing physically, he still needs our help. Perhaps in the future, depending on his medical progress and his willingness, leaving may be the only solution, but until then, I don't recommend it."

"Well then, what do we do?" Sarah asked.

"We wait," Daniel said. Sarah looked at him in surprise. "He may not get into college or he may decide not to go or he may decide he made a mistake once he gets there. I haven't given up hope he'll find his way back to us and eventually choose to baptize."

The bishop nodded. "I told Jacob the same thing. For now, the door is still open. We want him back and we will be patient. However, there is one thing you may need to do immediately."

"*Ja*," Daniel said. "Remove the source of the temptation."

WHEN TAYLOR OPENED her eyes Monday morning, she knew that day would be the last time she milked a cow or smelled manure. She would no longer help cook three meals a day for nearly a dozen hungry people, scrub floors, hang laundry, wash dishes by hand, light kerosene lamps, sit on a tree swing. She would no longer laugh at the twins' antics, chat with Becca in their beds at night, or feel like part of a family.

As Taylor finished helping clean up after lunch, Daniel nodded to his wife, then said to his family, "All of you, up to your rooms, except Jacob and Taylor."

The four sat at the kitchen table, Sarah's eyes downcast, Daniel's face stern but with a calm that comes from certainty, Taylor sad but resigned. Only Jacob seemed agitated and unsettled.

"You have betrayed our trust," Daniel said to Taylor. "We thought you were here to help Jacob find his future, not tempt him behind our backs down a forbidden path."

"Don't blame Taylor," Jacob said. "She wanted to tell you. It was my choice not to."

Daniel ignored him. "Right under our noses, you mocked and disrespected our values. You are no longer welcome in our home."

"*Dat*." Becca had been standing quietly outside the kitchen, listening.

Daniel whirled around. "Becca, this is no concern of yours."

"*Dat,* I have something to say."

Sarah touched Daniel's arm lightly. "Fine," he said. "What is it?"

Becca stood straight, trembling hands clasped behind her back, and locked eyes with her father. "You've made your decision about Taylor and it will be obeyed. But Taylor and Jacob didn't mock or disrespect you. Don't you see? It's because Jacob is so full of respect and love for us that he's been torn up about what to do. He was going down the wrong path before he met Taylor, drinking, smoking, and becoming a loner. It was Taylor who gave him back his life. *Dat,* if he can't be who you want him to be, isn't it better that he be who he wants to be rather than miserable?"

Daniel paused, surprised at his eldest daughter's outspokenness. "Becca, return to your room, now."

Becca glanced at Taylor, then Jacob, her eyes brimming. She turned and walked upstairs.

"Becca is right," Taylor said. "I know I have said far too much already but it is so important that you understand. Jacob's decision was not a reflection of his disdain for your way of life. His choice was an agonizing one. His devotion to you and to the Amish way of life is deep and his desire to move on is not without full knowledge of its ramifications, both for himself and for you and the rest of the family."

Sarah took hold of Taylor's hands. "We appreciate all you've done for us. There is so much we couldn't have done without you."

Taylor stood up from the table. "I have only profound respect for you, for all of you. I've cherished my time here and I believe what you've given me far outweighs what I've done for you. But I've overstayed my welcome and for that I am sorry."

An hour later, Taylor placed her briefcase, laptop inside, on the front passenger seat of the Lexus, along with her purse, plugged in her phone charger and BlackBerry, and then hoisted her suitcases into the trunk. Daniel had already said a brusque goodbye before he strode off to the barn and Taylor had said farewell to Levi and Mary before packing the car. Earlier in the kitchen, Sarah and Katie had hugged her and handed her a foil-wrapped packet of homemade sugar cookies and a jar of blackberry jam. Sarah had told her she was welcome to visit in the future, "but wait awhile until Daniel cools down."

"Thanks. Give my best to David and Anna when they return from Indiana."

As Taylor closed the trunk of her car, Emma and Joseph, standing forlornly by the kitchen door, ran over and hugged her. "It's our fault you're leaving," Joseph said.

"We're so sorry," Emma said.

"No, it is absolutely not your fault. You did the right thing by telling your parents."

"But who's going to read us books from the library now?" Emma asked.

"I will miss reading to you but I'm going to turn that job over to Becca."

Taylor turned to Becca. "Whenever you need or want me, just call or text. Or write me a letter if you decide to take a break from the wild side." She grinned.

"You taught me so much," Becca said. "My thinking is a little different now. I understand how small, in some ways, my world is."

She hugged Taylor and whispered, "I will miss you every day."

Jacob had waited patiently for his siblings to say goodbye.

"I guess it was inevitable that it would end this way," Taylor said as she sat in the driver's seat.

"This isn't over," he said. "I need to see this through."

"I know. We'll keep in touch by phone and I'll help you any way I can."

Taylor pulled out of the driveway, and while the twins and Becca and Jacob waved, Sarah watched from the kitchen window.

Taylor waited until she reached a red light on Route 30 and then made a phone call.

"Hi, Dad. I'm on my way home. For good."

⌢

WELL, I DID it. I stood up for Jacob and Taylor to Dat. I don't know if it did any good, but I had my say. I almost chickened out I was so nervous, but then I remembered Taylor giving that woman at the Images store in Philadelphia a piece of her mind and that gave me strength. I tried to be humble and respectful but Dat still looked surprised. He hasn't said anything about it to me so far, so that's good.

I have to be careful I don't get too full of myself, though. This afternoon at the grocery store I ran into my friend Mattie and her mamm (Fannie Gossip, we call her). We chatted a little and then Fannie Gossip said, "We hear Jacob wants to go to college. You all must feel horrible." She was right but it still got my dander up, so I said, "He's been through so much and if this college idea helps him to find his way, then I thank God for giving him the courage to try."

She looked at me strangely, and then Mattie said, "You think it's God's will that Jacob go to college?"

"I don't know," I said, "but I'm not ruling it out."

Fannie Gossip harrumphed and walked away.

Mattie walked with me up to the register. "Some people are saying just the opposite, that Jacob's giving in to temptation and displeasing God."

"What else are people saying?" I asked.

"A few are saying God has punished him for wanting more. But most people are giving him the benefit of the doubt, saying he's confused and not thinking clearly, after his accident and all."

I started to disagree then stopped, not wanting to give people another reason to think badly of Jacob, but then I spoke my thoughts anyway. I wanted to get the truth out there, my truth.

"Jacob is not confused. He's always known he wanted more education, even before the accident. Why would God give Jacob the desire and

the brains to further his education and then disapprove when he accomplished it?"

Mattie shrugged, then changed the subject and asked me about John.

So I probably gave the community some more to chatter about, which is not a good thing. I have mixed feelings about the whole situation. On the one hand, I want my brother to not feel conflicted anymore. Yet there's this tension within the family and when we go out in the community that I just want to go away. I don't like being the family everyone talks about.

22

TAYLOR GLANCED OUT the car window as she drove down four-lane Bahia Vista Street, fascinated at the scene before her and half listening to the GPS: "In point two miles, turn right." A small group of young women, in *kapps* and long dresses in a variety of colors and styles, but all wearing flip flops, stood chatting on a corner, and a bearded man with suspenders talked on a cell phone as he ambled by on a three-wheeled bike. Only two miles west of downtown Sarasota, but Pinecraft was another world.

She turned right onto Graber Avenue. The palm-tree lined avenue, like those surrounding it, sported tiny one-story white, tan or grey wood frame or cinder block cottages, with Amish names affixed on mailboxes or house signs: The Hochstetlers, The Weaver Family, Aaron and Susan Schwartz, even one that indicated the owners were from Ronks, Pennsylvania, in Lancaster County.

"It's 1545 Graber," Jacob said. "It's a white frame house with a King Family wrought iron sign on the front."

Two weeks after Taylor left the Yoder home, she and Jacob boarded a plane to Florida. He told Taylor that before he left for Florida, the mood in the Yoder household matched the mid-December weather: frosty. Sarah understood why he needed to get away and "clear his head," but flying to Pinecraft upset both she and Daniel.

"You could go somewhere closer and not have to fly," Daniel had reportedly said. "Why must you be so difficult?"

Although agog at his first sight of an airport, Jacob had incurred no boarding issues since he owned a Pennsylvania ID with photo, which had been required to take the GED tests. Though Taylor had briefed Jacob on the airport security process, he was uncomfortable with the pat down in his wheelchair due to his natural as well as Amish-bred reserve.

The first to board, Taylor wheeled Jacob to the open door of the plane, where he transferred into a skinny chair with wheels that fit down an airplane aisle. His wheelchair was taken and stowed in cargo. In first class he transferred to an aisle seat. Jacob wore compression stockings prescribed by his family doctor to prevent leg swelling and blood clots and the flight had been scheduled around his bowel movement, so Jacob felt free enough from worry to fully immerse himself in the flight, unlike Taylor who worried something would go wrong but kept it to herself.

Taylor joked that he was probably the only person on board actually listening with rapt attention to the flight attendant's seatbelt and exit spiel. She watched Jacob's face with amusement as the plane taxied down the runway and lifted into the air, his expression a mix of fear and amazement. During the flight, she lost count of the times Jacob leaned over her to look out the window, exclaiming, "Will you look at that!"

When they landed, they headed to the rental car agency and off they went in search of Pinecraft.

"The house must be right up ahead," Taylor said, driving slowly down Graber. "We just passed 1485. They really have the houses packed in here."

Jacob pointed out the window. "There it is, The King Family sign. Tobias told me Pinecraft is one hundred twenty acres split in two by Bahia Vista Street. The majority of the five hundred or so cottages—most not more than six hundred square feet with two bedrooms—are on one side, along Phillippi Creek. On the other side of Bahia Vista are several streets of houses and the creek."

Taylor parked the car in the driveway. "What's the attraction here? Why are all these Amish snowbirds in Pinecraft?"

"For one simple reason: to get out of the cold. Each winter, buses shuttle thousands of Amish and Mennonites from the ice and snow of Ohio, Indiana, Illinois, and Pennsylvania and they stay for a week or two. Retirees come, single folks come for a few months and work construction or in restaurants, and young families visit grandparents or other relatives. "

"But where are the horses and buggies?"

"Horses and buggies aren't allowed on the roads in Florida so the Amish rent adult-sized tricycles to get around, unlike in Lancaster where bikes aren't permitted. If they want to go fishing or to the beach or anywhere outside Pinecraft, they ride city buses."

Taylor retrieved the wheelchair from the trunk of the car and helped Jacob into it.

She took the house key from Jacob, opened the door, and wheeled him in. The house seemed slightly bigger than most, with three bedrooms instead of two, a family room, small kitchen, and two bathrooms. The cottage had electricity—"It's mandated by the county," Jacob said—and a washer and dryer, but no TV.

Taylor, standing in the middle of the family room and surveying the diminutive living space, joked, "The bedroom is in the family room which is in the kitchen."

Jacob laughed. "That's okay. We'll only be here three nights. No cows to milk, no five o'clock alarm."

"They must not have church services down here. The houses are too small to hold many people."

Jacob grabbed his travel bag, hoisted it onto his lap, and headed for one of the bedrooms. "Amish and Mennonites of

all faiths, Old Order to liberal, worship here in churches instead of in homes. It's a real melting pot of plain cultures.
Tobias said one church—the Mennonite Tourist Church—may
be the only one in the country where Old Order Amish and
liberal Mennonites worship together."

After unpacking and surveying his bathroom, which was
not conducive to handicapped use, he and Taylor decided on a
system. He'd be able to transfer from the wheelchair to the
toilet, but would need help getting into the tiny stall shower.
They found a metal folding chair in a closet, placed it in the
shower, and when the time came, the chair would be placed in
the shower and Taylor would help Jacob from the wheelchair
to the chair. "I'll wear my new bathing suit," Jacob said,
blushing, "so no one gets embarrassed."

That settled, Taylor ran out to the nearby pizza shop and
brought back dinner.

"Tomorrow I want to explore Pinecraft," Jacob said, as he
folded a slice in half and took a bite. "Tobias said there's a
park with picnic tables where everyone gathers to play shuffleboard and volleyball. And could we go to the beach?" He
looked sheepish. "I've never been."

JACOB POINTED WITH his spoonful of hot raisin oatmeal
across the packed six hundred-seat dining room of the Der
Dutchman restaurant, past the scurrying waitresses serving
what looked to be a mix of *Englisher*, Amish, and Mennonite
customers. "There's a back room section with a door off the
parking lot. Tobias said it's a popular early morning hangout
for Amish men. They group themselves in sections depending
on where they're from."

"I wonder if there's any Lancaster men back there," Taylor
said as she dipped homemade sourdough toast into her over-
easy eggs. "I should go back there and check it out and then

they can gossip all morning about that uppity *Englisher* woman who invaded their club."

"Please don't. I'll have even more trouble on my hands if it gets back to *Dat*. I need to keep a low profile."

They topped off their breakfast with fresh fruit and pecan sticky buns. As they were leaving the restaurant, Jacob stopped to inspect a rack of cookbooks displayed near the cash register.

"Look at this," he said, showing her *Simply Delicious Amish Cooking*, a spiral-bound book by Sherry Gore. "Nearly three hundred recipes from the locals and people who vacation here, and some unusual stuff like avocado egg scramble and fried alligator nuggets. This three-layer strawberries and cream cake sounds great. The author includes humorous stories along with the recipes. *Mamm* would like this. I'm going to buy it for her for Christmas. I'm also going to get a couple postcards for the twins, and Becca and Katie."

Later, Jacob waited in line to send the postcards at the tiny Pinecraft post office, which Taylor discovered online was the world's only Amish-run post office. She read that the Amish, for whom sending letters is a way of life, bought the building from the U.S. Postal Service when it decided to close the branch.

While waiting for him in the car, Taylor browsed delightedly through the village paper, the *Pinecraft Pauper*, priced at one dollar from the honor system yellow distribution box in the post office's four-space parking lot.

The twenty-two pages of the stapled-together paper was chock full of news, photos, human interest stories, resident profiles, puzzles, and cartoons. She read about an Amish grandma who fished in Phillipi Creek nearly every day, a recipe for squirrel stew, and an article about iguanas falling out of trees.

The line advanced and Jacob scanned the large bulletin board on the outside of the post office building, an obviously popular place judging from the amount of people gathered around it. The board was packed with job listings and scraps of paper from people looking for jobs; cottages for rent and for sale; ads for the Haiti Benefit Auction, the annual Christmas parade, the Pinecraft Pie Contest, and a garage sale to benefit the Amazon Mission; and fliers selling everything from a litter of kittens to used tricycles.

Once inside, the postal clerk, using a small calculator, handed Jacob a hand-written and hand-stamped receipt for the postage for the post cards.

"Did you know," Taylor asked Jacob as she helped him into the rental car, "that when the temperature falls below forty degrees, iguanas, because they're cold-blooded lizards, become comatose—a form of hibernation—lose their grip, and plummet to the ground from their tree perches?" Jacob looked at her in silence, then finally said, "Uh, no, I did not know that."

"I read it in the Pinecraft newspaper. The iguanas appear dead but will revive if the weather warms up."

"Interesting fact. Since it's in the low-seventies, I guess we don't have to keep looking up when we pass under trees."

"Go ahead, make fun of me, but I love local newspapers. They're the heartbeat of a community. I fear they're becoming extinct. People aren't reading them much anymore, especially the younger generation. They're either getting their news online or they're not paying attention to news at all, preferring online games, social media, or reality TV. That doesn't bode well for our society."

"That sounds a little harsh."

"It's true. Newspapers are society's watchdogs; they're supposed to be where we turn to get facts, layers of meaning, and analysis. That kind of detail isn't consistently provided on television anymore, the focus instead on weather or natural disaster coverage or ten-second sound bites that don't explain much but are attention grabbing. We have twenty-four hour cable news that offers immediacy but is often short on depth. We have television and radio stations with a right or left political slant rather than reliable facts. If we don't understand what's going on in our towns and our governments, how can we be informed citizens? And if we're not informed and engaged, democracy doesn't work well."

"You don't think newspapers have contributed to this lack of newsiness?"

"Not any of our papers, of course." Taylor laughed. "It's definitely a complicated issue. Editors are struggling to add more features and sports and lifestyle articles to attract readers, while cutting the number of reporters, foreign news, editorial content.

"Little by little, over the course of years—with the exception perhaps of a few large national papers and a handful of exceptional local ones—the news has been chipped away at until we're left with abbreviated content, and unfortunately, that has contributed to a less well-informed public.

"On the other hand, the public is not screaming for more comprehensive news. People have short attention spans. Hundreds of TV channels offer a dizzying array of options competing for viewers' time and attention. We've become a culture that values entertainment over substance. As a result, the media provides less in-depth news because the ratings or the readership aren't there. It's a vicious cycle and we're all the worse for it."

"So what's the solution?"

Taylor sighed. "For the news industry as a whole, I'm not sure. My father and I, though, can strive to be the best stewards of our media as possible, deliver the most substantive news we can, and at the same time try to develop an engaging but informative online presence that increases readership. So we can survive."

AS TAYLOR PULLED out of the post office parking lot, she noticed a commotion across the street. A crowd of about a hundred, on foot and on bikes, in cars and vans, milled about the parking lot of the Tourist Mennonite Church.

"Let's check this out," she said and pulled into a narrow alley next to the lot. She wheeled Jacob over to the crowd and they mingled, the excitement palpable.

"Looks like this is the place to be right now," Jacob said.

"Who drives the cars?" Taylor asked. "Aren't we still in Amish country?"

"From what I've seen so far, it looks like many different Amish and Mennonite sects visit here, some liberal, some conservative. Some Mennonite groups are more liberal than the Old Order Amish. They believe in higher education, dress more modern, and drive cars. If you look closely around this parking lot, you'll see different styles and colors of dresses and *kapps*, depending on which Amish or Mennonite group they're from and what part of the country."

Within minutes, a Pioneer Trails motor coach pulled into the lot. The crowd tensed in anticipation. When the door opened, the crowd cheered and shouted, as relatives and friends waved and found each other.

"Where are these people from?" Taylor asked a middle-aged woman standing next to her.

"This is the bus from Ohio. My sister and her family are joining us for a week. Oh, there they are. Franny, Franny, over here!"

The new arrivals piled pillows and suitcases into the metal baskets on the back of their hosts' trikes, or into the waiting vans or cars, or lugged them down the street to their accommodations.

Taylor asked an elderly man sitting nearby on his trike if he was waiting for family.

"Not this week. I'm staying for the winter and just like to come down and see if anyone I know gets off the bus. It's the highlight of the week."

No sooner did the Pioneer Trails bus pull out of the lot

than an Elite Coach pulled in, with another load of snowbirds, Taylor learned, from Lancaster.

"It makes me smile to see them get off the bus," she said. "They all look so buttoned-up and pale, the women with their black stockings and chunky shoes. In a day or so, they'll be in flip-flops, riding rented trikes, and getting sunburned."

"I understand why Tobias likes to come down here with his family," Jacob said. "It's like being in another world."

Back in the car, Jacob pointed to a stretch of sidewalk along Bahia Vista Street where about thirty bikes were chained to trees near a bus stop. "I bet that's where everyone picks up the bus to go to the beach," he said.

UNDER THE PICNIC tables at Pinecraft Park, giant Florida oaks draped with Spanish moss provided shade from the midday sun. Young boys rollerbladed deftly around girls meandering in long dresses and flip flops, co-ed teens cheered during an energetic game of volleyball on the sand court, while a small group of men concentrated on checkers. One group of elderly gents played shuffleboard, while another played a rousing game of bocce, bad rolls evoking a fervent, "Oh, for Petey's sake!"

At a picnic table under the park's pavilion, Taylor unpacked their takeout lunch from the picnic basket, a find from one of the King family's closets, and handed Jacob a chili dog and fries, a piece of Dutch apple crumb pie, a plastic fork, and a bottle of water. She took a bite of her grilled chicken wrap and watched the activity around her. She was only halfway through her wrap when she noticed Jacob was nearly finished his pie.

"What?" he said, as she grinned at him. "This weather makes me hungry. And it's fun to watch people enjoy themselves. It's been sort of somber at my house lately."

Taylor finished her wrap, took a couple bites of her key lime pie, and slid the rest over to Jacob to finish.

"I've been thinking about what we talked about earlier, about the state of the news industry," she said. "And I'm wondering, in general, what is success? Is success the quantity of newspapers you sell or the quality of those newspapers? Is success how much money you make or what you contribute to the benefit of society through your job? Do gobs of cash make you a success or just a person with gobs of cash and an inflated sense of self-worth?"

Taylor rose from the picnic bench and paced around the table. "There's a lack of correlation between the worth of a contribution, how meaningful it is to society, and compensation. I'm thinking, for example, of some reality TV stars. They contribute nothing to our lives, other than empty entertainment value—and by that I mean entertainment not based on real talent—yet they're making big money. As opposed to, say, our teachers, policemen, firemen, paramedics, or social workers who are vital to society but are in my opinion underpaid.

"And I wonder about all this because I look at you, and your family and community, and I see not much wealth but what I would consider a lot of success. Your work is meaningful and contributes to the community, both the Amish one and society as a whole, because we drink the milk you produce, eat your crops, purchase the furniture and crafts you make. Your families work, play, and stay together, you help each other as well as those outside the community, and you care nothing about, except maybe during *rumspringa*, what we *Englishers* find so compellingly meaningful: fashion, technology, celebrity entertainment."

Jacob shifted in his wheelchair. "You're on a roll today. Where's all this coming from?"

"I don't know. It's sort of bubbling to the surface and bursting out of me. I think I've been sleep walking for a long time. Now I'm waking up." She sat back down on the picnic bench.

"I see things a little differently," Jacob said. "I was born into the Amish lifestyle, and while there is much I appreciate about it, I have fought its restrictions for a long time. What I am by birth is only a part of who I am. I don't fit neatly into the Amish mold and I've struggled to please my parents and community while hiding who I am. I'm certainly not a success by Amish standards."

"Yes, I get that. What you were born into and what you do for a living should be only a part of who you are. I've defined myself solely by what I do for a long time. I lost the rest of me somewhere along the way." Taylor's voice cracked. "Probably when my mom died."

"What do you mean, you lost the rest of you? What is the rest of you that you've lost?"

Taylor watched an older gentlemen instruct a male teen on how to throw the bocce ball. The teen threw a shot, the ball smacking another ball away, and the other players yelled their encouragement: "Atta boy!" and "Way to roll!"

"I don't know," she said. "That's the problem. Who am I besides the vice president of Loden Media? I've neglected to develop interests or real relationships, other than with my dad, and more recently, with your family. I don't even know if I have a favorite color. I haven't lived with intention. I'm like a successful shell. There's a vacancy at my core."

Jacob took a long sip from his water bottle, then wadded up his trash and stuffed it in the picnic basket.

"What do you wish for or dream about?" he asked.

"I don't have dreams, literally. I used to dream about my mom after she died, but it was so painful to wake up and realize she was gone that I think I willed myself not to dream about her, or at least to not remember that I did. Since then, I can't remember the last time I woke up and remembered a dream. As for dreams for my life, I have goals I work toward at work, like increased newspaper circulation or TV station acquisitions, and I've always accepted I would be the heir-apparent when my father retires, but there is nothing I personally long for, no hopes or dreams or wishes." She gazed vacantly at the activity around her. "That's just sad, very sad."

"I CAN'T BELIEVE we're eating again after that huge supper we had at Yoder's," Jacob said as they waited in line at Big Olaf Creamery. "Fried chicken, mashed potatoes and gravy, peanut butter cream pie for dessert. How do we even have room for ice cream?"

"We're on vacation. We're supposed to eat everything in sight." Taylor scanned the menu. "Twenty-three flavors. How to decide? Do I want blueberry cheesecake or orange pineapple? What are you going to have?"

"Vanilla with brownie bits and caramel, in a waffle cone."

Aside from the line of waiting customers that stretched down Bahia Vista Street, the parking lot bustled as a blue grass trio set up for a concert. The gathering crowd sat on wooden benches and chairs on the patio in front of the creamery, or on lawn chairs they had brought, or on their trikes, some with toddlers asleep in the large square metal baskets on the back.

"Big Friday night at Big Olaf's," Taylor quipped.

While they waited in line, Taylor amused herself by Googling Pinecraft on her phone.

"Guess what? Pinecraft has a Facebook page," she told Jacob. "Lists all kinds of goings-on in town. Listen to this: 'Bahia Vista Mennonite Church semi-annual parking lot sale. All items must go. Parking lot stays.'" She chuckled.

Jacob watched her as she played with her phone.

"I think you do have longings," he finally said. "I think you wanted a family and that's why you maneuvered yourself into our family."

"Maneuvered?" she said, looking up at him.

"In a good sense." He smiled at her. "You needed more meaning in your life, so you took on my cause and Becca's *rumspringa*."

"Maybe you're right," Taylor said. "It's obvious I have a long way to go in the self-awareness department."

❦

THE SAND DOLLAR lay half buried in the sand, surrounded by bits and pieces of other shells ravaged by the sea, and it wasn't until Taylor gently pulled it out that it revealed itself to be intact and whole, a perfect specimen.

"Here you go. That's a good one to bring home to the twins," she said, handing the shell to Jacob. "I learned about the legends of the sand dollar when I was a kid. One was that sand dollars were mermaid coins or coins from Atlantis. The Christian legend is that it symbolizes the birth and resurrection of Christ: the petal shape is like an Easter lily with the star of Bethlehem in the middle and the holes represent the nails on the cross. If the shell breaks, there are small bony, boomerang-shaped pieces inside, which are really teeth, but to some represent doves of peace and goodwill."

Jacob looked at it closely, turned it over and over in his hands, then placed it gently in a Ziploc bag, already nearly full with a variety of shells they had picked up on their walk along the beach.

The late morning sun was starting to warm Lido Beach, a barrier island in the Gulf of Mexico a short distance off the central western coast of Florida and connected by highway from Sarasota. Taylor pushed Jacob in a special wheelchair, one with large, wide wheels that moved easily through the sand, that she had rented from a stand near the parking lot.

When they had first arrived that Saturday morning, only a smattering of other tourists and locals were sunbathing or walking the beach. Taylor was barefoot, her jeans rolled up, and though the temperature was in the high sixties, she had earlier tested the water, letting it lap around her ankles, and found it chilly.

Jacob wore a t-shirt and had insisted on wearing his bathing suit, and though it reached to his knees, it did not as easily hide the catheter attached to his leg bag as did long pants.

"I've never been to the beach before," he had explained. "And I may never go again. I want to be like normal people who wear bathing suits to the beach. The bag will be hidden by my suit, just the catheter will show a little and I don't care."

As they continued down the beach, they passed a cluster of Amish, barefoot women hitching up their long summer dresses to wade in the water, and a couple men in bathing suits, others dressed for the barn but with pants rolled up and bare feet. Jacob waved and exchanged greetings.

A little further down the beach, they stopped to rest and Taylor flopped down on the sand. "Do you want me to help you out of the chair and onto the sand?"

Jacob glanced around at the Amish group in the distance and other couples and families nearby. He shook his head. "Maybe later."

Taylor watched Jacob as he gazed at the ocean. He was absorbed and peaceful and for a brief moment seemed free from the worry and tension usually etched upon his face.

Taylor snapped a picture of Jacob with her phone and texted it to Becca. Within minutes, she texted back: 'Glad you're having fun on beach while we shovel couple inches of snow that fell last night!' She showed the text to Jacob, but his mind was elsewhere.

"The waves seem so calm and harmless as they break here on the sand," he said, "but I imagine them to be powerful and relentless further out."

Taylor put her phone in her jeans. "Is there something you want to talk about?" she asked, sensing his preoccupation.

"I feel like I'm a wave, the same repetitive motion over and over as it crashes on the shore, but am I really going anywhere? I've turned everyone's life upside down because I want to go to college, but what am I really going to do if I get there?"

Taylor sighed. "I've told you before you don't need to decide on a vocation or even a major now. Stop thinking that going to college is a waste of time unless you have a specific vocation in mind. A career can be determined later, after you take a variety of courses and see what jazzes you. But if you're set on having a plan now, I'll humor you. What do you most like to do? What gives you the greatest pleasure?"

"Reading."

"Ok, so with a passion for books, you could be a librarian, teach literature, work in publishing, or own a bookstore."

"But I can own a bookstore without college. I could probably teach Amish kids somewhere near home without college."

"Dig deeper, Jacob. Picture yourself in school. What about that picture invigorates you?"

Jacob was quiet, the sound of children laughing in the distance.

"When I was studying for the GED and the SAT, I realized just how much I didn't know. The more I studied, the more there was to learn. At times, it was overwhelming, but it was also energizing. I'm curious about lots of subjects mentioned by my teachers or that I've come across in my reading."

"Such as?"

"Biology. I want to learn more about cells and genetics and evolution. Chemistry. How does baking soda work and why do leaves change color in the fall? Astronomy and Physics. I want to learn about Jupiter's rings, black holes, the big bang, and look through a telescope. Anatomy and Physiology. How does my heart pump, how do my eyes and ears work? English. I want to read more great literature, contemporary and classic. And I know absolutely nothing about philosophy, psychology, archaeology, music, art. There's so much to learn and so little I know."

Taylor smiled at him. "You've just listed the core curriculum of a good liberal arts education, one that will provide you with the foundation to pursue any number of careers."

"My father would say it's a waste of time and money to learn so much and use so little on a daily basis in real life. But can any knowledge be a waste if it helps me understand how things work? Doesn't that make me a better citizen, even in my small corner of the world?"

"Absolutely," Taylor said. "Learning for the sake of learning is enough in itself. The power of education is not just in book learning but in the broadening and enriching of the mind, learning how to read critically, how to think issues through on more than a superficial level and to develop your own opinions and judgments, learning how to problem solve, how to rise to a challenge and stick with difficult material until you figure it out."

Jacob used his arms to shift his position in the wheelchair. "I understand the value of enrichment learning. You were able to approach education that way since you had a family business to join. But I'll be on my own eventually and will need to support myself, so I need to tailor my education in order to get a job. I'm having trouble deciding on whether to go to one college and what to do once I get there. You went to three. You have three degrees. I envy you."

Taylor stood up and brushed the sand off her jeans. "We need to return the wheelchair. I only rented it for a couple hours." She turned Jacob around and headed back down the beach.

"I have taken my education for granted," she admitted. "It was a given in my family, very little discussion except which college to attend for which degree. But I envy you. Your new life is just beginning and anything is possible."

❧

NEARLY ALL OF the early evening passersby waved at Jacob as he sat on the small front porch of the cottage and watched: bikers, walking couples, skipping or rollerblading children, groups of laughing teenage girls and guys on their way to visit friends or to the park or just out for a stroll. He had finished packing for the trip home the next day, he and Taylor had eaten a quick supper from Subway, and he had completed his nightly bowel routine. Once Taylor finished packing, they planned to head to another beach, Siesta Key, to watch the sunset, which according to Tobias King, was not to be missed.

Jacob waved back, but after a while, his view shifted off into the distance, his hands clasped on his lap, and he calmly contemplated his future.

THE POWDERY WHITE Siesta Beach sand was fine and soft, like walking on flour, Taylor thought. She had rented another big-wheeled chair for Jacob and parked it a few yards from the breaking waves; she had also rented a low-seat beach chair.

"I discovered a couple interesting tips while browsing the web on my phone," she said as she helped settle Jacob on a beach towel. "This sand is ninety-nine percent pure quartz, so it doesn't get hot." She carefully brushed sand away from Jacob and off the towel so it wouldn't get into his catheter. "Also, this is one of those places on the east coast where the sun looks like it's setting over the water rather than over land, but that's only because we can't see across the gulf to Mexico." She settled herself in the beach chair. "I know, I know. I'm just a font of information."

Jacob sat upright on the towel and dug his hands into the sand. He lifted up a handful and let it sift through his fingers. They sat quietly. Taylor had picked a somewhat secluded section of the beach. From either direction, they could see other couples in the distance sitting on the beach or walking along the water's edge.

"I want to feel the water," Jacob said. "Can you get me down there?"

Taylor jumped up. "You bet." She moved the wheel chair behind Jacob and held it firm while he grabbed the chair and lifted himself up into the seat. She folded the towel over the back of the chair, pushed him to the water's edge, then re-trieved the low-seat beach chair, setting it just up from the breaking waves, and helped him into it, making sure not to get his bag and catheter wet. The waves rolled up and swirled gently around his calves; he bent at the waist and trailed his hands in the water. She sat in the big-wheeled chair, the water lapping at her feet.

"Being away has been good for me, helped me clear my head," he said. "I've made a decision."

"Great. What is it?"

"Actually, it's a series of decisions. If accepted, I will go to college. I'm leaning toward a teaching career, but I'm not sure what I want to teach. But I think it might be fun to impart knowledge to young minds." He grinned.

"Teaching, terrific. An honorable profession. You'd be well suited for that."

"I'd like to try and get a job on campus to continue helping my parents pay off medical bills and to help pay my way through school."

"Jacob, I already told you I'd pay for college, anywhere you decide to go."

"I know, and that's more than I deserve. I don't even know how to thank you for that. But I want to help, I insist. I know I won't make much but I can contribute toward my books or other expenses."

"Fine. What else?"

"If I'm not accepted to college, I'll continue to work at King's Gazebos part-time to help pay off the medical bills. Maybe a full-time job will open up there. Or I could teach in an Amish school, but I don't know how well that would go over with the other parents, considering my reputation. It's probable, though, if I come back to the fold, all will be forgiven. Or I could start saving for a bookstore. There isn't one near where we live and I could offer books for kids and teens and adult fiction."

"Several solid options. Nicely done. If you don't get accepted to a college this year, you could apply again next year, but I'm almost certain you'll get into at least the community college. So I guess baptism is out then, if you do go to college."

Jacob dug a hole with his hand in the damp sand and watched it fill and disappear as the waves rolled in.

"The Old Order Amish would never accept me back if I went to college. I'd have to join a more liberal group, one of the Mennonite ones, that aren't opposed to higher education. But I wouldn't be shunned by my order since I'm not baptized, so I could at least return to the area and be able to see and be near my family."

"But if you leave your community, what happens if you have another medical emergency? The community won't be there to help raise money for your medical bills. Never mind, I'll answer my own question. I can research what state or federal resources you may be eligible for, we'll find you a health insurance policy, and I can help with any medical expenses not covered by insurance. Someday you may have insurance through your job."

"Once I'm independent, I'll do whatever is necessary to pay my own way. Hopefully, nothing major will happen in the near future."

"And if you don't go to college, what about baptism?"

"If I stay in the community, I won't be able to hold out much longer. I can't do that to my parents and the rest of my family. If I don't go to school, I'll baptize. And I'd be content teaching in an Amish school or owning a bookstore."

"But wouldn't that be settling? Not what you really want, but an acceptable substitute?"

"For a long time I saw only a narrow, dismal view of my job choices and my life if I stayed Amish. Because of you and the other teachers who have helped me, my view broadened, other options became possible. I want to go to college more than anything, and I'll do my best to get there. But if it doesn't work out, I'll be okay. I'll keep learning through reading."

Taylor looked out over the water, the sun starting to sink over the gulf.

"You've got a plan. Goals you've taken the time to choose consciously. Good for you. My work here is done." She laughed as she looked at Jacob, but then quickly glanced away.

They fell silent. Then Jacob said, "It's your turn now."

Taylor turned toward him. "But I don't know how . . . "

"Be still," Jacob said. "Stop running, slow down, just be."

They both gazed toward the gulf, the sky a deep tangerine interspersed with brooding charcoal clouds; the blood red sun sank slowly, slowly toward the water, and then it was gone.

23

D ANIEL DRAGGED THE fence post off the horse-drawn wagon and placed it in the hole where he had removed the old rotted post. He held the post steady with his hands while shoving small mounds of dirt with his boot into the hole around the post. Once the post was steady, he shoveled the rest of the dirt into the hole around the post and tamped it down until the post stood strong.

The post was the last of the three he had replaced that day on the fence surrounding his cow and horse pasture. Last week, the tobacco bales had been taken to the warehouse in New Holland and the check from the tobacco company already deposited in the bank. From then until spring, when planting would begin again, Daniel faced a winter of farm maintenance.

He turned toward his parents *Grossdaadi* house and saw David up on the roof, repairing shingles. He and Anna had returned a few days ago from their post-wedding visit to Indiana and he was helping around the farm while also working with his uncle John Esh to make repairs on his own farm and planning for the dairy operation he had decided to undertake.

At least one son's life was settled and going well, Daniel thought. The night after Jacob had returned from Pinecraft, he had informed the family of his decision to apply to college. Daniel had sat stone-faced, and later that night felt helpless as Sarah quietly cried herself to sleep.

Daniel lined the three damaged posts he had replaced in a row on the ground and picked up his hatchet; he could use the kindling for the wood-burning stove in the stripping room.

He swung the hatchet over and over, not pausing, not stopping for breath. Despite the December cold, he broke into a sweat, and still he continued to swing, splitting and splintering the wood until it lay in dozens of defeated pieces at his feet.

TAYLOR REVIEWED ONE last time Jacob's online application to Penn's College of Arts and Sciences, hit send, and closed the laptop on her desk at her office.

"Done," she said to Jacob on the phone, and sighed with relief. The application process was over. She pictured Jacob in his room on the farm, his face pensive.

Penn was certainly a reach school for Jacob but Taylor thought applying was worth a try; the academic challenges he had faced and overcome and the unusualness of his Amish background might make him an attractive candidate and worth the university taking a chance on. Plus, if he went to college in Philadelphia, she could easily keep an eye on him; to that end, they also applied to the Community College of Philadelphia.

In addition, they applied to Franklin & Marshall, Millersville University, Elizabethtown College, and the Lancaster branch of the Harrisburg Area Community College, all within a half hour of Jacob's home. Over the course of three weeks, she had advised him by phone and helped him apply online. He had written essays, requested letters of recommendations from the teachers who had helped him prepare for the GED and SAT, and had also applied for merit scholarships where applicable.

"Now what do we do?" Jacob asked. Taylor noticed his voice seemed lighter, less anxious. She guessed he too felt the pressure lifting.

She leaned back in her desk chair. "There's nothing left to do but wait. We wait for the decisions."

CONNOR STOOD IN the doorway of the Loden Media conference room and watched his daughter. It was late Friday afternoon and they had just finished a company meeting; Taylor had walked out of the room with a couple of her colleagues that had just finished a PowerPoint presentation on ideas to revitalize their newspaper websites.

"Great presentation," Taylor said to her co-workers. "You came up with clever options to attract readers online. I think we can move forward, at least with our larger papers initially, to update our websites and create mobile phone and tablet apps on a test basis and see how it goes. And we can also encourage our reporters and columnists to take advantage of Twitter to further create a following."

As Connor headed to his office, he heard Taylor say, "It's been a grueling week. Want to join me for a drink at Tria after work? It's a wine, cheese, and beer café I've wanted to try near Rittenhouse Square."

The group agreed to meet at seven and head to the café. Since Taylor had returned home and to the Philadelphia office, Connor had noticed a change. He had thought her leaving the Yoders would be another loss from which she'd have a hard time coping. Yet, although she missed the family, she seemed fine, and apparently her time there had done her some good. She was as productive as always at her job, but made an effort to socialize and fill some of her time with other activities, and not just with colleagues.

At least once a week, he and Taylor had dinner together—

sometimes at a restaurant but more often his daughter cooked simple meals for them at her place—and actually talked about things other than work: politics, current events, TV shows, books, even sailing, which she encouraged Connor to try. Once a month, at her initiative, they did something together: a day trip to New Hope, a symphony concert, an art exhibit, the theatre, or a movie. She also told him she struck up a conversation with a woman she frequently saw at the fitness center in her building and they enjoyed an occasional smoothie together after their workouts.

Connor leaned back in his leather desk chair and smiled. Baby steps, he thought, but nevertheless steps in the right direction.

THE BOX, BECCA'S address in the left corner, sat on the living room coffee table and Taylor slit it open with a pair of scissors. Inside, on top of several packages, was an envelope, which she ripped open, then sat on the couch to read.

Dear Taylor:

I miss you! We're busy here preparing for Christmas next week. Mamm's baking up a storm. Relatives and friends will be in and out all week and we'll be visiting them, too. Naturally, the twins couldn't wait until Christmas to open the gifts you sent, so we all thank you for the Lego Creator Lakeside Lodge 3-in-1 building set (twins loved!) and the board games: Scrabble, Pictionary, and everyone (even Dat) is excited to play Settlers of Catan. My friend Mattie has the game and we always play with her family. Now we have our own!

Along with this letter I'm sending our gifts to you. Hope you enjoy. Open them now so I can explain some things.

Taylor obediently set the letter down and pulled out of the box a package covered in grocery bag wrapping paper and tied with a red velvet bow. She unwrapped a homemade cookbook titled *Yoder Family Favorites*. The pages were hole-punched and held together with colorful yarn tied in small bows. Taylor flipped through the handwritten pages of recipes: blackberry cobbler, chicken corn soup, cheddar meatloaf, snicker doodle cookies, cinnamon bread, apple cake. She remembered family meals around the big kitchen table and felt sad. The box also contained two jars of blackberry jam, which brought back fond memories of the day they made and preserved the jam.

The last gift was a small box, also covered in paper bag wrapping but decorated with crayon drawings and stickers. Taped to the top of the box was a folded over piece of white paper. Taylor carefully unwrapped the package to reveal a cardboard box, its top and sides covered with seashells. Inside the box, on a piece of red velvet, lay a sand dollar. She opened the note:

"Taylor: Thought you might like a souvenir of our Pinecraft trip. Thanks for everything you've done for me. I can't possibly tell you how much your help and support has meant. You gave me hope. And I have no doubt you are much more than an empty shell. Merry Christmas. Jacob"

Taylor picked up the sand dollar, caressed it gently, then placed it back in the box and continued reading Becca's letter.

The cookbook is from the entire family; even David's Anna contributed her favorite snicker doodle cookie recipe. Emma and Joseph, of course, decorated the wrapping paper for Jacob's gift and also glued the seashells onto the box. The twins and glue . . . you can imagine. Emma insisted on buying a scrap of red velvet from the fabric store for the bow and because the sand dollar "needs a soft home."

In other news, Jacob's new buggy arrived yesterday from Weavertown Coach Shop. It took about three months to build and is a few feet wider than a normal buggy. The back folds down like a ramp, and instead of a full back seat running the width of the buggy, there are two side seats, leaving the middle open. Jacob can wheel himself up the ramp, through the buggy to the front, and then can strap down the wheelchair so it doesn't tip over if the horse rears. He can be either the driver or a passenger. The seat up front slides from one side to the other, depending on who's driving. Dat paid for it (reluctantly) with the donations from your newspaper articles and Jacob said all the family can use it, too.

Went for a ride last night, with Jacob driving. He said the buggy will give him "a bit more freedom" since he won't have to depend on someone else to help him and his chair into it. It was the first time he's driven me since the accident. I admit I was a little anxious but I tried not to show it. He seemed subdued, too, like he was also thinking about that last ride. Emma and Joseph rode in the side seats and had a grand time. It was all Katie could do to keep them from jumping up and down. Maybe they should put seatbelts in buggies.

Jacob seems less tense these days. He told us when he came back from Pinecraft about his decision to apply to colleges and to attend if accepted. Katie cried and Mamm and Dat didn't say much, but I know Mamm is heartbroken and Dat is frustrated and probably angry. Later, when it was just the two of us, Jacob told me if he doesn't get accepted to college, he'll stay in the community and baptize, maybe start a bookstore or teach. But he told me not to tell anyone because he doesn't want to get hopes up.

How do I feel? I ache for him. He must feel so alone. How brave he is to not only handle the pressure from our family and community but the paraplegia, too. I watch him sometimes when he doesn't know. His eyes are sad and far away. Even when he is with us he seems apart from us. I know he loves us but he has always been different. The life that satisfies us is not enough to fill him up.

Many in our community think that's because he's not trying hard enough, or he's looking for outside fulfillment rather than inner, or he's selfish, not putting God first. I don't think any of those things. I think that for whatever reason, God has chosen a different path for Jacob. I've been taught that Amish life is the way to best honor God, but that was before I saw that other people honor and worship Him in good ways, too. I'm not sure but maybe God doesn't care how we honor Him, so long as we do. So I want Jacob to honor Him the best way he can. And someday, I hope to see my brother's eyes smile.

Hope you have a good Christmas. I can't wait for the day when we visit each other again.

Much love,

Becca

CONNOR, PHONE IN hand, was conflicted. Should he make the call, or was it too soon? He sat on the plump brown leather couch in his den, a wood-burning fire crackling; outside the ice from the latest February storm still clung to the windows and snow lightly fell.

He had met Elena a few evenings ago in the lobby of the Kimmel Center, where he and Taylor had attended the symphony. Before his wife Alexis had died, they had traveled in the same social circle as Elena and her husband. Connor had heard not too long ago that she was a recent widow. Elena had attended the concert with some friends and they had a nice chat in the lobby during intermission.

After observing his daughter's attempts to cultivate a social life, Connor decided maybe he should do the same. He had looked up Elena's phone number online; luckily she still lived at the same address he remembered from years ago. He wanted to ask her to dinner. But maybe she wasn't ready to start dating yet. Maybe it was too soon after her husband's death.

Yes, he should just forget it; he didn't want to put Elena on the spot. But what about a drink after work, nothing too serious?

Hell with it, he thought. *Nothing ventured, nothing gained.* And he dialed the number.

WHERE IN SPAIN should she go? The medieval streets of Cordoba, the northern coastal city of San Sebastian, Barcelona, Seville, or the capital city Madrid? Guidebooks and maps cluttered Taylor's desk in her home office and she had just spent a couple hours perusing travel sites online. The March wind howled outside. Maybe the islands of Majorca and Ibiza, she thought, someplace warm.

She had decided to take a trip, by herself. She hadn't taken a vacation since before her mother died, and she had never traveled alone other than for short business trips. The thought of it scared her a little but she brushed the fears aside other than to recognize the precautions any woman traveling alone should take.

In the past month, she had also branched out in two other ways. She had joined a book club in her building—the book she was reading, *Please Look After Mom* by Kyung-Sook Shin, peaked out from under one of the travel guides of Spain—and she had volunteered at The Children's Hospital of Philadelphia to read to patients a couple hours a week and had donated books to stock hospital playroom shelves. She also decided she wanted to write—not news stories, that would be too close to work, but something fun, maybe a blog; she could start her own or pitch a blog to Huffington Post. Or maybe take a creative writing class.

It was time, she knew, to enjoy a *rumspringa* of her own.

THE CHOCOLATE CAKE cooled on the kitchen counter, nearly ready to be frosted. Daniel and Levi were due in from the barn for lunch shortly; a platter of deli meats and American cheese already adorned the kitchen table. When David stopped by earlier to lend a hand in the barn, Sarah had sent Katie and Becca to the store for more sandwich rolls.

It was an unseasonably warm late March day, a touch of spring in the air. From the kitchen window, Sarah could see Jacob sitting on the bridge over Stoney Creek, looking out over the fields; he had been there for some time, probably thinking and planning, as her eldest son was prone to do. She crossed the kitchen, opened the back door and called to David, who was just exiting the barn, to fetch his brother for the noon meal.

She began to frost the cake, her knife smoothing and swirling the frosting; she glanced out the window, saw David reach Jacob, saw him pause, then bend down to shake his brother, and then as she saw him fall to his knees, his head in his brother's lap, her knife clattered to the floor.

"IF WE OFFER the buyouts, can we avoid layoffs?" Taylor asked.

Connor leaned forward in his desk chair. "We avoid layoffs if we run our papers lean and mean. I want to cut fat, not muscle. Our TV and radio stations are profitable but to supplement our print revenue, we need to diversify online to attract advertisers. While we diversify, we need to conserve cash. So the strategy is this: We offer the buyouts to our newspaper employees, continue to revamp the websites, and roll out the mobile phone and tablet apps. For now, I'm willing to operate at break even or at a modest loss in order to keep the news core strong. Luckily, one benefit of being a non-publicly traded, family-owned company is we have no shareholders to appease. We just need to hang on until the digital strategy pays off."

"What about charging website readers? That could bring in some much-needed cash."

"Yes, we could offer a digital subscription option as well as a newspaper and digital subscription together. Worse case scenario is, and much as I would hate this, we may eventually have to sell or close our smaller papers in order to conserve resources for our larger ones."

"No, Dad, we can't do that! Some of those towns have only one newspaper. Where would our readers get their local news? There's got to be another way."

Connor shrugged. "Here's an example of a paper whose cord we should cut. We have a managing editor at one of our small suburban Maryland papers who's been with us for over thirty-five years and is in declining health. The circulation numbers haven't increased at that paper in the last five years and he's resistant to digital changes. You tell me what we should do if not sell or close that paper."

Taylor's cell phone rang; she glanced at it, saw it was Becca, and held her finger up to her father. "I'll just say hi and call her back later."

In a matter of seconds, Connor saw Taylor's face go white and she lowered the phone to her lap; Connor could still hear Becca talking.

"Taylor, what's wrong? Taylor?" Taylor sat motionless, looking at Connor vacantly.

Connor walked over and picked up Taylor's cell. "Becca, this is Connor. What happened?"

CONNOR ACCOMPANIED TAYLOR to her penthouse after Becca's call; his daughter hadn't said a word since the minute she heard the news. Connor tried to get her to open up; they sat on the living room couch together, and he said, "I know it's a shock, honey. Becca said he died of a heart attack. A doctor at the hospital said it sometimes occurs among spinal cord victims, even the young. They don't know why."

Taylor nodded, her hands clasped in her lap, face expressionless.

"Do you want to talk about it? It might help. Can I get you anything?" Connor floundered. He remembered Taylor had acted the same comatose-like way after her mom had died: no crying, no words. He changed tactics.

"I hope you don't think there's anything you could have done. Even if you had been there, it still would have happened. Becca said the whole family wanted you to attend the funeral the day after tomorrow. Do you want to go?"

Silence. Connor rose from the couch and walked over to the window wall; he looked out over the city skyline, not really seeing. He wasn't sure what to do or say, how to help his daughter.

"I don't think I can bear to go to the funeral," Taylor said.

"Okay," Connor said quietly, and on instinct, he waited, and it finally all came out in a rush.

"How could they leave me? I needed mom. I still miss her. And I wanted to help Jacob. He had so much life ahead. They weren't supposed to leave me yet." Tears welled in Taylor's eyes. Connor returned to the couch.

"I thought I was in control but I was wrong. Control is an illusion. Life just happens and all we can do is try to keep up." Tears rolled down Taylor's face and Connor took her in his arms.

She sobbed, for all the lost years since her mother died which she had spent, to no avail, trying to regain control; for all the years of stoicism and the constant work that masked the pain; for all the years she had lived in her own insulated world where no one could leave her again.

She cried and cried, and as Connor held her, he silently thanked Becca for opening her heart to someone lost and alone and searching for a connection, and he thanked Jacob, not for dying, but for providing a catalyst for Taylor to feel, to find meaning, and in the end, to open up and grieve, so that perhaps she could finally begin to heal.

THE FIELDS BELOW were in transition, the ground beginning to thaw but the soil not yet ready for spring planting, making for a drab brown panorama. Taylor sat in her car, pulled off the road, on a hill overlooking the Yoder farm. She hadn't thought she could endure mourning Jacob in public and so had decided instead to attend his funeral from afar.

Taylor saw the dozens of carriages parked at the Yoder's for the morning service, saw the freshly dug grave in the family plot at the far right corner of the property bordering Hickory Hill Road, beyond the house and pond and Stoney Creek. Jacob's grave was next to the grave of his stillborn sibling.

She had called Becca, explained she couldn't attend the funeral and expressed her condolences; she asked about sending flowers but was told that wasn't the Amish way. The funeral, held three days after Jacob's death, would be a simple affair, Becca explained. During the two days before the funeral, family and friends would visit the Yoders and view the body, dressed in white. Taylor couldn't manage any more conversation than that and so the phone call was brief.

Taylor saw the mourners exit the Yoder home and after a bustle of activity, she saw the hearse, a large black carriage pulled by a stately horse, set off down Yoder Lane, followed by a long procession of grey carriages.

She imagined the simple pine coffin in the hearse, Jacob dressed in white pants, shirt and vest; she imagined Daniel and Sarah and the rest of the family, all in black, in the first several carriages behind the hearse, and she felt dizzy, her stomach clenched, her hands gripped the steering wheel so hard it became painful.

The procession turned onto Hickory Hill Road, traveled to the corner of the Yoder property, and stopped by the side of the road; the carriages emptied for the graveside service led by Bishop Lapp. When it was over, many would return to the

Yoders for a meal prepared by other members of the congregation.

The Amish, Taylor had been told, don't believe in eulogies, preferring instead for the service to focus on God, with Bible readings about the creation and resurrection.

"So," Taylor said out loud, "I will eulogize you myself. Jacob, you may not have thought yourself a success by Amish standards, but you were by mine. You were brave and kind and smart, and even wise. You were my teacher and I learned far more from you than you learned from me. I will miss you and I will try to live my life in a way that honors you."

She wiped the tears from her eyes with the back of her hand, started the car, made a U-turn, and headed back to Philadelphia.

❦

The Daily Collegian
Independently published by students at
Penn State University

Column
Tribute to a Friend
Eric Richards

I lost a friend this week. He was a paraplegic like me. But unlike me, he was not in college, although he desperately wanted to be. He was a farmer's son, with five brothers and sisters. He was also Old Order Amish, so college was not a path open to him. It was a path he had to create for himself.

He was quiet and reserved but determined. With only eight grades of schooling, but with the help of some good people, he spent months studying for the GED and then the SATs, struggling to attain what most of us take for granted—an education.

His hard work paid off. He scored better than average on the SATs and applied to colleges. He died before realizing his goal.

In today's world, where girls in many countries are denied education, where teens drop out of school and see it as having no value, where others party their way through it or study the bare minimum, my friend simply wanted to learn.

His was a story of determination, of overcoming odds, of endurance and perseverance. Yet his accomplishments won't trend on Twitter or go viral on YouTube. A Facebook page won't be devoted to him. He won't be Time Magazine's Person of The Year.

But in his own understated way, he was a hero, to me and to many who knew him. I will miss who he was and mourn who he may have become. RIP, Jacob.

Eric Richards is a freshman journalism major.

24

Six Months Later

Dear Taylor:

Hope all is well with you. This letter is long overdue and I apologize. Things have been so busy here but that's no excuse. To be honest, I kept putting off writing because you remind me of Jacob's lost future and that's still painful, even now, for me to deal with. Maybe you feel the same since I haven't heard from you either. I miss you. I miss our talks. I miss seeing you around the farm. I feel like I lost two family members at once. Keeping busy helps. So here's the latest Yoder news.

Dat gave up the tobacco crop (without the subsidy and with David gone to his own farm, it was just too much labor for not enough profit), increased our cow herd by a few, and started growing soybeans, which we'll harvest later this month. Anna's younger sister Rachel works for Tobias King in Jacob's old job as assistant office manager.

David is doing well on his farm. He has cows and also goats and he and Anna are making artisan goat milk cheese. They belong to a cooperative that sells Lancaster cheeses to area farmers' markets, restaurants, and cheese shops. The best news is they had a baby boy two weeks ago. They named him Jacob. He's our pride and joy. Of course, Mamm and Dat are over the moon, as are Daadi and Mammi.

Another piece of good news: our hospital and Jacob's rehab bills have been paid. Tobias King auctioned off a property he owned and used the proceeds to pay the bills. The highest bidder still paid under market value for the land, which he'll be able to farm, and we are now free of the bills. A "win-win" for everyone, John King quoted his father as saying. I know this is a huge relief to my parents and in some ways they do seem lighter, somewhat.

I'm still seeing John. He will baptize in a couple weeks, and already gave up his car and joined the family gazebo business full time. I think we will marry. We've talked about it but I'm not ready yet for marriage or for baptism. I'm starting a bookstore, partially in memory of Jacob, but also for me. I want to contribute to the family income but I also want to contribute something to my community, and someday to my own family, that's all mine.

We're converting the tobacco shed into a bookstore; Dat is helping (I think I can thank Mamm for that) and David and Uncle John Esh, too, when they have time. I'm nervous about running a business but I'm fairly confident I can learn what I need to know to be successful. I'm getting bookkeeping advice from my quilt store aunts and Tobias King helped me find a book distributor. Katie will help me in the bookstore. She has started her rumspringa and joined a conservative gang, the Quakers. I don't think she has her eye on any boy . . . yet.

Maybe you're disappointed I won't be leaving my Amish world for your modern one. From what little I've seen, the world isn't as evil and immoral as many Amish believe. Leaving was an option, there are so many exciting and new things to discover in your big world, but I believe I can find what makes me happy and fulfilled here with my family and friends (and John). Plus, I absolutely can't imagine causing Mamm and Dat any more heartache. I would, though, like to travel and see more of the country, and maybe someday John and I will do that.

I have all the clothes and shoes you gave me stored in my hope chest. I'm still in my rumspringa but not sure if I'll wear them again. Someday I may donate them to charity but I'm not ready to part with them yet. I have so many fun memories related to wearing the clothes and I remember how pretty, and free, they made me feel. I know, I know, pretty is more than skin deep. I watched Mamm wash supper dishes last night, her hands red and callused from hard work, her apron soiled with food and dirt from the chores of the day. I realize she's getting older, her hair greying, her face lined and a little weary. But that face seems beautiful to me, her smile so warm and caring. When she talks to me I feel understood and loved. No clothes, no matter how expensive or fashionable, can make a person that good on the inside.

I also kept all the books Jacob had stored in his trunk. They're now in my hope chest (along with the books you gave me), and they make me feel close to him and to you (last night I armchair traveled to Agra, India and saw the Taj Mahal, and to Goa and its beautiful beaches).

I understand why Jacob loved reading so much. Reading is a way to understand myself, not, as my father believes, a temptation to a worldly life. I've been reading "To Kill a Mockingbird" to Emma and Joseph. It may be a little advanced for them but they call each other Jem and Scout (and named one of our new cows Boo Radley) and it has led to some good talks about prejudice.

Dat decided to sell Jacob's buggy. Even though it was useful for us, I think seeing it sitting in the driveway was too much of a reminder. A disabled man in a neighboring church district bought it at just about full price since it was only a few months old and Dat put the money away "for a rainy day."

You may be wondering how Mamm and Dat are doing. I finally told them about Jacob's plans to baptize and either teach or start a bookstore if not accepted at college, and it seemed to make a difference to both of them, the idea that he hadn't entirely given up on the Amish way. One hot July night, I came downstairs for a drink of milk and I heard them talking quietly in the kitchen. I'm ashamed but I eavesdropped. Mamm said she thought Jacob had given them a gift by not baptizing, thereby sparing the family the humiliation of him breaking his vows and a possible shunning and it was his way of at least trying to keep the family together. And Dat said, and this surprised me, "We think we know the way to God but only God knows best what He wants from us."

You remember that picture you texted me of Jacob on the beach in Florida? At his work one day, John downloaded it onto a USB stick and then we took it to Walmart and printed it. I know it's wrong to have, but I'm still in rumspringa and for now I'm keeping it in my hope chest. I can't bear to forget what Jacob looks like.

The other day I thought of something you told me once about people going to their graves with their music still inside them. I think Jacob had a symphony inside him.

I'm enclosing Jacob's mail, unopened, from the colleges. Mamm slipped the envelopes out of the mail before Dat saw them. She said she didn't want to throw them out because they meant so much to Jacob but she also didn't want to open them. So we decided to send them along to you. I'm also sending his GED diploma and our cell phones. Thank you for the phones but now that my John only uses his for work, I have no use for mine. You can still reach me on our shed phone. Or by mail. I'll let you know when the bookstore is open and ready for business. Maybe you will come and visit?

Katie and Mamm say to tell you "hi." Oh, and check my cell phone for two last texts.

Love,

Becca

P.S. Hi Taylor, it's Emma. Come see us. I don't think Dat's mad anymore.

P.P.S. This is from me, Joseph. Remember when you read to us during the hurricane? That was fun. We want you to visit.

Becca had sent everything in a box. The letter and GED certificate lay on top. The phones were wrapped separately in bubble wrap. Taylor unwrapped Becca's cell phone and retrieved one of the texts, a picture of a section of the Yoder garden, full of blooming sunflowers. "This year they made it!" the text said. The second text was a picture of baby Jacob: "I shouldn't have, and David pretended he didn't notice, but thought you might want to see him." Taylor assumed Becca used Jacob's phone to take the photos, then sent the pictures and texts to her phone.

Taylor stared at the baby photo a long time, thinking about the beginning of a new life, the loss of another. She was glad the Yoders had a new baby in the family to soften their heartbreak, but little Jacob, as adorable as he was, did nothing to dull her grief. Despite the daily busyness of life and her work which had helped mask her pain over the last six months, Becca was right: Taylor had avoided contact with the Yoders; for months, just the thought of them had been enough to cause a stab of pain as fresh as cow's milk.

At the bottom of the box was a large sealed envelope, which Taylor presumed contained the individual envelopes addressed to Jacob—from Franklin & Marshall, Millersville, Elizabethtown, Penn, the Harrisburg Area Community College, the Community College of Philadelphia—and as she held the package, she felt again the familiar sad ache.

For several days, she left the envelope on her home office desk, torn between opening it or not. She felt guilty because she had neither called the colleges and withdrew the applications after Jacob's death, nor checked online for the decisions, and the time had long passed for a response to an acceptance, if there was one. She felt an unease, a faint panic about how she might handle the emotions which either a rejection letter or, even more so, an acceptance, would provoke. Finally, one night, a glass of wine in hand, she placed the envelope in a desk drawer. Maybe someday when she felt braver, when her emotions weren't so raw, she would open it.

She then penned a letter to Becca. She wrote briefly about work—the online news strategy, though still a work in progress, seemed to be paying off—but more about her personal life: Connor was dating a lovely women he had known socially for years, and had bought a sailboat and was taking sailing lessons; Taylor's first solo vacation to Spain in July; the book club she had joined; her volunteer work at the children's hospital; and the "light" redecorating she had done to her penthouse. "Your quilt is on my bed and I had draperies made to match. Looks great," she wrote. She enthused about baby Jacob, congratulated Becca on the bookstore, and promised she would visit soon.

She did not tell Becca, though, about an idea she had presented to her father three days before. She wanted to take a leave of absence to help manage the small town Maryland paper and its ailing editor Connor had mentioned right before she learned of Jacob's death. She had argued she could increase circulation and bring the paper into the digital twenty-first century, thereby saving it from the cutting block and preserving a town's only paper. Connor was considering the idea. Taylor thought the challenge, although a detour from her current career trajectory of running their media empire, would broaden her skills, contribute directly to the bottom line, and most important, was a proactive plan. She no longer wanted to merely drift through life.

IN HER HOME office, Taylor had one final work email to respond to. She read the email again, reviewed the attached resume, and then forwarded the resume to three newspaper editors, with a recommendation to interview the college student for an internship. She smiled. Eric, Jacob's former Bayard roommate, would make a good reporter someday.

LATER THAT NIGHT, Taylor settled on her couch with a bowl of popcorn, looking forward to a quiet evening of reading, a recently purchased stack of novels on her coffee table. She looked around her living room, at the framed Susie Riehl watercolor on one wall, and at the newly framed photos of the Yoders, most of which she had taken surreptitiously with her phone, on the shelves surrounding her televisions: the twins washing the family buggy; Becca sitting atop the camel at the Philadelphia Zoo, on the beach in Rehoboth, and one of her sunflowers; Emma laying on her beloved Bessie as the cow lounged in the barn and one of her with blackberry-stained teeth from their morning of berry picking; Jacob at the Phillies game with his backward baseball cap and a five-by-seven of him at Lido Beach in Florida.

On another shelf rested the sand dollar and seashell box and a frame containing the hand-written note from Jacob, the colorful wooden fish from Emma and Joseph, and the hot air balloon glass figurine. That morning she had placed on the shelves surrounding her bedroom fireplace a dozen pictures of her mom and other family photos she had pulled out of photo albums and framed.

At last, it felt right, despite the heartache, to blend the memories of her past with her life going forward, and to try to live that last lesson from Jacob: to stop the frantic activity and be still. The resulting changes in her life were incremental but meaningful, as even small change can be.

Instead of reaching for a book, Taylor rose from the couch and stood for a moment before her floor-to-ceiling windows, appreciating the view of the city. Then she opened the piano bench, chose sheet music, and sat down. It was a full minute before she placed her hands on the keys. She began to play Beethoven's *Moonlight Sonata*, softly and languidly through the first movement, then faster and more lighthearted through the second, stumbling her way through the frenzied difficult third movement, but continuing on, lost in the music.

Acknowledgments

I am indebted to the works of Donald Kraybill, Stephen Scott, and Steven Nolt; to the Lancaster, Pennsylvania Amish entrepreneurs and families who graciously invited me into their businesses and homes; and to the Mennonite Information Center. Thanks also to Brad Igou for the herd of grazing horses anecdote. My special gratitude to Eric Potts for his insight on living with a spinal cord disability and for his courage and determination.

About the Author

 Sherri Schaeffer's professional background includes newspaper reporting and corporate law. *To Everything A Season* is her first novel. She lives in the Greater Philadelphia area with her husband.

To Famulare

LOV the

Leadership

Bob
Ricken

Made in the USA
Middletown, DE
30 September 2018